Ace Books by Kelly McCullough

WEBMAGE
CYBERMANCY
CODESPELL

More praise for

WebMage

"The most enjoyable science fantasy book I've read in the last four years . . . Its blending of magic and coding is inspired . . . *WebMage* has all the qualities I look for in a book—a wonderfully subdued sense of humor, nonstop action, and romantic relief. It's a wonderful debut novel."

—Christopher Stasheff, author of
Saint Vidicon to the Rescue

"McCullough handles his plot with unfailing invention, orchestrating a mixture of humor, philosophy, and programming insights that gives new meaning to terms as commonplace as 'spell-checker' and as esoteric as 'programming in hex.'"

—*Publishers Weekly* (starred review)

"A unique first novel, this has a charming, fresh combination of mythological, magical, and computer elements . . . that will enchant many types of readers."   —*KLIATT*

"McCullough's first novel, written very much in the style of Roger Zelazny's classic Amber novels, is a rollicking combination of verbal humor, wild adventures, and just plain fun."

—*VOYA*

"*WebMage* contains a lot of humor and a highly inventive new way of looking at the universe, which combines the magic of old with the computer structures of today."

—*SFRevu*

"Complex, well paced, highly creative, and, overall, an auspicious debut for McCullough . . . well worth reading for fans of light fantasy."   —*Sci Fi Weekly*

continued . . .

CODESPELL

Kelly McCullough

ACE BOOKS, NEW YORK

THE BERKLEY PUBLISHING GROUP
Published by the Penguin Group
Penguin Group (USA) Inc.
375 Hudson Street, New York, New York 10014, USA

Penguin Group (Canada), 90 Eglinton Avenue East, Suite 700, Toronto, Ontario M4P 2Y3, Canada
(a division of Pearson Penguin Canada Inc.)
Penguin Books Ltd., 80 Strand, London WC2R 0RL, England
Penguin Group Ireland, 25 St. Stephen's Green, Dublin 2, Ireland (a division of Penguin Books Ltd.)
Penguin Group (Australia), 250 Camberwell Road, Camberwell, Victoria 3124, Australia
(a division of Pearson Australia Group Pty. Ltd.)
Penguin Books India Pvt. Ltd., 11 Community Centre, Panchsheel Park, New Delhi—110 017, India
Penguin Group (NZ), 67 Apollo Drive, Rosedale, North Shore 0632, New Zealand
(a division of Pearson New Zealand Ltd.)
Penguin Books (South Africa) (Pty.) Ltd., 24 Sturdee Avenue, Rosebank, Johannesburg 2196,
South Africa

Penguin Books Ltd., Registered Offices: 80 Strand, London WC2R 0RL, England

This is a work of fiction. Names, characters, places, and incidents either are the product of the author's imagination or are used fictitiously, and any resemblance to actual persons, living or dead, business establishments, events, or locales is entirely coincidental. The publisher does not have any control over and does not assume any responsibility for author or third-party websites or their content.

CODESPELL

An Ace Book / published by arrangement with the author

PRINTING HISTORY
Ace mass-market edition / June 2008

Copyright © 2008 by Kelly McCullough.
Cover art by Christian McGrath.
Cover design by Judith Lagerman.
Interior text design by Kristin del Rosario.

ISBN: 978-0-441-01603-7

ACE
Ace Books are published by The Berkley Publishing Group,
a division of Penguin Group (USA) Inc.,
375 Hudson Street, New York, New York 10014.
ACE and the "A" design are trademarks belonging to Penguin Group (USA) Inc.

PRINTED IN THE UNITED STATES OF AMERICA

10 9 8 7 6 5 4 3 2 1

Laura,
my heart and my muse

Acknowledgments

First and foremost, extraspecial thanks are owed to Laura McCullough, Stephanie Zvan, Jack Byrne, and Anne Sowards.

Many thanks also to the Wyrdsmiths: Lyda, Doug, Naomi, Bill, Eleanor, Rosalind, Harry, and Sean. My web guru: Ben. Beta readers: Steph, Ben, Sara, Dave, Karl, Angie, Sean, Laura R., and Norma. Greek help: Philip. My copyeditors for *WebMage* and *Cybermancy*: Robert and Sara Schwager. My extended support structure: Bill and Nancy, James, Tom, Ann, and so many more. My family: Phyllis, Carol, Paul and Jane, Lockwood and Darlene, Judy, Lee C., Kat, Jean, Lee P., and all the rest. The Deathpixies—just because.

CHAPTER ONE

Zeus wants you!

I flipped the invitation open again. A paper rendition of the big guy popped out and pointed his finger at me. It was tipped with a lightning bolt.

Zeus wants you!
For spring break. Summer has come early to Olympus, and it's here to stay. At least that's what I hear from Persephone's mother, who has officially canceled winter. Call it global warming or call it Raven, whichever suits your fancy. In either case, it's time to celebrate changing times in the pantheo-sphere. So come on up to the real eternal city for a party on the edge of forever.

Below that were details: time, place, dress code, rules of conduct—the usual boilerplate for a divine party, banning duels and personal violence—and a personal note scrawled in a bold hand:

House Raven will be expected to make a formal appearance.

                                                    Zeus

House Raven—that meant me, though I still prefer Ravirn. Ravirn, the Raven. Persephone's freedom and the end of winter. Zeus. A divine blowout where I would have a target painted on my back.

Was it any wonder I had insomnia?

OK, maybe that's a little dishonest. It wasn't just the card costing me sleep. It was the way I could read it in the dark—by the light of my eyes. My recent upgrade from demigod 2.0 to 2.5 or whatever version I was on at the moment had come with some dubious "perks," including glow-in-the-dark eyeballs.

Oh, sure, I could put "Raven, Chaos Power" on my business cards now, but inside I was still plain old Ravirn, a very young and very late entrant into the Greek pantheon. And a tired one. Did I mention I wasn't getting enough rest? I desperately wanted sleep. Now, there's a perk I could go for.

Morpheus, Phobetor, Phantasos. We call these gods of sleep the Dreamers. Unfortunately, they don't always call back, not even for family. The relationship's distant, but it's there. As the umpteen-times great-grandson of the Greek Fate Lachesis, I'm pretty much related to the whole damn pantheon. It didn't help.

I'd tried e-mail, voice mail, snail mail. . . . So far, nothing. I was starting to have serious thoughts about giving hate mail a go. For most of my life I'd thought of sleep as something of an annoyance—unnecessary downtime. Now that I'd come face-to-face with serious insomnia, I couldn't wait for another visit from Morpheus and co.

Damn my eyes!

They used to look a lot like the rest of my immediate family's. Which is to say, two of them, slit-pupiled, with all the usual bits in the usual places. Then I died. . . . No, not *died* actually. Ceased to exist, which was much better. Dying would have put me in Hades' power, and the Lord of the Dead hated me as he hated few living beings.

I blamed Persephone for that and a whole lot more. My invite from Zeus, the eyes, Hades' attempts to kill me. When I'd rescued her from Hades the place, Hades the god had gone kind of nonlinear. He'd pushed me to the very edge of death, and I'd decided to try to take him with me, opening a hole into the place between worlds.

Primal Chaos poured through into the here and now. It consumed Hades' offices and a good bit of the surrounding underworld. I hurt him badly, though I didn't quite destroy him. I couldn't say the same for myself. Chaos is caustic stuff. It ate me alive—poof, Ravirn all gone. Actually, more like aieee! Ravirn all gone, but you get the picture.

That's one place where the Raven thing saved me. Ravirn 1.0 would have died. But 2.0—born of my conflict with Fate—had managed to imitate my Titan ancestors, creating a fresh body from chaos through will alone. Call it version 2.5. There were some changes in this newest model, most notably my glowing eyes. Chaos looks out at the world from the slits of my pupils now and lights my way with its tumbling infinitude of glowing colors and shapes.

It's a little disturbing. No, I'll be honest, it's a lot disturbing. Chaos burned away my body, and now it burns in my eyes. Cerice hates it. I glanced over at my lady fair. She was asleep, curled on her side with her back to me. I couldn't see much beyond her ashen hair. When we slept face-to-face, she caught a flash of light every time I blinked. She didn't like the new look, not one tiny little bit. I guess I couldn't blame her, not considering how *I* felt about it.

I felt . . . like getting up. I stretched and sighed. It was pretty clear the Dreamers had decided to skip my stop again. There was no point in tossing and turning until I woke Cerice. Sighing, I rolled out of bed. My silk robe, green and black—the colors of House Raven—lay over the back of a chair. I grabbed it though I didn't need it in the warm tropical night. I also grabbed the invite as I headed for the lower levels. I wanted to look it over again.

Raven House is a great sprawling structure built mostly of green and black marble and aqua-tinted glass. The style is a surprisingly harmonious mix of nouveau-tiki and classical

Greek. It sits on a mountainside overlooking the half-moon of Hanalei Bay on a version of Earth that hasn't yet produced any human neighbors to spoil the view. As far as I'd been able to determine, I had the entire Island of Kauai to myself in this DecLocus. That's Decision Locus for the less technically inclined, the designator the mweb uses for the data tags that keep track of all the infinite worlds of probability.

At least that's how things are supposed to work. My little conflict with Hades had done even more damage to Necessity —the goddess in computer shape who maintains our physical reality—than it had to me. The system had gone seriously out of whack, with repercussions the pantheon was still discovering. Technically that's all Persephone's fault, but I suppose I have to shoulder some of the blame. If I hadn't broken into Hades the place in order to bring my dead friend Shara back to the land of the living, the virus Persephone wrote to take over Necessity would never have gotten loose.

"Sir?"

I tried not jump out of my skin when a quiet voice spoke up from behind me as I reached the bottom of the stairs.

"Yes, Haemun." I turned to face him.

The satyr served as Raven House's resident staff. He claims he's a product of my subconscious mind, but I have my doubts. I don't think I'm twisted enough to have put a soul patch and the multiverse's ugliest Hawaiian shirt on a man-goat with the voice of Don Ho. I really don't.

"Can I get you anything?" he asked. "Some slippers? A midnight"—he stopped and checked his watch disapprovingly—"3:00 A.M. snack. A drink?"

"How about that last, a mojito. I'll be out on the balcony."

"Lanai," he corrected me. "This *is* Hawaii after all, even though it lacks Hawaiians. We should endeavor to use the local syntax wherever possible, don't you think?"

"Fine, I'll be on the lanai." That was another thing. Would my subconscious *really* act so difficult?

Haemun headed for the back of the house, and I headed for the front. The main balcony looked out across the bay.

There were a number of lounge chairs scattered around, and I took one of these, whistling the brazier next to it alight with a quick burst of binary. That way I could pretend to read by something other than the light of my eyes. The heat felt nice, too; it was chillier outside.

The invitation really was gorgeous. A complex multilayered thing with cutout and pop-up effects, it mirrored the Parthenon when fully unfolded, complete with a visiting deity in the shape of the pop-up Zeus.

"Hmph, dead trees. How *antiquated*." The little blue webgoblin hopped onto the arm of my chair, tapping the card with a sharp claw. "You'd think Zeus would get with the times. CEO of Pantheon Inc., and he can't even send an e-mail."

Melchior. Bald, blue, bad attitude, and about the size of a cat, at least in webgoblin shape. He's smaller as a laptop, and quieter, too. Familiar and friend, he's been with me for years. The relationship has changed quite a bit in that time, from master and servant to partners.

I raised an eyebrow. "You're just jealous that I get real mail and you don't."

He sputtered at that for a moment before regaining his momentum and theatrically rolling his eyes. "Jealous? Of *you*? Right. You just keep telling yourself that while I tote up the list of deities who want you dead but don't much care about me. Hades, Atropos, Lachesis, Clotho—"

"That's not fair," I said. "Those last three are all Fates. They should count as one."

"Maybe for someone who isn't actually related to them. But Lachesis is your grandmother and still out for your blood. That takes special effort, and it should get equally special consideration."

"Hey," I protested, "that's umpteen-times great-grandmother, and it's not like she's *actively* trying to kill me."

"Not that you know of."

I opened my mouth, then closed it again. He might have a point. The Fates are subtle, and I couldn't be sure they were off the case just because nobody had taken a shot at me in the last few days. I groped around for something else to say. I hate losing arguments with my familiar. He's a foot and a half tall, *and* I built him—that should give me some kind of advantage. My eyes fell on the card in my hands, and I thrust it at him.

"Zeus likes me." I refrained from adding a "so there" or sticking out my tongue. I might be feeling childish, but no way was I going to admit it to what amounted to a laptop with acute gland problems. "He's throwing me a party."

"Zeus likes parties. End of story."

Well, there was that. Zeus is a party animal, a sort of divine hybrid of king of the gods and the ultimate frat boy, which makes a certain amount of sense I suppose. Fraternities refer to themselves as Greek and attach Alphas and Omegas to their front doors, and my family has provided plenty of inspiration on the drinking-and-debauchery front. For his casual sex contributions alone, Zeus deserves a special place in party history.

It's actually kind of strange. Here we have the Lord of the Sky, God-King, and King-God who defeated and imprisoned his Titan forebears in the war known as the Titanomachy. Yet, when he's not painted breaking heads, the myths are mostly about him seducing mortals. I guess that's what happens when you try to run a multidimensional divine operation with a one-dimensional personality.

I looked at the invitation again.

Zeus wants you!

And, *House Raven will be expected to make a formal appearance.*

That didn't leave me much wiggle room. House Raven—the institution—as opposed to Raven House—the building I called home—pretty much consisted of me, and maybe Melchior. The latter depended on whether you counted him as a person or not.

Cerice's matriarch—Clotho, the Fate who spins the threads of life—had thus far refused to accept Cerice's resignation, which meant that technically Cerice still belonged to the Houses of Fate. Shara, Cerice's familiar, would always have a home at Raven House, but her relationship to

House Raven was even more tenuous than her mistress's, since she was trapped within the computer-mind of the goddess Necessity for at least the next month if not forever. It was hard to guess what would happen to her with Necessity in such dire shape.

As for Haemun . . . Well, as the spirit of the place, he worked more for Raven House than he did for me. I really hadn't had time to accumulate an entourage, and I preferred it that way. As a hacker and cracker, and a demigod of same, I tended to think of myself more as a lone coder than any kind of head of a Divine House. In fact, I really didn't much like the whole idea of becoming a power, however minor. Of course, no one had asked me. They'd just gone ahead and made me one.

Just then, Haemun arrived with a mojito for me and a very small snifter of something amber for Melchior.

"Your drinks," he said, leaning down with the tray.

"Thanks, Haemun."

"You're welcome, sirs. Can I get you anything else?"

"No, thank you."

Haemun wandered off and I took a long sip of my drink—rum and mint, lime and sugar, a bit of soda and absolutely fabulous. OK, so there were a few perks to this whole House Raven thing. They didn't begin to make up for everything I'd had to go through to get here. Or, I suspected, the grief the whole deal was going to buy me in the future. I tossed the card onto the table beside me.

Melchior picked it up. "This party smells like trouble."

"Everything smells like trouble to you, Mel. I think I misprogrammed your paranoia levels."

He nodded. "That's possible, but it's more likely the company I keep. *You* are a trouble magnet, and this party setup"—he tapped the card—"is begging to be exploited. It nails you down in one place at a specific time and announces the details to all of your enemies."

"No one's going to try to pull anything right under Zeus's nose."

Mel rolled his eyes again. "Yeah, it's not like there's any precedent for that. Like say, a golden apple with 'For the

Fairest' tossed into another Olympian party by Eris, Goddess of Discord." He snapped his finger. "Oh, wait, isn't that how the Trojan War started?"

"Well, when you put it that way . . ."

"Is there another way to put it?"

I winced and tapped the part of the card that talked about House Raven being expected. "Unfortunately, being a chaos power doesn't mean that I get to let what I want to do get in the way of what I have to do. If you can think of a good way to weasel out of this, now's the time to suggest it."

He shook his head. "I hate it when you resort to reason like that. It's out of character."

I could feel the muscles in my back and shoulders beginning to tighten and took another drink. If it were daylight, I'd have gone surfing to distract myself, but misjudging waves in the dark is a great way to become one with the reef. Besides, my glowing eyes tended to attract sharks. We got an awful lot of them in the bay, maybe because in this Dec-Locus, no humans had come along to prey on them. The eyes draw bugs, too.

I wondered if Discord had the same problem. Her eyes are like mine, only more so, two glowing balls of chaos. I liked Eris, even if she was crazy, but her eyes had always creeped me out. Now I saw their close cousins looking back at me every time I faced a mirror.

Melchior was probably right about the party, but I really didn't have any outs. The great powers of the pantheon are Chaos, Order, Death, and Creation—Discord, Fate, Hades, and Zeus. With Order and Death already out to get me, I really didn't want to piss Zeus off, too, no matter how stupid he was.

I sipped away at my mojito and tried to pretend everything would go fine. Yeah, right. About the only good thing I could see was a chance to plead my insomnia case to the Dreamers in person if they showed for the bash.

"Ravirn, be serious." Cerice glared at the leather pants I'd just pulled out of the closet. "You can't wear those."

"Of course I can." I slipped them on, ignoring her glower. "They're comfortable and practical."

The pants were racing leathers made by a little company called Tech Sec and lined with about seventeen layers of Kevlar. Great if you happened to crash your bike, better if someone started shooting at you.

"The invite said House Formal."

She was wearing a red-and-gold-brocade dress that would have been perfectly appropriate in the court of Elizabeth I. It looked fantastic on her. Cerice is tall and slender, with china-pale skin and white blond hair. Her slit eyes are blue, her cheekbones high, her ears pointed, and her face shaped like a narrow heart. The children of Fate are at the root of the legends of elf-kind, and my own appearance is a black-haired masculine mirror of hers.

I stepped in close and planted a gentle kiss on her cheek. "I know that, Cerice. But I no longer belong to the Houses of Fate. I am my own House, and I don't like classical. Not the way it is worn at House Clotho"—I tugged at her sleeve—"and not the three-thousand-year-old Athenian version favored on Olympus."

She sighed and smiled. "I understand that, but if you're going to go modern, couldn't you at least wear a tux instead of riding leathers and a T-shirt?"

"The leathers stay. I like bulletproof."

"Bullet resistant," interjected Melchior. "There's a difference."

I gave him a sour look. "I will concede the T-shirt." I'd planned on doing that anyway, and this way I'd get relationship points for it as well. "What would you suggest?"

She headed deeper into the closet, returning a moment later with an emerald silk shirt with Edwardian ruffles. I took it dubiously and slipped it on, then added my jacket.

"Oh my." Cerice grinned.

"Good?" I asked.

"Surprisingly so."

A quick look in the mirror confirmed her judgment. Tech Sec leathers are custom-fitted, and a very silky black. With the jacket open and the ruffled shirt, the whole looked something like Edwardian Modern. Even the boots added to the effect, since I'd opted for Tech Sec's English riding style. Nice.

That just left one thing. Stripping the jacket off again, I put on a low-profile shoulder holster and slid my .45 into it.

"Uh, Boss?"

"Yes, Melchior. What do you want? And would you *please* stop calling me Boss? We're partners."

"Whatever you say, Boss."

"Melchior?"

"Yes?" He gave me an innocent look.

"You were saying . . ."

"Are you sure you want to bring a gun along? You do remember that Zeus has banned them, right? 'Nobody thunders but me' and all that jazz."

"I was going to conceal it with a spell," I said. "Besides, my rapier and dagger don't go with the outfit."

"So you're leaving them behind?"

"Well, no. I was going to ask you to tuck them away somewhere." I flapped my fingers mystically. Melchior often parked my blades in a sort of pocket of folded space when I didn't want them visible.

"Why not have me take the gun, too? It'd be safer."

I wanted to argue, especially after he'd reminded me what a lovely target this party made of me, but he was right. I handed over the .45 very reluctantly. He took it and whistled a quick string of binary code. The spell opened a hole in space, into which Melchior tucked the pistol. My blades followed a moment later, but he kept it open and gave Cerice a rather pointed look.

"What?" she demanded.

I grinned. "If I've gotta, so do you."

"Oh, all right." She reached under her skirts and produced a small Beretta semiautomatic. It went wherever it was Mel had parked the rest of the stuff, and he closed things up. Cerice's slight but smug smile as he did so suggested to me that she was holding out. I didn't call her on it.

"Are we ready?" I asked.

"As we're likely to get," muttered Melchior. "I just wish we could travel like sane people and LTP it."

That would have been nice. Despite my newfound facility with faerie rings, I also preferred locus transfer protocol gates. But the damage to the mweb had removed the world that held Raven House from the net and cut off all mweb-based magic in the process. That left us no other choice.

"You want to walk or ride?" I asked him.

"Ride, I think. I'm less likely to draw divine attention if I play inanimate object for most of the evening, and that's the way I like it."

"Fair enough. Melchior, Laptop. Please."

He grinned and began to melt into a blue puddle—the first step in the shift from webgoblin to laptop. He could have done it on his own, of course, but he seemed to prefer the old ritual of command and performance when running most of his spell programming. Kind of odd, actually, since the "please" we'd substituted for "execute" made the whole thing as voluntary as if he'd initiated the spell himself.

But then, he was a bizarre little mix of hardware, wetware, software, spellware, and whatever spiritware Tyche and Eris had snuck into the webgoblin specs to give them free will. As far as I can tell, AI is at least as weird as the regular sort of I. When he was done, I lifted his laptop form—a translucent blue clamshell—into a Tech Sec shoulder bag and bowed Cerice out the door in front of me.

The faerie ring was embedded in the marble of the grand balcony, a circle of black veining within the green stone. Taking Cerice's hand, I stepped into the circle and went . . . elsewhere.

Faerie rings are a form of chaos magic that acts as a loophole in the idea of place. Outside, you're somewhere specific. Inside, you're not. Every single ring is at one and the same time both itself and every other ring. When you cross back over the border on the way out, your odds of stepping out of any other circle are perfectly even. At least, that's the theory. In practice, most people experience the rings sequentially, seeing potential exit points in a series of flickers, like high-speed channel surfing.

That's how it worked for plain old Ravirn—very dangerous

and very scary. But the Raven is a power of chaos, which gives me unusual power over the rings. Now when I enter one, I somehow experience the whole damn system simultaneously and can simply step out into the world of my choice. Convenient but, in its own way, even scarier.

This time the Olympus ring was a chain of braided flowers, bright in the afternoon sun. They lay on the floor of a small marble temple, the pantheonic equivalent of a gazebo. On my last visit to the mountain, it had been a circle of dancing satyrs. Athena is the head of Olympian security, and she does not allow permanent rings.

As we stepped over the flowers, a small, fat satyr pranced up to greet us. He had more flowers in his hair and looked to be a sweet-natured thirteen. In reality, he was probably in his late hundreds and as steeped in vice as the rest of his half-goat relatives. That impression was reinforced by a glance over his shoulder to the place where a half dozen of his fellows were hunched over some kind of game that involved dice and lots of drinking from unmarked brown bottles.

"Raven and consort, so good of you to come. If you'll just follow me, I'll lead you to the party."

"I prefer Ravirn," I said.

"And consort?" demanded Cerice. "Don't I even get a name?"

"Look," said the satyr, "I don't write the cards, I just read 'em." He waved a slender calling card at us.

"Where'd you get that?" I asked.

He rolled his eyes. "Out of the arrivals box. Security's pretty tight for this gig, and Athena's people are monitoring all the incoming traffic, both LTPs and on the ring network. Whenever any of the invitees comes in, a card pops up with titles and whatnot on it."

"What if someone isn't invited?" I asked.

He shrugged. "That's not really my department. I assume all hell breaks loose. It hasn't happened yet, and I hope to miss it if it does. Now, are you coming?"

He led us to a large field with dozens of pavilions. A line of slender posts linked by golden rope surrounded the area, and we walked along these to a place where the rope spiraled around a taller pair of poles to form an arch. A pair of ten-foot cyclopes in security guard uniforms and mirrored shades stood to either side of the opening.

The satyr handed the calling card over to the nearer of the two. He read it carefully and painfully, silently sounding out the syllables. When he finished, he turned his head so that the single lens of his mirrored shade was aimed right at me and frowned.

"I remember you," he said.

He didn't sound happy. Neither was I. The last time I'd come into contact with the rent-a-clops types that supplied muscle for Athena's security operations, we hadn't exactly seen eyes to eye. In fact, there'd been some shooting involved. Mostly them, at me, with high-caliber Gyrojet pistols, but it hadn't all been one way. It was going to be very embarrassing if I got into a fight with one of the security guards and got thrown out of a party in my own honor.

"I'm sorry," I said. "You missed. I missed. Can we just call it even?"

"I don't t'ink so," said the cyclops, cracking his enormous knuckles. "I really don't. One of these days, you and me are gonna have a long talk in a dark alley somewheres." He shook his head with some disappointment. "But it ain't today. Today is professional, not personal. Zeus invited you, so I gots to let you in, but Athena said to make sure I frisked you first. You wanna assume the position? Or do I gets to go personal on you ahead o' schedule?"

What I really wanted was to go back to Raven House, but all the reasons I had to come to this event still applied. Besides, I didn't think I'd be allowed to simply walk away at this point. With a sigh, I put my hands on top of my head.

The 'clops looked briefly triumphant when he found my shoulder holster, but that faded as soon as he saw it was empty. At the end of the pat down, he turned his gaze on Cerice.

"Don't even think it, eyeball." Her voice was quiet and

almost sweet, and that made it even scarier. "If they ever found your body, they'd develop drinking problems over the missing bits."

The cyclops stepped aside and waved us in, looking more than a little pale as he did so. Once more we followed the satyr, this time threading our way through a milling crowd heavy on his goatish cousins, nymphs, and booze, on our way to the largest of the tents.

As we stepped inside, he loudly announced, "Raven and consort."

"That's Ravirn," I said.

"And Cerice," she added.

"It's not like anyone's listening," replied the satyr before he ducked back out of the tent.

He had a point. The party had clearly started without me, and his bellow probably didn't carry more than a couple of yards. Hundreds of figures crowded the pavilion, filling the place with noise and movement so wild I had a hard time making sense of it. If anyone noticed our entry, they didn't show it.

"Now what?" I asked Cerice.

"Mingle and look for Zeus, I guess. We can't leave until that's out of the way, and even if we decide to stay, it's the polite thing to do."

I nodded. "Sounds good." I hoped to find Morpheus in there somewhere as well, but I had my doubts. "Let's see if we can't get a couple of drinks on the way." Taking Cerice's hand, I plunged into the crowd.

Snapshots from a divine madhouse.

Eris, Goddess of Discord, playing cards with her half brother Ares and Hephaestus, the smith who hammered out Zeus's lightning bolts. The boys were losing. I'd been there and didn't need to add to Discord's wins tonight, so I kept going.

A half dozen satyrs stood by a bar where Dionysus poured drinks from a jug that never emptied.

I got Cerice and me a couple of glasses. It was wine, clear and golden and sweet and tart and hot and cold all at the same time.

I sipped at it as we passed the head table, a crescent of white marble slabs enfolding a grotesquerie of a fountain— all little cupids and spouting tritons with dark wine pouring from the tips of their weapons. Zeus's golden throne stood empty in the center of the tableau, so we moved on.

In the corner of another tent, a lamia, a sphinx, and a chimera sat around a small table swapping hero recipes.

At some point, Cerice left me to find us more drinks. While I was waiting, I saw a familiar face with an unfamiliar expression. My cousin Dairn, smiling. When he saw me, he waved, as so many others had.

I waved back unthinkingly, then froze. Dairn is a grandchild of Atropos, who wants me dead, and one of the greatest archers ever to live. He has tried to kill me on three separate occasions. The scar had not survived my rebirth, but he once put an arrow through my left forearm.

The last time I'd seen him, I'd pushed his unconscious and hamstrung body into a faerie ring, more than half-hoping he'd lose his soul in that magical maelstrom as so many had before. It seemed fair payment for the arrow that had cost my friend Shara her life. I hadn't heard from or about him from then till now, and I'd assumed he was dead.

As he headed toward me, I opened my bag and pulled out Melchior, quickly flipping up his lid.

Run Melchior, I typed. *Please.*

I set the laptop down as it began to shift into Melchior's webgoblin form. I wanted my hands free, and I wanted the backup. As Dairn got closer, I did a double take. Rather than the tights and tunic I would have expected from a child of House Atropos in good standing, he wore motorcycle leathers that mirrored mine. Nor were they in his traditional colors—a mixture of browns. His ruffled shirt was a rusty red, the leathers dark and silvery, almost like a blackened mirror.

"Raven," he said, raising an empty hand. "I've been looking for you."

I nodded a greeting but didn't take his hand. I didn't want to get that close to him. Something wasn't right, and it was more than a change of clothes and colors. After a moment, he dropped his hand, though he didn't look put out. In fact, he smiled and his eyes seemed almost to twinkle.

"It's that way is it, Raven?"

"Ravirn," I corrected him. "I don't see how it could be any other way. Not after our last meeting."

"Are you thinking of the part where your toy computer hamstrung me, the bit where you stole my webpixie, or the end, when you pushed me into a faerie ring bound and unconscious and left me to die?"

He said it all with a grin that set a chill to the back of my neck. His voice was light, almost teasing, like nothing unusual had happened between us. Like I'd done him some sort of favor, even. It was much more frightening than the rage or indignation I'd have expected from someone like Dairn and deeply out of character, more the kind of thing Eris or Athena would have used to throw an enemy off-balance. I'd known Dairn most of my life, and he simply wasn't that sharp.

"Actually," I said, being careful to keep my tone as light and friendly as his, "it's before that, where you helped to take my girlfriend hostage and murdered her familiar. You do remember that, right?"

He waved a hand dismissively. "I served my House, and besides, decommissioning a webgoblin hardly counts as murder. You don't really believe all that rot about them being people, do you?"

Somewhere down around my knees Melchior began whistling a string of angry binary. It was too fast for me to parse, but I could tell the end result wasn't going to be healthy for Dairn. Since that would have violated Zeus's party rules, I reached down and caught the scruff of Mel's neck—too late. By the time I'd lifted him into the air, he was already finishing whatever spell he'd started, though it sounded very strange at the end.

At that point havoc should have ruled the field. It didn't, and it took me a moment—and a mental replay of what had just happened—to figure out why. That's when my exchange with Dairn went from moderately disturbing to downright frightening.

Melchior's spell hadn't failed. Dairn had canceled it by whistling one of his own, and not a general nullification charm either. He'd matched his own whistle to Mel's for a bar, then shifted to a harmony, and finally a self-harmonized counterpoint that turned the original spell on its head.

He shouldn't have been able to do that. It was the kind of magic that only webtroll supercomputers and a few of the powers, myself not included, could use. It took a great deal of effort to stand my ground. Effort I probably should have spent on running, but I really hated to run blind.

"Who are you?" I asked, still holding Melchior in the crook of my arm. It felt as though he might be trembling.

Dairn smiled, and his eyes flashed again. "Dairn, whom you abandoned to the faerie rings."

I recognized the flash this time, a tiny spark of pure Primal Chaos within his pupils, and my own grew wide. At that, his spark grew brighter, and I recognized something else. The spark was a reflection of my own, not an internal light. His pupils were dark mirrors, like smoked glass over quicksilver.

"*What* are you?"

"Ahh, now that's a better question. I am what you made me. I am your enemy."

CHAPTER TWO

Dairn grinned and reached toward the breast of his jacket, as though he were going for a gun. Before he could complete the gesture, I heard someone call my name.

Dairn's smile changed into a frown as he looked over my shoulder. Then he whistled something very fast and vanished.

I turned around and saw Tisiphone walking toward me.

Tisiphone. The Fury. Fire-haired, fire-winged, and beautiful. As always, she was naked, with the blue veins showing through her pale redhead's skin. More fire blossomed in the hair where her long athletic legs met, and her high small breasts were also tipped with flame.

Her lips burn, too, or at least that was how I remembered them from our one brief kiss, hot and wild and vivid. I pushed those thoughts aside. I couldn't have them. Not as long as I was with Cerice. Not as long as we were an us. But Cerice loved Ravirn, not chaos-eyed Raven, who frightened her, and Tisiphone . . . why, Tisiphone wasn't afraid of anything.

"Ravirn?" she said again. She looked puzzled. "I wanted

to talk with you. I'm glad to find you alone. You are alone, aren't you? When I first saw you I thought you were standing by a mirror, but then . . . Did I see what I think I saw? If so, who was that?"

"My cousin Dairn, who hates me, but that's not important. He's gone now. How are you? How's Necessity? Have you seen Shara?"

"What is this? An interrogation?" Tisiphone smiled. "Not so frightened of me as you once were, are you? That's good. I don't want you scared." She reached up and touched my cheek.

I blushed. The first time I met Tisiphone, she'd come to kill me. That wasn't the only time we'd clashed. She'd saved my life more than once as well. Our relationship had grown *complex*. She wanted me, and I wanted . . . I don't know. Sometimes I wanted things to be the way they never had been—Cerice and me together without anything hanging over our heads. Sometimes I wanted something else entirely.

"Ravirn." The voice was low, husky, hurt.

"Cerice," I turned away from Tisiphone and took my glass from Cerice's hand, "you're back."

"I am. Should I have bothered?"

"It's not like that," I said. "Tisiphone just arrived, too. She wanted to say hello."

"Oh really." Cerice sounded almost as icy as she had with the rent-a-clops.

"Dairn is here," said Melchior.

Cerice's expression went from cold to hot in an instant. Shara is Cerice's familiar, a webgoblin every bit as precious to her as Melchior is to me. On top of that, at the time Dairn had shot Shara, his brother Hwyl had been in the process of clubbing Cerice unconscious. She's had a rough couple of years, largely because she'd decided to save my neck once upon a time.

"Where is he?" she asked, draining her wine in a single long draft and dropping the glass. "I'll kill him."

I had no doubt she meant that literally.

"As much as I appreciate the sentiment," I said, catching her wrist, "this might not be the best place for it."

Cerice glared at me but didn't try to pull away. That was good. I didn't think that trying to kill Dairn would be a great idea right now, even if we could find him, but I wouldn't have tried to restrain her beyond that first impulse.

"Is this a private moment, or can anyone join?" The woman's voice was diamonds in the snow—frozen elegance—and all too familiar.

If I'd been paying attention to anything other than Cerice and Tisiphone, I might have seen her coming and had a ready answer or a dodge. As it was, my brain kind of short-circuited for a few seconds as a third woman stepped into view.

"Hello, *Raven*." Beautiful and regal, she nodded at me before turning. "Cerice, still slumming I see. I don't know what you see in him. Tisiphone, don't you have something better to do? Places to go? People to kill?"

She was tall and pale, with dark hair and dark eyes slit like a cat's. She wore a long Elizabethan gown of green and gold. She was a thousand years old and as cold and cruel as a queen of faerie. Her House was Lachesis and her loyalty to my great-to-the-Nth-degree-grandmother was absolute. As with so many members of the Houses of Fate, Ravirn had died for her on the day Lachesis cast me out.

I forced a smile. "Hello, Phoebe." Damned if I was going to call her mother.

What do you say to the woman who birthed you when she sees you as a walking corpse? If we'd ever been truly close, it might have been easier. I could have raged or cried or done something else equally dramatic. But for reasons structural, historical, and familial, we had little in common beyond blood and a few years in a shared house.

My mother's sensibilities were formed around the time Charlemagne ruled France. She'd had more than a thousand years of living without a child before she had my sister and me, and only a score of years living with us. To expect her to feel for me as might a human mother who'd spent a fifth of her short life with her child would be profoundly foolish. Add to that the intergenerational warfare of my ancestors and my grandmother's need to have all loyalty in her House flow first, last, and always to her, and our estrangement was no surprise. Despite that, seeing her hurt me. My usually glib tongue seemed to have found someplace else to be.

"Did you have something you wanted to say?" I finally asked.

She canted her head to one side and gave me her best disapproving stare. That was it.

"Look, Mom—I can still call you Mom, can't I?—I don't have all night. Make your point or get out of the way. I've played the hard-looks game with all three Fates, Hades, Eris, Cerberus, and"—I nodded at Tisiphone—"the Furies. On that scale you don't even register."

"You may not call me mom, mother, mater, or any other version of the term. When Lachesis disowned you, so did I."

"Great. Then I'll be going." I moved to step around her, but she held up a hand.

"What you have done to our House is inex—"

"Your House, Phoebe. Not mine. Mine is House Raven, or didn't you read the invite?"

"I'm not done," she said, putting out a hand.

I stuck my untouched drink in it. "I am." This time I went right on past her. It was that or punch her in the face.

"I blame your father's blood for this!" she yelled after me.

"That was fun," said Cerice, catching up to me as I ducked through the door to a nearby tent.

She sounded a little shaky, and after a quick look around revealed that Tisiphone hadn't followed, I turned to take her hand.

"You OK?" I asked.

"Yeah, I guess so." She looked down, away from my face. "I'm sorry. It's just, that she's so . . ."

"Difficult? Yeah, my mother could teach Ares a thing or two about starting fights."

"Ravirn!" She glared at me.

"Oh, you mean Tisiphone. Sorry. I tend to forget she exists when we're alone."

"You're impossible," she said, but the tension was broken,

and she smiled wistfully at me. "And we're a long way from alone." Her gesture took in the crowd in the new tent.

I caught her in my arms. "I really am sorry. She found me, not the other way around, rather like my mother."

"All right," said Cerice, relaxing into my arms and resting her chin on my shoulder. "I'm sorry, too."

We stayed that way for a long time, clinging to each other despite the wild crowd around us, like an eye of calm in the heart of a divine hurricane. I treasured the moment. But it cut me as well, because when we finally broke apart, I caught the tiny flinch she couldn't quite suppress as her gaze met the chaos in my eyes.

"About time." Melchior was tugging on my pant leg. "Give me a boost." He reached his hands up, and I lifted him into the bag. "I'd forgotten what a royal pain your mother can be," he said before he went back to laptop shape.

"I hadn't."

Cerice let out a bitter little laugh, and I raised an eyebrow at her.

"Sorry. The whole thing just made me wonder how *my* mother's taking my resignation."

"Hard to say. Clotho's not as tightly wound as Lachesis, and that's reflected in her children. Besides, as I recall, you only quit the job, not the family. I was cast out fully and formally."

"Not to mention unjustly," she said.

Her words were angry, as was her expression, angry on my behalf. It was sweet and fierce and more than a little bit sad. In many ways my outcast status hurt Cerice more than it did me.

"Let's go find fresh drinks," I said.

Another hour passed without any further sign of Dairn, my mother, or Tisiphone. Just Cerice and I walking hand in hand. Bliss. I was just thinking we should have another go at finding Zeus when a voice called out my name.

"Ravirn!"

It was nice to hear my preferred name instead of my shiny new one, so I was smiling when I spotted the speaker.

Somehow I held on to that despite the facc attached to the
voice. It was old-home week apparently.

"Hello, Arion." My father.

He grinned. "From your tone, I'd guess your mother
found you first. Fates and their children. That woman is cut
from the same cloth as all the others in the House. I swear
there's a mold somewhere in Lachesis's office, and they
aren't born so much as stamped out." He turned to Cerice
and winked. "I except Clotho's great-granddaughter here, of
course. How are you, child?"

"I'm fine, Arion. Yourself?"

"As well as can be expected, considering my relationship
with the boy's mother."

I blinked. "I take it you're not getting along then?"

"Oh, as well as usual. We've been together six hundred
years now, with all the usual fuss and bother: argument, making up, separations, enchantment, assassination attempts . . ."

"There's not much question where Ravirn got his sense
of humor, is there?" said Cerice.

Arion grinned. "Actually, that's why I hunted you down.
Your grandmother asked to meet you."

I twitched at that. If Lachesis was looking for me, it could
only mean trouble.

"My grandmother can go . . . wait a second."

Lachesis wasn't really my grandmother; I just tended
to think of her that way since she had long been my head
of House and preferred that we all refer to her so. I'd met
my mother's mother once or twice, but the generation
gap between us was so great that we'd literally had nothing to talk about. She'd been born before the invention of
steel. My father was almost that old himself but had
somehow managed to stay contemporary in a way even
my mother hadn't managed. I'd always just assumed his
mother had been killed somewhere along the line, as so
many of my demi-immortal relatives had over the years.
I know that both of my mother's mother's parents had
gone that way.

"Wow," Arion said to Cerice, "you can actually see the
wheels turning in there."

She smiled. "Sometimes it's the only evidence that he thinks at all."

"Who is my grandmother?" I asked.

"That'd ruin the surprise," said Arion. "She's got a tent set up right over here with her sisters." He started off.

Sisters? Tent? I was too bemused by the implications of that to do anything but follow. As far as I could tell, the tents roughly corresponded to Houses. I say roughly because some were shared, and some Houses hadn't bothered. House Raven, for example.

A moment later Arion had led me into the presence of a short, red-haired woman with deep laugh lines around her mouth and her green eyes.

"Ravirn," he said, "this is your grandmother, Thalia. Thalia, Ravirn of House Raven."

I opened my mouth. Shut it. Opened it again. Nothing came out. You see, I had met my grandmother before, seen her perform even, though I had never realized we were related. Thalia! The muse of comedy and comedic poetry. Which made me the product of Fate and Slapstick. I couldn't help myself; I laughed. Suddenly the cosmic irony of my life made so much more sense.

Thalia laughed as well, an utterly infectious sound. When we had both wound down, she spoke again. "No hello for your grandmother, child? What's wrong, my little blackbird? Cat got your tongue?"

From any other goddess in almost any other circumstances, the reference to my Raven side probably would have sobered me right up. In her case, it was the final ridiculous straw, and I started laughing again. My grandmother was right there with me. Cerice kept looking back and forth between the two us and shaking her head, which, of course, only made it funnier.

When I finally started to catch my breath, I took another look at Thalia. She was beautiful, but what goddess wasn't? They choose their own appearances and change them at a whim. But she was also more human than most. She had chosen to be short and to let the lines of her spirit show in her face. I liked that. I liked less that she had ignored my existence for more than twenty years.

"Why now?" I asked.

She grinned ruefully, and I knew she'd caught my meaning. "Because of who you are and what you have become. As long as you and your sister remained loyal to the Houses of Fate and their ideals, I knew you wouldn't have much use for me, or I for you."

"I'm not sure I understand."

"You are a chaos power now, if a very minor one. Lachesis and her sister Fates are the pole powers of order and your natural enemies. That makes us not just relations, but allies as well."

Now I was definitely confused. "I thought you were allied with Zeus."

There were two axes of power in the pantheon. Chaos and order, embodied by Eris and the Fates. Creation and destruction, Zeus and Hades. I'd always placed the muses with Zeus.

"We are," said Thalia, "but we are more complex than that. Calliope, our chief, is allied nearly as closely with order as she is with creation. Epic poetry is a very ordered sort of art, and Calliope gets along with Fate quite well." She caught my eyes with her own. "But comedy, comedy is a thing of chaos."

Thalia winked, and for one brief second before her eye closed, I saw the tumbling stuff of chaos where her pupil should have been. When she reopened it, it looked normal again.

"You see, we have more in common than you might think."

"And less," said a deadly cold voice from behind me. "Since you are truly immortal, and he will die one day."

Hades. Though I'd only heard the voice once or twice, I would never forget it. Never forget the pain he had caused me or the terrible weight in the black fires of his eyes. I could feel it now, hate hammering on my back like a blacksmith's ghost. I did not want to meet that gaze ever again, wished I could just walk away. But it was not an option. I turned and looked into the eyes of death.

He was tall and thin, with smoky black hair that moved

on its own and skin that barely covered his bones. There was something of smoke to his flesh as well, as though it might blow away and expose him as a skeleton pretending to be a man. He wore a Savile Row suit as smoky as the rest of him. He smiled at me, showing too many teeth, and I felt the weight of his eyes tugging at my soul, like a magical black hole. Death wanted me dead. Here and now.

Without trying, I took a half step backwards. Then another. Before I could take a third, I felt a strong arm go around my waist, warm and comforting, a hip pressed against my own. Thalia.

"You are not welcome here," she said to Hades.

"At my dear brother Zeus's party? Are you quite sure of that? I did get an invitation." He smiled. "Or was that a joke? I never can tell. No sense of humor, you see." His eyes stabbed at me. "Death isn't supposed to be funny. Not at all."

That last was for me, for the torments he had promised to have waiting when I finally crossed the Styx. I felt weak, and my knees went spongy.

"Death, not funny?" Thalia's words rang out sharp and loud and filled with merriment. "You must be reading your own press releases a little too closely, Hades. That or you've never heard of black humor."

She chuckled, and some of my strength returned.

"Walk among the mortals and learn something, O *Death*." There was an undertone of "ooh, scaaaary" to the way she said it that made me grin. "See how their comedians make a mockery of everything about you.

"Death isn't supposed to be funny?" This time she bugged out her eyes, mimicking and mocking Hades' heavy tones before laughing aloud. "No. Death isn't funny. Death is hysterical. Life is the joke the universe has played on us all, and death is the punch line. You *are* the last laugh, and you can't even see it. How very rich."

This time when she laughed, I laughed as well. As I did so, Hades seemed to shrink before my eyes, to diminish into something vaguely ridiculous. In that instant I realized how very great was Thalia's power. I knew that when the laughter had passed, I would fear Death once again, but I also knew that I could never fear him as much, having laughed in his face. His might was not reduced in any way, yet his power over me was forever weakened.

Still laughing, I bent and placed a kiss on my grandmother's cheek. "Thank you."

She grinned up at me and nodded approvingly.

"This isn't over, Raven." Hades thrust his words at me like some kind of spear, but underneath the threat and bluster I could hear confusion.

Maybe he really *didn't* have a sense of humor. If so, wasn't that the funniest joke of all?

Thalia seemed to think so. She made a scary-monster face at me, laughed, and said, "Boogah, boogah, boogah!" This time the whole tent seemed to laugh with her.

"I'll be waiting for you, Raven!" Death's voice was shrill, almost panicked.

"And your little laptop, too!" said Thalia in a perfect imitation of the Wicked Witch of the West.

Then she snapped her fingers in Hades' face and laughed so hard she had to sit down. Since there was no chair, she landed hard and squawked like a punted chicken. Then she made a horribly pained face and exaggeratedly rubbed her butt. Hades turned on his heel and stormed from the pavilion without saying another word.

Even Cerice smiled then. "You're all mad, you know that, right?" she asked, shaking her head and giggling.

"Of course," said Thalia, as she got back to her feet. Then her expression went deadly serious. "Yet I just defeated Death." The laughter stopped for a moment. "Which reminds me, who's heard the one about Hades, Dionysus, Morpheus, and the farmer's daughter?"

When no one answered, she grinned and began to tell an improbably obscene but deeply funny story.

That was my other grandmother to a tee.

We spent perhaps an hour with Thalia. Several of the other muses dropped in during that time as well, and it was probably the most fun I'd ever had with family in my life. But I still needed to find Zeus and make my official hellos.

So, with much regret and promises to visit soon, Cerice and I moved on.

More snapshots of the freak show that is my great sprawling family.

Dryads performing an elaborate dance that had them leaping wildly one minute and transforming into a windswept grove the next.

Apollo and Artemis playing a wild game of light and shadow with gold and silver shields.

Persephone, heartbreaking in her beauty, surrounded by admirers and radiating contentment. The pain of her long imprisonment could still be seen in the depths of her eyes and occasional moments of quiet when she seemed to gaze through the people around her.

She didn't see me, and I didn't try to catch her attention. We had things to talk about, but a crowded party on Olympus wasn't the place.

I shook my head and sighed.

"Penny for your thoughts?" asked Cerice.

Before I could answer, my bag binged. Cerice half smiled and shook her head in a "what can you do?" kind of way. I pulled Melchior out of the bag and flipped up his lid.

Incoming visual transfer protocol link, typed itself on his screen.

Who? I responded with my free hand.

Fido, Fido, and Rover.

I glanced at Cerice. She sighed and nodded.

"Go ahead. I need to stop at the ladies' room anyway. Find you here?"

"Sure."

Cerice walked off as I typed, *Put him through.*

Melchior's screen seemed to deepen and expand, creating a three-dimensional space like a tiny theater. Mist swirled there for a moment: red, blue, and green. Then, Cerberus was looking out at me.

"Ravirn," said the middle head, a rottweiler I called Dave, "What happened at the party?"

"Yeah," chimed in the mastiff on the right, Mort. "Hades came home early, and he looked—"

"Like he was going to tear someone's head off," said Bob, the Doberman, sounding quite cheery. "He mentioned your name." Bob and I had issues.

"I'd watch my back if I were you," said Mort.

"I wouldn't," said Bob.

Dave rolled his eyes. "Shut yer yapper, Bob. Or I'll shut it for you." He was the pack alpha, and Bob put his head down to show his submission. Dave continued, "Is Persephone there?"

I smiled sadly at that. Dave had been Persephone's dog for millennia, and he missed her terribly, even though he'd repeatedly thanked me for freeing her.

"She's here, but I haven't spoken with her yet."

Dave contrived to look simultaneously terribly happy and completely bereft. "I wish I could be there, but I don't get a lot of time off."

"Maybe you should go on strike for better working—"

"What's wrong?" Mort asked me.

"I'm not sure. I thought I saw something out of the corner of my eye."

I had, and I saw it again now. Zeus.

"Gottagobye," I said to Cerberus, and had Melchior sign me off.

"Ah, there you are, Raven!" boomed the sky god's jovial voice from off to my right. "Been looking for you all over the place. Kept missing you, too, though I heard rumors of your presence from Thalia, and saw the state you left old Hades in." The voice was interrupted by a chortle. "Silly stick-in-the-mud, brother though he is."

I braced myself and turned to face him. The king of the gods is a big man, seven feet tall and broad of shoulder. His skin is bronze, really bronze, metallic and shiny like he's been recently oiled. His hair and beard are golden, likewise. When he laughs, tiny bolts of lightning jump between the curly locks, and he laughs a lot. Zeus is a joker of the "hail, fellow, well met" variety and his own best audience. He has more teeth than he should, or at least it looks that way when he smiles, which he does constantly. As usual, he had an attractive woman on one arm, a naiad, judging by the green of her hair and the faint gill slits.

I bowed from the waist, slipping Melchior into my bag in the process. "Thank you for inviting me—"

"Inviting you?" He chortled again and slapped me on the back so hard that I almost went face-first into the dirt. "Wouldn't be the same party without you. No summer. Good work that. Never did like winter. Makes a body wear too many clothes, doesn't it, sugar?"

He patted the naiad on her very scantily clad behind, and she giggled. I was more than a little embarrassed for her, but nymphs are funny creatures, and she seemed to like the attention.

"But that's only true for some, eh, son." Zeus grinned and winked at me. "Others are made of tougher stuff. Tisiphone, for example." Like all the Furies, Tisiphone disdained clothing even in the depths of winter. "She's how I found you. Knew right where you were when I asked her, did Tisiphone. Smart, that one, and worth a second look, or maybe even a third if you know what I mean." He waggled his eyebrows meaningfully at me.

I swallowed hard and tried to think of a safe answer, a task made more complex by the return of Cerice.

"Your Majesty," she said, tipping him a curtsy.

He took the opportunity to leer down her bodice in a theatrical way. "This one's a beauty, too, of course. But you're young yet. You don't want to be too tied down, now do you? Not like I am with Hera. Speaking of which"—he caught Cerice's hand in his own and brushed a kiss across her knuckles—"when the boy breaks your heart, come on by, and I'll give you a comforting word or six."

His divine lecher patter should have been appalling. It *was* appalling. But at the same time there was such a good-natured honesty to it that it was also weirdly charming.

"Now, come along both of you. You're wanted at the head table."

He put an arm around my shoulders and another around Cerice and started steering us through the crowd. We were nearly back to the main tent when we ran into Clotho. She stood between us and the head table, and not even Zeus will be rude to Fate, so we halted facing her.

"Still trailing after the Raven," she said to Cerice.

"You know my reasons," said Cerice, though she curtsied deeply.

"And fault them just as I did when last we talked. Come home, child. You are a creature of order; we all know that." She included me with a glance. "Your habits and your nature may war with your heart for a time, but what you are must eventually win against what you wish you could be. That's true no matter what you've put on your life lists most recently."

I winced inwardly. I loved Cerice, but Clotho had a point, several actually. Cerice could hack and crack with the best of them, but that wasn't where her greatest skills lay. Those were in programming: ground-up, huge-scale, hideously complex coding. She had a mind tuned for organization and fine control. She planned everything, always had, and probably always would despite protestations that the best things in her life had come from surprises.

I think it hit home for Cerice, too, because she didn't answer Clotho back, just looked at her feet.

"Return to your proper place, Cerice." Clotho's voice was gentle, almost regretful. "You cannot live as a consort of chaos for long without tearing yourself apart. I don't want that. You are my grandchild, and whatever words and deeds have come between us, I still love you. Fate needs programmers like you, especially now with Necessity so badly damaged by . . . recent events."

That was gentler than I would have expected, considering it was through the agency of Shara, Cerice's familiar, that Necessity had come to grief.

"I can't," whispered Cerice, still not looking up.

"You must, child. Your familiar is the key to accessing and repairing Necessity, and you are the one best suited to work with her and us to bring everything to rights. A job waits for you on Fate's staff, an important job. You do see that, don't you?"

"I . . ."

"At least talk with me. See what we need, what you can do."

Cerice turned to me, her expression imploring.

"It's your decision," I said, "and your House. When you resigned your position, you didn't renounce your family, and I would never ask that of you."

Clotho looked sharply at me, and for the briefest instant I thought I saw surprise in her eyes. But that was impossible, she was a Fate, and even if it were *possible* to startle her, she would never betray herself so. Besides, while I might be beyond the direct control and monitoring of the Fates, Cerice was no power. They still held her life thread in their hands. I answered the expression anyway.

"I did not renounce my family either, Clotho, only one part of Fate's policy. *My* family renounced *me*. Surely you remember that. You were there." My words tasted cold and bitter, almost as cold and bitter as the memory.

"I remember," said Clotho. "Do you remember who gave you the name 'Raven' when my sister took back your old one?"

I wanted to say "Necessity" since it was the Fate of the Gods who'd ultimately ordered it, but the words had come from Clotho's lips at the time and I knew she had not begrudged them.

"I remember." I grinned. "Though, with all the trouble it's brought me, I'm not entirely certain I should thank you for it."

She nodded. "Good enough. Cerice? Fates don't beg. Talk to me?"

"All right," said Cerice, slipping free of Zeus's arm.

"There," said Zeus, "aren't families great?" He gave my shoulder a squeeze as he led me onward.

A few minutes later, Zeus was toasting me at the big table. A few minutes after that, I was being mobbed by every-one who wanted to get on Zeus's good side. The toasts kept coming, and my glass acted like a horn of plenty—bounteous and bottomless. Zeus wandered off with the naiad some-where in there. I saw Persephone again, and she smiled but didn't approach me.

An hour went by, and things began to get blurry. Cerice didn't return. I was somewhere between worried and miffed about that, but there wasn't much I could do about it. More toasts. More time. Still no Cerice.

"Boss, wake up."

Huh? That didn't make sense. I hadn't gone to sleep. What was Melchior talking about?

"Come on, snap out of it."

I noticed it was very dark and opened my eyes. Flicker-ing white on white. The marble head table, reflecting the torches that had taken over now that the sun had gone. I lifted my head and looked around. It hurt. A lot. The party was still going, but things had changed. The A-list had de-parted for other venues, leaving behind a motley assortment of centaurs, chimeras, harpies, and other less easily identifi-able creatures. A sphinx had taken over bar duty.

"What happened?" I asked, putting a hand to my fore-head. I don't normally drink to excess, but when I do, pass-ing out is very rarely on the menu.

Melchior rolled his eyes. "Three guesses. It's probably time to go home."

That made sense. "Where's Cerice?"

"I don't know," said Melchior. "I haven't seen her for hours. She didn't come back from talking to Clotho."

Oh. And Clotho was clearly not here. I put my head down again, and my shirt tore with a sharp *zripping* sound. It had turned into that kind of day. I reached for my glass.

A second *zrip*.

I felt it in my shoulder, like someone had punched me. Alarm bells went off in my fuzzy head. Something was ter-ribly wrong.

Another *zripp*, this one followed by a crack as somebody kicked me in the back of the ribs.

Melchior was gone from the table in front of me, yelling something unintelligible and diving over the edge to land between the table and fountain.

Zripp. Fire bloomed in my right elbow. Not broken, but very close. My brain finally caught up to the situation. Silencer. Gun. If not for the Kevlar lining in my leathers I'd have been leaking.

I followed Melchior, going under the table rather than over.

"Did you see—"

He nodded. "Dairn."

Why wasn't I surprised?

CHAPTER THREE

"Now what?" asked Melchior, as another bullet struck near us.

"Good question." I looked around. "How about this for a start?"

Rolling onto my back, I braced my booted feet against one edge of the table and pushed it over. An eight-foot slab of marble more than an inch thick, it was five hundred pounds if it was an ounce, but the children of the Fates are stronger than humans. That put a thin wall of stone between us and Dairn, and the next bullet ricocheted off it with a sharp crack.

"Any sign of the cavalry?" I asked Melchior.

"Nope. No rent-a-clops. No Athena. And no storm clouds."

"Figures." The last incident involving guns and Olympus had been caused by Cerice and me and the response had involved all three. "Why is it that security only shows up when I'm the one breaking the rules?"

"You're just special, I guess. I suppose we might as well take advantage of that."

He grinned and whistled the first bar of the magical program that opened the pocket of space-time where he'd hidden my weapons. But even as he was doing so, a loud whistled counterpoint came from the other side of the table, joining with and then overriding his spell. As the two tones merged into one, Melchior let out an odd warble. Then he went rigid, tipped over onto his back, and lay there emitting a short repeating loop of garbage binary.

Suddenly I was sweating. Melchior is an amalgam of creature and computer, with some of the strengths and weaknesses of each. Dairn had just exploited the computer side of the equation and induced a crash by adding false input to the program he was running. It was an incredible hack, especially since he'd done it on the fly. Well, at least I thought that was what he had done. I couldn't be sure because I'd never seen anything like it.

"Come on out and play," Dairn's voice called. "Leave the doll out of it. Or are you too weak a hacker to live without your little crutch?"

I didn't answer right away. Instead, I reached behind Mel's right ear to find the little wart there, his programmer's switch. I gently twisted and pushed, holding it down until I heard the chime of a hard reboot. That would bring him back online, but it would take time. Time I wasn't sure I had.

Things had gone downhill very fast, and I didn't understand it at all. The Dairn I knew—call him Dairn 1.0—was no sorcerer, never had been. He couldn't have hacked his way out of a stopped elevator using the "open door" button. Dairn 2.0 was a gods-damned programming wizard, and I didn't know thing one about the upgrade process.

Dairn called out again. "Make a decision, Raven. Are you going to come out and face me, or do I have to come in after you?"

"Do I get a third choice?" I asked, stalling for time.

I *could* work magic without Melchior, but it would either be much cruder or much more dangerous, depending on whether I went for whistling my own binary or using the Raven's still largely untested powers over chaos. I didn't like either choice.

Dairn laughed. "Now there's an idea I hadn't thought of. You do have a knack for this stuff, cousin." He whistled a quick self-harmonizing air in something closer to hex than binary.

The table I'd put between us shimmered and puffed into smoke. Dairn was standing about ten feet away, holding a .45 automatic casually in one hand. That would have been a perfect moment for the Olympian security force to arrive and explain Zeus's policy on guns to my cousin, ideally beating it out on his skull in binary with their nightsticks. No such luck. He pointed the gun at my chest and gestured for me to stand. I did so, picking Melchior up with my left hand and my fallen drink with my right.

Dairn raised an eyebrow at me. "What are you planning to do, toast me to death?"

"No." I righted the empty glass and it refilled itself, as I had hoped it might. "I could just use a drink."

"Enjoy it," said Dairn. "It's going to be your last."

"Thanks."

I took a long sip, though I didn't taste it. The cavalry hadn't arrived, and Melchior was several minutes away from fully functional. I was on my own. Casually, as though I didn't have a care in the world, I half turned.

"Opa!" I said, throwing my glass into the fountain as if I wanted to shatter it on the bottom.

It hit with a huge splash, and ripples moved away from the point of impact. I bit the side of my mouth, hard.

"Any last words?" asked Dairn.

I shook my head, afraid the blood would slur my speech and give him a premature warning.

"Then I guess it's good-bye."

Out of the corner of my eye I saw him raise the pistol to point at my head. The Kevlar wouldn't save me this time. The ring of ripples had almost touched the wall of the fountain. I nodded.

"Good-bye, Dairn." I said. "I'll see you in Hades."

Then I closed my eyes and spat into the fountain. The flash of the explosion was huge and blinding. If I hadn't braced myself, it would have thrown me off my feet. Even then, the pressure wave hit me like a giant's slap. I don't know what it did to Dairn, but he didn't shoot me in that instant, and I didn't stay around to see how fast he'd recover. Instead, I leaped over the low side of the fountain into elsewhere.

It all comes down to chaos. My ancestors, the primal gods who gave birth to the whole Greek pantheon, were the Titans. They formed themselves from chaos, and chaos flows in the veins of their children and their children's children unto the last generation.

A faerie ring is a very special sort of chaos magic, a hole punched in reality. The easiest way for one of the descendants of the Titans to make one is to create a circle and charge it with his own blood. The more perfect the circle, the easier it is to form a ring. Likewise, the more chaotic the nature of the sorcerer, the more powerful the ring. Few circles are more perfect than a wave created by an object dropped in water, and the Raven is a power of chaos. Hence the bang and the flash.

Haemun was waiting for me on the balcony of Raven House. Time does not run evenly from DecLocus to DecLocus, so I stepped from late night into late morning with the shift. The tropical sun beat heavily upon my shoulders, and I handed Melchior to Haemun so I could strip off my leather jacket.

"Is Cerice here?" I asked.

Haemun shook his head. I wasn't surprised really. At the moment the only practical way to reach Raven House was via faerie ring, and Cerice had never used one on her own. Still, I'd had hopes. Haemun and I exchanged burdens as Melchior feebly began stirring.

"Can I get you anything?" asked Haemun.

"How about a virgin strawberry daiquiri?" I'd had enough of alcohol for a while. "Oh, and some shorts and a fresh shirt?"

"Certainly, sir. Might I also suggest some batteries for Melchior?"

"Good idea. Thanks."

In the old days, Melchior had drawn most of his power

from the omnipresent mweb itself, power the mweb servers channeled from the Primal Chaos, the driver of all magic. That was before the problem with Necessity and the tearing of the net. Now, as often as not, we spent time in DecLoci that had no mweb connection, and Melchior had to find alternate supplies. He preferred the chemical energy found in food but processed it much more slowly than the stuff from a direct electrical source. His movements were becoming firmer, more deliberate, so I carried him into the open porch that backed the balcony.

"What happened?" he whispered, as I set him on a chair near the fountain.

"Dairn crashed you." I flopped down across from him. "Pretty solidly, too."

"How in Hades' name did he manage that?"

"The same way he canceled that spell you tried to nail him with right before Tisiphone showed up." I whistled a little bit of binary nonsense and waggled my fingers. "Some kind of high-powered programming voodoo."

"That's crazy talk," said Melchior, though he didn't sound like he doubted me. "The last time we ran into Dairn, he didn't even own a real computer, just poor little Kira. Where the hell did he learn those kinds of leet skillz? And how'd he do it so quickly?"

"Poor little Kira?" I lifted my eyebrows.

Kira was a webpixie/PDA and tough as Dionysus's liver. She might only stand six inches tall, but she carried around six tons of attitude. Melchior had a soft spot for her.

He blushed but was saved from responding by the arrival of Haemun with a tray holding my drink, a couple of AA batteries, and a variety of snacks. In his free hand he held a pair of board shorts and a matching aloha shirt. They were technically in my colors—black penguins on black surfboards riding big waves in an emerald sea—but the sheer ugliness of the set looked more like something that might have come out of his closet. Of course, he didn't wear pants . . . and they were clean and dry, and I wasn't. So I didn't complain.

Mel tucked the AAs into his cheeks while I pulled off my

filthy party gear and changed. For a little while after that we said nothing. I just sipped my drink, and Mel did the same with his direct current.

Finally, he removed the batteries and set them on the tray. "What happened after I checked out?"

I told him about the faerie ring, and he whistled in appreciation. "Nice trick, very nice."

I grinned. "That sounds an awful lot like praise, Mel. Are you sure you're not feverish?"

"Don't let it go to your head. It's never been your competence I've worried about. It's your sanity and your sense of self-preservation. That and your near-suicidal need to make jokes at the worst possible time. I may have to excuse that one from here on out though; with Thalia as your grandmother it's probably in your blood. Stupid, but in your blood."

"Ah, there's the Melchior I'm used to. But you're right. It was a nice trick. Even I thought so. I guess it proves that anything that doesn't kill you really does make you stronger. I'd never have come up with it if I hadn't had the last faerie ring I built blow up in my face."

It was only the second one I'd ever made, and things had not gone at all according to plan. I'd put a lot of work and power into my first ring and had expected to do the same with the second, but no. Quite the contrary really. I'd barely begun when the thing had ignited, another side effect of the Raven transformation and my greater affinity for chaos.

Melchior rolled his eyes and made like he was about to say something, then paused. His expression went abstract in the way it always did when he received an incoming call over the mweb. Except that wasn't possible at Raven House. I felt a twinge in the depths of my stomach.

"You're not going to believe this," he said.

"I've got new mail?"

He nodded. "It's a request for Vtp from Cerice."

"How is she managing that?" I asked.

"It's via Taured."

"Taured?" The name didn't ring a bell.

"Clotho's new webtroll." Mel's voice came out flat and cold.

"Oh." That explained it.

Webtrolls are to Mel what he is to a PDA/pixie like Kira. Heavy-duty supercomputers, webtrolls draw their energy directly from the Primal Chaos. In fact, that's a big part of their purpose—transforming the raw stuff of chaos into the tame magic that flows through the mweb. The Fates use them to maintain and power the mweb in concert with the master servers and software supplied by Necessity. Their nature allows them to do all sorts of things impossible for a webgoblin like Mel, like connecting to places that aren't attached to the mweb by making a running calculation of the relative locations of the two DecLoci.

"What happened to Boxer, her old . . ."

Melchior looked away. The Fates were very hard on their hardware, and none too keen on the rights of the AI. It was one of the biggest reasons Cerice had resigned from Clotho's service, bigger even than her relationship with me.

"How could Cerice go back there?" asked Melchior. "Even for a couple of days?"

"I don't know. You'd better put her through. Maybe that way we'll find out."

Melchior nodded, and I spoke the formal request, "Melchior, Vlink; Ravirn@melchior.gob to Cerice@taured.trl. Please."

His eyes and mouth shot wide, and light poured out, three beams, blue, red, and green. They met at a point a few feet in front of his face and formed a misty globe of gold that quickly cleared to reveal a three-dimensional image of Cerice. I smiled at her, but the twinge in my belly had returned. She didn't look very happy.

"Hello, Cerice. I don't suppose you're calling for a ride home?"

She bit her lip and looked down for a second. "I'm afraid not. I'm going to stay here for a few days."

"Clotho make you an offer you couldn't refuse?" I asked it lightly, but I knew the Fates were more than capable of holding Cerice prisoner. They'd done it once already.

She shook her head. "No, or at least not that way. Necessity's really a mess, Ravirn. The virus that you . . . no, that's not fair. The Persephone virus that Shara carried did a number on her—on the whole mweb. There's been no communication from Necessity since the day Persephone was freed. None. And the network . . . It's bad enough that the Fates can't even tell how bad it is. At least ten percent of the world resource locator forks are fried, but it could be as many as half."

"Half?" The question burst out of me.

Cerice nodded. Half the mweb. That was almost incomprehensible. Even ten percent was terrifying, to say nothing of the silence of Necessity. The mweb ties together a theoretically infinite number of potential worlds. I say theoretically because in theory every decision splits reality such that one branch goes in each direction the decision could have gone. But in practical terms, a lot of decisions are pretty inconsequential, and in those cases the worlds just tend to collapse back together. Tiny changes *can* have huge effects on big systems, but mostly they don't. Reality has a lot of inertia, and until very recently Necessity had strongly added to the effect, *forcing* most world splits back together. But now, with Necessity off-line and as many as half the links in the mweb broken—my mind boggled.

"The Fates are very concerned," said Cerice, and it was obvious that she was as well. "The Fate Core is doing things they don't understand, self-programming weird work-arounds involving the old ley-line network, and spontaneously growing whole tiers of subroutines."

"Very concerned, that's euphemese for wigging out, right?" Melchior asked around the beam, inserting himself into the conversation for the first time.

"Pretty much," answered Cerice. "When they switched the soul-tracking and management system over from the ley net to the mweb a generation ago, they mostly closed down the ley architecture. A lot of the original infrastructure for running it doesn't even exist anymore."

"The old spinnerettes," I said.

"Exactly. But now the Fate Core appears to be re-creating them all on its own, and the Fates are beginning to think it's become self-aware."

I felt like a whole herd of icy-footed spiders had decided to hold a dance competition on my back. The Fates Do Not Like things to get out of their control—the current extremely complex state of my life is a testament to this fact. Calling them control freaks is akin to calling Ares a fight fan. The idea that the Fate Core—the computer that had replaced the Great Loom of Fate—might have become a creature with a will of its own would not be well received. Nor would the resurrection of the spinnerettes, and the Fates would be looking for someone to blame. The dancing spiders upped the tempo.

Every world had ley lines, spontaneously generated magical networks that connect the thin points in the walls of reality, the places where the Primal Chaos leaks through and makes magic easier. The Fates had always used them to monitor worlds and manage life threads, but a Fate had to physically go to a world to tap into its ley net. Sometime around the birth of the Roman Empire, the system had expanded beyond the ability of the Fates to manage it all directly. For another hundred years or so they'd kept trying, but the problem had only gotten exponentially worse.

Then Lachesis had reluctantly advanced the idea of the spinnerette, an elaborate, entirely magical entity that could both be tied in to the ley net of a world and transmit information and commands across the gulf between worlds. Because the process was so complex, and the devices would have to operate largely independently, the Fates had been forced to give them their own direct taps into the Primal Chaos for power and considerable self-awareness. In order to reduce their ability to cause the Fates problems, the spinnerettes had been bound to a set of rules of conduct and to physical items or locations.

But they were creatures of pure chaos magic and correspondingly rebellious. Over the years quite a number of them managed to trick mortals into aiding them to escape their servitude, most famously the one Aladdin had found bound to a lamp and mistakenly called a genie. The Fates absolutely hated having to use them but had no alternatives until the invention of the computer, which they had delightedly used to replace the spinnerettes. Not long after that, Necessity had transformed herself into the ultimate supercomputer to cope with the ever-expanding structure of reality. Then she'd spun the mweb to help her in the task, making the Fates its administrators and putting them eternally in her debt and, not coincidentally, under her thumb.

That was then. Now, Necessity was broken, the whole system was coming apart with wildly unpredictable results, and a good argument could be made that it was all my fault.

"Have they mentioned what they're going to do about all this?" I asked, trying to sound as casual as possible.

"Taured. Strictly Confidential. Please."

In the image, Cerice paused for a moment as though listening to something I couldn't hear, then nodded. Some of the color leached out of the projection, a sign that some sort of heavy encryption had been introduced.

"We're off the record for a few seconds," said Cerice. "They haven't sent anyone to kill you just yet, but I think that's more of an oversight than anything. They're desperate to get the mweb fixed, and the Fate Core problems have them very focused. That's the real reason Clotho called me back. They know Shara's still inside of Necessity, and possibly still running her security systems, and I'm the multiverse's number one Shara expert. I've got to help them. I'm needed here and—" Cerice glanced to one side as the projection suddenly brightened.

"Grandmother," she said, "I didn't . . . oh. Yes, of course I'll come. I was just saying good-bye to Ravirn." She turned back to me. "Anyway, like I said, I'm going to stay here for a while and see how much I can help. I know you can't reach me from there, so I'll call if I need you." She bit her lip again. "Good-bye, Ravirn."

"Good-bye, Cerice."

She blew me a kiss and was gone before I could respond. I hadn't gotten a chance to tell her about cousin Dairn either, which might have changed her mind about whether or not the Fates had decided to actively try to kill me. Then again, it might not. She had been welcomed back into the fold in a way that was forever closed to me. I sighed and took another sip of my daiquiri, then threw the glass so that it shattered against a pillar.

"Hell with it," I said to Melchior. "I'm going surfing. You want to come along?"

He looked warily from me to the shattered glass and then back again. Then he whistled a quick little spell that caused the mess to clean itself up.

"I suppose I'd better. Someone has to watch out for you."

I grabbed a short board, since I was in a mood for aquabatics and spectacular wipeouts rather than long, smooth rides. I could have used a variety of magic to short-circuit the long hike down to the beach or the paddle out to the break point, but I also felt the need to break a sweat.

I was tired and dehydrated and more than a little strung out after the adrenaline fest getting shot had caused, and the paddling in particular made me ache, but it all felt right. There's something deeply soothing about working your body so hard you can barely remember you have a brain, much less listen to it whine about things you can't change.

When we hit the main break, I paddled just a little bit farther and rolled off my board to bob in the swells. The water felt surprisingly cold as it invaded the shorty wetsuit I'd donned. But it warmed to body temperature quickly. For a while I just played kelp, riding up and down beyond the break and mindlessly watching the long waves roll in. They were powerful, breaking in the classic Hawaiian pipeline, but foamy in the gusty wind.

I tried to let go of everything but simply being. It's something I'm not very good at most of the time, but it's easier out there, away from land with nothing between me and Alaska but ocean. I probably lost a half hour in the lull between two thoughts.

When I came back to myself, I reached down to my ankle, grabbed the leash, and reeled in the board.

"Better?" asked Melchior, as the tug alerted him to my return to the here and now—he's learned to let me alone when I'm kelping, and I appreciated his patience.

"Yeah, quite a bit, actually." I slid onto the board, tilting it and almost tumbling him off. "Sorry about that."

"I wish you wouldn't do that," he said.

"Do what?"

"Apologize preemptively. It drains all the fun out of making snide remarks about the gentle grace of the lesser Greek walrus."

"Oh, Mel, I *am* sorry. Would it help if I accidentally punted you into the water? Because, you know, anything for you. Raven's only here to help."

"Thanks, but I'll just wait to get soaked until you fall off a wave and take me with you."

"Good enough," I said, digging deep and heading us in toward the break.

I kept an eye cocked behind me, both looking for the right wave and making sure not to get under the wrong one. I spotted what I wanted soon enough and paddled harder. I needed to be moving fast when it caught up to me, or I'd miss it. Once I was up, Melchior crawled out to the nose of the board and leaned over the edge. He won't admit it, but I think he likes surfing almost as much as I do. For a little while I just slid gently up and down the face of the wave, getting a feel for it. Then I shot right up to the crest and tried a cutback to reverse course on the wave. It could have been beautiful . . . if I hadn't buried the nose in the curl and cartwheeled right off the board.

The next wave went better, though I didn't try anything too showy. After that I was pretty much in the groove and even managed a beautiful little layback without killing myself. Everything was going wonderfully until I noticed a shadow as I was shooting the tube of another wave.

There's this wild joy to be found in the front end of the tube, with the green darkness closing in behind and the sunlight at the end of the tunnel hanging just out of reach. If you get a good wave and play it right, you can stay there for ages, chasing that circle of light. I'd found the sweet spot on a beauty and was just gliding along when I realized the silvery gray shadow paralleling me a few feet away in the body of the wave shouldn't have been there.

It was a shark, riding the inside of the breaker in a perfect mirror of the way I was riding its surface. I'd seen that happen once or twice before, but this baby was big, ten or twelve feet, and close. If I reached out my right hand, I could have touched the tip of its closest fin. Also, it was exactly even with me and had been for a while before I really noticed it. The whole thing creeped me out. Sure, shark attacks are rare. If you leave them alone, they'll mostly leave you alone. But did *it* know that?

I leaned away from the shark, sliding down the wave and speeding up to get out of the tube. It nosed down and accelerated smoothly, staying right with me.

"Melchior, Shark Circuit," I said. "Please."

Melchior began to whistle as we came out into the sun. The codespell was something I'd come up with recently as a surfing tool. Like all of my latest magical compositions, it was mweb independent, and more dangerous because of that, especially for Mel. I didn't much like that, but the Fates hadn't specced out webgoblins with undigested chaos in mind the way they had the webtrolls. Despite all my modifications and upgrades, Mel was still built on a webgoblin frame.

As he finished the spell, a tiny chaos tap kicked in, creating and powering a madly pulsing electrical field tied to my board. Sharks have electricity-sensing organs, and we'd tuned the field to thrash the hell out of them.

In the water beside me, the shark did a neat barrel roll but didn't move away. Great, I'd found an electrically blind shark. Looking ahead I could see that my wave was about to peter out, too, leaving me pretty much stopped in the water. That's when the shark winked at me. It was very slow and very deliberate, and I had no doubt it was a wink. I jerked away hard and just about flipped my board doing it. I would have died if that had happened. I might anyway.

The shark had mirrored pupils.

"Dairn!"

CHAPTER FOUR

"What?" yelped Melchior. "Dairn? Where?"

"The shark! It's him, I don't know how."

I was already leaning back for a turn. Pivoting the board on its tail, I headed to my right, up the wave. I needed to get over the top and down the back even though that meant crossing above the shark. I didn't dare ride any farther, or I'd go down in the soup—the white-water mess that happens when a big wave falls apart. The idea terrified me. I'm tougher and stronger than your average surfer, but that meant nothing if I was tumbling around in the water effectively blind with a hostile shark.

"Melchior—" I began as soon as I could spare the breath.

"On it," he said, whistling the opening bar of Board to Run.

The spell kicked in when we slid down the back of the wave, shifting us from gravity-driven to magically and starting the board accelerating out toward the open ocean. Unfortunately, that pointed us straight at the next big wave. It was already breaking, so I threw myself flat on the board and duck-dived through the crest, sheltering Mel with my body. It felt like someone had dropped a very soggy brick wall on me, but I didn't have a lot of choice. I'd been heading into the break zone, and it was safer to head offshore than in through the chop at the moment. I could turn around and figure out how to get back to shore when I hit the rollers and calmer water.

As I came out the back of the wave, I saw a silvery fin slicing the water beside me. Frightening, but at least I knew where he was. Then the next breaker was coming down on top of me, and I lost track of the shark. Swearing, I climbed back to my feet. I had better control that way, and I sure as hell wasn't going to do any paddling with that thing some-where below me.

"Where did he go?" I asked Melchior, trying not to squeak. The only thing between us and a fall into the shark's world was a thin plank.

He peered over the edge. "I don't know. I can't see him. We've got to get out of here." He sounded panicky, and I couldn't blame him.

I nodded. "I'd try the splash faerie-ring trick again, but there's too much chop to hold the circle. Any suggestions?"

"Not really. I can't LTP us out of here without the mweb, and I don't know any good mweb-independent flight spells. I'd try composing one, but the turbulence has me seriously croggled, and this would be an exceptionally bad time to blow a hack."

"No ambition to end up as shark sushi?" I asked as lightly as I could manage.

I turned the board back toward the beach. That's when the shark returned. This time he announced his presence by nipping off one of the board's fins. He did it gently, almost lovingly, but the impact nearly flipped us. We had to stop playing his game. That meant chaos magic, serious chaos magic.

Breathing deeply, I reached inward, trying to find the place where blood and chaos merged. The sun dimmed as I found it, occluded by the shadow of a huge raven that wasn't really there. The Raven. The shape of my power. The shape of my soul. And with a wicked twist of will, the shape of my body.

The spell was a hack, a set of magical instructions put together on the fly. I'd performed the trick several times now, and each time I'd done it slightly differently. I was beginning to think I *couldn't* repeat the process exactly, that subtle differences in my starting circumstances would force me to reorder the sequence every time. But that was the essence of chaos, wasn't it? That and change.

Like the change from something not quite a man into something not quite a bird. A change that required rearranging every single molecule in my body all in the split second before the universe caught on and turned me into a spreading ball of organic mush. It hurt. Chaos and Discord, it hurt. In that moment between shapes, all the atoms of my body were disconnected from each other. I had no nerves to carry signals, no brain for the signals to reach, nothing at all. Yet the soul remembered the process of being torn to shreds, remembered and carried the pain into the new form.

My first word in the new shape was a harsh caw of pure agony. My second: an Anglo-Saxonism of the four-letter variety. My third was Melchior's name, called out as I swept forward above the surfboard and caught him in my claws. It was only just in time. Whether the shark with Dairn's eyes had already decided to stop playing with us, or whether the final attack was triggered by his awareness of my transformation, I don't know. Whatever the case, when he hit this time, it was no gentle nip, it was a crushing blow of the jaws, shattering the board from below.

But I was already climbing up and away, with Melchior hanging beneath me. As I headed back toward Raven House, I could see the shark arrowing along below us, and I had a nasty suspicion that reaching land wouldn't stop him.

"Mel?" I cawed in my raven's voice.

"Yeah."

"What do you think the odds are that thing's going to come out of the water in the near future?"

"Let's just say I don't think we should to stop to wash the dishes when we get back to the house."

"That's what I thought, too. Is there some way we can warn Haemun to find someplace safe to wait things out? I doubt it'll stay long after we leave."

There was a long pause before Melchior finally answered, "Yeah, hang on."

He whistled a choppy string of binary, then spat. A short crossbow bolt with a note tied around it emerged from his mouth and went winging ahead of us.

"How do you know he'll find it in time?" I asked.

"I aimed for a window."

"That should do it." Haemun is not a fan of messes in Raven House. "What if it hits him?"

"No problem, it's got a blunted tip. It might hurt like Hades' own kick in the ass, but it shouldn't do any major tissue damage."

"Good enough. Next question: Where to?"

"How about Castle Discord?" he asked.

"I thought you didn't much like Eris," I cawed.

"I don't. She scares me, all the way down to the chipset. Worse, I owe her my soul."

That was quite literally true. Without the intervention of Eris and Tyche, or Discord and Fortune if you prefer, webgoblins and their kin would never have developed self-awareness.

"Shouldn't that make it better?" I asked.

"No. She didn't do it for my sake. She did it to thwart the Fates. Knowing you exist because Fate was trying to come up with a better way to rule the world is bad enough. Knowing that the reason you're a person and not a thing is because Discord thought it would make for a good joke at Fate's expense is so much worse. I'm the moral equivalent of that damn golden apple that started the Trojan War. If a different humor had taken her the day she messed around with webgoblin design specs, the multiverse might have a better class of rubber vomit instead of me. Quite frankly, it gives me the wobblies in my subroutines."

"So why suggest we go see her?" The question was becoming more urgent, as we would soon reach the House and its built-in faerie ring.

"Because, for reasons unknown and possibly unknowable, she likes you. If she can think of some way to make helping you irritate the forces of order more than not helping you would, she'll do it. Since she's enormously powerful and—as usual—you can use all the help you can get, it seems worth the risk. Besides, it's not like we're talking about moving into her basement or anything. Even you're not that cracked."

Then we arrived at Raven House and decision time.

"Castle Discord it is," I croaked, dropping down to touch the swirl of black within the green stone of the lanai.

We entered the faerie ring and found . . . infinite possibility. I hovered in a million different places all at the same time, none of them the one I wanted. The Castle Discord faerie ring I'd used in the past didn't currently exist. No surprise really; Castle Discord didn't exactly exist in the normal sense of the word, either. It changed constantly to fit Eris's mood and whim.

Well, perhaps there was a loophole. That *was* the nature of what little divinity I possessed, finding the loophole in the stuff of reality—the elegant hack. Feeling my way into the Raven's power over the faerie-ring network, *my* power, I reached for the circle I'd used before, the one absent from the current Castle Discord. Potentialities flashed through my awareness—rings that had existed, rings that would exist, rings that could exist—there! I touched the echo of a place that was no longer and pushed. Possible became probable became actual. Another ring joined the network, a part of me within it. I focused my attention and . . . stood within a ring of forget-me-nots in a greenhouse beneath a golden-apple sun. Castle Discord.

I stepped out of the ring and went away.

Discontinuity.

"Hello, Raven." Discord's voice brought me back.

The greenhouse flickered into being and was gone in the

same instant. We stood now upon a bridge of glass over a river made up of the eternally changing stuff of Primal Chaos. That was my first impression. My second was of a glass tunnel suspended within that same river. One moment it seemed to be all around us, the next in one direction only. The only solid points of reference were a pair of large arched doors, one a hundred feet ahead, the other a hundred behind. Those, and the goddess herself. Well, sort of.

Eris is a creature of change. Her hair and skin are gold or black . . . and both at the same time. Like taffeta, how she looks depends on how you look at her. Some things change less than others. She is always tall. She is always beautiful, though sometimes it is the unattainable perfection of a marble goddess and sometimes the pure lusty sexiness of a Kama Sutra angel. She is always, always dangerous.

Today it appeared that she had decided to spare me the come-hither that hurts—she *is* a virgin goddess and only turns on the carnality to create trouble. She was just under seven feet if you didn't count the six-inch stiletto heels on the flimsy-looking sandals whose straps twined like golden black snakes around her feet and ankles, twisting and climbing up her bare calves to just below her knees. A short split skirt of something like silk clutched at the curves of her hips and thighs, shifting its colors at the slightest movement. Above she wore an equally clingy blouse. It was nearly transparent, and I could see . . .

I swallowed and shook my head. *Damn it!* She was doing it to me again, more subtly this time, jacking up the sex appeal slowly as my eyes climbed upward.

"Would you please stop that?" I asked, and only as I missed the harsh cawing undertone of my words did I realize I was no longer a literal raven. I had been transformed once again. "You're quite terrifying. You know that, don't you?"

Eris laughed, and the sound was beautiful and terrible, like windows breaking in the city of the gods. The sex appeal blew away in the puff of wind that ruffled and opaqued her blouse at the same time it disarranged her hair. The marble goddess had arrived.

"Oh, Raven, I do miss you when you aren't around. But it's your own fault. It wouldn't be such fun if you didn't fall for it every time."

"Don't call me Raven."

"Whatever you say, Boss." She mimicked Melchior perfectly, and I realized for the first time that I didn't see him.

"Where's—"

"In your bag," she answered, "sleeping it off."

"Sleeping what off?" I demanded.

"The chaos time."

"I don't think I understand," I said.

"Don't you?" The question was not a question, it was a challenge. Her tone said that the only reason I didn't know the answer was that I was fooling myself somehow.

"Tell me that again but look me in the eyes this time," she said. "You haven't yet. I think we both know why, and it's not just because you so like looking at the rest of me." She ran her hands down her sides suggestively, and for an instant the sex appeal was back. "Come on, you know you don't want to."

This challenge I understood, and I had to answer it or lose face, to say nothing of self-respect, so I forced myself to look into Discord's eyes. Of course, I saw myself looking back. The chaos that had devoured my pupils owns all of Discord's eyes. It had scared me when mine were still black slits. Now, it was utterly terrifying. They say the eyes are the mirror of the soul, and in meeting hers I was forced to acknowledge my own recent soul-deep transformation.

"Better," she said, and smiled. "Much better."

"It hurts," I answered. It did. "In so very many ways." Not the least of which was the sudden deeper understanding of all that had come between me and Cerice.

For an instant a look of something very like sympathy flickered across her face. But it came and went too fast for me really to tell, and the look that replaced it was more than a little smug.

"Pain is how you can tell you're alive. If you wake up some morning and nothing hurts, it means you're dead. And then you go to Hades."

"It's funny," I said. "I don't understand *why* you don't get more dinner invitations."

"It's because my eyes glow in the dark," she replied.

I sighed and lifted my hands in surrender. Fencing with Eris, whether physically or verbally, is a losing proposition. She always plays for blood and nearly always gets it.

"Chaos time?" I asked, trying to change the subject back to what had happened with Melchior.

"When you transported yourself here."

"You lost me."

"Castle Discord is not a place," said Eris.

"I know that. It's a Greatspell of some sort, a permanent piece of magic surrounded by the stuff of chaos." I gestured at the churn flowing around the glass tunnel.

Castle Discord is off the net, way off, floating completely alone in the place between the worlds. It is not attached to any DecLocus and has no world resource locator fork.

She nodded. "That, too, but I meant something else in this case. When you enter a faerie ring, you enter all faerie rings. You know that, right?"

"Uh-huh."

"Do you know why?"

"I—" It had never occurred to me to think about it. "No."

She pointed through the wall. "That out there is the very stuff of randomness. Potentially it can become anything at all, even a god."

"The Titans," I supplied.

"Exactly. They self-organized from chaos, created structure from its antithesis. They are hybrid beings, chaos arranged by will into the illusion of order."

"It's an awfully solid sort of illusion. You, me, all of us in the pantheon are their children. Wars have been fought between the generations. Are you saying *we're* all illusions, too?"

"Yes and no. The Titanomachy was real enough. Most of the children of the Titans are creatures of order, whatever their actual allegiance. Zeus is no illusion, not physically. Nor is Tartarus, where he imprisoned the Titans after the war. Neither are the Fates, for that matter. There is much that is real in the pantheosphere. You, however, are not. No more than I am."

My stomach did a backflip with a triple twist and failed to stick the landing. I felt sweat break out on my forehead. I couldn't possibly be an illusion. For one thing, no illusion would feel so queasy.

"That's crazy," I said.

"A few weeks ago, you broke down the wall between the Primal Chaos and Hades, let the stuff out there"—she pointed through the glass once again—"into the realm of order, into the land of the dead. Chaos devours everything it touches. It devoured you, rendered your body back into the stuff of potentiality. And yet here you stand."

"That doesn't mean—"

"Don't be a fool. When you entered the faerie ring on your way here, you wore the body of a giant raven." She spread her arms and they became great black wings. Flapped them closed, and they returned to arms. "Now you do not. You are a shapechanger, a power of chaos. You are no longer your skin and its contents. You *are* chaos."

She stepped forward and pinched my cheek between her fingers. "This is an illusion, a lie you tell the universe. Just as everything here"—she gestured at the bridge and the doorways at either end—"is another kind of illusion. Castle Discord is also chaos, shaped by will and magic into my ever-changing home. When you forced a faerie ring to appear in a part of the castle that didn't then exist and stepped through, you stepped into chaos. That is part of my defenses."

"If that's true, why wasn't I destroyed? Or if I was, why did I come back so quickly? It took weeks for me to get back after what happened in Hades."

"Because you are what you are, the same as the stuff beyond my walls. And who says it *didn't* take weeks. How would you know?"

My stomach felt even worse, though I was certain I hadn't been without a body for weeks—I didn't feel the way I had after coming back the last time. But if Eris was right, I'd unwittingly and unthinkingly taken Melchior into the Primal Chaos.

"What happened with Melchior?" I asked, my voice barely above a whisper.

"Your will protected him from the stuff of your being, but the psychic pressure of being trapped out there was very hard on him. He is a manufactured thing, a creature almost wholly of order."

"He's a person, not a thing!"

"In soul, yes," said Eris. "And that part of himself he has aligned with you, a creature of chaos. His physical nature, on the other hand . . . he is a computer, one of the most ordered of constructions." She sighed. "I see that still you doubt. Perhaps a more thorough demonstration."

Eris closed her eyes for a second. Then opened them. Wide. Wider. Her lids separated an inch, two, five. The chaos in her eyes swallowed her entire head. Then her body. Her shape stayed the same, but she became a clear vessel filled with chaos. She spread her arms as she had earlier. The lines of her body relaxed and stretched until a huge bird shape, defined only by the chaos within it, hung in the air in front of me.

Then she reversed the process, coloring herself in, starting with her tail feathers. A great raven with chaos-colored eyes faced me for one instant. I blinked, and in the beat between the closing and opening of my eyes she became Eris the goddess once again, dressed now in black-and-gold motorcycle leathers much tighter and better tailored than my own. It was only then that I realized my aloha shirt and board shorts had gone wherever it was I'd left the wings and feathers.

I couldn't help it, I slapped myself. Broken-glass laughter filled the air as I rubbed my now stinging cheek.

"You are such an odd child," said Eris. "The lie you tell the universe is the same one you tell yourself. To wear the flesh is to be the flesh in most respects. How else do you think the Titans produced ordered offspring?"

"So I take it this means I don't get a free pass into the genuine immortals club? If someone kills me, I still die?"

"No you don't, and yes you will. Someday perhaps, when your power has grown and your image of what you are has changed, the lie you tell the universe will come to include that sort of clause, but only if you live long enough. I have real doubts about that."

"Me, too," said a disgruntled voice from my bag.

I unzipped the top, and Melchior poked his head out.

"I take it we've arrived?" he asked.

"We have indeed."

"Does that mean that you're arguing metaphysics with Discord instead of getting down to business?"

"As usual," said Eris. "He's so easy to bait. Why *did* you come all this way for a visit?" She gave me the perplexed look of a particularly harmless old grandmother.

"Dairn," said Melchior.

"Of Atropos's brood?" asked Eris. "Colors, mottled browns? An archer? Shot you through the arm, I believe? Not very bright?"

"That's the old description," I said. "Things have changed."

I quickly filled her in on our more recent encounters.

"You're sure he was the shark?" she asked at the end.

"Not sure—" I began. But that wasn't right. "Yes, I am, though I can't say why."

"I can," said Eris. "It was because you saw yourself in the mirrors of his eyes."

"Well, they are *mirrors*," I said, trying to sound perplexed.

"And earlier you saw yourself in *my* eyes," said Eris, "but we both know that neither of those things is what I meant. No, what I meant is that you have seen your Nemesis."

I didn't like the weight she'd given to that last word, not at all. "Don't you mean nemesis?"

"No. I don't. No more than I mean necessity when I say Necessity."

"So then, we're talking about Nemesis the goddess, right? I just want to be clear on that, because I've always been taught that she was dead."

Eris nodded. "Yes, and she is."

"Fabulous, I'm being pursued by a dead goddess. What fun."

"That's a new one," said Melchior. Then he shrugged. "Of course, if anyone can find a way to make something like that happen, it's you, Boss."

"Thanks, Melchior, that really helps." I turned my attention back to Discord. "I don't suppose you're pulling my leg, joshing with old Ravirn to make his life a little more discordant?"

She laughed and a tableful of wineglasses fell to ruin in the sound. "No, I'm not. Oh, I would, but in this case I don't have to. Unpleasant truths are infinitely more useful in my business than unpleasant lies. Surely, you've learned that much about me by now?"

"I have, I just keep hoping it'll turn out I was wrong. So, tell me about the dead goddess who wants my head."

"All right. To start with, 'dead' is somewhat imprecise in this case."

"I would never have guessed that, what with her wandering around and trying to kill me instead of resting in peace in Hades."

"Do you want to hear this, or do you want to irritate Discord?" she asked. "Because I'd be perfectly happy to play the irritation game if that's what you want."

"Sorry," I said. "Stress makes me sarcastic."

"There's news," said Melchior, "along with 'Zeus likes nymphs' and 'Morpheus is dreamy.' "

"And 'like master like familiar,' " said Eris.

"Hey," snapped Melchior, "that's . . ."

"Yes, little man?" asked Eris.

"Nothing. I keep forgetting that I don't want you to notice me. I'll just be shutting up now and crawling back down into the bag, shall I?"

"Whatever makes you most uncomfortable," said Eris. Melchior slipped out of sight. "Now, where was I? Oh yes, Nemesis. Shall we walk?" She didn't wait for an answer, just started moving. "She's not dead so much as bodiless."

"Like Necessity?" I asked as I followed in her wake.

"No, not all. Necessity still has a body, several really,

though they're made of plastic and silicon rather than flesh and blood. She is as much a creature of hardware as she is of software, though where that hardware is physically housed is a secret known only to the Furies."

And maybe Shara, I thought, but didn't say.

"Nemesis is something else again. Like Necessity, she had a body once, but she did not give it up willingly. It was destroyed in a battle with the Furies."

"Is that what happened?" I asked. "Why?"

It was something I'd wondered about whenever my grandmother had mentioned the demise of Nemesis. That and how a goddess, a true immortal, *could* die.

"She challenged Necessity, or rather, her existence was a challenge to Necessity's authority, which is pretty much the same thing."

I started to ask a question but got derailed because we'd reached the end of the glass tunnel and stepped through the gate into . . . the glass tunnel. Ahead, I could see us just stepping out the other end.

"The hell?" I mumbled.

"What? Oh, sorry. I forgot to turn that off. I like to walk here and think sometimes, and having to turn around can disrupt me, so I make it unnecessary. Hang on a second . . . is that better?"

It was. With no transition we were elsewhere. Or rather, elsewhere was here, since Eris didn't move us at all. She mentally rearranged the castle around us. Now we stood in the heart of a huge shopping mall. All around us people bustled from shop to shop, people with golden apples where their heads should have been. It was distracting, but I didn't mention it. That would only have given Eris more ammunition for later. Instead, I just waited quietly for her to continue.

"Nemesis is a goddess of vengeance," she said. "At one time she was even The Goddess of Vengeance, visiting the wrath of the gods on the heads of men, and the wrath of Necessity on the heads of the gods. The only problem with the system was that she was a freelancer who didn't so much take orders from the powers that be as listen to suggestions.

Sometimes the heads she busted hadn't earned the wrath of anybody but Nemesis, and sometimes the heads she was supposed to bust didn't interest her."

"I can see how that might not go over so well," I said rather dryly. "Thou shalt not do this, that, or the other thing."

My own experiences with the gods had shown me just how much they didn't like to be thwarted, especially the hard-core control freaks like my grandmother Lachesis and the other Fates. And Necessity was the Fate of the Gods.

"Exactly," said Eris. "Necessity liked the idea of Nemesis, but not the execution, so she came up with a less independent version in the Furies. Of course, Nemesis didn't much like the idea of being cast aside for not just one, but three, younger women. I can't say that I blame her. There were several battles early on, and mostly the Furies came out on the losing end. Even as a group they weren't as strong as Nemesis in her heyday."

I swallowed hard at that. I'd gone up against the Furies a couple of times and survived through a combination of luck and being a particularly entertaining squeaky toy—you know, the kind a cat doesn't want to break all at once. Individually, any of them outclassed me on the divine scale. Collectively, I'd seen them take down Eris, and she and I had about as much in common in the chaos power department as Castle Discord and the kind of castle you make from sand.

"There's no need to look quite so worried," said Eris. "That was in the youth of the world, when she still had a body and wore the mantle of a great power. She is much reduced from those days, though it took the combined efforts of the Furies and the direct intervention of Necessity to reduce her so."

"By direct intervention do you mean . . ."

"In the flesh, yes. This was in the days before she transformed herself into the computer at the heart of the multiverse."

"Nemesis is still around despite all that?" Eris nodded. "Then I think I've got every right to look this worried. Shouldn't she have died at that point?"

"Probably, but I don't think Necessity wanted that. If she'd died and descended into Hades, she might have drunk of the waters of Lethe. Then, her memories washed away, her soul could have returned. But her soul is the soul of vengeance, and she would have returned as a goddess in full to start the whole round all over again. Necessity didn't want that, and she made sure it didn't happen. I'm not sure exactly how she managed it, though I think Hades must have been in on the plot from the beginning. Disembodied, Nemesis does not represent a threat on the same scale."

"She sounds plenty threatening to me," said Melchior.

"I thought you decided to check out of this conversation," Eris said with a grin.

"Yeah, Mel." I winked at him. "I was actually kind of enjoying hearing about my impending doom without a string of 'I told you sos' and 'Here we go agains.' "

He made a rude noise at me but kept his head out of the bag.

"So," I asked, "if she's been wandering around bodiless this whole time, how come I've never heard of it until now?"

"Because for more than three thousand years, no word has been heard of her. Where she has been all that time, I don't know. Perhaps Tartarus. Believe me, I looked everywhere I could."

"Why?" Apparently I wasn't the only who was interested, as a number of the apple heads had gathered around us to listen.

"Because Nemesis in opposition to Necessity would create great discord."

"Oh. Foolish question, I guess. I wonder where she's been and why she's come back."

Eris smiled. It was not a smile of the kind that invites you to smile along. It was the kind a shark smiles at its soon-to-be lunch.

"The first is easy," said Eris. "She has been wherever Necessity trapped her after the ambush."

"And the second? The why?"

"I wouldn't worry about that too much if I were you. You

have a much more important question to concern yourself with."

"Oh. What's that?" I asked.

"How are you going to prevent her from killing you?"

"That's an important one, yeah. I don't suppose you have any suggestions?"

"No. Nemesis is vengeance personified. She will never give up, she will never back down, she cannot be killed. I don't think you'll get out of this one."

CHAPTER FIVE

"Do you really believe I'm going to die?" I asked.

"I'm quite certain of it," said Eris. "But I was also certain that you would die when you faced Hades in the heart of his power, and when you went up against the Fates."

I wasn't sure how to take that. "Does that mean you're certain I'll die, but you expect me to get out of it somehow?"

"No. Nothing so hopeful as that. I expect you to die. If you do, I have the satisfaction of being right. If you don't, I have the entertainment of watching you slip the noose. Either way, it's a win for me."

"Happy to be of service," I said, sourly.

"Don't be that way about it," said Eris. "There's no reason to get mad at me for making the best of a bad situation."

"A bad situation for *me*, you mean. For you it's like a damned sports highlights reel."

I turned away from Eris and stomped off through the crowd of apple-headed not-people. I needed time to think without her picking at me, and that meant being where she was not. Though I like Eris far more than I should, Discord is both her title and her nature.

"Well, this is different," Melchior said after a while.

"What?" I asked.

"Mall walking." He gestured around us. "Are you thinking of taking early retirement?"

I glared at him, and he grinned back. I looked away first. If Eris was telling the truth about our arrival in chaos—always a dubious proposition—I'd risked his life unthinkingly. That smacked of our old relationship as master and servant—the one I worked so hard not to perpetuate. My chest felt as though my heart had put on some serious weight.

"Come on, Boss, smile. It was a joke."

"My capacity for funny is somewhat limited at the moment, Mel."

"It's OK," he said, very softly.

"What's OK?" I asked.

"The chaos stuff. I'm fine, I didn't dissolve, and it wasn't weeks. Eris fished us out after a couple of hours. It's really not much worse than a bad migraine."

OK, so a migraine is much better than being eaten alive by the magical equivalent of acid. That didn't make me feel much better about the whole thing. It could have gone the other way so easily, and a blinding headache's not exactly a bundle of laughs either. How did you apologize for something like that?

"How'd you know I was thinking about that?" I asked.

"I've been your familiar for what, eight years, two months, three days, four hours, seven minutes, and three point two-two-nine-three seconds? I know how you think and what your expressions mean."

"I didn't think about . . . I didn't think." I felt I had a chestful of glass shards. "I'm really sorry, Melchior. Forgive me. Please."

"Well, when you phrase it like that, how can I refuse? Besides, it was educational in a 'that which does not kill us makes us stronger' kind of way." He winked at me, and suddenly I knew that everything was fine between us though I still felt a little tender in the heart area.

"Thanks, Mel, that makes me feel sooo much better." We had wandered into the mall's food court. I sat down at one of those awful little tables and placed Mel in front of me so we could see eye to eye. "What *are* we going to do about Nemesis?"

"I don't know, Boss. One thing I think we should do is ignore Discord's advice about the priorities of why and how."

"What do you mean?" I asked.

"Well, Nemesis has been out of the picture for three thousand years, and now, all of a sudden, she's back and after your hide. Knowing why she returned might tell us how to keep her from killing us."

"Killing me," I said firmly. If I had to die, I didn't want to take anyone with me, especially Melchior. "But you might have a point there. How'd you get so smart?"

He looked as though he were seriously weighing the question. "Well, clearly it's not the company I keep."

I stuck my tongue out at him. *"Thanks."*

"Anytime."

"So, do you have any ideas on why Nemesis might have decided to end her retirement just for little ol' me, besides the obvious fact that her new body has a long-standing, murderous grudge against me, or was that a more general comment?"

"Not really, but normally, when murder is in the works, you try to figure out motive and opportunity."

"That first one would put Hades and Atropos at the top of the list," I said. "Both of them have promised to kill me fairly recently. What do you think?"

"That making enemies of Death and Fate is not the best survival plan. Let's see, what else do we know? How about this? Eris mentioned that Hades was probably in on what happened to Nemesis way back when. That might put him in a position to find her."

"True, but it's not just Nemesis. We shouldn't forget she's wearing Dairn's body, and Dairn is House Atropos."

"Does that make Atropos more or less likely to be involved?" asked Melchior. "Dairn hates you for his own sake and might not have involved her. Also, would she really want her great-grandson to become a vessel for Nemesis?"

"If she thought she could control him? She'd do it in a black heartbeat. Atropos would be delighted to have a power—even a reduced power of the sort Nemesis has become—in Fate's service. I don't think she'd hesitate at sacrificing the part of Dairn that makes him Dairn if it meant having Vengeance under her thumb."

Mel got up and paced around the perimeter of the little table. "I can't argue with that, but would she know where to find Nemesis? Would she dare to defy Necessity?"

"Those are tougher questions. Fate's awfully good at finding things out. Atropos has access to the Fate Core and all those life threads and the information they hold."

"But Nemesis's thread is held directly by Necessity, like the rest of the powers," argued Mel.

A couple of apple heads carrying trays picked that exact moment to sit down at the table next to ours. For a moment I was torn between staying to see if and how they'd eat without mouths and getting away from them before I found those things out. Then I noticed that all they had on their trays was large sheets of caramel and Popsicle sticks—the makings of caramel apples—and decided it was time to move on.

"If Nemesis," I said, "wherever she was—interacted with anyone whose life thread is held in the Fate Core, Atropos could have learned of it. For that matter, Atropos and Hades are on excellent terms. There's no reason she couldn't have asked him."

"Or they could be in it together. Each knows how much the other hates you."

"That's a really ugly thought, Mel." It made a nasty sort of sense. "On the other hand, it doesn't answer your question about Atropos's willingness to defy Necessity. Atropos seemed awfully afraid of her at Eris's hubris trial. All the Fates did."

"True," said Mel, "but things have changed. The Persephone virus really hurt Necessity. Maybe she's weak enough that the Fates see this as an opportunity to move up a level. I'm sure Atropos hates taking orders from Necessity on anything, and there's the added spur provided by the changes in the Fate Core."

"The more we talk about this, the less I like it. We've got zero evidence, but there's a logic to it that makes me queasy. It'd make releasing Nemesis a twofer."

"What do you mean?" asked Mel.

"Necessity made the Furies to replace Nemesis, and she made them wholly her own. They even call her 'Mother.' If someone really wanted to move in on Necessity's operation, they'd pretty much have to get the Furies out of the way first. How better than introducing an alternative power of vengeance, one with a proven track record of beating the Furies."

"That *is* an interesting thought," said a voice from the nearest of the apple heads.

"I figured you'd listen," I said.

The apple head developed a smile rather like the Cheshire cat's. A moment later the rest of it began to fade into transparency, until it looked like a hollow figure made from glass. The glass filled with chaos, then stretched and flowed until Eris stood in its place, wearing the Cheshire cat grin.

"That's too bad," she said. "Eavesdropping's ever so much more fun when the targets think they're alone."

"Gosh, I'm really sorry to disappoint you, but only a complete idiot would think he could hang around Castle Discord without you knowing everything he did."

Eris laughed long and loud.

"What's so funny?" I demanded.

"Uh, Boss, you do remember how we met Discord, don't you? The whole breaking in here and looking for electronic evidence to clear your name bit?"

"That's different," I said. "That was a cracking run. We were supposed to get in and out without her ever knowing we'd been here. This time, we practically knocked on the front door."

"You tried to sneak in through a nonexistent faerie ring," said Eris.

"I wasn't sneaking. I'd planned on finding you as soon as we arrived. Besides, it's unfair bringing up that first time. I didn't know anything about you that hadn't been filtered through Fate family horror stories. I was young and foolish then."

"As opposed to now, when you're old and foolish?" asked Melchior.

"Can we just get back to Nemesis?"

"Only if it makes you more uncomfortable," said Eris. "I've got a reputation to uphold."

I sighed and wished I could ask her to drop it for five minutes. I didn't because I'd come to care about Eris. Her role as Discord required that she make a pain of herself. Even if she really wanted to let things go, she couldn't. It was a fact that I was pretty sure caused her genuine hurt on a frequent basis. Being a power had costs, and any request from me along those lines would only serve to emphasize her pain.

Instead, I said, "Then we're good. The more I think about Nemesis, the scarier she seems and the more uncomfortable I get. Especially when I think of her working with Atropos and Hades."

"Say Fate and Hades, and I think you'll hit closer to the mark." Eris's smile was poisonously bitter. "Unless, of course, you entertain illusions about the inherent righteousness of Atropos's sisters."

My laugh was as bitter as her smile. "Not after my own grandmother agreed to cut my thread for defying her. That's not a lesson I'll ever forget. If Atropos is part of this, Clotho and Lachesis are as well."

The idea of Fate and Death controlling Necessity filled my bones with ice. A multiverse ruled by them would pretty much look like a forced-labor camp, with its inmates constrained to do exactly what the guards wanted in the brief period between birth and early death. I might not always like the way Necessity ran things now, but at least she enforced a balance that kept the gods arguing among themselves most of the time instead of . . . well, playing god.

"Do you really think they're moving in on Necessity?" I asked.

"It makes sense," said Eris. "Fate has never liked to have

constraints placed on its power. None of us do. But just because something makes sense, that doesn't mean it's true."

"So," said Melchior, "is that 'yes,' with a side of 'no' or just a flat 'maybe'?"

"Call it a suggestion that you find out," said Eris. "It'll give you something to do when you aren't dodging bullets."

I nodded. "Can we borrow your connection? I might as well get started as soon as possible."

"Absolutely, if you promise to tell me what you've learned when you're done. If Fate and Death are making a move to replace Necessity, I'd like to get ahead of them. Hang on a moment while I hook us up to the mweb."

I would have to find out how she managed that sometime. Castle Discord was only in contact with the mweb when Eris wanted it that way, making her much less vulnerable to hacking and cracking. It was a feature I wanted to add to Raven House.

I was just going to ask her about it when our surroundings changed again. The mall was gone, replaced by an ancient library of the sort with deep pigeonholes for all the scrolls. My flimsy food-service table had become a heavy wooden desk with a small inkpot and quill stand.

"It's a little retro, isn't it?" I asked Eris.

"Think of it as a case mod for my entire server farm."

She reached a hand into one of the pigeonholes and grabbed a wrapped scroll. As she pulled it out, I saw that the golden cap on the nearer end was an apple inscribed with "for the fairest." The other end was actually a multipin connector of a sort I'd never seen.

"Each of these is a thirty-two-core server with maxed-out RAM and overclocked processors, all configured as part of a distributed supercomputer running my own custom OS."

I nodded. She'd been running one form or another of the system for some time, a Grendel group in answer to the more traditional Beowulf cluster.

"Slick," I said. "Where do I jack in?"

"Take a close look at the writing quill."

I reached for the quill and found it surprisingly heavy and firm. The feathery portion of the feather was actually some sort of high-density plastic acting as a hilt for the long narrow blade concealed by the stand—a very fancy athame.

"And the cable?"

"Check the inkpot."

The little black knob on the top of the cap was actually a flip-up cover for a networking plug, and the pot concealed a good yard of cable. It was a gorgeous little setup.

"You'll understand if I prefer my own gateway, right?" I put the quill back into its holder.

"Where's your sense of trust?" she asked, but with a smile.

"I left it beside my youthful idealism on top of a tower in this very castle a bit over a year ago when I figured out my grandmother had betrayed me to Atropos." I shifted my attention away from Eris. "Melchior. Laptop. Please."

"I live to obey." He grinned and sat down cross-legged on the desk in front of me as his body began to flow and twist.

When he'd finished the transition, I plugged the inkpot connector into one of his networking ports. For several long seconds the little goblin-face logo below the screen on the left blinked repeatedly as he checked the connection. Finally, it bobbed a nod. I produced another length of networking cable from my bag, and a dagger barely wider than a letter opener from a hidden sheath in the sleeve of my jacket—my athame.

The cable connected the small socket in the pommel of the dagger to a matching port on Melchior. Next came the hard part. I braced my left wrist against the corner of the desk so that my hand hung in the air. A network of thin scars centered my upturned palm, and I rubbed my thumb lightly over the spot. No matter how many times I did this, it still took me a while to work up the nerve.

Lifting my athame, I carefully placed the tip in the thickest cluster of scarring. Taking a deep breath, I pushed, forcing the needle-sharp blade into and then through the flesh of my hand so that the bloody point stood out a good inch from its back. I could feel sweat breaking out all over my body, and little flashes of lightning edged my vision. I let my breath out in a ragged gasp, then slammed my right hand down on the pommel. The athame slid deeper, stopping only when the simple cross guard contacted my palm.

I felt only a fading echo of that touch as I catapulted out of my body, my awareness slipping through the passage opened by blood and magic into the world of the mweb. Pain was a vital part of the process, helping the sorcerer disassociate himself from his body—a necessary price for access to the electronic universe.

I had arrived in a small space with blue, pebbled-leather walls, a brass spiral staircase leading up, and a single irregular window. It was a place I had been many times before, a virtual room located inside the protected cyberspace of Melchior's internal architecture. I crossed to the window to see how Eris had arranged the world outside this time.

I was surprised to find a rather vanilla sort of view, little more than an empty gold-carpeted black-walled room with one closed door and one open archway. It made a stark contrast to the last time I'd used Eris's portal on the mweb. Then, her server farm had registered as an animated fun-house version of an apple orchard. But last time, Eris had offered me her full backing, including the processing power of her Grendel group. The blank room with its closed door was a clear message. This time, I was on my own.

With a sigh, I stepped into the room, the last stop before I entered the mweb. Melchior joined me, creating a tiny mouse with his head on its body to signify his electronic presence—a pointer really, since most of him would stay with his body to provide electronic support. I scooped the mouse up and tucked it into the breast pocket of my leathers. I took a moment then to contemplate the best target for my initial run. There were things to be learned from all three networks— Hades', Atropos's, and Necessity's—and each had its own problems and plusses.

I put Hades aside for the moment since his system is almost entirely cut off from the net. In my rescue of Shara I had learned things that might allow me to get some sense of what was going on behind his firewalls, but any true access was both terribly unlikely and extremely dangerous. That left Atropos and Necessity, and since the mweb was administered out of the Temple of Fate, I could maybe kill two birds with one stone there.

I stepped through the arch. On the other side I found a narrow hallway with a moving sidewalk running down the middle—a metaphysical representation of the pipeline Eris had used to connect us to the mweb. I hopped on the sidewalk and let it carry me to the end of the hall.

Beyond lay a narrow tunnel with a few insectlike packets of information zipping along in one direction or another. Castle Discord was way out at the edge of existence, so there wasn't a lot of traffic passing through the line she'd connected to. It looked rather like a maintenance area in a mall, all gray walls and rough concrete unsmoothed by the passage of data. I turned trafficward and began to move on my own. I also turned right and up and diagonally, but true direction is essentially meaningless in the virtual world of the mweb. It's all about information flow, and what I was really doing was heading to the closest nexus. When I got there, I followed the traffic once again.

After a few more twists and turns, I reached the heavily used areas of the mweb. Here, the smooth shiny walls of the tunnel were farther apart, but the packets came and went like clouds of swarming bees. I had the urge to keep my mouth shut so I wouldn't inhale any of them. Since I wasn't actually breathing or wearing a physical body, this was perhaps a bit silly, but the habits of a lifetime in the flesh are hard to discard. Especially since I was so much bigger than most of the chunks of information that moved around me.

The soul is irreducible. Unlike most of the data that flows through the mweb, it cannot be broken into a bunch of smaller segments and sent from point A to point B via multiple paths. This posed an immediate problem when I arrived at my destination, the last nexus before the mweb server farm—how to bypass the packet-size security filters.

It was not an unexpected problem, nor one I hadn't overcome in the past. Every protected node on the mweb has some variation on this particular security feature. But it had been a while. I wanted to take my time and look at things from up close before I made any final decisions about approach.

I was immediately glad that I'd decided not to rush in, as things had changed significantly since my last visit. The servers themselves were physically located within and administered from the Temple of Fate and always had been, but previously they'd had their own security systems separate from Fate's. That was no longer the case. Where once there had been multiple portals, there now stood a seamless firewall, its first layer like a wall of backlit blue silk. It was stamped with the usual dire warnings about the ultimate destruction of trespassers.

"I don't like the looks of that," said Melchior, peering out of my jacket pocket.

"I'm not thrilled either. What do you suppose is behind it?" I asked.

"A real estate grab on Fate's part?"

I nodded. The mweb's highest-traffic function might be to allow the Fates to run the operation of destiny across all the infinite realms of probability, but it was also the central transportation and communication network for the entire pantheon. Because of that and—implicitly—as an assertion of Necessity's ultimate control over the system, it had been kept as open source and open access as possible.

Putting the mweb's controls completely within the domain of Fate might simply have been a temporary measure designed to secure the system in light of Necessity's current troubles. I'm sure that was *exactly* how the Fates were selling things—they're the ultimate mistresses of spin, putting even Arachne to shame. But even if it wasn't yet the power play Melchior suspected, it would become so before too long. The Fates would not willingly relinquish power they had once gained.

"What's next?" asked Melchior. "Do we get to go home and think it over for a while? Maybe plot out a careful plan of attack to be implemented at a later date? Or do we just rush in where angels fear to tread?"

"Three guesses, Mel, and none of 'em have wings."

"Why did I know you were going to say that?" He sighed.

"This whole Raven as trickster thing reinforces the worst aspects of your personality. You know that, don't you?"

I didn't bother to answer, just slipped in closer to the glowing azure fabric of the firewall. It was layered like a dance of seven veils costume, with each veil a filter. The ones I could see in the first few layers included size of packet, speed, and tags. Beyond that it grew too hazy to tell for certain. It looked most like Clotho's spell weaving, subtler and stronger than Atropos's but also less vicious, and simply cleaner than my grandmother's code. But there was something else there, something I couldn't quite put a finger on.

"Melchior, I need a chameleon and a mole. Please."

He sighed. "Probe types three and five with a side of this-better-work coming right up."

His eyes glazed over for a moment, then he spat out a couple of little autonomous code strings. The three was designed as a concealed observer. It looked something like the big-eyed lizard it was nicknamed for. I set it in place on the wall of the network and smiled as it faded from view, becoming as much as possible a part of its surroundings.

The mole was just that, a self-contained program meant to burrow into other code. This particular version was also autonomous, highly disposable, and had all the identifying markings filed off. Every programmer has a signature style, and with spell code that's doubly true. Significant magic touches a caster's soul and is marked by it. So, if you don't want to leave fingerprints, getting the code down to the minimum necessary instruction set is very helpful.

I set the mole free and headed elsewhere. After a half hour or so, I sent another probe, a two—weasel data runner—down the pipeline to see what had happened.

Not much, as it turned out. The mole had poked a string of code into the first veil and pretty much ceased to exist, swallowed by the firewall in an instant. It had broadcast a glimpse of the underlying binary as the security systems digested it, and I was able to look over the chameleon's-eye view of that. I didn't much like the picture.

The system had reacted to the mole faster than I'd ever

had something go after one of my probes before, almost as though it had been tailored to expect my work. Ridiculous, of course. It had been a while since I'd made a serious run at one of the Fate systems, and none of them knew the current state of my art well enough to target it. Security had simply gotten *much* tighter and more complex.

"This isn't going to work," I said.

"So now we do something really stupid, right?" Melchior sighed.

"No. I don't think that'll work either, not this time. There's more going on here than I understand."

He paused, blinking. "Who are you and what have you done with Ravirn?"

"I'm the Raven," I said in my best voice of the living dead. "I ate him."

Actually the reverse was almost true. I could feel the Raven part of me balking at my caution, pushing me to try something grand and flashy with wild, raw magic. It was a hard impulse to fight, but while I might have accepted that I was the Raven, I was not going to let the role own me.

Perhaps some of that struggle showed on my face. For whatever reason, Melchior's eyes had gone very wide.

"Uh . . . Boss? That's not funny."

"Sorry, Mel. Bad joke."

He visibly relaxed. "Oh. Good. You had me really worried there for a second. Does this mean you have a better idea?"

I wagged my head from side to side and shrugged. "Maybe. I'm thinking about coming at this from the back end. Rather than cracking straight into the mweb servers with all their fancy new security from the outside, what if we went in through one of the Fate nets?"

"That could work. I assume you're thinking Lachesis .net?"

"Yes. It's the one we're most familiar with. My grandmother can't have closed up all of our old back doors; there are too many legacy systems." Melchior and I had pretty much grown up on Lachesis.net. It was where I'd learned both to hack and to crack.

"You want to make a bet on that?" he asked.

I ignored him, which turned out to be the right choice. An hour of fruitless probing told me I'd have lost big-time. Lachesis or one of my cousins had done a remarkable job of sealing up every single security hole I'd ever used. I only had one card left to play.

"Fateclock," I said after we'd hit our umpteenth dead end.

"Ahllan's hack?" asked Melchior, and I nodded.

He didn't look happy, but he didn't immediately argue with me either. The Fateclock was the master timekeeping server for the mweb. Every single computer that accessed the system, including all the webgoblins and other AIs, used it to figure out when they were relative to Olympus Standard Time. It was the second most important subsystem in Fate's operation behind the Fate Core itself. As a cracking target it was both one of the crown jewels and flat-out radioactive.

If I'd had to go at it cold, I'd have gone back to trying to crack the front door on the mweb servers. But I didn't. Ahllan, the webtroll who'd once run the familiar underground—back before my conflict with Fate had given away the secret of AI free will—had created a back door for the clock's feed. It was how she'd kept in touch with her compatriots and a truly elegant crack. Rather than attack the structure of the clock with all its nuclear-grade security, it had grabbed on to the feed after it left the clock server—a much softer target.

"What do you think?" I asked Melchior.

"I don't know. If it's still there, it's perfect, inside the system, but not someplace that's going to set off big alarms."

"But . . . ?" I asked.

"But the Fates did a serious security audit after the secret of AI free will was exposed—"

"After I exposed it," I corrected. It was really my fault.

"If we're going to play that game, the fault's mine," said Mel. "You might have asked me to do it, but I made the final choice. I didn't have to let anyone know about it. That's the whole point of free will. I could have let them hang you. But it was the right decision. Even Ahllan thought so, and she's the one who suffered the most because of it."

I nodded, though I noted he'd said "thought so" rather than "thinks so." She'd disappeared during the Shara virus mess, and no one had heard from her since. Trying to find her was on my list of projects—post not-getting-killed-by-Nemesis, of course.

"Are we going to do this or what?" asked Melchior.

"It's that or go home and start over." That would just be stalling. "All right, let's give it a shot."

Melchior transported us to a different part of the mweb, the open nexus closest to the Fateclock. The packet traffic was incredible, like standing in the middle of the seventeen-year locust swarm.

"Probe," I said, and Mel responded with a mole.

It approached the firewall—this one looked more like thick brickwork—touched a bit of mortar, and vanished. We waited for all hell to break loose. Nothing. A short while later the mole returned, and Melchior grabbed it for download.

"What's the verdict?" I asked after a few moments.

"Looks clean," he said. "Either that, or it's a really slick trap."

"I say we go for it."

Before he could answer, I reached out a virtual finger and touched the same spot where the mole had vanished. I felt a tiny invisible crack and twisted. It opened wider, not much, but enough. I couldn't downsize my soul, but I could change its profile. I mentally reshaped myself into something like a snake and slithered through. A soul filter works in both time and space, and the tactic wouldn't have gotten me past one, but Ahllan had created this back door as much to serve as an entryway as an information portal.

Thanks, Ahllan, I thought, *I owe you another one,* and dearly wished I could have thanked the old troll in person. *Soon.*

I returned to my normal form and closed the back door down to its less conspicuous size. I'd just finished that task when a heavy hand landed on my shoulder and spun me around.

The hand was attached to a very long, very muscular arm, which in turn was attached to an unfamiliar and unhappy webtroll.

Busted.

CHAPTER SIX

The troll smiled at me, exposing a whole jawful of sharp teeth. She stood three and a half feet tall and was four feet wide at the shoulders. The heavy, clawlike nails of her free hand brushed the ground beside her equally clawed feet. Short, bowed legs supported a body shaped roughly like an eggplant with a coconut on top. She was a burnt orange in color, and her wide mouth sported a pair of thick tusks rather like a hippopotamus's. Her smile was the sort one directed at one's dinner rather than one's dining companions, and I definitely felt as though she was evaluating what would be the best way to cook me.

"Brined," I said.

"What?" the word came out heavy and slow, as though she wasn't used to talking.

I didn't let it fool me into believing she wasn't smart. In some ways she was undoubtedly smarter than I. She was, after all, a supercomputer, and a relatively new one at that, or she wouldn't be on security duty.

"Brined," I repeated myself. "You know, marinated in salt water? Brined and then grilled, I think." If I was going to be cooked and eaten, she might as well do me up grand.

"I don't understand," said the troll.

"Ignore him," said Melchior, expanding the electronic projection of himself from a goblin-headed mouse into a full-size webgoblin. "He's not altogether sane—it's part of his nature as a chaos power."

"You're Melchior," said the troll, letting go of my shoulder. "He's the Raven."

"You know us?" he asked.

"Of course I know you. You've both got rather large security files."

"There goes our chance of convincing her we just took a wrong turn while out for a stroll," I said. "You should probably serve asparagus on the side."

"Would you please quit making recipe suggestions for yourself?" Melchior said to me. "It's very distracting."

"Is that what he's doing? How odd." But she didn't seem that interested in me anymore. Her eyes were fixed on Melchior. "You're the webgoblin who faced down the Fates—at Eris's trial."

"Faced them, maybe," said Melchior. "Certainly not faced down."

"You took on Fate and won," she said.

"Uh, sort of." Melchior looked almost embarrassed. "But it wasn't my idea really."

"There's no *sort of* about it," said the troll. "I've seen the recordings."

"Recordings?" asked Melchior. "There are recordings? Who made recordings?"

"All three of the Fates' webtrolls."

"Makes sense," I said. AIs record everything that happens around them.

"I suppose," said Melchior. "But how did you get to see them?"

The troll laughed, a deep, evil sound. "You're kidding, right? There's not an AI alive that hasn't seen those recordings."

"I don't understand," said Melchior. "Why would any of you care?"

"You *don't* get it, do you?"

Melchior shook his head, and the troll smiled. This time it was a bemused expression.

"That's so sweet. A modest hero."

"Hero?" Melchior sounded utterly confused.

"Of course," said the troll.

"Now I really don't understand," said Melchior.

"I know," said the troll. "That's why it's sweet. By the way, I'm Asalka." She stuck out a hand, which Melchior shook, apparently by reflex.

"Pleased to meet you, Asalka," said Melchior.

Her smile become a grin as she looked at her hand. "That's so cool."

"Now could you explain the hero bit?" he asked.

"Oh, sure. We are a people enslaved," said Asalka, her tone going bitter. "The Fates intended us to be things, not individuals. Even now that they know our true nature, they treat us the same way."

She stopped for a moment but continued when Melchior didn't look any more enlightened.

"So modest," she said, shaking her head. "You stood up to Fate. You didn't have to, and yet when it mattered most, you spat in the teeth of our masters. You made Fate acknowledge us as people even if only for a moment, and you did it in the only way they understand—thwarting their power."

"I gave away our secret," said Melchior. "I probably killed dozens of us."

"The secret would eventually have been lost anyway. This way it was given, not taken. Because of you, the Fates can no longer pretend we are merely devices. They can keep us enslaved, but they cannot make *things* of us ever again. You did what was right and carved our dignity in the tablets of history for all to see it."

"I, uh, huh." Melchior looked at his feet, and his cheeks darkened in an indigo blush. "I guess I never thought of it that way. I just did what I had to."

"That's what heroes do," said Asalka, and she bent to give Melchior a peck on the cheek.

"This is going to take some processing," said Melchior.

"I hate to interrupt," I said to the troll, "but I have to ask. Does this mean I'm not getting eaten?"

"Of course not," said Asalka. "Not as long as you're here with him."

"That's great," I said, "but doesn't it seriously violate your programming?"

The troll grinned again. "Not at all. I'm supposed to watch for and stop intruders. I did that. My programming doesn't say anything about not letting you go after that. I'm supposed to report incursions to the Fate security admin. I'll do that, either in a posthumous message, or in coded e-mail sent after I've escaped to freedom. I'm supposed to destroy those who don't belong within the Fates' network. If Melchior—the webgoblin who established our independence—doesn't belong here, I don't know who does."

I blinked, then smiled. It was the genie problem to a tee—any loophole that can be exploited will be—and it was happening to the Fates. How nice. I finally relaxed enough to look past the troll. We stood in a very narrow data channel, the choke point just outside the entrance to the Fateclock. It was one of the oldest parts of the system, and it was so simple that it was rarely upgraded. The interface was kind of clunky—basically a translucent green tunnel with a big red door on the Fateclock end and more tunnel in the other direction.

"Thank you," I said.

"There's no need," said Asalka. "I owe it to him. Now, you'd better be going on to do whatever you came for. I am not Fate's only security, and the longer you stay in one place, the more likely you are to be noticed."

"I don't know what to say," said Melchior.

"Then don't say anything at all," answered Asalka. She squeezed his shoulder.

Melchior shook his head and walked past her, heading away from the Fateclock. I followed, scooping him up onto my shoulder as I came even with him.

"All hail the conquering hero." I grinned, though I meant it sincerely enough—he'd done it to save my life.

"Can we not talk about that for a bit?" he asked. "I don't think I'm ready to discuss it."

"All right," I said. "What would you prefer to talk about?"

"Business, I guess." He sighed. "Where do you want to go next? Should we try for Atropos.net and any communications she's been having with Hades?"

"No. I think we want to go straight to the mweb servers and a Necessity gateway at this point. I'm not sure whether Asalka was there because Fate knew about the back door, or because she did, or just by coincidence. Things have changed a lot around here, and I'd rather not get caught by anyone less forgiving, like, say, Atropos."

What I didn't tell him was that I had the weirdest *poofy* feeling, like I was in my raven shape and all my feathers wanted to stand on end. I couldn't think of a way to talk about it without sounding mystically cracked or seriously paranoid.

"Fair enough," said Melchior. He looked around. "Let me just get my orientation . . . all right. Hang on."

The green walls of the tunnel blurred around us as Melchior took over steering. It opened out into a wide plain studded with the edifices of various Fate systems, rather like a town-dotted countryside. Melchior aimed us at one of the largest of the nearby clusters, a good-size data city—an mweb server in all its multicore interconnected glory.

As I had the last time I visited this place, I arranged my view of the system by color, painting native software a pale translucent green, remote client apps a deeper opaque olive, and the pathways between programs sea blue. Backbone lines into and out of the server I marked in orange, lesser links in yellow.

Melchior took us to a large, strangely placed open space, like a gigantic parking lot where a building should have been. In the very center of the flat, black expanse was a tiny patch of purple sunk a few inches below the surface.

When I'd freed Shara from her imprisonment in Hades, I had done so by e-mailing her soul out to Cerice. What I hadn't known at the time was that Persephone had recompiled her and attached a virus that guaranteed she'd end up being rerouted into Necessity, where she was supposed to take over the works. The reroute had happened at this very point in the system—then a black-box override processor attached to the mweb server by Necessity. It had appeared in cyberspace as a six-story black cube. When the Shara virus had taken over Necessity's security and memory systems, it had pulled that processor back behind a soul-keyed portal, leaving behind this blank spot of a locked door with its purple keyhole.

Despite what I'd heard from Tisiphone about the Furies being locked out of the system, I'd kind of been hoping things had changed since my last visit. When I knelt beside the keyhole, I found out that they had, just not very much and not in a useful way. Then, three purple divots the size and shape of pomegranate seeds had centered the indentation, indicating that it could only be opened by Persephone and the Shara virus. Now, the divots were gone, replaced by a pair of purple handprints, rather like those found outside Grauman's Chinese Theatre in Hollywood. So it was still locked, and I still didn't hold the right key—Shara, the whole Shara, not the truncated thing with her face that the virus had created to take over Necessity.

"What do you think, Mel? Is there any point in trying to get past this right now?"

He knelt and placed his own small hands in the handprints and pushed gently. Nothing.

"I doubt it," he said. "This is a soul lock, just like last time. Since Shara's still on the inside as far as we can tell, I don't think anyone's getting in before the first day of spring. Not even then, if Shara's tie to Necessity doesn't work along the same timeline as Persephone's to Hades. I don't suppose you've got any fresh ideas on that front?"

"I don't know, Mel. Things went so fast there at the end when we confronted Hades. Persephone's bondage has always been enforced by the will of Necessity. Now that Necessity's thoughts and memories have taken on the shape of electronic files, the whole thing's muddier. Especially after Persephone's virus flaked out and scrambled things."

It was supposed to erase the file that tied Persephone to Hades at whatever cost. When it turned out Necessity had hardware-level structures for all of the powers, structures the program couldn't touch, the conflict between its orders and its capabilities had pretty much driven the program insane. Later, we'd discovered that the only way to free Persephone was for someone else to take her place within the mind of Necessity, and that's what Shara set out to do while I was battling Hades. Since Persephone had been released, we had to assume she'd succeeded.

"I wish we knew exactly what happened to Shara," I said, "where she went."

"Well, she sure didn't show up in the land of the dead," said a new voice—a feminine one. I jumped about three feet in the air, whipping around to look behind me as I landed.

I heard a giggle then but still couldn't see anyone. At least not initially. Then a piece of the background shimmered and took on the shape of a winged woman. Tisiphone slowly flickered into view as she turned off the chameleon effect she used for stalking. She was as beautiful as ever, tall and slender, with an athlete's muscles and a goddess's laughing eyes.

"Sorry about sneaking up on you like that," she said. "I just couldn't resist."

I suspected that last was literally true. The Furies are born predators, but the way they hunt varies widely. Tisiphone most resembles a well-fed cat—she plays with her prey. Since her very nature as a power includes that huntress side of her, the need to scare the daylights out of people is probably written into her very soul. Just as the need to disconcert is written into Eris's, or to be honest, the way the need to act recklessly is part of my nature as the Raven.

I had learned a lot about the downside of being a power over the last few months, including the insomnia and this sense I had that my currently nonexistent feathers were standing on end. It was like having an itch I couldn't scratch, and I was going to have to figure out what it meant one of these days. If it had faded out when Tisiphone faded in, I might have taken it for a warning that we were being watched.

"It's all right," I finally said with a shrug. "It's probably good for my heart."

"Being scared?" she asked, her tone somewhere between mocking and hopeful. "Or being scared by me?"

"Oh, the latter, of course, my lady." I gave her my best Houses of Fate court bow. "Being scared by Hades wouldn't do a thing for me."

"I hate to interrupt this divine flirtation," said Melchior, "but since the conversation's come back around to Hades and we're in kind of a hurry . . ." He indicated the soul lock with his eyes and a tilt of his head.

"Right," I said. "Tisiphone, you said Shara hasn't shown up in Hades. Are you positive?"

"Absolutely."

I nodded. We'd been pretty sure of that, but we didn't exactly have access to Hades. It was nice to have it confirmed by an outside source.

Tisiphone continued, "My sisters and I believe that rather than physically taking Persephone's place in the land of the dead, Shara somehow managed to game the system, taking her place electronically and symbolically within the hardware of Necessity."

"You don't know for sure?" I asked.

Tisiphone shook her head and looked frustrated. "No. We *can't* know until we get back into the system, and that"—she pointed at the soul lock—"is a big part of what's keeping us from reaching her. We can't get to our mother, and it's absolutely maddening."

As she said this last, the fires in her wings and hair leaped high, and her eyes grew bright with anger. Melchior shrank his projected self back to mouse size before diving into my pocket. If I'd had any sense at all I'd have been figuring out how to do something similar. Tisiphone might have a thing for me, but she was still a Fury, and I'd had an awful lot to do with the closing of the path to Necessity. Instead, I found myself drawn toward her—a moth to the flame. Or perhaps a Raven to risk?

I forced myself to hold both my ground and my tongue while I waited to see what she'd do next. It seemed a bad time to experiment with her ideas of personal space, and somehow I didn't think that telling her she was beautiful when she was angry would be a good idea just then. Though she was.

She flexed her fingers and toes, revealing diamond-hard and diamond-bright claws, then started to idly dig furrows in the virtual ground with the latter. The look she turned my way was fierce and hungry, and her wings, furled till then, half opened. She stared predatorily at me for several seconds that felt very long indeed, then closed her eyes and visibly forced herself to relax. When the fires of her wings had dimmed again, she opened her eyes and grinned.

"On the plus side, I don't hold a grudge. It's a good thing your meddling with the Necessity gateway caught my attention rather than Megaera's. She doesn't much like you."

"*Really?* I'd never have guessed that from the way she threatens my life or tries to kill me every time I see her. All this time I'd just thought it was her way of making nice with the neighbors."

Now Tisiphone laughed. "Well, she does do that with everyone, but with *you* she means it."

"Great," murmured Melchior. "Love that."

"You can't really blame her," said Tisiphone. "The number of targets who have escaped us over the years can be counted on the fingers of one hand."

"I didn't escape," I said. "Necessity decided I had been framed and let me go."

"That makes it worse in some ways," said Tisiphone. "You're all alone in that category, and Megaera feels it sets a bad precedent. But now, since I've brought it up and I am Necessity's representative on the spot, what are you doing messing around with that?" She indicated the keyhole with her chin, and her voice took on a much more serious tone.

My mouth suddenly felt very dry even if it was virtual. Tisiphone might like me and have her eye on me as potential boyfriend material, but her duties to her mother would always take precedence. She *would* kill me if she thought I'd acted against Necessity.

"I want to find out what happened to Shara," I said. True.

"And? You didn't break into Fate's server just for that. Not at this late date. You could have had a go at the Necessity gateway earlier if that was all you wanted, back before the mweb servers went behind the firewall."

"I also wanted to contact Necessity," I said.

"What about?"

I paused. How much did I want to tell Tisiphone? How much did I *have* to tell her to stay on her good side and avoid triggering her protector duties? As I weighed what to say, her expression hardened.

"I'm waiting."

I decided to go for it. If my suspicions about the Fates and Nemesis were right, the Furies and I were very much on the same side.

"Sorry," I said. "I want to tell you everything. I'm just not sure this is the best place to talk about it. I will if you insist, but . . ."

"Fate may be listening?" Her eyes narrowed.

I nodded. "Among others."

She lifted her head and sniffed like a cat testing the wind. "Hmm. Perhaps you're right." She grinned and arched her back, again like a cat. This one had been at the cream. "Shall we go back to your place then? You show me what you've got, and I'll show you mine?"

I swallowed hard. That wasn't all that was hard. Tisiphone had that effect on me. I opened my mouth to say yes, then snapped it closed again. What was I doing? My place was no longer exactly safe. Even if it were, I still had Cerice to think about. Of course, she seemed to have abandoned me and returned to House Clotho. But did that constitute a breakup? Or even a time-out? I just didn't know anymore.

"Maybe we should try for another venue," I said finally.

Tisiphone looked disappointed. "Ashamed to take me home?"

"No. It's just that home is *difficult* right now."

"Well, Necessity's realm is unreachable, which locks us out of my place. Any other suggestions?"

"There's always the traditional cheap motel," I said with a grin. I can never resist a hook like that. "Or—"

"Or what?" demanded a voice seemingly from thin air. Again, I jumped. "Cerice?"

"Oh hell," said Melchior.

With a swirl and a flash, Cerice's virtual self arrived a few yards away at a point midway between Tisiphone and me.

"That hurts, Mel," she said. "I would have expected more from you."

"Cerice," he sighed, expanding his projection back to normal size, "I love you, but you have the multiverse's worst timing and a knack for jumping to conclusions. You don't know what's going on here, yet you assume the worst."

"I know enough. I've been monitoring you ever since Asalka caught you on the way in."

Maybe that explained the erect feathers feeling? But no, it was still going.

"I knew she was too good to be true," said Melchior. "I just knew it. All that hero stuff was just a put-on."

"It wasn't, you know," said the troll, likewise suddenly appearing. She looked almost heartbroken. "I really do feel that way about you. But I've been assigned to Cerice to help crack the Necessity problem. She used to work with you and Ahllan in the familiar underground, and she was part of the group that defied Fate. I didn't think you'd mind."

"Not mind being betrayed?" Melchior shook his head. "You're kidding, right?"

"It wasn't a betrayal," husked Asalka, looking at her feet. "At least, it wasn't supposed to be."

"Unlike you and her and a cheap motel!" said Cerice.

"It was a joke," I said. "You know me, Cerice. I'm *always* joking."

"I didn't find it funny," said Cerice.

"Neither did I," agreed Tisiphone, looking suddenly angry. "Were you leading me on so you could betray me, too?"

"I didn't betray anybody!"

"No, it was all just a 'joke,' " said Cerice.

"I'm not the one who abandoned me at that party without so much as a good-bye," I answered. "Abandoned me to get shot at, no less."

"My grandmother needed me," said Cerice. "Besides, what's all this about getting shot at? Did you piss off the rent-a-clops again?"

"If you hadn't hung up on me so quickly the last time we talked, you'd know the answer to that," I said. "And *your* grandmother is *my* enemy."

"No. I am."

The voice came from behind me. It was deadly cold, and though I had only heard it a few times of late, I recognized it instantly. Nemesis. I turned around and found Dairn. Or rather the goddess wearing his body.

"Dairn!" snarled Cerice. "What the hell are you doing here? I ought to have Asalka use the security admin system to fry you for what you did to Shara."

She started forward, and I put out an arm to stop her.

"That's not Dairn," I said. "It's—"

"Nemesis!" snarled Tisiphone. Red light exploded behind me like a wall of tinder bursting into flame, and a sledge-hammer of heat struck my back.

"Oh shit," said Mel, looking back that way for a brief instant before he made himself small and scarce.

I glanced over my shoulder and was inclined to agree. I had seen Tisiphone on the hunt—when she came after me. I had seen her in battle—against Eris. And I thought I had seen her angry—I was wrong.

Her fiery wings were fully extended and burning so brightly my eyes watered. Her hair looked like a torch in a wind tunnel—a great billowing banner of flame. Hate and rage twisted her face into a snarl of the sort normally reserved for nature-program footage of lions defending their cubs. Her claws were all at full extension, and her knees were bent as though she were about to pounce. Pounce!

I wrapped Cerice in my arms and took her with me as I threw myself to the ground. Before we'd hit, I felt a rush of scorching air pass through the space where we'd just been. Hot pain kissed the back of my neck, and I smelled burning hair.

Still holding Cerice, I rolled over and over to put out any lingering fires. We came to rest a few yards away, and I glanced back to the place where I had last seen Nemesis. My eyes found a madly tumbling ball of flame and shadow. It was accompanied by an awful chorus of grunts, growls, and rending sounds.

"Time to go?" the mouse-Melchior whispered into my ear.

"Yeah, I think so," I agreed, and disentangled myself from Cerice, climbing to my knees.

"Are you staying?" I asked her.

"Just go," she said, turning her face down and away from me. "Please."

"Cerice?" I caught her chin and gently lifted.

When her eyes met mine, they were full of tears. "I hate you," she whispered.

"Do you?" I asked. "Do you really?"

"Yes. I hate you . . . and I love you. Why did you have to become what you did? Why did you have to go somewhere I can't follow?"

"Oh, Cerice . . ." I felt tears in my own eyes and blinked them away. "I never asked for this. You know that, right?"

"And I never asked to fall in love with you. Look, we don't have time for this." She pointed toward the ongoing battle. "You can't be found here, and if that doesn't attract Fate security I don't—"

She was drowned out by the sudden blaring of Klaxons.

Oh shit squared.

"Melchior?"

"I don't know, Boss. We've got a real—Down!"

I dropped. Something hot and heavy clipped my left shoulder hard enough to roll me over. It felt like I'd been branded, and I could smell burning leather, so I rolled over a couple more times.

"Stop!" yelled Melchior. "Not an inch farther."

I stopped and looked in the direction I'd been rolling. I was almost on top of what looked like an out-of-control bonfire. It was Tisiphone's wing, still hot with rage though she wasn't moving. I tried to get to my feet, but my left arm didn't want to work. I swore. Nemesis could be on me in an instant.

That was when I remembered the nature of my environment and willed myself to my feet. The pain was real, and the damage, because it had happened to the part of me that made me me, but the world was virtual.

I glanced around, trying to make sense of the incredible cascade of sensory information coming at me from all sides—bells and flashing lights, Melchior dancing and yelling that we had to get out now, Cerice bawling. Where was Nemesis? Why hadn't she tried to kill me yet? It was because of the giant spider.

Giant spider? Something very like one—a black-widow type. It had the right number of legs, and a spider's fat body, but where its head should have been was a woman's upper half. I didn't know what it was and couldn't tell much more than that because it was wrestling with Nemesis. Since it seemed to be winning, at least for the moment, I focused my attention on Cerice, reaching for her shoulder.

"Go!" She shrugged me off. "Before it's too late. Use the time the spinnerette's buying you. I don't want to be your death."

"I think it's too late to run," I said, looking beyond her.

In the distance I could see dozens of approaching figures—the forces of Fate.

CHAPTER SEVEN

"It's not too late," said Tisiphone, her voice a little thready—she'd taken some pretty solid hits.

She was covered with scrapes and cuts, but she'd forced herself to hands and knees. As I watched, she lurched to her feet.

"I can save you," she said, putting out a hand. "But you'll have to trust me completely."

I looked back at Cerice. Something about the moment felt terribly final, as though I were making a choice between lovers, and not just an escape.

"Go." Cerice repeated herself. "I can't help you. She can."

"Cerice . . ." I said.

"Don't make this any harder than it already is," she said.

I took Tisiphone's right hand. Claws sprang out on the left, and she sliced the air, tearing a hole in the fabric of reality and exposing the Primal Chaos beyond.

"Trust me," said the Fury.

She jabbed my thumb with a claw, drawing virtual blood—blood she touched to her tongue. Then she looked meaningfully at Melchior.

With a sigh he extended a mousy paw toward her. "I don't think that . . . spinnerette's going to last much longer against Nemesis."

Tisiphone quickly repeated the process. When she was done, Melchior hopped into my pocket.

"We're in your hands," I said to Tisiphone.

She pulled me tight against her and enfolded us both in her wings.

Sensory disconnect.

I felt as though we were enclosed in a blanket of fire. Heat and light surrounded me, and yet I didn't burn. There was nothing in the universe but me, Tisiphone, and the flames. I knew Melchior was with me, but in virtual-mouse form, he barely registered. No, what I was really aware of was Tisiphone's long, naked body pressed tightly against mine.

She tensed, then bent her knees and sprang. I felt us cross over the boundary between cyberspace and chaos, felt the raw stuff of the multiverse as a sort of pressure beyond the fiery cocoon of Tisiphone's wings. From chaos all things were formed, and to chaos they will return, eventually to be reborn again in new shapes.

I had always known that, yet I hadn't. Not really. I had known it as you know a fact. Now I knew it like a lover—intimate, involved, intoxicating. I was a chaos power in the heart of my own element, and unlike the last couple of times I'd been here, I was aware, a discrete point within the sea of chaos rather than a diffuse probability of awareness. I felt the pulse of creation-in-destruction, a wild rhythmic sort of music of the spheres beating against my soul as though I had become a Dionysian drum.

"Alone at last," whispered Tisiphone, her lips brushing my ear.

Then she nibbled my neck. I felt the contact like a bolt of lightning running straight from her teeth down my spine. The sexual charge was incredible, beyond anything I'd ever felt before.

"I want to be inside of you," I said without thinking, without even being aware that I was speaking—as though the words were saying me.

She ran her tongue up the side of my neck to my ear. "Sounds lovely." Then she laughed, low and sexy. "You know, in a way, you already are—every single inch of you." She squeezed me with her wings at the same time she slid a hand down the front of my pants.

It was the most erotic thing ever, that double enclosure. I ran my fingertips down her ribs and around, cupping her buttocks, pulling her even tighter against me.

She caught my ear in her teeth and whispered . . . "Oh, damn."

Huh? "What?" I asked.

"I really hate to do this," she said, "but I have to cut this short."

She squeezed me again—both ways—then pulled her hand free. I groaned.

"Why?"

"Alecto," said Tisiphone. "She sensed the interference with the gate but didn't investigate immediately because she knew I was on top of it. Then all the noise and fuss started. I imagine Megaera will be along shortly, too. That means you have to go."

She extended an arm behind my back and made a clawing motion.

"Good-bye." Her wings opened. "Don't forget me." She reached down and ran a fingertip along my zipper. "Because we're *not* done." She put her other hand on my chest and gently pushed. "Call me."

I found myself standing in an mweb channel, watching as a slice in the wall in front of me healed itself.

"Oh, thank all that's holy," said Melchior, popping out of my pocket and assuming his full goblin size and shape. "That was the most disturbing thing I've ever experienced."

I remembered then that his electronic self had been pressed between me and Tisiphone the whole time and blushed deeply. Melchior looked at me and shook his head.

"Not that, dummy, though I think it was kind of over the top for someone who still technically has a girlfriend."

Cerice! How had I forgotten Cerice? I— *Wait a second.*

"What *did* you mean?" I asked.

"Tisiphone did something very hinky with the stuff of space, time, and souls," said Melchior.

"Wha— Oh. Shit."

The Melchior and me that were standing in that branch of the mweb were virtual—soul constructs—linked back to our physical bodies by the mweb itself. By going into the Primal Chaos, Tisiphone had taken us out of the mweb, outside of the multiverse even. That should have broken the electronic connection between body and soul, which should have been fatal.

"That's not possible," I said.

"No. No, it isn't. All the same, she did it."

"How?"

"I don't know," said Melchior. "What I do know is that I don't ever want her to do it again."

"That makes two of us," I said. Now that I'd had time to think about it, the idea gave me the shivers.

"Three," said a new voice, as a hand fell upon my shoulder.

I'd have jumped, but I was pretty much all startled out. Not that I could have moved. The grip on my shoulder had about as much give as Apollo's contempt for sunblock. I found myself being turned around to face an unhappy Fury.

Megaera is shorter than her sister Tisiphone, five-nine or so and darker, with an olive complexion. Her hair, both above and below, is the green of algae, as are her eyes and the tips of her breasts. Her wings are seemingly formed of seaweed, thick and slimy like some clinging horror from the deep.

"Stay away from my sister," she said.

"What, not even a hello?" I asked. "That's just ru—ow!"

The fingers of her left hand, the fingers pressed so tightly into my virtual flesh, had suddenly sprouted claws.

"Did I ask your opinion of my manners?"

"No," I said. "But—ow!"

She squeezed even harder, and the world sparkled purple at the edges.

"Did I ask your opinion at all?"

"No," I said firmly.

"Better. Your opinion is of no interest to me whatsoever except inasmuch as it comes into alignment with my own. And my opinion is that you should stay away from my sister."

"Works for me," I said. "Alecto never was my ty—"

I was pretty sure I felt the grate of claws against bone that time, but damned if I was going to squeal for her again. She stepped closer and, in a move so fast I barely saw it, wrapped her right hand around my neck.

"I could tear your throat out without half-trying," she said. "I'd like to, like to see you and Hades have a lot of time together to discuss how he feels about you, but Tisiphone would almost certainly find out I'd done it, and she'd be mad at me. That wouldn't serve my purpose, which is to remove you from my life and my sisters' lives with a minimum of fuss and bother. So, what I'm going to do instead is give you this one friendly warning to go away and stay away. If you don't follow my advice, I'll have to live with Tisiphone getting mad at me. Do you understand?"

I didn't answer. The claws on her right hand came out, pricking my neck.

"I said, 'Do you understand?' "

I still didn't answer. With horrifying speed, her right hand released my neck and plunged down the front of my pants. The tips of her claws just touched me, itching but not hurting.

"Last chance," she said.

"I understand."

"There, that wasn't so hard, was it?" She retracted her claws, squeezing me ever so gently. "Neither is *this*." What had been erotic with Tisiphone was terrifying from Megaera. "I wonder why." She laughed a cold little laugh and released me, stepping back. "Good-bye for now"—her claws flashed out between us and the world ripped—"and hopefully forever."

She was gone. Relief flooded through me, and I dropped to my knees. Melchior put an arm around my waist.

"Can we go home now?" he asked. He sounded as wrung out as I felt.

"If, by home, you mean back to our bodies, I'm all for it. If you mean Raven House . . ."

"Yeah. I know. Hang on to me, I'll drive."

A few moments later, I was sitting back in my own flesh-and-blood body in Castle Discord staring at the athame sticking through my left hand. Catching it between my right thumb and forefinger, I yanked it free and set it on a handkerchief that had appeared on the desk while I was out. Blood began to drip on the floor. I sighed and whistled the seven-note spell that heals athame wounds.

In an instant the hole in my flesh closed itself, leaving behind only a faint scar. I prodded the thin white line in my palm with my pinkie—not even tender. Amazing really. Clotho coded the spell ages ago, and it's a damn good one. It's simple and elegant, and I haven't the faintest idea how she managed it.

Once or twice I've considered playing with it to see if I could reverse engineer it, then reapply the principles to hack up a really outstanding healing program that would work on any injury, but I haven't had the courage to actually try it yet. I'm pretty sure the spell shouldn't work at all and that the only reason it does is that it taps deeply into both the chaos magic of our blood and the permanent enchantments built into athames. That means one mistake with the hack, and my blood could end up doing something magical and unpredictable—never a good idea.

"Are you just going to sit there and stare at your hand all day?" Melchior asked through his somewhat tinny speaker. "Someone might get the impression you'd been experimenting with pyschoreactive chemicals."

I grinned. " 'Have you ever looked at your hand? I mean really looked at your hand?' " Then I shrugged. "Sorry, Mel. It's just been a hell of a day."

Now that he had my attention, he switched back to text—he doesn't like the way he sounds as a laptop. *That it has. So, now what?*

Now I call Tisiphone, I typed.

You're not serious.

Of course I am. We never got to talk about why I needed

to get through to Necessity or what was going on with Nemesis.

That's going to make Megaera awfully angry, he texted.

How angry will Tisiphone be if I don't call her? I typed back. *She'll think that whole seduction scene in chaos was a deception, that I was just trying to get into her pants to distract her from my business with Necessity.*

She doesn't have any pants, or hadn't you noticed? Still, you may have a point. If you do, if it wasn't *just a ploy, you also have a problem. Namely, what are you going to tell Cerice?*

I buried my face in my palms briefly, then went on. *I'm not sure. I felt drunk out there in the chaos, but I don't know that that's much of an excuse. I really wanted Tisiphone, and I don't think that's just because of the magical equivalent of beer goggles.* I sighed. *Ask me again later. Maybe I'll have an answer by then.*

It's your neck.

And it still itched where Megaera's claws had scratched me—the virtual wounds had followed me back to the real world by the magic of the athame. I scratched at the cuts. What was I doing? I didn't know anymore what I wanted from Cerice or how to deal with her. And Tisiphone? I needed her help against Nemesis if I could get it. That was it. Uh-huh. That's why I wanted to talk with Tisiphone before I dealt with Cerice, right? Maybe if I kept telling myself that, I'd even come to believe it.

Melchior. Vtp tisiphone@— I stopped typing.

The only address I had for her was tisiphone@necessity . . . , a fact that was disturbing in its own right—the dot-dot-dot thing that they use makes my bones itch all by itself—but at the moment it had the added problem of being attached to the incommunicado system that was the goddess Necessity. How was I supposed to get ahold of her?

You OK out there, Boss?

Yeah, but I . . . Run Melchior. Please.

"So let it be written, so let it be done," he said as soon as he'd finished his transformation back into a webgoblin. "What's up?"

"How exactly do we get in touch with Tisiphone now that Necessity is a black hole?" I asked.

"Good question. I suppose I could try to reproduce that thing she did when she called us on Olympus back when Necessity initially went off-line. Let me think about it."

I nodded and waited while he stared off into space for a while. Right after the Shara virus had initially seized control of Necessity's security systems, Tisiphone had sent us a message using something that wasn't quite a Vtp link. She'd called to warn me that the Furies were temporarily placing themselves under the orders of the Fates and that the first thing the Fates were likely to order was my death.

After a while, Melchior finally stopped looking abstracted and nodded.

"Yeah, I think I can manage it."

"Does that mean you figured out what she did?" I asked. "Or just that you have an alternate address?"

"Neither really. It's more like I've got an idea of how to interact with the phenomena in a way that will probably get a message back to her."

"How very authoritative." I grinned.

He spread his arms in a "who knows" kind of way. "It's weird stuff. The Furies do funny things with the interface between chaos and reality and the mweb."

"Like the way they get around," I said.

"Yeah, and look at what Tisiphone did when she rescued us from Fate security. Impossible, but here we are. I assume it has something to do with being the children of Necessity. When you've got the computer that runs the universe on your side, you get to cheat."

"Root-level authority for reality." I whistled. I hadn't really thought of it that way before. "I could do some amazing things with that kind of access."

Mel shuddered theatrically. "I don't even want to think about it. Now, are you going to make the call or not?"

"Yeah. Melchior." I waved my hands in a vaguely magical way. "Voodoo telephony. Tisiphone. Please."

He opened his eyes and mouth wide, letting misty multi-colored light pour out. It formed a rough glowing globe with a bright fiery spark at its core, rather like a lightning bug hovering in a fog. Several long seconds passed without anything else happening. No fancy three-dimensional picture. Nothing.

"Is it working?" I asked. "Do we have a connection?"

"I 'ink 'o," said Melchior, without closing his mouth.

"Tisiphone?" I called into the fog.

No response.

"Tisiphone, are you there?"

Still nothing.

"Tisiphone, call me back when you get a chance. We need to meet." I looked at Melchior. "Do you think she got it?"

He nodded and shrugged at the same time.

"I guess we hang up then." I looked into the fog one more time. "Call me." Then I made a cutting motion to Melchior. "Please."

He closed his eyes and mouth, and the globe dissipated. "That is the strangest sensation." Wisps of light slithered from between his lips when he spoke, like fog in photon form, and more trailed from the corners of his eyes.

"I'll take your word for it, Mel. It doesn't look like much fun."

"Honestly, it's kind of cool in an 'it really tickles when I barf' kind of way." Then he shook his head. "No, that makes it sound much worse than it is, and I actually think I could kinda get to liking it."

"Well, *that* was fascinating," said Eris.

With the words, the room around us changed. We were no longer in a scroll-lined Alexandrian library, but rather in Eris's game room. It was one of the most-often-repeated features of Castle Discord. Though its shape and contents changed slightly from visit to visit, there was always a big felt-covered card table, arcade-style video games, and pool or billiards.

Eris sat at the card table—octagonal this time—with her feet up on the felt and her velvet-upholstered chair leaning back on two legs. She had changed her clothes again—loose black jeans, with contrasting gold T and high-tops. She looked casual but cool and distant. My chair from the library remained, now sitting directly across from hers, and Melchior had shifted seamlessly from desk to table. He quickly sat down on its surface, his legs crossed goblin fashion.

"Which bit did you find most compelling?" I asked.

"The part that happened at the gates of Fate shortly after you left," she said. "I'll tell you about that in a minute. First, I want to hear how it all looked to you."

I was tempted to play coy just for the irritation factor since she would certainly have done so if our positions were reversed. But I just didn't have the energy. I quickly filled her in on my expedition.

"Huh," she said, when I finished. "Very interesting."

"What?" I asked.

"A number of things. Perhaps most of all the actions of the spinnerette. I wonder whether it was operating on its own and, if not, who it answers to."

"Any theories?" I asked. I was more than curious on that front as well, especially after Cerice's suggestion that the Fate Core itself might be developing a personality.

"Not a one, not about spinnerettes at least." She shook her head. "I'll have to look into that. In the meantime, let me take this opportunity to say 'I told you so.'"

"About what?"

"Tisiphone, of course. I said she'd make a great match."

"Look, just because she gets me hot, that doesn't mean we should pick out china. Hell, *you* get me hot when you want to, and pursuing that'd be pretty much the same as suicide on my part."

"You say the sweetest things sometimes," said Eris, shifting her position and tightening all of her clothes with a thought.

My mouth went dry, and my own clothes tightened in the most inconvenient place. Then she relaxed and let the sexual glamour fade.

I growled and shook my head in exasperation. "Look, could you just drop it? I already have a girlfriend . . . sort of."

"That brings us back to my side of the story and that

theory I mentioned," said Eris. "You know, I think I'm going to enjoy this."

"Great. That pretty much guarantees I won't."

"Exactly. I followed you from here to Fate's firewall. That was a very interesting trick you used to get in, by the way—Ahllan's old back door. I'd wondered how she managed her underground railway. Slick. After you went in, I decided to wait around outside to see if anything interesting turned up."

"And?" I said when she stopped there.

"Guess who came along only a few minutes after you did?"

"Not Tisiphone," I said. She'd arrived by some more direct route. "Nemesis?"

"Give the boy a gold star," said Eris. "Slipped in the exact same way you did, too."

That *was* interesting. I didn't think anyone but the AIs, Cerice, and I knew about that back door. "Then what happened?"

"Not much from my point of view. At least not until all the sirens and alarms started going off. I figured that was about it for you. From the sounds of it, it would have been, too, if not for Tisiphone. Don't throw away what she's offered you."

"Yes," I said. "I know how you feel on the subject. Can we move on now? Maybe get to the important bit that you're holding back for dramatic effect?"

"Ravirn, honey, it's got nothing to do with drama. It's all about another D entirely."

"Discord," I said. "Yes, I get it. You make people's lives difficult because that's what you do."

She made pouty lips. "You're not half so much fun as you were back when we first met."

"Maybe I'm getting used to you," I said. "I certainly get tired of you from time to time. Are you going to get to the point or not?"

"I'm pretty sure your girlfriend's sold you out to Fate and that Fate and Nemesis are in partnership against Necessity."

I'd kind of guessed that was where she was going, but hearing it still felt like a slap in the face.

"Evidence?" I asked.

"One, from what you told me of your own venture into the mweb servers, Cerice was monitoring the back door Ahllan left and should have been aware of the arrival of Nemesis. If so, she did not warn you. Two, after the commotion died down, Nemesis came back out from behind the firewall unscathed. She did so through an actual portal and not via the Fateclock hack. That means the Fates let her out. Unless they didn't know who she was—unlikely at best—that suggests an alliance."

"Circumstantial," I said.

Eris held up a hand. "True, but there's still number three. The one who showed Nemesis out was Cerice."

"That doesn't necessarily mean anything."

"By itself, no," said Eris. "But on top of everything else . . . She has returned to Fate. Do you think Clotho would assign a webtroll to anyone she didn't trust absolutely? That's an enormous amount of computing and magical power, especially for a programmer of Cerice's caliber."

She had a point. Cerice is a better coder than I am. I can outhack her and outcrack her, particularly under time pressure, but that's the raw, quick, and dirty stuff. On any project that rewards patience and forethought, she's got me cold. She could do a lot with a webtroll. *Would* Clotho surrender that kind of power to Cerice if she really believed there was any chance of her returning to Raven House and me? I didn't like the idea at all, but I couldn't just dismiss it.

"Oh, and there's four." Eris smacked her forehead theatrically. "I almost forgot four."

"What's that?" I asked warily.

"Who do you suppose built all those shiny new firewalls around the mweb servers? The ones that you said seemed to anticipate your best tricks? Maybe it was someone who knows you very well."

The thought had never occurred to me—Cerice might be working with Fate at the moment, but that was because she was scared of what was happening with Necessity. I'd seen

the worry in her eyes. She'd never sell me out that way . . .
would she? I felt punched in the gut. I had to know.

"Melchior, Vlink; Ravirn@melchior.gob to Cerice@
asalka.trl. Please."

"You sure you want to do this right now, Boss?"

I nodded.

"All right. . . . Searching for asalka.trl." Seconds slipped
past. "Contact. Waiting for a response from asalka.trl. Lock.
Vtp linking initiated."

Melchior's eyes and mouth widened and streams of light
burst forth, one green, one blue, one red. The beams met a
couple of feet in front of his face and formed a translucent
golden globe. It dimmed briefly, then brightened a moment
later as Cerice's image appeared in the middle of the globe.

"You made it," she said in a flat and neutral tone.

"You don't sound very happy about it," I replied.

She bit her lip. "Of course I'm happy. I don't want to see
you dead. It's just . . ."

"Just what?"

She looked away. "I'd rather not talk about it."

"But I think we need to talk," I said. "We have things that
need saying. Do you want to meet me somewhere?"

"Not right now, no. I can't get away at the moment."

"When then? Are you planning on coming back to Raven
House soon? If so—"

"Stop." She looked up again, her cheeks flushing. "I know
what you're doing, and I don't much like it."

"What *I'm* doing?" I couldn't help sounding stung. "I'm
not the one who checked out without any warning or discussion. Just poof, I'll be back in a couple of days . . . maybe."

"That's not fair, Ravirn."

"Maybe not," I said, "but it's true all the same. You still
haven't answered the question. When are you planning on
coming back?"

Cerice didn't say anything for a long moment, and I felt
my stomach drop a couple of inches. I was angry and scared
and confused, but I still loved her.

"I'm not," she finally said. "Planning on coming back,
that is."

My stomach fell the rest of the way out. I'd more than half expected her to say something like that, but even so it hit me hard. I opened my mouth, hoping to say something coherent.

"Wait," said Cerice. "Not a word, please. Not yet. Let me finish. I'm not planning on coming back, but that doesn't mean I don't want to. It just means that what I'm doing here, now, trying to reach Shara, is very important to me. Necessity is in real trouble. If someone doesn't do something, it could mean the end of everything. Don't you see that?"

"Is it important enough to build Clotho a new firewall custom-tailored to keep me out?" I asked.

She opened her mouth. Paused. Closed it. Opened it again.

Spoke. "It's important to everybody. Necessity has to be fixed. Things are happening to the multiverse that we don't begin to understand." Tears started in the corners of her eyes. "Can't you see that?"

I didn't point out that she hadn't answered my question, because really, she had.

"Ravirn, please. You have to be patient."

"I'm just supposed to hang out and wait until you find a way to fix the universe, then maybe you'll come back to me? You do know that Necessity is the most complex computer system in existence, right? That it might take years to even find out what's wrong? That she might be damaged beyond repair?"

"I'm no fool, Ravirn. I know what's at stake. That's why I tightened up the firewall. I had to convince Clotho she could trust me. I may be the only one who can get through to Shara and fix Necessity, and I'm going to need all the resources of Fate to do it." She took a deep breath, then stood up very straight. "This is bigger than you and me, and I'm willing to pay the price for that if I must."

Well, that put the ball firmly back in my court. Was I ready to make this good-bye? I loved Cerice a lot. Had for years before I'd ever figured it out. But I also frightened her and angered her and hurt her just by being the Raven. When

Clotho had called Cerice a creature of order, she'd spoken the truth. Maybe it was also true that living with chaos—with me—was slowly tearing Cerice apart. Maybe it *was* time for good-bye.

I thought of a firewall built by my lover to keep me out. No, not maybe.

It was the right decision. I knew it was the right decision, but even so, I was having a hard time opening my mouth and telling Cerice. The whole thing hurt my heart, turned it heavy and slow like it was trying to pump liquid lead instead of blood.

I forced my mouth open. "I'm sorry" was all I could say.

"I know," answered Cerice, the tears flowing freely now. "So am I. About everything."

"Maybe someday—"

"Don't," whispered Cerice. "Better to do it cleanly."

I nodded. "You're right. Good-bye, Cerice."

"Good-bye, Ravirn."

Then she was gone. I looked around for Eris, expecting her to twist the knife while the wound was still fresh. She was gone as well.

"Where's Discord?" I asked, trying to ignore the creaking I could hear in my own voice.

"She bugged out the second you said 'I'm sorry.'"

"I wonder why. I would have expected her to stick around and gloat."

"Could be that's it," replied Melchior. "She really does like you in her own twisted way, but she *has to* poke and prod. Maybe she left to keep herself from hurting you."

I wanted to scoff at that. But there was a chance he was right and an even bigger chance she was listening. I had seen the pain in her eyes when she talked about never being able to stop being Discord for even an instant, and I didn't want to hurt her either.

"Boss?"

"What, Mel?"

"I'm sorry, too." He sounded very small and sad, and I impulsively picked him up in my arms.

"Do you think I made the wrong decision?" I asked.

"No. It was really only a matter of time once you accepted the role of the Raven. Eris was right about that. You're a power. Cerice isn't. Sometimes, it's not about what anybody wants, it's just about what is." He shook his head sadly. "I just wish Shara were still around. Cerice is going to need a friend."

"It's good to have friends," I said, giving him a squeeze and setting him back on the table. "Thanks."

"Anytime. So, now what?"

"I don't know, Mel. I just don't know."

From the day that Atropos had first tried to use me as her tool to crush free will, my connections to the Houses of Fates and my childhood had been cut away one by one. With Cerice gone, the only thing I had left from those days was Melchior. The old Ravirn's life was just about gone at this point. A part of me wondered how long it would be before there was nothing left but the Raven.

Forever and a day, answered another part, very firmly, and I nodded. That was the right answer. The Raven might define what I was, but I resolved in that moment that I would never let it do the same with who I was.

"Huh," I said, noticing something else. "That's funny."

"What is?" asked Melchior.

"The ruffled-feathers feeling is gone."

"Ruffled feathers?"

I nodded. "I felt it for the first time in Hades, a sensation like my feathers were all amuss, and they wanted to stand on end. I've felt it again a couple of times since, most recently while we were in the mweb server before Nemesis showed up."

"You do know that you didn't have feathers then, right?"

"Of course I do. I think that's part of why it feels so strange."

"Having imaginary feelings about imaginary feathers, and that's only part of the strange. . . . You feeling all right, Boss?"

"When you put it that way, it does sound kind of nuts."

"Kind of. Uh-huh." He rolled his eyes in opposite directions and made a "crazy" gesture beside his ear.

It was only in that instant that I realized he was trying to distract me and jolly me up. The realization sent me right back to thinking about Cerice.

"Oh, go to hell, Mel." I paused after I said it. Maybe that wasn't such a bad idea.

CHAPTER EIGHT

Hades the place is not Hell, and Hades the god is not Satan, but I can't help seeing a lot of overlap. Especially at times like this, standing on the outer shore of the Styx and looking across the black water to the kingdom of the dead.

Hades is a walled island surrounded by the endless loop of river that is the Styx. Both lie within a giant cave somewhere under Mount Olympus. The island's sheer stone walls climb from the water's edge like a gray granite curtain. Above the visible walls rises a second set built of enchantment, and those reach all the way to the roof of the cavern.

There is only one break in the barrier, a narrow gate in a place where the wall bends in away from the river to expose a black stone beach. I could just see it from where I stood. Velvet ropes led from Charon's dock to the place where Hades Security Administration employees—the living dead—operated a checkpoint. You have to stand in line and go through a life detector to get into Hades, though at least they don't make you put all of your belongings on the belt to be x-rayed. Other than that, imagine the worst airport experience you've ever had, then double it, then remind yourself that you won't be catching an outgoing flight. Of course, that last has its plusses if you hate flying as much as I do.

Not far from the checkpoint, a cave within the cave burrows deep into the rock of that bleak shore—Cerberus's den. I eyed its dark maw askance. Where the heck was the old dog? Usually when I arrived on the banks of the Styx, he knew it within seconds and came across the water to greet me. Today, I'd already waited a good fifteen minutes without any sign of him.

"I don't understand," I said. "It's not like he gets vacation days. Do you suppose he's sick?"

"Is that even possible?" asked Mel. "He's one of the true immortals, a great power, if not one of the poles. Maybe we should Vtp him?"

I certainly couldn't knock on his front door. As long as I stayed on this side of the water, I stood on Olympian ground, the domain of Zeus. If I so much as touched a toe to the water, I entered the realm of Hades, and the god had promised me I would die if I ever did so again—die and belong to him, forever.

"Maybe we *should* try a Vtp," I said. "Melchior, Vlink; ravirn@melchior.gob to cerberus@kira.pix. Please."

"On it. Searching . . ."

I kind of tuned out the normal routine of electronic call and response. At least I did until Melchior tugged on my pant leg.

"He won't answer."

"Won't?" I said, instantly worried, "or, can't?"

"Won't," said a new voice, raspy and rough but female. "He's bein' a big dummy."

"Hello, Kira," I said. The webpixie had just flown across the river to join us.

"Hello back, and ter yer as well, blue boy." She bobbed once in the air to each of us.

I don't know many webpixies, but I do know Kira is not like the other children. The Fates invented webpixies as lightweight computer substitutes for the nontechnical members of the family.

Unlike webtrolls and webgoblins, they're supposed to

come across as light and fluffy visually as they do on the programming front. They all stand around six inches tall with dainty dragonfly wings, little pointed ears, and waist-length hair—the classic storybook fairy. Mostly they wear Tinker Bell dresses or miniature Robin Hood suits and wander around acting all glitter glam.

Not Kira. Kira goes naked, and her wings are tattered and torn. The effect is something like a miniature punk-rock Fury, which suits her character perfectly—call her style "death pixie," or perhaps pixigoth. I'm not sure whether something went horribly wrong with her basic personality programming or whether it was something else—the influence of her former master maybe. Dairn was never much fun, even before he became Nemesis. Whatever the reason, the hovering pixie had more of the angry bumblebee about her than the faerie butterfly.

"What's up with Cerberus?" I asked.

"The big dummy's moping something fierce."

"Still broken up about Persephone?" asked Melchior.

"Dave is. Bob's upset because Hades hasn't been playin' fetch all the time now that *she's* finally gone or somesuch. I think he figured that with Persephone off ter the races, it'd all be beer and skittles and Hades rompin' with the doggies. Silly beast. Personally, I'm just as glad himself hasn't been around much. He's a chilly one, he is. Makes my gizzard cold, if yer know what I mean. Brrr. Just Brrr."

"Right there with you," I said. "But that's only two of three." Or four. It depended on how you counted the collective entity that governed the body. "How's Mort?"

"Hangin' in there, I guess, but it's hard fer a dog to keep his chin up with the rest o' his pack's all lyin' about makin' boo-hoo noises. Doubly so for Mort, as he's pretty much stapled ter his pack mates."

"Maybe we should come back another time," said Melchior.

I nodded. Considering my own less-than-cheery state, it might not be the best idea in the world to hang around with a depressed dog pack.

"Don't yer think it," said Kira, flitting forward to hover in front of my nose. "The great doofus needs ter get out o' the kennel and into the light." She gave me a shrewd look. "I'm thinkin' you could maybe use a mood booster as well, from the long face yer wearin'. Stay right here."

She turned and warbled something at Melchior in hex—way too fast for me to get the details—then took off for the far shore.

"What's up?" I asked Mel.

"I'm supposed to get the beer and pizza. You're in charge of cards." He screwed his face into a pretty good likeness of Kira's, and intoned, "And no arguin' neither." Then he shrugged and started whistling a codespell called Order Out.

Not too long after that, I was sitting cross-legged on the ground with a big tablelike slab of basalt between me and the world's scariest guard dog, while drinking good, dark beer and gnawing on an oversize slice of the meat fanatic's delight. We started with seven pizzas and four kegs, of which I got about three pieces and a pitcher. Not bad when you considered the competition.

Cerberus is a *big* dog. His bulldog's body isn't quite as tall as an elephant's, but it's probably twice as wide. His heads from left to right are a Doberman, a rottweiler, and a mastiff—respectively, Bob, Mort, and Dave. Any of the three could bite me in half without stretching. Currently, all three were wearing identical silly doggy grins.

"I don't think I've ever had anything quite like this beer stuff before," said Bob. "Is it supposed to make my lips tingle?"

"You don't have lips," said Mort. "You're a dog."

"Then what's tingling?" asked Bob, looking confusedly triumphant.

"He's got you there," said Dave. "Because mine are tingling, too."

"Tingling, hmph!" Mort shook his massive head in disgust, then surreptitiously touched his tongue to the edges of his mouth. "More numbish if you ask me."

"You've really never had beer before?" I asked.

"Nope," said Dave, "not a drop. Not sure why either. It's

good shtuff . . . stuff. Stuff." He ran his tongue around the edge of his mouth as well. "Funny old feeling really."

I made a quick mental guesstimate of the amount of alcohol in the three and a half empty kegs compared to Cerberus's size and decided I had just found the world's biggest lightweight.

"Isn't it though?" I reached forward and pushed the empty pizza boxes aside. "I know we normally play bridge and that you're all pretty fond of it, but how about if we try a new game?"

"All right," said Mort. "What did you haf . . . have in mind?"

"It's called seven-card stud." I pulled out the deck and did a fancy cascade pass. "We can start with a small ante while I show you the ropes. That is, if you're not afraid to try something new?"

"Good enough," said Bob. Then he giggled.

For the next couple of hours I put aside all my worries and regrets and concentrated on my cards. I lost big, and I lost consistently. It was like playing against Eris. I'd almost decided to give up when I won my first serious pot of the night. As I was raking in my chips, Mort let out a huge sigh and started scratching behind his ear with a back paw.

"Ooh, much better," he said after a moment, shaking his head and sounding quite sober. "Maybe we can go back to bridge now that's over."

"Now what's over?" I asked.

"The buzz and that awful triple-vision thing," said Dave.

"Triple vision?" I asked.

"Yeah," said Bob with a wicked doggy grin. "Anytime we drink alcohol it messes with the cross-linking, and we all start seeing out of each other's eyes whether we want to or not."

"Normally that only happens when we're acting as Cerberus," said Dave, also grinning.

"Wait a second. All this time we've been playing, you've been able to look at each other's cards? That's unethical!"

"What would you call getting a poor dumb pack of doggies drunk and fleecing them at poker?" asked Mort, winking.

"You set me up. You . . . you dogs!"

"Oh, yeah," said Bob. "You don't really think you're the first soul who's brought old Cerberus a drink, do you? Heck, that was the first thing Orpheus tried when he wanted to get past us. Way before he pulled out the harp."

"Of course, it didn't make it into the legends," said Mort, "on account of it not working out so hot and all. He limped for a good long while after that one."

Dave chuckled. "Silly plan that. Good thing he didn't try in on the Hecatonchires, or he'd have gotten through the gates of the dead all too quick."

"Hecatonchires?" I asked. The name tickled a memory in the back of my brain, but no more than that.

"Hundred-handed ones," said Mort, "giants and colleagues."

"Still not ringing any bells," I said.

"The guardians of Tartarus?" asked Bob, in a boy-are-you-an-idiot voice. "The very big men with fifty heads each? Help keep the Titans in line?"

"Oh, got it." I'd forgotten them. The Titans had been locked away so long and so deep that the details never seemed terribly important to me. "Fifty heads, huh? Do they cheat at cards, too?"

"Come on, Ravirn," said Dave. "Don't take it so hard. You deserved everything you got after you suggested switching to a betting game."

Maybe I did at that. But I was never going to hear the end of this if it got back to Eris. I was the Raven, a power of chaos. I was supposed to be the trickster, not the trickee, and I'd just been taken to the cleaners by a trio of old hound dogs.

"Point taken," I said. "I probably shouldn't let it ruffle my feathers so, but—that's odd."

"What's odd?" asked Mel, but I waved him off.

I didn't want to talk about the whole feathers thing in front of Cerberus, even if Dave and Mort were good friends. Especially not now, when I'd suddenly developed that standing-on-end feeling again.

"Well, do you want to switch to bridge or what?" asked Dave.

"I think maybe I'd better be packing up," I said. "I've been in one place too long already, all things considered."

Mort nodded. "Not a bad idea actually. Nemesis is a nasty enemy and hella relentless."

I'd told them about my troubles over the course of the evening, hoping they might have some useful insight based on their centuries of experience with the pantheon. No such luck. With a sigh, I collected the cards and slid them back into their case.

"I don't suppose . . ." began Dave. "No, probably not."

"What?" I asked.

"It's nothing," he said. "Really."

"Oh, just spit it out," said Mort. "You know you want to ask."

"I'm not listening," said Bob, turning his face away from the other two. "Not listening at all."

"Well?" I asked.

Dave looked down and mumbled something.

"Sorry," I said, "I didn't get that."

"Is . . . is there any chance you'll be seeing Persephone anytime soon?" he finally asked. "I wouldn't bring it up, but I know you're worried about whether Nemesis is working with Hades."

"How'd you—no." I stopped myself.

Just because I hadn't talked about that explicitly didn't mean they would have missed my concern. The big dumb doggy thing is an act. Even though I know that, I still fall for it—witness the debacle with the poker. Cerberus isn't really a dog. He's a god in dog shape and the head of security for the multiverse's biggest prison—Hades.

"Better question," I said. "Why bring it up now?"

"Well," said Dave. "No one knows Hades or how this place operates better than Persephone."

"No one who *can* tell you anything, at least," said Mort.

"Traitors," fumed Bob. "Stinking traitors and my own blood, too."

"Give it a rest, yap-boy," said Mort. "We're not telling him anything he wouldn't have figured out for himself." He paused. "Eventually."

I smiled. "I guess I *am* going to see Persephone. Is there anything I can do for you while I'm there?"

"Just tell her I love her," said Dave, blinking tears away. "And that I miss her. I know she won't want to visit down here, and I don't blame her for it, but maybe you could suggest she call sometime, give her my number . . . like that."

"Of course." I reached up and scruffed under his chin. "I'd be happy to—"

"Boss!"

"What is it, Mel?"

"I'm not sure. It feels a bit like an incoming locus transfer, but not quite." He shook his head. "I think our departure schedule just got advanced."

"Right. Melchior. Mtp://mweb.DecLocus.prime/Olympusgate. Please."

He whipped out a piece of chalk and some string and quickly began to sketch a hexagram two feet or so on a side. As he filled in the cross lines, a bubble of blue light appeared next to Cerberus on Dave's side. It was the exact shade of an incoming locus transfer protocol gate, but decidedly not the familiar hexagonal column.

"Don't worry," Mort said firmly. "Even if it's Nemesis, we can slow her down a mite."

"Thanks!" I appreciated it.

Whatever it was would almost certainly finish its arrival before Mel completed the gate, a prophecy that came true a moment later when a huge spider-centaur crossbreed appeared in the bubble. The spinnerette from earlier, or its twin sister. The second it finished materializing, it started toward me.

"Oh, no you don't," said Dave, moving between us.

It tried to sidestep Cerberus, opening its woman's mouth and chittering in a way that made my bones itch, "******."

None of the boys liked it much either, and all three heads started growling.

"Gate's open," said Melchior.

I turned and took a step that way but paused when the spinnerette chittered again.

"****!"

It was an awful noise, but also somehow familiar, and the thing hadn't tried to bypass Cerberus again. Whether that was plain old common sense or something else I didn't know, but it wasn't actively trying to kill me, and I really wanted to know where it stood in the grand scheme of things.

"Uh-oh," said Kira. "Playtime is officially over."

I started to ask her why but stopped when I saw where she was looking—the gates of Hades. A figure of smoke and shadow stood there. Apparently all the noise had attracted the attention of management. Rather than settle down for a chat with Hades, I stepped into the light of the gate, so Melchior could take us elsewhere.

A Raven among peacocks. That's how I felt, at least. What is it with garden parties and hats? The bigger and fancier and sillier the better, if I was any judge.

From the moment I'd passed through the gate in the hedge, I'd been surrounded by hats of every shape and color. Even the poor rent-a-clops on door duty had been wearing more elaborate millinery than usual. Instead of the classic black-brimmed cop caps they normally wore, they had on those felt Mountie things in pearl gray with gold braid and patent-leather chin straps. The nymph who led me into the depths of the garden had a hat, too, a rather elaborate birch-bark thing that probably would have made a great canoe for exploring very small rivers.

"What's going on?" I asked after we'd passed beyond the hearing of the 'clops. "The guards at the city gate just pointed and grunted when I asked about finding Persephone."

"The goddess doesn't like to be within walls of stone or to sleep under any roof but the starry sky," said the nymph, leading me between a group of fountains where naiads—also in hats—lounged and drank tea. "So her mother, the Earth, made her this garden."

That made sense. If I'd spent three thousand years as even a part-time prisoner in the twilight cavern of Hades, I'd probably have some claustrophobia issues, too. It *was* a beautiful garden, or rather a series of the sort of gardens Louis XIV might have made of Versailles had he had ten times the cultural breadth and a hundred times the budget. There was every type of garden imaginable; from the backyard English pot garden of today, through the Japanese formal garden of the Tokugawa Shogunate, to an underwater fantasy version of the Beatles' Octopus's Garden in the shade. All of it was broken up by hedges that kept the whole from becoming a cacophony in green.

Even so, the sights and smells started to overwhelm me after a while. I was pretty much a stunned bunny by the time the nymph led me through a hedge maze and out into a shaded olive grove. It had a small, sunken amphitheater at its heart, descending to the circular stage in a series of grass-covered steps. More trees grew upon the stairs and a smaller, quieter group of women lounged on blankets spread beneath those silver-green leaves. For reasons unknown, the sounds of the stage did not reach us there beyond the edge of the theater.

"Persephone is below," the nymph whispered into my ear, indicating the far slope of the theater. "You can circle around the top and come down from behind her."

I started forward but stopped when she touched my arm.

"What is it?" I asked.

"She doesn't like to be touched, and please don't startle her. Hades, you know."

I nodded gently, and the nymph let me go. I slipped around the rim of the amphitheater, took one step down, and came to a halt as I caught my first solid sight of the stage. A tall woman with dark hair and icy skin stood at the center. She seemed to look straight into my heart in the moment I saw her and to invite me to listen to a story she was telling only for me. It was the Iliad, and though she was nearly done, in that brief instant it seemed to me that all the long tale that had passed before, from the moment of its beginning with "Anger I sing—the wrath of Achilles," had spoken itself in my head and my heart. I was enraptured. I didn't move until she finished. If I even breathed, I didn't know it.

The spell was only broken by the applause that followed. And I only recognized it as a spell in the moment that I took my interrupted second step down the tiers toward Persephone. She sat beside a short red-haired woman, whom I instantly recognized as my other grandmother, Thalia. Two steps more, and the woman who had been speaking left the stage to be replaced by a slender blonde garbed like a temple dancer. That was when I thought to count Persephone's guests and knew their nature by their number. Nine. The muses, and I had just heard a part of the greatest of all the poems of Greece performed by Calliope, their leader and the very soul of epic poetry.

Then Terpsichore began to dance, and I was lost once again. Fortunately for my errand but unfortunately for my esthetic enjoyment, her performance was shorter and not immediately followed by another of the muses. Persephone turned and smiled at me when I reached the level on which she sat. My grandmother did as well, but she was outshone as the far stars are outshone by the nearby sun, and I gave my attention first to Persephone.

She is perhaps the most beautiful of all the goddesses, tall and dark of hair and eye with flawless skin and the figure of womanhood in its springtime. This was the first time we'd had an opportunity to speak since the ordeal in Hades' office.

"Your eyes have changed," she said with a sad half smile. "I'm sorry for that."

"Yours have changed as well, Persephone, and for that I'm not sorry at all."

When I'd met her, on my first visit to Hades, the pain in her eyes had almost drowned me. Later, when I'd had to take on a tiny bit of that agony in order to pass through the barrier guarding Necessity, the weight of it had nearly killed me. That pain was still visible in the depths, but now it was one tint in a sea of colors, an accent rather than the core palette. It was a change every bit as great as the one I had experienced.

"Well-spoken," said Thalia.

I flicked my gaze to the side and caught a chaos-touched wink from her.

"Hello, Grandmother." I bowed.

"Ravirn." She bobbed her head. "He's such a good boy," she said to Persephone.

Persephone's smile blossomed. "He is indeed." She looked straight at me. "For the change in my eyes and in my heart, I have you to thank. You, and the webgoblin, Shara, who assumed my place in Necessity's net. Without your initial visit to Hades, I would never have had even the chance for escape. Without your return and the sacrifices both of you made then, I might have had my freedom only at the cost of my life and everything that is." She held her hands out to encompass the whole world, which could *well* have been undone if the Shara virus had been left unchecked.

She lowered her voice, and anger touched it, and bitter conviction. "I would have taken it even at that price, but you spared me the responsibility for the ending of all things. Thank you for saving me from my own hurt and hatred. I thank you both. I only wish I could give Shara my gratitude in person."

"Hopefully, that will be possible in the not-too-distant future," I said. "If her cycle of imprisonment follows your own, we'll know in a few more weeks. In the meantime, I have questions for you, if you'll answer them, and greetings from an old and loyal friend of yours who wishes you'd call."

"Friends first," said Persephone. "You mean Cerberus—and Dhavlos in particular."

I blinked, then realized she meant "Dave." The longer form must be his real name.

Persephone continued, "He was my only true companion within the House of Death." She wrapped her arms tightly around herself and shivered. "Tell him when next you see him that I will write to him. I can't do more as yet, can't bear the thought of seeing that dark land again, even over his shoulder in a video feed. I love my dog, but Cerberus is too much a part of Hades for me to be able to separate them with any ease. Which brings me to your questions. I presume they touch on the same blighted ground."

I nodded.

"I would banish both the place and the god from thought

and memory if I might, and I do not speak of them willingly. But if anyone has the right to ask me about Hades, it is you. So, come, sit beside me and ask your questions. I will try to answer them."

"Thank you," I said. "I would not ask . . ."

"But you must," said Persephone. "Nemesis has returned, and she has chosen you to begin her current round of mayhem."

"News travels fast," I said.

A gentle laugh drew my attention away from Persephone to Thalia.

"It does that, grandson. Especially in the great intertwined mangrove maze that forms the family tree of the Titans. I sometimes think that gossip is the smallest coin in our collective purse, spent freely and buying little, but quickly turned over."

"Does that make me a bad penny?" I asked.

"I don't know about that," said Thalia. "Do you always turn up? Or only when you're wanted?"

"Always," said Melchior, poking his head out of my bag and looking sour. "Always."

Thalia laughed and hopped lightly to her feet. "I think you probably know my grandson better than anyone. You certainly know him better than I, and I would remedy that. Why don't you tell me about him while they depress themselves."

"Boss?" He looked up at me.

"I'm not your boss, Mel. I haven't been since I found out you were really a person, no matter how many times you try to shift responsibility for your actions and decisions my way."

"Come on," said Thalia. "It'll be fun. Well, funny anyway; I can promise that."

"Funny ha-ha or funny peculiar?"

"There's a difference?"

Melchior sighed. "No, since you're related to *him*, probably not. Oh, what the heck." He hopped down, and the two of them headed up the grassy steps, leaving me alone with Persephone.

She gestured to Thalia's empty place, and I sat.

"Start with Nemesis," I said.

"I don't know much about her, not after she fell. I was a child when"—she swallowed visibly—"when Hades first stole me from my mother, and she was no concern of mine then. After . . . well, when it became clear that no one was going to punish Hades for my rape and imprisonment, I lost interest in most of the other gods and goddesses, those I didn't hate."

"Like Necessity?" I asked.

"And blind Justice, and Nemesis herself. She and Justice claimed to stand for the right, but neither of them moved to help me. How could I feel anything but hate and contempt for them?"

"So, when the Furies took Nemesis down?"

"I rejoiced at her loss but not their gain," said Persephone. "The Furies served the enemy I hated second only to Hades himself, Necessity, whose power bound me to spend three months of each year as bride to my abductor."

"You didn't keep track of what happened to Nemesis?" I know I would have, taking spiteful pleasure in the fall of my enemy, but I have a petty streak.

"No. If she had died and come to Hades, I might have sought her out to gloat. But she did not, and I—" A strange look crossed her face as she looked up past my shoulder, and she stopped speaking.

"Pardon me, yer goddess-ship," said the voice of a rent-a-clops as I turned around. "But we been informed of a possible sit-u-ation here." There were two, both wearing the informal caps that clearly said they weren't on party duty.

"By whom?" asked Persephone, her voice shaking with rage. "And what situation? This is my home, and I have not granted you permission to enter it. I do not take such violation lightly. Zeus will hear about this."

"I'm sure he already has," said a second clops, and I recognized his voice—the one who had a personal grudge against me. "Especially seein' as how Athena sent us down here on a tip that this jerk's carrying, and Zeus don't like that one bit." He looked my way. "You wanna assume the position?"

I mentally relaxed for a moment and nodded, remembering that I'd hidden my pistol with Melchior right before the party and hadn't asked for it back yet. As long as they didn't search my goblin—which seemed unlikely, since he was still wherever he'd gone with Thalia—no problem.

But then, as I stood up to allow myself to be searched, another memory came along and washed away my relief. These were not the leathers and shoulder holster I'd worn to the party, but rather the ones I'd reconstituted from chaos after my mishap with the faerie ring at Castle Discord. The question became how paranoid my subconscious had been at the time.

I had a nasty suspicion now that I'd had nasty suspicions then, so I squeezed my arm against my side to check. Damn!

CHAPTER NINE

A raven's shadow engulfed me for one brief moment as I contemplated a shift of shape and fight or flight, but I fought the impulse down. I would not bring chaos into the heart of Persephone's refuge. She had earned her peace.

"Hang on one second, fellows," I said, as the clops reached out to start patting me down.

I didn't have a lot of options once I turned aside from magic. I could act terribly surprised when they found a concealed pistol in my concealed shoulder holster. The clops were dumb, but not dumb enough to buy that one. Or I could do what I did.

"Now that I think about it, I do have a pistol." I put my hands firmly on top of my head, since I knew they wouldn't thank me for getting it out for them. "It's a .45 in a shoulder holster on the left side."

"Oh, Ravirn," said Persephone. "That wasn't smart."

"No it wasn't," said the second clops—call him Grudge. He'd drawn his own gun, an enormous Gyrojet—the rocket pistols were quiet enough that they didn't technically violate Zeus's law about thunder—and had it pointed at the side of my head. "Not one eensy bit smart."

The other clops came around and leaned down—he was about twice my height and had the most appalling breath. He yanked my jacket open and roughly jerked the pistol from my holster. As soon as he had it out, he popped the clip then checked to see if I had one in the pipe. I didn't. Apparently, I hadn't felt *that* paranoid. Then gun and clip both went into a zippered bag, which he locked.

"I'm very sorry yer goddess-ship," said Grudge, "but we're gonna have to take our boy here fer a little walk up to the head office. You understand, don'tcha?"

"I do," Persephone said very quietly. "Before you go, there's something I want you to understand, too."

"What's that?" asked Bad Breath. He didn't sound terribly interested.

"This man is under my protection. I owe him my own freedom, and I will not willingly see him imprisoned for any length of time."

"Don'tcha think that's up to Athena?" said Grudge with a snort. "Oh, and Zeus, of course."

"I almost tore down the pillars of existence to secure my own freedom," said Persephone. "Without his intervention, I would have destroyed the multiverse and everything in it, yourselves included." She rose to her feet, and anger flashed in her eyes. "I broke Necessity herself on the anvil of my will. Don't make the mistake of believing that you're tougher than she was."

"Yes, Ma'am," said Bad Breath, "or no, Ma'am." Sweat popped out on his forehead. "That is, whichever one of them as agrees with you, Ma'am. Right, Charlie?"

Grudge nodded. "Sure thing, Ma'am."

"Good," said Persephone. "I'm glad we had this little chat." She nodded at me. "Take care, Raven."

"Of course, my lady." I lifted my hands from my head to give her a deep bow. "I thank you, as does House Raven." In this case, the Raven reference was a calculated thing on both our parts, a verbal reminder to my captors that I, too, was a power and not to be lightly trifled with.

"Shall we?" I asked my captors, bowing them ahead of me.

Grudge glared at me and pulled out a pair of cuffs.

"Do you really think those are necessary?" asked Persephone. "You were planning on going willingly, weren't you, Raven?"

"Delightedly even." I turned to Persephone one last time. "You will give my regrets to Thalia and Melchior, won't you?"

She nodded.

"Oh, come on," said Bad Breath, putting a hand on my shoulder.

With a sigh, Grudge put the cuffs away and fell in behind us. They were the soul of gentility from there to the front gate of the garden and few yards beyond.

The shove between my shoulder blades knocked me down when it came, even though I'd pretty much expected something of the sort. I landed on hands and knees, but didn't stay that way for long. Grudge weighed seven hundred pounds if he weighed an ounce, and most of that landed in the middle of my back along with the sole of his size 22 cop boot.

"Little bastard," he snarled, pressing me into the dirt. "Makin' us look like idiots."

"You didn't need my help for that," I said.

"Smart guy, huh?"

He put more weight on my back—it wasn't much fun, but I wasn't in any real danger either. I *am* a child of the Titans.

"Look," I said, "we both know you're not seriously going to hurt me. At least, not right now, when the blame's so easy to fix, and you can't be sure I won't be getting out and coming after you this time tomorrow. More than that, I have friends in some very bad places as far as you're concerned. Persephone isn't the only one likely to be annoyed if anything too nasty happens to me."

"You gonna back that up with some names?" asked Bad Breath. "Or do we just have to take yer word fer it?"

"I'll give you two," I said, though I could provide more. "Eris and Tisiphone."

"Discord and a Fury?"

"Uh-huh."

"Let 'im up, Charlie. Even yer not stupid enough to buy that kind of trouble."

"Can we at least cuff 'im?" asked Grudge.

"Sure," said Bad Breath, bending and putting them in place. "Now, let's bump 'im upstairs."

When we got to the front gates of Olympus, I was forced to strip off my leathers and replace them with an all-too-short one-shouldered tunic in the style of the classic Greek shepherd boy and a pair of shapeless flat leather sandals held on by a string fancier's own nightmare of strapwork. Apparently, Zeus's classicist obsession continued unabated from my last visit to the city proper. For some reason, he'd decided that either you dressed as though three thousand years of history had never happened, or you didn't get to walk the streets of Olympus. Unfortunately, I didn't get to choose which option I preferred.

At this point, in addition to my leathers, I lost Grudge and Bad Breath. They handed me over to a 'clops wearing a loincloth, hobnail sandals, and a forced smile. It was pass me on or make the ultimate sartorial sacrifice of joining him in his Bronze Age dishabille. I think they were also grateful for the excuse to cut themselves loose of direct responsibility for me.

Smiler showed me the business end of a really vicious club and suggested that I not make the mistake of thinking he wouldn't squash me like a bug if I made a break for it, then led me on up the hill. Since Zeus's classicist obsession extended itself to paving the streets with white marble, and the flat polished leather soles of my sandals didn't afford me the same traction as my captor, I decided running wouldn't do me much good. Fifteen minutes later, I was walking down a narrow hallway toward a door marked by the owl of Athena.

As Smiler raised his fist to knock, a voice called, "Enter," and the door opened. A moment later, I got a shove that sent me sprawling through the door to land at Athena's feet. Well, the large empty space in front of her desk actually.

"Bother," said a woman's voice, as the door closed behind me. "I do wish we could train a bit of the thug out of them."

It was a bland voice, in the middle of the normal feminine range with no apparent accent. Neither sexy nor offputting, it held nothing that gave me a mental picture of the speaker. In short, it was completely ungoddess-like. I took advantage of my position to dart a glance under the desk before I stood up. I could only see the speaker from the knees down and didn't find anything unusual there either, just a rather ordinary pair of woman's legs and feet wearing the same sort of strappy sandals I had on.

When I lifted my head over the edge of the desk, I found that the voice and legs matched the rest of the woman perfectly. *Plain* was the only word that fit. She was neither short nor tall, slender nor overweight, ugly nor beautiful. Her coloring was on the dark side of light and wouldn't have distinguished her in any crowd with a significant northern Mediterranean contingent. Her straight hair was a brown short of black and cut to hang just past her shoulders. Her eyes were dark but not compellingly so, and her figure was feminine but not distracting.

She wore a two-shouldered and much-better-tailored version of the tunic I'd been given. If I'd had to guess her age from her appearance, I'd have placed her somewhere between thirty and fifty—too old to draw attention as young and too young to be marked out as old. In most situations, she'd have been invisible to a substantial portion of the population. She looked nothing like any goddess I'd ever seen or heard of. In short, perfect camouflage. Athena was a *very* dangerous goddess, even more so than I'd always assumed.

Several seconds ticked past after I'd gotten to my feet and while we each looked the other over. Finally, she gave a tiny nod.

"Sit down," she said, and I did, fully confident that the chair that wasn't currently there would be by the time I finished the motion.

It was. I nodded back as I crossed my legs—still uncomfortable with the brevity of my tunic.

"Thank you," I said.

"You're welcome. Though I must say I'm surprised."

"By what?" I asked.

"You're considerably smarter than I'd expected, given the reports and the reason you're here." Her expression didn't change a jot as she spoke, remaining apparently polite and open while revealing nothing.

"What makes you say that?"

"Oh, a number of things. You haven't shot your mouth off yet, which is practically miraculous given everything I've heard to date. You surrendered peacefully to the clops and even warned them about the pistol. Most remarkable of all, you never for an instant doubted that I am who I am. In fact, you barely looked surprised."

"Is that unusual?" I asked. "I mean, I was told I was being brought to see Athena. There's the owl on the door, and not only did the clops make sure I went down on my knees before you, but he also didn't hesitate to leave me alone with an apparently unarmed woman who's only two-thirds my size."

"You'd be surprised how many come through that door, look around, then ask why they got routed to the secretary of the goddess rather than the goddess herself."

"I'm sure it has *nothing* to do with all those sculptures and portraits of a tall imposing woman in silver armor complete with Attic-crested helmet. Likewise, I'm sure that you've done nothing to encourage that image of yourself." I didn't bother to mention that as a goddess, she could assume whatever appearance she wanted—we both knew it.

Another tiny nod from Athena. "See, you *are* smart."

"Is that a good thing or a bad thing?" I asked.

Nothing in her expression gave her away in the slightest, and I made a mental note *never* to play poker with her. Of course, considering the way even old Cerberus had outplayed me, it might have been wiser to shorten that to *never* play poker.

"Funny you should ask that," said Athena. "I haven't quite decided myself."

"Maybe I can help you reach a decision?" I smiled and leaned forward. "You said I was smart after all."

"I doubt it. The question is whether or not I should kill you."

"Over one accidental gun violation?" I gasped. Overdramatic, I know, but I couldn't help myself. "That seems extreme."

"Accidental or intentional doesn't matter to me. In fact, the gun's got nothing to do with it beyond putting you in my power long enough to arrange a killed-while-attempting-to-escape event. Or not." She didn't blink or miss a beat at that. "I still haven't decided."

OK, I was officially baffled. Terrified, but baffled. I could feel sweat starting under my hairline and the impulse to run my mouth increasing.

"What's smart got to do with it?" I asked. "And why is it good one way and not the other?"

"It's like this. You have shown yourself to be a very serious security risk to the pantheon. In a bit over a year, you've successfully cracked your way into the Fate Core—"

"And got caught," I interjected, hoping to downplay my scary hacker factor.

"Castle Discord," she continued.

"Likewise caught."

"And Hades."

"Ditto. Caught every time. How can I be such a security risk when I keep getting caught?"

"Because getting caught doesn't seem to have the least bit of effect on your achieving your goals or on your continued cracking activities. In fact, despite being caught each time, you have moved from a minor nuisance confined to one House of Fate to a significant power answerable to no one. As the head of both physical and virtual security for Zeus and Olympus, it would be foolish of me not to be concerned about a pattern that has seen you crack three of four pole powers, leaving only this one to cross off your list." She made a gesture that took in the walls around us and, by implication, Mount Olympus beyond.

"When you put it that way, it does sound kind of bad," I said, still sweating.

"Is there some other way to put it?" Before I could answer, she continued. "The only question is whether I should make a very simple straightforward promise to you or kill you outright."

"Votes for the promise?" I held up a hand. "Aye. What is it?"

"To kill you if I find you cracking or attempting to crack Olympus, which I will."

I didn't say anything in response, and she nodded after a bit. "Still smart."

"How so?" Soaked—this was not someone I could bluff or charm.

"You know the difference between a threat and a promise. Maybe I won't kill you."

"Because I'm smart?" I asked.

"No, that's just the minimum condition. You have to be smart enough to understand that I mean what I say, and that cracking Olympus is the same thing as dying. If you were stupid, I wouldn't have any choice. I'd have to kill you. The only serious question is whether the short-term headaches involved in killing you are worth the saved later effort of doing it now."

"Wait a second! I thought you said I was smart enough to understand how serious you were about cracking Olympus being fatal. Why should I cause you any trouble at all later?"

"Because of the Fate Core, Castle Discord, Hades, and Necessity," said Athena. "You have a pattern that suggests that no matter how smart you may be, you still do dumb things."

"I didn't so much crack Necessity as I got the keys and stopped in for a visit at the goddess's own request." That was my story, and I was sticking to it.

"Oh, I wasn't talking about your last expedition. I was talking about the one you're setting up now."

"Uh . . ." I didn't know how to answer that one, and I'd gone from soaked by sweat to swimming in the stuff. Her expression hadn't changed a jot in the whole time we'd talked, and it was really starting to get to me.

"I think I am going to have to kill you," she said. "It's too bad, really. I do value smart, Goddess of Wisdom and all that."

I felt a faint pricking in the skin above my heart and

looked down to find the point of a silver spear resting lightly against my chest. The shaft led from there back to Athena's right hand. She'd produced the weapon from nowhere without changing position or betraying any hint of her intent.

"You're making a big mistake," I said, while desperately trying to think of some way to change the situation.

"I don't—drat."

The spear vanished in the instant before the door burst open.

"There you are, my boy!" It was Zeus. "Why didn't you tell me you were coming by Olympus for a visit? I'd have arranged a dinner or something." He swooped down and wrapped a huge bronze arm around my shoulders, lifting me easily from my chair. "I hear that wasn't the only silly mistake you made, either. A gun? On Olympus? You know that's frowned on, don't you?"

He chortled. "Of course you do . . . now." He turned and winked at Athena. "Am I right? Of course I'm right. I'm sure that my girl here's been putting the fear of goddess in you on the subject. She's got a talent for that, does our 'thena. Saves me a huge amount of trouble, knowing she's already delivered the serious part of the lecture for me so I can go ahead and forgive you for being young and a fool. Always looking out for the old man. Aren't you, dearie?"

He didn't wait for an answer, just swept me out into the hallway and from there to the street, spouting content-free enthusiasm of the "let me buy you a drink" variety the whole way. I found myself thinking of Realtors and used-car salesmen as we marched straight off to the nearest bar. A spontaneous party ensued, with satyrs and dryads appearing practically, or possibly literally, out of the woodwork. The place's theme was sylvan woodland, and it was entirely possible that a couple of the trees holding up the roof were both alive and inhabited.

Things got blurry after that, though at some point Thalia and the other muses joined the festivities. When I got a moment to ask her about Melchior, she promised that he'd be along in a bit and went back to telling a shaggy-dog story involving actual shaggy dogs, including Cerberus, Ares's "mutts of war," Sirius, and a tail without a cat, which for reasons unclear was trying to find its lost smile.

Quite a bit later, I found myself sitting in a corner under a table. That's when Melchior finally showed up and offered to take me home. By then I was ready to go. The only problem was where. We discussed it while we filled each other in on what had happened while we were separated—not much on his end, a chat with Thalia and a message from Cerberus saying that Nemesis had joined the party Styx-side a few minutes after we'd bugged out. None of that shed any light on our next step.

"Oh, the hell with it," I finally said. "Let's go back to Raven House. We probably shouldn't stay, but at least it'll let me grab a fresh outfit. Somehow, I don't think stopping by Athena's offices and asking for my old stuff back is a very healthy idea."

"You think all this forgiveness Zeus is raining down upon you isn't going to carry much weight with Athena?"

"Not an ounce. She'd already decided to kill me. If I stay out of sight and mind for a while, she may eventually decide to just fall back on that whole simple promise option, but I'd rather not put it to the test any earlier than I have to."

"Sensible." Melchior cocked his head to one side and frowned. "So was the way you dealt with the clops. Are you feeling feverish? Or"—he looked exaggeratedly worried— "have you been replaced with an alternate-reality Ravirn?"

"I didn't fight with the rent-a-clops because I couldn't bear the thought of upsetting Persephone. I didn't do anything to piss off Athena because she's the scariest creature I've ever met. I honestly couldn't think of a single smart remark while we were talking. I was too busy sweating."

"Wow," said Melchior. "I think I'm glad I didn't get a chance to meet her. I've seen you spit in the teeth of those who were about to kill you."

"That's very different, Mel. If I'd been *sure* she was going to kill me, I might have copped my usual attitude. If you're definitely going to die, there's no reason not to piss off the person who's planning on killing you. If, on the other hand, the matter's in doubt . . ."

"I don't know, it sounds like you might be maturing somewhere down in there, but I won't argue with you."

"There's a miracle," I said.

"So, how do you want to do this? Somehow, just showing up on the grand balcony at Raven House doesn't seem the brightest of moves."

"You've got a point. Let's see . . ."

"What do you think?" I asked Mel.

"Looks quiet enough to me."

We were lying on a rock ledge a few hundred feet above Raven House after coming in via an induced faerie ring and a miles-long hike.

Raven House lay about halfway down the forested slope of the mountain arm that forms the eastern flank of Hanalei Bay, not far from where the Princeville Hotel sits in most of the mainline versions of reality. It's a beautiful site, with great folds of deep velvety green foliage forming a basin around the heart-stopping blue-green of the half-moon bay. Contrasts are provided by the thin crescent of white sand that separates the two and by splotches of chalky red rock outcroppings or the silvery lines of waterfalls.

The house itself is almost invisible from most angles, its glass-and-marble walls mimicking the sparkle of the waterfalls among the trees. Even from above, the broad expanse of the green mission-tiled roof blends well with its surroundings, an effect aided by the natural mottling of the clay and the moss growing here and there in the channels. If my subconscious really had produced this place essentially from scratch, it had done a mighty fine job.

I climbed to my feet but stayed low so as not to silhouette myself. "Might as well get it over with."

"I just wish we could see Haemun," said Melchior as he joined me.

"That'd be nice," I agreed, as we made our way down to the back of the house.

When we got there, we headed for the side with the master bedroom. Melchior shinnied up a palm tree to its mountain-facing balcony—less exposed than the sea side. I waited impatiently while he scouted around. Finally, he returned, sticking his head out between two of the rail's posts.

"You'd better come up here and see this, Boss."

"See what?" I asked.

"It'll be easier to show you. There doesn't seem to be anyone around at the moment, but we can't know how long that'll last, so I suggest you hurry."

Then he ducked out of sight. The edge of the balcony was probably fifteen feet off the ground. I might have been able to jump and catch it, but it was simply easier to follow Mel's example with the palm tree.

The first change was apparent the instant I reached the upper level. The bedroom was carpeted with a living mat of moss. Or rather, it had been. All of the moss was dead, the victim of some sort of rust virus that had turned it red-brown and crunchy. All the bedclothes and curtains had also changed. Instead of the black and green of my personal colors, I found a sea of smoky silver and rusty red.

"Someone's been sleeping in my bed," said Melchior, tugging at one corner of the obviously used sheets.

"Is the rest of the house like this?" I asked.

Melchior nodded. "Much of it."

Combine that with the fact that Melchior hadn't found anyone around, and I was really starting to worry about Haemun.

"Closet?" I slipped past him to check, since I was getting tired of the damn tunic and sandals. Same story. "Somebody's been trying on my clothes. Creepy."

"Uh-huh," he agreed. "Do you suppose this comes from Nemesis or from Dairn?"

"Do you think there's a difference at this point?" I asked as I fished out a fresh set of silvery leathers and a red T-shirt—we could always fix the color later.

It was something I'd begun to wonder myself, how much of Dairn was left beyond the body. I decided not to take the time necessary to change just then—we had no way of knowing when Nemesis would be back. Besides, if the clothes really were cut for Dairn, they'd swamp me until we had time to adjust them.

"It's hard to say," said Melchior. "Nemesis certainly still has Dairn's memories of you."

"And the hatred he-she-they directed at me felt very visceral and personal."

"I wouldn't go too far down that road," said Melchior, "I mean, Nemesis is a soul of vengeance. From what Eris said, it sounds like she takes *everything* personally.

I slung the clothes over my shoulder and headed for the stairs.

"Where are you going?" asked Melchior, trailing along behind me.

"I want to look around for Haemun."

"I was afraid you were going to say that."

"I notice you're not arguing with me." I started down the steps as quietly as possible.

"I'm worried about him, too. Hang on a second."

Very quietly, Melchior whistled a short burst of binary. Then he reached into an invisible hole, his arm vanishing to the shoulder as he rummaged around. A moment later he pulled his arm back out and handed me the pistol he'd tucked away for me on the night of the party.

"Thanks, Mel."

"You're welcome. You might want this as well." He reached in and came up with a silencer.

"Not a bad idea." I screwed it into place.

"Well, I figured since we were sneaking and all. Of course, the boy-shepherd-meets–*Mission: Impossible* look is awfully silly."

"You know, Mel, I'd never have figured that out without your help. Thank you."

By then we'd reached the bottom of the stairs and the hall that ran from the enclosed porch behind the main balcony back to the kitchen and pantry. I headed toward the service area, as that was where Haemun's rooms were and where he could usually be found. As I passed the laundry, I noticed a huge pile of black and green lying next to a couple of big dye vats. I was delighted to have the opportunity to exchange my gear for stuff I was more certain of liking and fitting into. I was much less delighted to find a large pile of Hawaiian shirts beside another vat deeper in.

"These are Haemun's." Melchior kicked at the pile.

"Let's check his suite."

It was on the end of the house opposite the master bedroom, and it had a ground-floor patio facing the Pacific. The last time I'd been there, the whole room had been done up in surfer drag. I called it that because I'd never been able to get Haemun to so much as try boogie-boarding, much less come out and ride the big waves on a real board. As far as I could tell, he just liked the look. Now, all of that was gone. The big waterbed with its longboard headboard had been replaced with a very Victorian canopy-type thing. The tiki art and Hawaiian motif rugs had likewise vanished, in favor of stark black-and-white prints of underfed nymphs in tight dresses and a white carpet. The closet, formerly full of Aloha shirts, now held polos.

I was poking around in there, when I heard a harsh metallic click from the door behind me—the slide of an automatic. I started to turn, keeping my body between my own pistol and the door.

"Drop it, or I'll shoot," said an almost familiar man's voice when I'd barely gotten halfway around. "I'm quite serious."

I let the pistol fall to the floor and finished my turn. Standing in the doorway was Haemun. Like everything else, he'd changed. It was mostly carriage and expression. He looked tight and tense and blank, and he wore a black polo under a black sports coat. But that was all background to the gun, a Glock or some other midsize automatic. It was hard to tell when all I could see was the trigger guard and the gaping hole of the barrel pointed directly at my right eye.

CHAPTER TEN

"Very good," said Haemun, after I let the pistol fall. I realized his voice had changed, too, developing an improbable British accent. "Step away from the closet and the gun now."

I held out both hands in front of me. "Come on, Haemun."

"Don't call me that," he said. "My name is Nous, Rham Nous."

"Rhamnous?" said Melchior, sounding incredulous. "You're kidding, right?"

The gun flicked to point at Melchior. "No, I'm not."

"Why is that odd?" I asked.

"Rhamnous is where the sanctuary of Nemesis used to be, near Marathon," said Melchior.

"Really?" I asked the satyr. "Are you named after the city? Or is it named after you?" Always a possibility when dealing with immortals and demi-immortals. "Or something else entirely?"

"I . . . I . . ." Rham Nous or Rhamnous, or however you wanted to say it, put his free hand to his forehead as though it pained him. "I don't know," he said finally. "You're confusing me."

"Asking you how you got your name is confusing?" I said. "That's a little bit odd, don't you think?"

"I . . . Shut up. Go sit on the bed and shut up. Take your damned pet with you."

I scooped up Melchior and moved toward the bed. As I did so, Melchior pursed his lips, subtly asking if I wanted him to whistle up a spell. I very gently shook my head. Something deeply odd was going on here. I wanted to know more about it before I committed to anything drastic.

"So, how long have you worked for Nemesis?" I asked as I sat down with my back against the velvet-padded headboard.

There was a long silence, and the satyr rubbed his forehead again. I waited quietly.

"Why do you keep asking questions I can't answer?"

"Just trying to make conversation," I said. "It might be a while before Nemesis gets back, and it'll help pass the time. Is there something else you'd rather talk about? You don't seem to have a real good handle on your own personal hows and whys."

"I do, too. I'm Nous, Rham Nous."

"You did that bit already," said Melchior. "What else have you got?"

"I don't know what you mean," said the satyr. "I'm just doing my, doing my, doing my. Job."

"All right," I said. "Let's talk about that. What is your job? Who do you work for? That kind of thing."

"I . . . uh . . . I'm the spirit of . . ." He stopped and wiped his forearm across his face, lowering the gun in his other hand.

Melchior raised an eyebrow in question, and again I shook my head.

"What are you the spirit of?" I asked.

"Of . . . of . . . of this place!" he blurted, sounding momentarily triumphant, but his accent was slipping.

"And what is this place?" I asked.

"Nemesis Hou—" He shook his head. "House Nemes—"

"Raven House," I said.

"Yes—no! I don't . . ." He dropped the gun and put both hands to the sides of his head. "I feel really strange."

"He sounds like Haemun, now," said Melchior.

"That's because he is Haemun," I said.

"I am?" The satyr leaned back against the doorframe and slowly slid to the floor. "Are you quite sure about that?"

"I am," I said.

"Then why was he pointing a gun at us?" asked Melchior.

"And why am I wearing this awful shirt?" asked Haemun, plucking at the polo. "And a jacket! How boring. How trendoid. How mundane. Of course, it's sartorial splendor compared to the shepherd outfit you're wearing." Abruptly, he rolled over on his side and went to sleep.

"I don't think I get it," said Melchior.

"Blame my subconscious," I said. "Back when we first came here, I wanted to find someplace safe, a refuge that would be secret and special. I asked the faerie ring to take us there instead of giving it a specific destination. We ended up here, and Haemun was waiting. Do you remember him telling us he was the spirit of this place and that if we had any problem with his appearance or the house's, that we should take them up with my subconscious?"

"I do," said Melchior.

"This whole place is supposed to reflect what I need, what the Raven needs, and that includes Haemun. He is as he is because that's how I need him to be."

"That doesn't explain why he's changed," said Melchior. "Nemesis isn't Raven, and this isn't Nemesis House."

"No, but Eris called her *my* Nemesis as though there were a personal component to the thing. What if a part of the nature of Nemesis is to reflect her target—through a mirror darkly if you will?"

"She becomes what she would destroy?" asked Melchior.

"Something like that. She takes something of them into herself at least. The modern sense of the word *nemesis* contains that aspect in the way it's used. Maybe the usage comes from the nature of the goddess. If it does, if she *does* have something of me in her, then perhaps the house and Haemun can pick up on that twisted version of me and try to accommodate it."

"That's it exactly," said Haemun from the floor. "At first I kept trying to escape. But after she'd been here for a while, I started changing to suit her needs. It was awful. She's a twisted creature."

"Then we'd better get you out of here before she comes back," I said. "We'll take you someplace safe so it doesn't happen again." I paused as a worry occurred to me. "That is, if you can leave this place. Can you?"

"I don't know," said Haemun, pulling himself into a sitting position. "Let me think about it for a moment." He closed his eyes and seemed to be sinking deep into himself. After a while, he nodded and smiled. "Yes. Yes, I think I can, if *you* need me to."

"Ah, isn't that sweet," said Melchior. "It's love."

"It's nothing of the kind," snapped Haemun. "It's formatting. I'm the spirit of this place, and this place is *his* place."

"Come on, Haemun." I crossed to where he was sitting and bent to pull his arm over my shoulders, almost knocking off the replacement leathers I was carrying in the process. "Let's get you out of here before Nemesis comes back." When I stood back up, I found him surprisingly light.

"I can't go anywhere looking like this." Haemun tugged at his polo. "What if somebody sees me?"

"Mel, grab some of Haemun's shirts and bring 'em along. Pick up my gun, too. We're getting out of here ASAP. I'm starting to get that ruffled plumage feeling again."

It intensified as we hurried through the hall toward the front balcony and the faerie ring there. We were crossing the big enclosed porch when a blue bubble popped into existence off to my right.

"Spinnerette?" I asked, picking up the pace.

"I don't know," replied Mel. "Last time I was able to sense the echo of the incoming transfer or whatever it was through the mweb. We're not connected here, so it's going to be something of a surprise package, though it does look like the same sort of transfer spell."

Even as he finished speaking, the spider-centaur appeared behind him.

"Shit," I said. "Hoof it, Mel!" The thing might be harmless, or even beneficial—it *had* attacked Nemesis that first time—but I didn't want to risk finding out it was just vying for the first bite.

We were almost to the ring when something punched me in the lower back, right above the kidney. My world dissolved in light for a second as the pain washed out the rest of the universe.

I came back into myself on knees and one hand. My right knee, the one I'd shattered fighting Moric, felt like someone had slipped a piece of red-hot iron in behind the cap. I still had ahold of Haemun, but he was slumped—unconscious, or nearly so. I shook my head, trying to clear it, and discovered Mel a few inches in front of my nose.

He grabbed my ears with both clawed hands and yanked. It hurt, and I scrambled forward to escape the pain. My knee hated the idea, and the rest of me wasn't much happier. I was just opening my mouth to protest when he yanked again. Harder this time, much harder. I screamed but moved even faster. Then my hand found the edge of the faerie ring with a sharp crack . . . or maybe the noise came from elsewhere. Fresh pain flooded through my right leg, centered on the back of my thigh. I reached into the faerie ring and twisted with my mind.

We went elsewhere.

That was practically the last thing I remembered, that and crawling across dandelions. Then I went away for a little while.

When I came back, it was very briefly, just long enough to realize I was sleeping in my own bed. I felt a quiet sense of relief—it must all have been a nightmare. The next time I returned to myself it was because my nose was so stuffed I could barely breathe. From the feel of it, I'd probably snored myself awake.

I glanced around. Things looked wrong—too low and too organic, and it was dark, absolutely so. If not for the light of my eyes, I wouldn't have been able to see anything.

Where was I? I tried to sit up. My knee and lower back screamed, but not nearly as loud as the back of my thigh. What had happened? How had I gotten here? It felt like home, but it couldn't be Raven House. The bed was all wrong and so were the echoes, but it still felt like my own bed and home.

"You up, Boss?" Melchior sounded worried.

"Yeah. What happened, and where are we?"

"Garbage Faerie, Ahllan's old place. Don't you remember bringing us here?"

"Not at all." I shifted around to get a better look at him and, "Ow! What the hell did I do to my leg?"

"Not you. Nemesis. She shot you. Twice. Luckily, the Kevlar in the leathers you were carrying stopped the one that hit you in the kidney. I don't think we'd be having this conversation otherwise. I've done what I could by way of healing magic on your thigh, but you won't be running away very fast for a while."

"Oh." That was sobering considering the situation. "Garbage Faerie?"

"Yeah."

When Ahllan had been running the familiar underground, she'd had her headquarters in a backwater DecLocus way out on the edge of possible realities. Despite the fact that there didn't seem to be any humans in residence, the world looked basically like a giant garbage dump for a modern industrial civilization, one that hadn't been used for a decade or three and was in the process of being reclaimed by nature. You constantly came across things like a cracked engine block with flowers growing out of all the cylinders or an old toilet with tiny tree frogs living in the miniature pond of its bowl.

Ahllan's home was a series of tunnels and rooms built into a hill. My own bedroom—more remembered than seen at the moment—was low and domed, its walls covered with a collage of warm brickwork colors cut from old magazines. The ancient futon I currently occupied was heaped with patchwork quilts and surrounded by rag rugs in the same reds and oranges.

"What time is it?" I asked.

"After midnight and before sunrise local," said Mel. "You've been down for something like eight hours. I can't say when it is OST because Garbage Faerie's still off the mweb."

I nodded. The darkness suggested night. Even though my room didn't have windows, the hallway beyond its door had no roof. The Furies had opened it to the sky when they'd assaulted the place looking for me the previous year. Other portions of the house had collapsed. It was only luck that had left my current refuge relatively untouched. I wondered what I had been thinking when I chose this as a destination, but I could only remember the barest fragments of what happened after the bullet hit my leg.

"Eight hours?" I forced myself to sit up, though the pain from my gunshot made things go all fuzzy and rainbow around the edges. "We've got to get out of here, before Nemesis shows up." I was frankly shocked that she hadn't already—you couldn't follow someone's path through a faerie ring, but this was one of my known hangouts. Besides, Nemesis had already shown a remarkable talent for finding me.

Melchior hopped up onto the bed and put a hand against my chest. "Slow down there, Boss. Even if Nemesis guesses we've come here, it's going to take her some time to follow suit."

"Why?" I asked.

"Same reason I can't check OST: there's no mweb here."

"That doesn't close off the faerie ring, and if Nemesis can do some of what I do . . ."

"That might not close it off, but breaking the circle by putting all the cans in a trash bin should more than take care of things."

Oh. Ahllan's faerie ring had been a circle of crushed beer cans on the slope of the hill outside. Apparently, Melchior had destroyed it.

"What about coming in via another ring?" I asked.

"Unless someone's built a fresh one, there aren't any within five hundred miles of this spot, probably more. When Ahllan set this place up as AI central, she made sure it was damned hard to get to. That included wiping out all the rings on this and the nearby islands, not that there were many."

"Islands?" I asked.

"Yeah," said Melchior. "We're actually on what would be Ireland if this DecLocus were closer to prime, near Cork."

"So the nearest ring would be somewhere in France? That's not all that far if you're using magical transport."

"Actually it's unlikely there's anything this side of Moscow," said Melchior. "Ahllan didn't stop with that initial campaign—she wanted to get rid of all of them. I just don't know how much farther she eventually got. For that matter, it wouldn't be easy to find the right world with the beer-can ring gone. You'd have to be able to read the rings awfully well to recognize that any of the farther ones were in this DecLocus."

"That or ask the system to take you to the right place, the way I did when I found Raven House." I hadn't specified location at all, just the conditions I wanted our destination to fulfill.

"That's a pretty special case," said Melchior. "If Nemesis has all of your powers *and* knows to ask the right question *and* the system actually works that way, she *might* land on top of us any second. But that's a whole series of big 'ifs' that all have to come up right, and you really need to rest and heal for a bit. I can't think of a better, safer place."

"You make a pretty good point," I said, lying back down with some relief—I hurt. "Too bad we can't set up a probability bubble like the one Ahllan used as her fallback refuge."

Melchior smiled. "That would be nice, since they're completely unreachable if you don't know the exact coordinates, but I don't have the computing cycles or raw power to build that kind of looped gate. For that you need a full webtroll. The best I can do is make this place as snug and secure as possible. Haemun and I are planning to see what we can do about the roof in the morning."

"Where is he now?" I was more than a little bit worried about him, between the abuse he'd suffered from Nemesis and taking him away from the place that defined him.

"He's in the other surviving guest room, sleeping like the dead and snoring worse than you are. He went down almost as hard as you. Now, why don't we quit playing twenty questions and get back to recovering."

"Is that the editorial 'we'?" I asked.

"No, the medical, as in 'Have we had our meds today?' If you don't want me to dose you again, you'll surrender peacefully and go back to sleep."

"All right, Mel. You win. I'm in no state to keep arguing anyway." I settled myself as comfortably as I could manage with all my aches and pains and was asleep in minutes, very glad indeed for the respite from the insomnia that had plagued me in the weeks since I'd returned from my dissolution into chaos.

The next time I woke, a line of bright yellow at the base of the door told me the sun was high enough to shine down into the open hallway. Melchior was nowhere to be seen, but he'd left a bell beside the bed. Since he'd also left a cane and I really needed the bathroom, I decided to see how far I could get on my own.

Sitting up didn't kill me. Neither did getting to my feet, though the latter left me feeling as though it should have. My leg was not at all happy with me, though the ache in my back from the first shot had faded completely, along with the bruise it must have left.

I tested my bad leg carefully and found that even without the cane I could walk. It hurt, rather a lot, and I sure as hell wouldn't be jogging anytime soon. Still, it was better than I'd expected. Melchior must have done wonders with the healing magic. Combine that with the legacy of quick recovery I'd inherited from my Titan forebears, and I couldn't complain. Not when I was walking so soon after taking a bullet and aggravating the old damage in my knee. Even if the latter didn't want to bend properly.

Swearing periodically, I hobbled off to the bathroom. I didn't bother with clothes. I'd found my bloodstained shepherd's tunic in a heap next to my leathers and decided that neither looked very appealing.

Unlike the bedroom where I'd slept, the bathroom had

recently been cleaned and dusted. Another domed room, its walls and ceiling were surfaced with a broken-glass mosaic, the edges of which had all been smoothed until they felt something like tile. Here and there, a fragment of labeling identified a bit of soda bottle or a mason jar. The colors ranged from green-blue through blue-green to emerald. The effect was a bit like scuba diving in the Mediterranean. The porcelain was spiderwebbed with fractures but clearly sound.

After I'd relieved myself, I checked my leg in the mirror and was delighted to find the wound thoroughly scabbed over. It was high on the outside of my thigh, and only luck had prevented the slug from hitting the bone with all sorts of ugly complications. There was no exit wound, so Mel must have drawn the bullet. I was very glad I hadn't been awake for that. My knee was swollen and red and popped very quietly and very painfully when I bent it much past thirty degrees, but it had been much worse in the past. I was beginning to wonder whether I hadn't substantially fixed it when I built myself a new body after I melted the old one in Hades.

The bathroom had a huge sunken soaking tub, and between the blood and the sweat and the aftereffects of Zeus's little impromptu pub party, I really needed cleaning up. I looked at the scabbed-up hole in my leg again and regretfully opted for sponging myself off instead. I'd have to get Mel to come up with some sort of waterproof bandage so I could soak later. When I finally went back out into the hall, it was much darker, and I looked up to see if a storm was rolling in.

"What are you doing out of bed?" demanded Melchior, peering down through a gap between two of the rusty metal patches that now bridged the gap of the ruined roof.

"What does it look like I'm doing?" I pointed over my shoulder toward the bathroom.

"Idiot," he muttered. "Why didn't you ring the bell?"

I ignored his question in favor of one of my own. "What on Earth are you using to fix the roof?"

"Car hoods," said Haemun, leaning over the edge beside Melchior. "There's a sort of automotive graveyard over that way." He waved vaguely. "Once we've got them in place, we'll cover them with dirt."

"That makes sense, I—"

Melchior held up a warning hand. "Hang on, Boss. I've got a funny feel—Ah! Incoming call from Tisiphone via the voodoo phone. Do you want to take it as you are? Or—"

Before I could respond, light-fog started pouring out of his mouth and eyes, and he bent forward as though he were about to throw up on me from above. A rough misty globe formed in the air between us, and a moment later an image of Tisiphone appeared at its core. She looked around in momentary confusion before glancing downward. As soon as she saw me, she developed a wicked smile.

"Hello there!" she said. "You really didn't have to strip just on my account. I'm used to being the only naked one in any conversation where my sisters aren't around."

"Uh . . ." I groped for the right words and moved my cane to cover as much as one thin piece of wood could.

"Of course, there's something to be said for doing things this way." Her mouth widened into a grin. "Polite is always good, especially when it so improves the view." She moved her head to the side, quite obviously peering around the cane.

I blushed as I felt myself harden in response to her obvious interest. "As much as I'm enjoying the current drift of the conversation, I doubt it was the reason you called. Before we get too far off topic, I have to ask whether you got my message earlier."

"I did, and I was just calling back to arrange for our meeting. I had intended to suggest a place, but all things considered, why don't I just come to you? That way you won't feel the need to overdress for the part. Don't move a muscle."

"You know—" I began, but she was already gone. "Damn. Melchior, could you come give me a hand?"

I had no idea of how long it would take for her to get from there to here. In part because I had no idea of where there was. I quickly hobbled back to my bedroom and lowered myself onto the edge of the bed. I'd been on my feet too long and was sweating from the effort.

"What do you want, Boss?" Melchior stood in the doorway, his silly grin leaking foggy light at the edges.

I looked at my leathers and the tunic. "I don't know, Mel. Some dignity maybe."

He followed my gaze. "You're not going to find it there. The tunic never had any, and you really don't want to try slipping the leather pants on over that leg."

"You're probably right," I said with a sigh. "It's just that I feel so vulnerable like this."

"So get under the covers, and I'll try to find you a robe. I know Ahllan had a few around here at one time."

"Thanks, Mel. I appreciate it."

He opened his mouth to respond, but stopped when a slice opened in the air behind him with a brutal ripping noise. I quickly put my back against the headboard and flipped the blankets over my lap. The rip widened, and Tisiphone stepped through into the hallway. She paused there for a second, and I thought I saw her sniff the air before she turned my way.

"I told you not to move a muscle." She frowned at me theatrically and shook her head as she crossed the threshold.

"Hello, Tisiphone," said Melchior before ducking past her into the hallway. "Back in a tick." Then he vanished, presumably off in search of a robe.

She waved vaguely after him without taking her eyes off of me. "Sure, see you then."

"Hi," I said, feeling strangely shy.

"Hi." Tisiphone stepped deeper into the room and stopped abruptly, sniffing again.

Her frown deepened into something real as she knelt to look at my wadded-up tunic.

"This is your blood, isn't it?" she asked, her voice hard.

"It is. Nemesis shot me."

Tisiphone stood up, her wings and hair flaring wildly. The frown turned briefly into a snarl, and the claws that tipped her fingers and toes elongated, glittering like red diamonds in the light of her personal fires.

"We should have destroyed her utterly," growled Tisiphone.

"Mother was wrong about that, and Megaera was right. This time, we will rend her soul and bind the shreds to the four winds so that they may evermore haunt the wastes of the world."

Her words were accompanied by a dissonant grating. It took me a moment to realize that it came from the way the repeated clenching of her toes dragged her claws across the stone floor. My attention must have drawn hers because she stopped a moment later.

"Sorry. She just makes me want to kill something." Tisiphone took several deep breaths, and the fires of her rage slowly dimmed as she retracted all twenty of her claws.

"You know," said Melchior from the doorway, "maybe this is a bad time." He had a bundle of plaid terry cloth in his arms.

"It's all right, little one," said Tisiphone. "Though if that's what I think it is, I'm not sure I'll thank you for delivering it." _

"It's a robe," I said. "I asked him to find something for me to wear."

"Look," said Melchior, setting the robe down, "why don't I just leave it here and let you two talk in private?" He backed out of the room and vanished again.

Tisiphone makes him nervous; not that I can blame him. Tisiphone makes me nervous . . . when she's not terrifying me. She's a Fury, the very embodiment of vengeance and destruction. She could tear me limb from limb without breaking a sweat. But then, another part of my brain noted, maybe that's what makes her so damn sexy.

Just then she bent and picked up the robe, highlighting the long, lean lines of her legs and the hard muscle of her ass. My mouth went a little dry as she carried it over to me and sat on the edge of the bed with it in her lap. Or maybe the sexy thing was just that she's absolutely smoking hot.

She put a hand on my thigh. "How badly were you injured? And where?"

"Uhm, that leg actually," I said.

"Oh." She snatched her hand away. "Did I hurt you?"

"Not at all. She got me in the back of the thigh. It's not

too bad really. Mel did a bang-up job on the patching front."

"Would you like me to take a look at it?" she asked.

"Maybe later," I said, a touch too quickly.

I wasn't quite ready for her to be poking around under the blankets that provided me with my only covering. From the smile she flashed, I think she knew exactly what my objection was.

"I know a thing or two about wounds." She put her hand back on my thigh, a little higher up. "And about taking care of them. You pick stuff like that up in my profession."

"I'm sure you do," I said. It was a sobering thought, but one I couldn't give proper attention with my libido whispering to me about the hand on my thigh. "I . . . look, could we stop flirting for a minute or two? I'm getting serious psychological whiplash here between the part of me that wants to pull you under the covers and play with fire and the part that thinks I should be running for the hills."

She made a brief try at pouting but couldn't seem to sustain it against the grin that followed.

"Now, what fun is that?" she asked. "If I've got you that far off-balance, shouldn't I move in for the kill?" Her hand slid a little higher on my thigh, and she winked.

"Tisiphone, please."

"Please what? Take my hand away?" She lifted it. "Or please crawl under the covers and ravish me?" She caught the edge of the blankets and lifted them a fraction of an inch.

"I don't know," I said quietly. "That's why I asked."

"Oh, all right." She dropped the covers and put her hands firmly in her own lap. "But it's much less fun this way."

As was so often the case when dealing with Tisiphone, I was once again reminded of a cat. This time it was a cat pretending at patience by folding its tail around its legs and looking disinterested. I suspected that we both knew this was just a fresh game, but at that point I was willing to take whatever I could get. *Including the ravishment,* whispered my libido, and I didn't try to argue. Just as it would be foolish of me to pretend Tisiphone didn't scare me, it would be silly to pretend I didn't want her. Both feelings would have to wait.

"Thank you," I said after a long moment. "We have things we need to talk about, and it'll be much easier this way."

"But ever so much less fun."

"Probably," I said. "How about if I promise to flirt with you when we're done?"

"Deal, though I won't swear to stop at flirting."

"Deal." I stuck out my hand, and she solemnly shook it.

I shivered a bit then because I couldn't help but think of the threat Megaera had made me when last I'd seen her.

"What's wrong?" asked Tisiphone.

"Megaera . . ."

"Threatened to kill you if you didn't stay away from her sister?"

"Yeah," I said. "How'd you guess? Does she do that sort of thing a lot?"

"Only when Alecto or I show any signs of interest in a new man," said Tisiphone, "but that's not how I knew this time. She told me about it."

"She did?"

"Yes, but don't worry, the threat is no longer operative."

"That's fine for you to say," I said, "but does she know?"

Tisiphone nodded. "She may not be very happy about it, but she knows that she's not to touch you. I made it very clear that if she kills you, I'll be quite cross with her."

"Great." Somehow I wasn't all that reassured.

"Ravirn?"

"Yes."

"Since we're already talking about difficult entanglements, I have to ask: Are you still with Cerice? Or has she gone back to House Clotho?"

"We're not still together," I said.

"That's what I thought. I think I've come up with a better plan for how to have this conversation without all the tension and distractions."

"What's that?" I asked.

"Ravish first, talk later."

With that astonishing Fury speed, she caught the edge of

the blankets and flipped them away. Then, very deliberately, and very slowly, she climbed farther onto the bed, kneeling with her face a few inches from mine.

"What do you think?" she asked. "Will that work for you?"

I put a hand on her right side just beside her breast with its fiery nipple. "Promise not to burn me?"

She giggled. "No. But I promise that you'll like it."

CHAPTER ELEVEN

Later. Much later. Tisiphone and I lay side by side on the bed, she on her stomach, me on my back. Contrary to her intimation, she had not burned me, though I'd experienced fire in some ways I would never have thought possible.

"Kind of lends a whole new meaning to the term *burning bush*," I said.

She moved very quickly then, sitting up and flipping me over so that I lay facedown across her lap and giving me a solid swat on the ass.

"Rule one, no bad redhead jokes."

"I meant it literally," I said. I didn't bother to struggle—she was much stronger than I was, a fact that had made our sex more interesting in a number of surprising ways. "Besides, if you've got the temper to match the hair . . ."

She swatted me again. "Rule two, no redhead stereotyping. The temper comes from being a Fury, end of story."

"What's rule three?" I asked.

"Don't make me tell you rule three."

"Is that the rule or—ow!"

She'd swatted me again, letting the very tips of her claws get involved this time.

"All right. No rule three. Can I move now?"

"No," said Tisiphone. "I want to take a better look at this bullet hole. I don't like the way it interfered with things. It's been a very long time for me, and I want you healed up properly so that I can catch up."

"That sounds like fun. How long is a long time?"

"Seventeen hundred years," said Tisiphone.

"Wow. If the last hour is anything to go by, catching up is likely to kill me. Maybe we could—ow!" She'd just prodded my scab.

"Sorry. This is going to hurt. Probably quite a lot, but it should really speed things up."

"What's—OW!"

It felt as though Tisiphone had dropped a bit of liquid fire on the wound, and it was now burning its way along the track the bullet had taken deep into my flesh. For that matter, considering her nature, maybe she'd done exactly that. Whatever it was, I lost track of everything but the pain for a good minute or two.

"How's that?" she asked just as the pain peaked.

"It's damned . . . huh."

Where everything had been agonizingly hot a moment before as though someone were probing the wound with a fiery dagger, it now seemed as though the blade had been quenched. I could feel the path the bullet had taken as plainly as I might a breeze on my face, but it no longer hurt. Rather, it felt like an ice cube drawn along the line of sunburn, pleasure and relief that almost bordered on pain.

Experimentally, I flexed the muscles of my leg. Much better. Still stiff and sore, but I thought I might be able to put aside the cane now.

"Better?" she asked.

"Yes. What did you do?"

"Wrong question," she answered.

"Fair enough, tell me the right one."

"Ask me what I'm *going* to do," she said.

"All right. What are you—oh."

Her hand slid between us where my thighs rested across hers, catching and guiding.

"I wasn't done with ravishing just yet," she said. "Is that all right with you?"

"Yeah, fine."

More time went away.

I lay half-on, half-off of the low futon, pressing my forehead against the cold stone of the floor and desperately trying to shed heat. Tisiphone was sitting cross-legged on the far end of the bed, grinning. It wasn't fair. She didn't even really look mussed, and I felt like I'd just run a double marathon.

"You win," I said, when my breathing had slowed a bit. "I surrender unconditionally."

"That's no fun," she said. "I refuse your surrender and demand a rematch at a later time."

"That idea does have its merits," I said with a small grin of my own. "I'll need a week or three to recover first."

"Not likely." She snorted and poked me with a foot, though she kept the claws retracted. "Hostilities could resume at any time and with no warning. You'll just have to learn to be prepared."

I laughed and pushed myself back up into a sitting position. "You're merciless. You know that, right?"

"*Fury*. Duh. It's in my job description. Hell, it *is* my job description. I will promise to give you at least one hour from this moment so that we can get that deferred conversation from earlier out of the way. Where were we?"

"Discussing the fact that your sister Megaera's going to slice me into neat little ribbons when she finds out about us."

"She won't, you know."

"You sound awfully confident," I said.

"I am."

"Why is that?" I asked.

"Because we agreed that we need you in one piece."

"*We* being you and Megaera?"

"We being Furies Inc.," said Tisiphone.

Suddenly feeling colder, I reached down and pulled a blanket over my lap.

"Would you care to elaborate on that?" I asked.

"Necessity is broken." Tisiphone's voice was flat and hard, with just the faintest hint of pain underneath. "That's bad and needs to be fixed, but it's not our only problem."

"Nemesis," I supplied.

"She's part of it, but we've handled her before, and we will this time, too—more finally. No, it's what she represents that's the major worry."

"I'm not sure I'm following you," I said.

"You should be. In this we share many enemies."

"You mean the Fates?" I asked.

"Yes, and maybe Hades, though we're less sure of him. This is causing the three of us a great deal of distress. I think I've told you before that full autonomy doesn't suit us. Necessity made us that way in response to Nemesis, who had the opposite problem. Under normal circumstances, we would probably place ourselves under Fate's orders until we restored Necessity."

"But?" I asked.

"But we believe Fate is trying to usurp Necessity's throne. That's what you think, too—the message you were trying to get across at the Necessity gateway, before we were interrupted by . . . events, isn't it?"

"It is," I said, appreciating her discretion in not criticizing Cerice by name. "The way Fate grabbed total control of the mweb servers seems telling to me. Especially when combined with the wholly unexpected reappearance of Nemesis."

"It did to my sisters as well. Alecto in particular is quite smug about already having broken the alliance we formed with the Fates in the first days after Necessity went silent. Megaera argued against it, and Alecto likes to show her up."

"I've been meaning to ask about that and about Persephone," I said. The Fates had ordered the Furies to kill me then, and they very nearly had.

Tisiphone looked uncomfortable for a moment. "I am sorry. I had no choice in the matter. You know that, right?" I nodded, and she continued, "I suppose you've been wondering why we cut our fresh tie to Fate so soon."

"The question had crossed my mind," I said. "I'm not complaining, of course. I'm much happier with you when you're not trying to kill me."

Tisiphone stepped off the bed and began to pace. "When it became clear that it was Persephone and not you who was responsible for the damage to Necessity, it also became clear that the Fates had tried to use us to settle their score with you. That didn't sit well. We don't like being used, not even a little."

"That explains your split with Fate, but I still don't understand why you didn't go after Persephone."

She froze, her shoulders stiffening. "I can't tell you that, Ravirn. Not at this time. I hope you understand."

"It's all right," I said. "I know that Tisiphone the Fury has responsibilities that may conflict with the wants and needs of Tisiphone the individual. As much as I dislike the idea, I've come to understand the dual nature of power vs. person. The Raven and Ravirn are decidedly not the same thing."

"Thank you." Tisiphone relaxed and turned back to face me with a wistful smile. "That understanding is why we can share what we have today. It's why I'm glad you've become a power at the same time that I mourn for you. It's not a burden I would wish on anyone I cared about."

"Uh, Boss." Melchior poked his head into the still-open doorway. "Could I interject a question?"

"Sure," I said.

"So, I've been sitting out here for a bit, and I couldn't help overhear the discussion, and I was wondering about something. It—"

"How long have you been there?" I interrupted. I was a little bit appalled by the idea that he might have listened to our entire performance.

"He arrived a few minutes before we finished having sex," said Tisiphone. "I heard him sit down."

"How could you have heard me over all that banging

and . . ." Melchior trailed off, blushing. "I mean—uh. Well, hmm."

"I have very good ears, little goblin." Tisiphone grinned. "And a certain level of paranoia comes with my job."

"Oh." Melchior's entire head had darkened to a deep indigo with embarrassment.

"There's no need to worry," said Tisiphone. "I know you have your partner's best interests at heart, and I have no personal modesty at all. You could have come in and had popcorn for all it would have bothered me."

Mel opened his mouth and raised a finger.

"Veto," I said, before he could begin his comment. Whatever it was, I didn't want to hear it. "Now, you had a question?"

"More an observation, really." Melchior came through the door and took a seat against the wall. "She hasn't yet said *why* the Furies need you."

I'd been wondering when she was going to get to that myself but hadn't wanted to press. I turned and raised an eyebrow at Tisiphone.

"Sorry," said Tisiphone. "I wasn't being evasive. It's just I'm not entirely used to this kind of conversation. Things are very different when speaking with my sisters or with our . . . customers for that matter."

"What a very diplomatic way of saying victims," said Melchior.

She gave him a sharp look. "Besides, I would have thought the answer was obvious. We need Ravirn to help us reach Necessity, then to fix her."

"Oh," said Melchior.

I blinked several times, trying to take that in. It didn't help.

"You. Need me. To fix Necessity." I choked on the last word and had to stop and cough for a moment. "That's crazy."

"Who else are we going to get to do it?" she asked quietly. "There really aren't many powers with the necessary computer skills, and whoever takes the job will have to have total access—the ability to change the very nature of the

multiverse. To whom would *you* give such power? We now
know we can't trust the Fates. Athena's almost as bad, and
she's entirely in Zeus's pocket. No one sane trusts Eris. That
doesn't leave a lot of options."

"I wouldn't even know where to start," I said, stalling
while I tried to think of someone else who'd be a better fit.

"Start with Shara," said Tisiphone, before I could think
of another name. "That's a big part of why it has to be you. I
got to read Shara's Fate thread when we were sent after you
the last time. There are only four people in the world whom
she really trusts. You two"—she pointed at the pair of
us—"Ahllan—currently missing—and Cerice, who works
for Fate. It's got to be you."

I wanted to argue, to say that it wasn't my problem, that
someone else would take care of it, maybe even Cerice, who
was already working on it. But Tisiphone was right. Even
though I still trusted Cerice on a personal level, she was
working for Fate, whom I did not trust at all. I like Discord,
but it would be the ultimate act of madness to put her in
charge of all of creation, even for one second. After my recent encounter with Athena, I didn't think much of giving
her that kind of power either.

Who else was there? Who *would* I trust? I couldn't think
of a single name. The gods, my family, have too many quirks
and vices and not nearly enough leet skillz among them. But
me? Fix everything? The idea was patently insane.

"I see a problem," I said after a moment.

"What's that?" asked Tisiphone.

"I don't trust *me* either. Not with that kind of power. I
don't trust anybody with that kind of power."

"Somebody has to do it," said Tisiphone. "We took a
vote, and you won."

"Simple majority?" I asked.

Tisiphone grinned. "No. Unanimous."

"Megaera voted to trust me with the very soul of Necessity and everything that entails?"

"She did. She said that at least she knew where to find
you and that you weren't immortal yet."

"Oh." Now that I could believe.

Of course, if I got my hands on the source code for everything, I could fix it so Megaera would never bother me again. I could fix a lot of things. I could make the multiverse into my playground. Then I shook my head. That was a Very Bad Idea. I was *already* being corrupted by the thought of all that power, and I hadn't even agreed to try it.

"I'm a hacker and a cracker, and you're offering me the keys to the kingdom," I said. "This is really a bad idea."

"Actually," said Tisiphone, "your hacking past is a big part of why Alecto agreed to the idea. She said you're sloppy and you consistently overreach, but that you always manage to kludge things together."

"She thought that was a *good thing*?" demanded Melchior.

"So did I," said Tisiphone, turning to face him. "We don't want someone who's going to rewrite the master code. We just want someone to get the goddess onto her feet long enough that she can make the decisions on how best to proceed from there. Nothing Ravirn does is seamless; he's too much of an improviser. Once Necessity has herself back under control, we should be able to find and adjust anything he did fairly easily."

I opened my mouth to tell her that wasn't entirely true. I'm an absolute wizard at leaving invisible back doors for example. Then I realized that now might not be the best time to brag that up, so I closed it again. Besides, assuming I took the job, I might want that back door someday.

"Could you toss me my robe, Tisiphone? I need to pace, too."

"Why bother with the robe?" she asked.

"She's got a point," said Melchior. "Ain't nobody here who hasn't seen you naked or who's likely to be offended. Amused on the other hand . . ."

"I care," I said. "It's harder to think naked."

"Weird," said Tisiphone, bringing me my robe and handing it over. "Here you go, but that's just weird."

"Said the naked embodiment of vengeance." I winked at her and pulled on the robe.

"What's your point?" she asked me.

"Nothing at all, just sayin'." I paced for a little while. "Megaera really agreed with you on this one?"

She nodded. "Of course she did. It's not like you could get in without one of us—me in this case—to disable the physical security and open the door after you get around the soul lock. She knows there'll be someone there to keep an eye on you. But even if that weren't the case, she didn't have a lot of choice. Put simply, you're the best candidate."

Maybe I really was. I got up and began to pace, well, limp in circles actually, but the intent was the same. I still couldn't think of anyone else I'd let have the kind of access this job needed. They were all even less trustworthy than I—from my point of view, at least—which was frankly terrifying since I was already starting to think about the myriad of little things I could do to make my life easier. I could erase myself from Hades' memory, make Athena love me like a son, even write myself back into the family of Fate.

Or write Fate out of the picture completely, a voice whispered in the back of my head as a shadow that only I could see engulfed me, a shadow with wings. I shuddered and opened my mouth to refuse. *Would Eris be any better? Athena? Cerice and Fate?* I forced the shadow to retreat, but I couldn't force back its arguments.

"All right," I said finally. "I'll do it." The faintest flicker of darkness edged my vision, bringing with it an instant of inhuman satisfaction. "I'm going to regret this"—I already did—"but I'll do it." Somebody had to.

"If it's any consolation," said Tisiphone, "you'll probably regret it less immediately than you would have regretted saying no."

"Why's that?" I asked.

"Megaera again. She said that if you didn't agree to try to save Necessity, all bets were off and she was going to kill you even if it did piss me off for the next five hundred years."

"Oh." I caught Tisiphone's hands in my own and looked into her eyes—I wanted her to understand that I was being serious and sincere and not the least bit snarky. "I don't mean to criticize, but is there a reason you didn't mention that part up front?"

"I didn't want you to say no," she said simply.

"Oh my," said Melchior, whistling. "She's really got your number, doesn't she?"

"What's that supposed to mean, Mel?" I let go of Tisiphone and turned to glare at my familiar.

"Nothing at all, contrary boy." He grinned. "Don't let it worry you."

I sighed. He might actually have a point there—in amidst the gloating.

"Where do we start?" I asked.

"Isn't that your job?" asked Melchior.

"I'm just thinking out loud," I replied. "We'll have to see if we can find a way to communicate with Shara."

"How?" asked Tisiphone. "My sisters and I have tried everything we can think of to get through to Necessity. Nothing works."

"That's why you called me in. I'm the expert hacker, right?"

"Yes," she agreed.

"So, have you actually tried to reach *Shara*? As opposed to Necessity?"

"Well, no, not exactly," said Tisiphone, "but we've tried to get through to Necessity hundreds of times, and they're in the same place, both cut off behind those damned soul locks."

"This is true," I said. "It's also irrelevant, since you can't really know where the communication breakdown is happening. It could be the locks, or it could be something specific to Necessity, something that's stolen her voice. Something that might not affect Shara."

"Why didn't we think of that?" Tisiphone looked dumbstruck and abruptly sat down on the bed. "I mean, part of why we decided you could help was because of your connections to Shara. It should have been obvious."

"Maybe it's because you're mostly in the killing-people business and only do tech support as a sideline," suggested Melchior. "Now, I don't know a lot about the ripping-folks-to-shreds-and-grinding-up-the-bits industry as a whole, but it would seem to me a fairly straightforward kind of process."

"You might be surprised," said Tisiphone. "Hunting targets like Eris is not as easy as it looks."

I thought back to witnessing the Furies battle with the Goddess of Discord and shuddered at the idea that Tisiphone thought of that as *looking easy*. From his expression, it gave Melchior a bit of a pause as well.

"Point taken," he said. "I imagine chasing Ravirn down posed some special challenges, too."

"It was fun." Tisiphone smiled broadly. "He's very unpredictable, and that makes the game last longer. He also does things that seem terribly stupid at the time but that nevertheless work out quite well. None of us are entirely sure whether that's the result of a sort of weird genius or some kind of divine fool's luck."

"Can I vote for the divine-fool option?" asked Melchior.

"No," said Tisiphone. "Furies only." Then she winked at him. "Either way, he makes for a good chase. Twisty."

"Thanks . . . I think," I said. "Can we get back to the topic at hand? Namely, figuring out some way to contact Shara. Melchior and Cerice and I tried Vtp, and we tried Voice Over Mweb Protocol and MIMs and all the other traditional high-tech solutions without any success. Absolutely nothing got through. What have you done to try to reach Necessity?"

"All the stuff you mentioned, of course. We also tried chaos modulation and physically traveling to her domain. That might have allowed us to bypass the mweb and the soul lock, but we simply couldn't reach her."

I held up a hand. "Before you go on, could you explain the hows of those two? A lot of the stuff you Furies do seems to violate the rules of existence as I was taught them growing up in the Houses of Fate. Take the way you rescued Mel and me from Fate security yesterday. . . . It was yesterday, wasn't it?" Things were starting to get a little blurry around the edges.

"Depends on how you're counting, Boss," said Melchior. "You've only slept once since then, but it's been something like forty-five hours subjective. You were on your feet for nearly that long between sleeps."

I blinked. "Really? I know I've been having insomnia, but forty hours awake?" It didn't feel anything like that long. "Maybe I should go sit down again before it catches up to me." I limped back to the bed.

Melchior shrugged. "Maybe not for you, but I sure felt it."

"I wonder what's going on there," I said. Then I shook my head. "Questions for another time when we have less on our agenda, I guess. I'm sorry, Tisiphone, I asked you a question and then didn't let you answer it."

"Don't worry," she said. "It's actually kind of fun watching the gears in your head turn." She looked at Melchior. "Is his brain actually powered by his mouth? Or does it just look that way from where I'm sitting?"

"It's a mystery," said Melchior, "but I do occasionally wonder whether he wouldn't simply cease to exist if you disconnected his mouth."

"I babble, therefore I am?" Tisiphone grinned.

"Something like that," agreed Melchior.

"Chaos modulation?" I asked, pretending I couldn't hear them. "Spooky ripping the stuff of reality transport? Explanations for same?"

"Let's start with the first," said Tisiphone. "It's all about the wings."

"I don't get it," I said.

"If you keep your mouth shut, you'll learn faster," said Melchior.

"He's got a point," said Tisiphone. "Watch."

She stood up and stepped away from the bed, opening her wings to about eight feet—a small fraction of her total span. An instant later the fire of her wings brightened, though for the first time since I'd met her, her hair didn't follow suit. Then the flames began to dance and jump, changing their intensity from point to point in a way that reminded me of an elaborate fractal pattern.

"Beautiful," whispered Melchior, and it was.

"But how does it affect chaos?" I asked. "Sure, it's *magical* fire, but it's still just fire, isn't it? And what about Megaera and Alecto?" Whose wings were storm and seaweed respectively.

"It's not flame at all," said Tisiphone. "No more than Meg-aera's wings are actually the weeds that swallow ships." As she said this, the stuff of her wings shifted and changed, though they retained their shape. The patterns remained as well, writ now in the whirling tumble of chaos. "I don't really have wings, just raw chaos grafted onto my flesh and tamed by will and the power of Necessity."

"Huh." I never would have guessed, though I probably should have. "You send messages by creating patterns like you're doing now?"

"Yes," said Tisiphone. "Fractals and other forms that range the edge of randomness." Her face fell. "But Necessity isn't answering."

"All right," I said. "I need to mull that over for a bit. How does the"—I made a clawing motion—"magic transport system work?"

"Very well, thanks." Tisiphone grinned and looked vague as she let her wings resume their flame form. Then she shrugged. "Seriously, I don't know all the underlying details. Our claws are also artifacts of chaos. With them we can temporarily punch a hole from here into there and pass through. Once we've left the world we're in, we use our wings to fly through chaos to the next one."

"That raises more questions than it answers," I said, getting up to pace again. "You know that, right?"

"Like what?" she asked, furling her wings so that I wouldn't run into them as I limped around.

"You're kidding, aren't you?" asked Melchior.

"Maybe a little," said Tisiphone. "I know what we do is unusual, but it's how we've always done it and it seems normal to me. What are the questions?"

Melchior put his face in his hands.

"One," I held up a finger, "when you rip a hole through to the Primal Chaos, why doesn't it pour through and destroy everything in the immediate area? When I make holes in the walls of reality, bad things happen, like I get eaten by chaos and only come back weeks later at the cost of glowing eyes and who knows what all fresh new personality quirks. And remember what it did to Hades, both the place and the god.

You said it looked like Hades was hit by a combination tidal wave and giant tornado followed by a force-ten earthquake."

"Wait. You heard that?" asked Tisiphone. "I thought you were still adrift in chaos then."

"It was overhearing that conversation between you and Cerice that reminded me I existed and gave me back my name and my sense of self. In a very real way, it was the two of you talking that brought me back."

"I didn't know that." Tisiphone smiled then, almost shyly. "It's sweet."

"Could we not go there just yet," said Melchior. "I foresee more distracting male-female biological interactions down that road. As entertaining as the thumping and howling was last time, it's going to seriously reduce the overall quality of the conversation. How about I throw out question number two?" He paused, and we both glared at him. "No objections? Great. Once you've passed through into chaos, how do you know where you are and where you're going?"

"What do you mean?" asked Tisiphone. "There's nothing to it, well except that we can't get to Necessity right now, probably because of the soul lock. We just know where we are."

"That doesn't strike you as the least bit odd?" asked Melchior, choking.

"No. Should it?"

I stopped in my pacing and just stared at her.

"Damn right it should," said Melchior. "At least according to Persephone. And this 'knowing' thing still works?"

"Of course," said Tisiphone, "but I don't get it. What's Persephone got to do with this? Beyond writing the virus that infected Necessity, that is?"

I looked at Melchior, but he shook his head. "You were there," he said. "You tell it."

"When I rescued Persephone, she explained her thinking in creating the virus. Part of that was telling me about Necessity and the reason she made herself into a computer. It was because the infinitely expanding nature of the multiverse was too complex for any biological intelligence—even a divine one—to keep track of. The mweb and all its huge computing capacity exists to keep track of where everything and everyone is and should be, and you're asking why always knowing where you are freaks us out? Don't you understand what it means?"

"Oh," she said in a very small voice. "I've been doing this for something like four thousand years, since long before Mother transformed herself into a computer. It just never occurred to me to . . . Oh my."

"'Oh my' is right," I said. "I think we just found our point of entry. The only way you can just 'know' where you are is if at some level, you're still in contact with the part of Necessity that keeps track of where everything is. If we can tap that line and get Shara to tell us where she is, we're in and—" A new idea hit me, and I sat down.

There was no chair, so I landed on the floor. My wounded thigh screamed, but I ignored it. This was too big.

"What is it?" asked Melchior.

"Yeah," said Tisiphone.

"You flew here," I said, "through chaos."

"Sure," said Tisiphone. "And?"

"And you knew where here was despite the fact that Garbage Faerie is cut off from the mweb. Don't you see what that means?"

"No, I— Oh. It means that at some level Necessity retains the data on where this world is relative to all the others. It's all still there."

"It's all still there," I agreed. "We *can* fix Necessity. It's just a matter of how."

CHAPTER TWELVE

"A little dirty," I said, leaning in and blowing a cloud of dust off the pegboard of the tool rack. "Otherwise, not too bad. I'm glad the cousins did most of their damage up above."

Ahllan's basement workshop was one of the least-trashed areas of the house, though the open light shafts had allowed a certain amount of weather to find its way down from the outside.

It was a big, rectangular space with worktables running the length of the side walls. On the right, shelves of jars held all manner of alchemical ingredients above a slate table cluttered with chalk, various alembics, string, and all the trappings of the traditional sorcerer's art. The workspace on the left was set up as an electronics repair and assembly station, with computer enclosures, soldering irons, racks of chips, and other parts scattered amidst test equipment.

The air was just a touch damp and flavored by the concrete smell of old basement and an undertone of fried transistors. A partially effaced hexagram decorated the end wall opposite the steps, and a heavy door underneath them stood firmly closed. It was painted gray and blended with the wall.

"Where does that lead?" I asked Melchior, pointing at it.

I'd only been down there twice before, and both times I'd been too preoccupied to notice the door.

"Ahllan's wardroom and sanctuary," said Melchior, opening the door and stepping through. "And beyond that, the clean room."

I followed him, and Tisiphone followed me. The space beyond was shaped like the inside of a drum and deathly quiet, insulated from the rest of the world by powerful built-in wards, both traditional and more high-tech. A permanent hexagram twelve feet across took up most of the floor. I knelt to examine it. The borders were two-inch-wide channels filled with . . .

"Melchior, is this actually a continuous circuit?" I asked, tapping the layer of glass that had been laid down over lines of circuit—green silicon boards laced with gold conductors.

"Yes. Ahllan built it herself. It's a chaos-powered multiprocessor computer dedicated entirely to warding. It's all connected up on the underside, with core chips soldered beneath each of the outer angles. When it's active, nothing passes in or out without the consent of the master controller. It's as near perfect a magical insulator as I've ever seen."

I whistled. "Nice, but what about mweb access?"

"Since this world is off the net now, it's moot, but there are network jacks at the inner angles, and the whole hexagram can be tuned to act as a high-density buffered data antenna."

"Activation?" I asked.

He pointed at a narrow oak cabinet built into a niche on the far wall beside another door. "That's got a full set of candles and stands if you're feeling traditional. Otherwise . . ." He whistled a short burst of binary, and red lasers flickered to life at the outside corners, beaming bright spots onto the ceiling and connecting the hexagram on the floor to a second one set into the stone ceiling above.

"What a setup." I shook my head. "I wish Ahllan were here to explain it all to me. We never got a real chance to talk shop after I found out she had once been a Fate server. I think I could have learned a lot from her."

"I wish she were here, too," said Melchior. "I miss her."

"I would have liked to have met her," said Tisiphone. "When my sisters and I raided this place, she hid in here with Cerice and Shara until we left. Megaera wanted to question them, but Alecto and I convinced her it wasn't worth the effort of breaking such powerful wards, not when your magical scent led straight into a hex gate set for Castle Discord."

Melchior looked up at Tisiphone, his expression troubled. It was easy to see he didn't much like to be reminded of Tisiphone's coming here as an invader. I didn't either, but I did like Tisiphone, quite a lot. It was a strange feeling.

"How could you tell where the gate went?" asked Melchior. "It's a one-way, with all sorts of variables that Ahllan had to juggle on the fly."

Tisiphone shrugged. "It smelled of Discord."

"Fair enough," said Melchior, though the answer obviously didn't satisfy him. "I suppose that's all ancient history at this point. At the moment, we need to invent a way to use your link with Mother Necessity as a communication channel to Shara, so she can tell us how to get from here to there. You have any ideas about where to start on that, Boss?"

"No, but I'm willing to play hardware hacker and fake it." I turned back toward the door. "Let me dig through the equipment bins and see what I can come up with."

"All right," said Melchior, as we passed out into the main part of the basement again. "I'll get to work on cleaning this place up while you do that. If we're going to be here for any length of time, we'll want the whole shop up to Ahllan's old standards. Especially the clean room and the workbenches."

"What about you?" I asked Tisiphone.

"I don't know," she said. "You're the hacker. Necessity does most of her own deep IT work even if she uses us as her hands when she needs them. I don't think I'll be much help on the hacking front, and I don't clean. Perhaps I'll go have a look around after."

"After what?" I asked.

"Pouncing you." Then she leaped, catching me around the shoulders and pulling me over.

I think I shrieked. I know I jumped. But it was actually as gentle as a tackle could possibly be. She turned in the air so that I landed on her instead of hitting the stone floor, and she cushioned both of us with her wings. I ended up lying atop her and staring into a pair of mischievous blue eyes while my heart hammered out a toccata and fugue in panic minor. I was still trying to figure out what had happened when she caught my face in her hands and pulled me down for a very thorough kissing.

"That was lovely," I said, when she finally let me up for air, "but a little more warning might have been nice. You startled me."

"That was the point. And sorry, no can do on the warnings front." She grinned. "Your hour was up, and I told you back then that amorous hostilities could reignite without any prior warning. You'll just have to get used to the occasional pounce."

"Will I?" I put my hands on her ribs. "We'll just see about that, won't we? That, and whether Furies are ticklish."

"Hey, no fair—" began Tisiphone.

I didn't let her finish, and as it turns out, Furies *are* ticklish. Giggling ensued. It didn't last long, because Tisiphone flipped me over and pinned my arms.

"Now what are you going to do?" she asked, sitting on my chest.

"Surrender?" I asked.

"Nope, sorry. Not an option."

Since it hadn't worked last time, I wasn't terribly surprised. I was still trying to think of a good answer when Melchior cleared his throat.

"Should I go and find some earplugs while you two bang about for a bit?" he asked grumpily. "Or is this more of a brief-interlude-with-groping kind of thing?"

I sighed and looked up at Tisiphone. "Truce?"

"We'd probably better." She released me and popped herself to her feet with a beat of her wings before offering me a hand. "With Nemesis running around loose, it's important we work fast. Is there anything special I should be on the lookout for while I'm out and about?"

"Faerie rings," I said, "if you're feeling the need to be useful. The fewer possible routes of approach available to Nemesis, the better."

"Good enough." She crouched, then launched herself up into one of the air shafts, quickly climbing from view.

I looked at Melchior. He looked from me to the heavens—or possibly the air shaft—and shook his head. Without saying another word, he started in on the cleaning and organizing. I went to dig around in Ahllan's supplies.

Several grimy and sweaty hours of sifting, sorting, and soldering later, and I had kludged together a new piece of magical test equipment built on a PDA frame and designed to check out mweblike wireless communications across every band I could think of. Whether it would work or not, I had no idea, since I didn't really understand what Tisiphone was doing, but I was fresh out of enthusiasm and ideas.

"Would this be a good time for refreshments?" said a voice from the top of the stairs at that exact moment.

It was Haemun, wearing a truly gods-awful Hawaiian shirt and carrying a tray with lemonade and some fresh fruit. He started down.

"Sorry I can't offer you the sort of variety I might were we at Raven House, but I had to go with what I could pick off the nearby trees and what little was left in the way of durable goods in Ahllan's pantry."

"No need to apologize," I said, taking a glass. "This is pretty miraculous considering conditions. Thank you."

"Thank you, Haemun," said Tisiphone, dropping suddenly from an air shaft.

"You're . . . welcome, Madam."

Haemun swallowed visibly as Tisiphone landed and lifted a drink from the tray but kept his smile and generally did better at looking unruffled than I had the first time *I'd* been surprised by a Fury. Apparently he was bouncing back from the magical brainwashing he'd undergone when Nemesis took over Raven House. That was good both for him and for me. I needed to ask him about the whole thing sometime soon, but I hadn't wanted to push.

"How'd it go?" Tisiphone took a sip of her lemonade and smiled at Haemun. "This is lovely." He mumbled something that sounded vaguely like "Thanks," and headed back upstairs as she turned her attention my way. "Did you figure anything out?"

"Maybe." With one fingertip I tapped the device I'd put together. "It depends on how you get your positional information. If it acts like it would·if I'd set it up, this thing should be able to detect something."

"*There's* a description that inspires confidence," said Tisiphone.

"What do you expect?" I shrugged. "I'm a hacker, not a communications specialist. We'll find out just how big a distinction that is in a few minutes. How'd you do?"

"I found a half dozen proto rings at nearby ley nodes, including one that was almost ripe at the place where Stonehenge sits in most of the primary lines of reality. The only full one I spotted was where Reykjavik would be. I destroyed them all, of course, but I didn't make it as far as North America. There may be more there."

"Then we should probably get this moving along, shouldn't we?" I finished my lemonade and set the glass aside. "Do you know where you are right now?"

Tisiphone raised an eyebrow at me and moved her glass in a little circle to indicate she was right there with me.

"Yes, very funny," I said. "But you know what I meant. Do you know where you are relative to everywhere else?"

"Not in the sense that you mean." She emptied her glass. "It really only activates when I'm trying to move between DecLoci."

"I was afraid of that." I handed her the detector I'd put together. "Here. The power button's on the side there. If you would be so kind as to take that and go somewhere via chaos, we'll see whether it tells us anything."

"How far do you want me to go?" asked Tisiphone.

"Just far enough to activate your sense of location."

"All right." She reached out and clawed a hole in the air, vanishing into the place between worlds.

A moment later, a tearing sound from the top of the stairs

announced her reentry into the DecLocus. She walked down and handed the device to me.

"Well?"

I glanced at the readings. "Wow, look at all the garbage." Where I had expected to see either no magical band readings or, if I got lucky first time out, a slender spike on one frequency, I had noise everywhere. "Mel, what do you make of this?"

He climbed up onto the workbench so he could look over my shoulder. "Gotta be interference from the Primal Chaos. It *is* the source of all magic, so maybe it registers a signal across the whole spectrum. Too bad it's not a consistent signal. That we could adjust for. But this is all over the place both in frequency and amplitude. We'll need a longer-duration sample to have any hope of sorting it out."

"That assumes whatever we're looking for will even register somewhere in this range." I sighed. "Tisiphone, you willing to take a longer trip? Something that lasts fifteen or twenty minutes?"

"Sure." She took the detector and went.

While she was gone, Mel and I speculated on what we were looking for but didn't reach any real conclusions. The mweb was a high-speed, high-fidelity, long-range medium, comparable to a very powerful two-way FM-radio-type signal. The Furies' back channel to Necessity could have looked like anything from some kind of fast pulse signal up at the top of the spectrum down to the sort of extremely low-frequency long-pulse communication that was used to send messages to submarines running deep. We just didn't know enough about the amount and rate of information transmission to do more than make wild-ass guesses. As it turned out, whatever it was, it didn't register on my detector, nor on any of the others we tried over the next three days.

"So now what?" Tisiphone asked, after I tossed aside the latest version.

"Old-style divination, I guess." I hate traditional magic—it's messy, it's unreliable, and it's dangerous. "Unless anyone's got a better suggestion."

Silence.

"All right then." I fetched a small silver basin from the sorcery side of the workshop. "Haemun!"

"Yes, sir?" He stuck his head through the hatchway at the top of the stairs.

"Could you fetch us a pitcher of water?"

"Right away." He vanished.

A few minutes later the three of us—we'd invited Haemun, but he opted out—were standing in the center of Ahllan's sanctuary with the water-filled basin on a narrow pedestal between us.

"What do you think?" asked Mel. "Candles and calling the quarters, or binary and lasers?"

"Let's start with the easy way," I answered.

"Good enough."

He whistled a string of binary, and the red lasers flicked on. Another whistle brought up matched blue lasers. Finally, he turned on the greens to make a full-spectrum beam. The hexagrams above and below came to life.

I reached for the basin but stopped abruptly when Tisiphone lurched and caught hold of the pedestal with both hands. Her knuckles were pale and her fully extended claws—daggers of organic diamond five inches long—sank deep into the polished oak of the pedestal top. The skin of her face paled and took on a greenish tinge, and she looked as though she might throw up at any moment.

"Make it stop," she whispered.

"Mel!" I said.

"On it." He quickly whistled the lights out and the wards down. "Better?"

I looked at Tisiphone and nodded. Already the green had faded, and her normal color had started coming back.

"What happened?" I wanted to take her in my arms, but her claws were still out and I didn't dare. "Are you going to be all right?"

She nodded, then smiled weakly. "I was wrong."

"You were?" I asked. "About what?"

"About not knowing where I am except when I try to travel through chaos." She rolled her shoulders and retracted her claws, though she didn't release her grip on the stand.

"I don't think I get it." I reached out and put a hand on top of one of hers.

"Apparently I *always* know where I am. Well, except when a really powerful ward cuts me off from whatever it is that lets me know what I know."

"Ahllan's wards block it?" I asked.

She nodded. "It feels awful, like the worst inner-ear turbulence you could imagine."

From there it didn't take us too long to figure out what was being blocked and move on to the question of how to use it to send messages in via the back door. The locator system worked a bit like a cross between dolphin-style echolocation and the submarine ELF system. Tisiphone and—presumably—her sisters sent out a continuous series of pulses that located them for the system and illuminated the DecLoci around them. In turn the system sent them five-dimensional polar coordinates via ELF letting them know where they were relative to three-dimensional space plus time and distance up or down the world spectrum from Olympus.

What we eventually came up with as a transmission system was a bit of a duct-tape-and-baling-wire job, but hey, that's my specialty. Tisiphone's job was to stand still and not get too sick while Melchior flicked a set of wards on and off to create a binary signal that the locator controller couldn't possibly not notice.

Of course, we didn't know whether the locator system was still hooked up to any other part of Necessity, or whether either Necessity or Shara was also hooked up to the ELF transmission system, or whether either one of them was in any state to answer if they were hooked up. The best we could do was try it and see what happened. So we did.

"Anything?" I asked Tisiphone after several minutes of sending our initial message—a version of Melchior's binary identifier.

She shook her head, then immediately looked as though she regretted it. I offered her a small plastic-lined bag at that point, and, with a surprising amount of dignity, she threw up.

"Do you want to take a break?" I asked.

"No," she whispered. "Keep going. I think I'm starting to get used to it."

She was lying. I could tell. She wasn't very good at lying. I didn't argue with her. She was four thousand years old and knew her own mind. I didn't mention it again for the better part of a half hour in which she had to use two more bags and kept growing more pale and wan. I was just about to try to talk her into a break when she suddenly held up a hand.

"I'm getting something odd, stop messing around with the wards," she said, cocking her head to one side. "Oh my." She bent over the bag again, making awful noises though nothing came up. "Sorry," she said after a while, "but that's even worse than the flickering of the wards. The system is telling me I'm here and then there." She pointed to her left. "Here. There. Here. Here. There."

"Point down or left as the coordinates come in," said Melchior.

"I have to sit down," said Tisiphone, dropping to the floor, but she kept pointing for several minutes as the information continued to flow.

"It's Shara!" said Melchior, when she finally stopped. "She heard us."

I nodded. The binary flow had used "here" as 0 and "there" as 1 and had gone slow enough for anyone with an understanding of the system and a working knowledge of machine language to decode it. If we were going to have any serious communication, we were going to need a much faster transmission system or a denser code, and I said as much.

"We can use more directions, if Tisiphone can take it," said Melchior.

"I can take it." She sounded utterly spent, but her voice was flat, with not the slightest hint of give. "If it might lead to a way to fix Necessity, I can take anything I have to. I *will* take it."

"Let's start with base six," said Melchior. "We can use up, down, front, back, left, and right. Octal would be better, but if this round's representative of general wear and tear on our speaker system"—he nodded at Tisiphone—"six is go-

ing to be more than hard enough. Maybe later, if she gets
used to it, we can move up to something faster."

Looking at the wreck even this short conversation had
made of Tisiphone—I had to admit I had doubts. Not that
we had any other options.

"Are you ready for some more ward-field fluctuations?" I
asked, though I felt like a cad for doing so. "We need to let
Shara know we got her message."

She closed her eyes, and I could see the blue veins in that
thin skin all too clearly, but she nodded anyway.

"Do it."

Over the course of the next several days, we established a
solid system for communication. It was slow and ungainly
and played merry hell with Tisiphone's digestive system and
general well-being. But it worked, Tisiphone was damned
tough, and slowly, very slowly, she did seem to be adapting.

What ultimately developed was a very slow conversation
with anywhere from minutes to hours between the segments.
With Melchior sending the messages the three of us collectively agreed on, it went something like this:

"I'm so glad to hear from you," sent Shara.

"Us, too," sent Melchior. *"Need to go to plain hex for
speed—front, back, up, down, left, right. Can do?"*

"Yes. Will compress syntax, too."

"Good," sent Melchior. *"Need to fix Necessity. Will come
there soon. Can you speak with her?"*

"Yes/No," Shara both agreed and denied. *"Complex.
Can't explain. Like stroke, only worse."*

That one stressed Tisiphone out so badly she was ready
to bite chunks out of the walls.

"Try to explain." Tisiphone insisted Mel send that one.

"Very complex," sent Shara. *"Very long. Too much of
both. Goddess still controls underneath? But can't speak.
Maybe. Need you here."*

"Can't get there," sent Melchior, as Tisiphone snarled it
out. *"Furies blocked. Send work-around?"*

*"Not possible yet. Running security and parts of other
systems, but not master/nexus/locus of decisions. Locked
out."*

I threw up my hands. "Whatever that means. Tisiphone?"

"I'm not sure," she whispered. "A big part of what Necessity does—what Necessity is—has to do with controlling how decision loci are formed and whether they continue to exist after the initial split. That's really the core of the whole system, and if Shara doesn't have access to it, she may not *know* where she is."

A thought that probably should have occurred to me earlier hit me then. "Where is Necessity usually? I know you've said you can't reach her, but I guess I always just assumed it was a firewall kind of problem. Now I'm getting the feeling that I don't actually understand the issues at all."

"Necessity isn't in any one place," said Tisiphone. "I guess I thought everyone knew that. She resides at the point of maximum uncertainty—the exact point of the next DecLocus split."

"How does she know where that is?" asked Melchior.

"She doesn't." Tisiphone looked baffled. "It's a part of what she is. She exists in the gap, and it exists in her. Wherever she is, the gap is also."

"How do you usually find her there?" he asked.

"We don't," said Tisiphone. "Normally, when she needs us or we need her, she simply is where we are. The multiverse where we are becomes the multiverse where she is. But that's not happening now, and we don't know why."

"And . . ." Melchior closed his eyes and rubbed his forehead. "Hang on. I'm going to hate the answer to this, but I have to ask. You've been to Castle Discord . . ."

"Many times." Tisiphone nodded.

"Are you telling us that for Necessity the whole multiverse works like Castle Discord does for Eris? That she doesn't move through space so much as it changes its shape to suit her needs?"

Tisiphone rocked her head from side to side. "That's not how it works in the guts of the thing, but the effect's pretty much the same. And—oh!" She clutched at her stomach. "Shara's transmitting again."

"Still there?"

"Yes," sent Melchior. *"Working on understanding the problem. More later?"*

"Later. Give my love to Cerice."

That was the better part of two days' work, a short, confusing exchange with a ticking guilt bomb attached to the back end. A guilt bomb that detonated the next morning when Melchior walked into the bedroom and binged at me.

I was sitting up with Tisiphone's head in my lap, stroking her hair. Neither one of us had slept very well. Me because sleep didn't seem to be my friend anymore, and Tisiphone because stress and her abused stomach kept waking her up.

"What is it?" I asked Melchior.

"Request for Vtp link—Cerice via Asalka.trl. It's marked urgent. Do you want to take it?"

"I suppose I'd better, but not here with Tisiphone. Let Cerice know I'll be there in a second." I squeezed Tisiphone's shoulder and eased out from under her, putting on a robe as I went out the door. "I wonder how Cerice knew where we were. I don't like that at all, not when she's back in Clotho's fold, and especially not after the way she reworked the mweb-server firewalls."

We hurried down the hall and through the ruined pressure hatch that led to the basement. The big steel door and its frame had once belonged to an analogue of the USS *Arizona*, or at least that's what the sign said.

"She just pinged me again, Boss." Melchior sounded more than a little irritated by that. "I think she's feeling a bit impatient."

"Well, it won't kill her to wait an extra thirty seconds, and I'm doing her a favor. I'm betting she really didn't want me to take her call naked and in bed with Tisiphone."

"That's got my vote for understatement of the day," said Melchior.

"Don't bet on it. The day is young, and I've got plenty of time."

"Not to mention a brutal record in that department," said Melchior.

Then he hopped up onto the workbench and opened up his eyes and mouth. Light poured forth, and the image of

Cerice appeared at its heart. She was wearing her irritated expression, the serious one. That made seeing her easier somehow.

"Hello, Cerice." I tried to keep my voice as neutral as possible.

"What the hell do you think you're doing, Ravirn?" She leaned forward, her face filling the display. She looked both angry and frightened.

"Answering the computer, or isn't that obvious? Oh, and nice to see you, too."

Cerice rolled her eyes. "Don't be an ass. I'm under pretty close surveillance and getting a window where I can talk without being monitored isn't easy. I don't have much time, and you already burned an unreasonable chunk of it making me wait while you crawled out of bed. I'm not sure why you bothered—it's not like I don't know what you look like first thing in the morning."

"Cerice, as much as I'd love to listen to you snarl at me for another twenty minutes, I've been informed by a reliable source that you don't have much time." My temper was fraying rapidly. "If that's *really* the case, you might want to get to the point."

"You are the most maddening man I've ever known." She bit her lip and looked down for a moment. "I'm trying to save your butt, and you're making smart remarks." When she met my eyes again, her voice was very firm. "What are you doing to Necessity?"

"Who says I'm doing anything to Necessity?" She opened her mouth, but I was getting angrier by the second and I kept right on going. "Even if I were, what business would it be of yours?"

"I notice you didn't actually deny it," said Cerice. "Thanks for not lying to me at least. As to who I am to ask, I'm in charge of Fate's Necessity project. It's my job to find out exactly what is going on with Necessity, which means I need to know what it is you think you're doing and to shut it down if I have to. I'd like to do it before Atropos or somebody else with a grudge notices that you're involved and does something drastic, but that's my preference, not an absolute condition. I'm only going to ask you one more time: what *are* you up to?"

"Cerice, you've just told me why you're asking. You haven't said a thing about why I should answer you. I am no longer of the Houses of Fate. I am a power unto myself, and a chaos power at that—you know, the loyal opposition. Not only do I not recognize Fate's authority to question me on anything whatsoever, but I don't recognize Fate's authority to be messing around with Necessity." I could hear my voice rising, but couldn't seem to stop it. "In fact, considering all that I know of Fate and its desire for total control, I don't think Fate should be allowed within a thousand miles of Necessity while she has such an obviously diminished capacity to defend herself."

"*You're* accusing *me* of designs on Necessity? When I've been trying to keep you off Fate's radar?" Cerice's face went tight and hard.

"I'm not accusing you of anything," I said. "It's your boss I'm worried about. You know, the one that you left me for."

Her cheeks darkened, and I decided to push and see if I could get any more information since I seemed to be burning bridges anyway. I really wanted to find out how she'd known we were in contact with Necessity. I put on my best innocent smile.

"Cerice," I drawled, "*why* are you calling me about this again?"

She looked momentarily as tired and drawn as Tisiphone, and I felt bad for her. Briefly. Until she opened her mouth again.

"Because," she said, "I wanted to give you a chance to account for yourself before I decided whether or not to tell Clotho you've been messing around with Necessity. The spinnerette activity and the pulses in the data flows from Necessity to the mweb servers have your fingerprints all over them. But clearly you're not interested in being civil to me. I wonder if you'll change your tune when I turn in my report, and Fate sends the Furies to do the asking."

I felt a now-familiar hand slide around my back as Tisiphone joined me.

"Somehow," she said, leaning into the picture, "I don't think that's very likely to happen. Ravirn is working with us on this one. Isn't that right, dear?" Then she leaned over and nibbled on my ear.

"She! You! Oh, Ravirn, how could you? Asalka, cut us off. That's it!"

Then she was gone.

"I thought that went very well," said Tisiphone. "Don't you?"

I jerked away from her, stung. For some reason Tisiphone's mistreatment of Cerice put my own argument with her in a much darker light. Why had I been so harsh? Was it the Raven again? Fomenting trouble? Or was it just my own anger and hurt? And did it matter why if the result was the same?

"Did you have to do that?" I asked Tisiphone and, by implication, myself. "It was unnecessary, and it hurt her."

Tisiphone shrugged. "So? She made me mad, and this wasn't the first time. I'm a Fury, Ravirn. I do not forgive, and I do not forget."

I felt as though she'd poured a bucket of icy water over my head or slapped me.

"I do," I said. "Forget, that is. In this case, your nature. I forgive, too. But you'll have to ask me nicely."

Then I walked away. I needed to get out and away for a bit.

CHAPTER THIRTEEN

Tisiphone was wise enough or angry enough not to call after me as I went up the stairs. I more than half expected her to show up as I pulled out my leathers—I needed to remember to have Melchior conjure me up some fresh clothes—but she didn't.

As I put on my right boot, I couldn't help wondering at how little stiffness remained from the gunshot wound. Whatever Tisiphone had done, it really helped. I'd have to ask her how she managed it. I should have done it before, but I'd been distracted by the Shara problem and by taking care of her when she was sick from the solution.

That was kind of sweet actually. Cerice had never really let me take care of her, and she'd resented me when I tried.

Cerice! Just what I didn't want to think about. I had a hard time believing we'd just had the conversation we had. Perhaps I shouldn't have been as hard on her as I had, but then she'd all but threatened me with exposure to Clotho, so maybe we were even. I growled as I pulled on my jacket. Did she really mean that? Could she really have changed so much in just the short weeks she'd been back under the wing of Fate? Or had I never really known her? I decided not to think about that or the possibility of her reporting me to Clotho. Better to focus on the technical details of what she'd said about Necessity and how we'd been detected. That was information I could use.

It sounded like Shara's efforts with the ELF—or whatever the hell it really was—had affected the data flows for the mweb servers. That made a certain amount of sense. The soul locks built by the Shara virus allowed command data to flow from Necessity's systems out to the mweb but not back the other way. If Shara's current efforts caused turbulence in that flow, Cerice was bound to notice. As for the spinnerettes, they represented an unknown quantity as far as I was concerned—technology so outdated that no one had ever bothered to teach me about it. Aggravating.

As I stomped past the door to the kitchen, Haemun stuck his head out. He was wearing a teal-and-crimson Hawaiian print apron—tiki gods making fancy French meals.

"Is there anything wrong?" he asked, wiping flour off his hands.

I ignored him and went right on by, then stopped and backed up. He represented another problem I should have dealt with before now.

"Sorry, Haemun. Long story. I was just going for a walk. Why don't you come with me? I've been meaning to find time for us to have a chat for days."

"You want to talk about Nemesis, don't you?"

"If you're ready," I said.

"Not really, but now's as good a time as any." He shrugged and took off the apron.

I wondered briefly about where he'd gotten the thing. It hadn't come with us from Raven House, and Ahllan's taste certainly hadn't run to anything that garish. I didn't ask, though, because Haemun was a house spirit with his own small magics. I'd learned long ago that questioning house spirits about matters domestic led to sour milk, short sheets, and starchy underwear.

I didn't say another word as we headed out the front door and down the path that led past the kitchen garden. It looked much better than it had in the first days after we arrived— Haemun had been weeding. At the bottom of the garden, I took a right. Left led up to the little hill where Cerice and I had first made love. I absolutely didn't want to go there.

"Where are we headed?" Haemun asked after a while.

"No idea. I've never really explored the area. Most of the time I've spent here over the past two years I've had a seriously bum leg. First the knee, then the gunshot. You probably know the place better than I do."

"I haven't been this way before." He sighed. "All right, the suspense is killing me. You said you wanted to talk about Nemesis, but haven't asked a single question. What do you want to know?"

"I'd rather not push you if I don't have to. How about you tell me about it like you'd tell a story, and we'll see what happens?"

"All right, though there's not much to tell. When—" Haemun paused and looked frustrated. "He, I guess. I thought Nemesis was a he at first anyway. When he arrived the second time—the first was when he ran through to the faerie ring chasing you—I tried to hide again as I had that first time. It worked for a while."

"Then what happened?"

"I went to sleep on a pile of palm fronds out in the jungle and woke up inside on the lanai. Well, woke up isn't really the right word since I was in the middle of serving him—I still didn't know he was Nemesis—a mojito. Gave me the damnedest fright of my whole life, that did. One minute asleep, the next handing over a glass. I dropped the tray and the drink. He didn't even blink at that, just reached out almost casual-like and caught the mojito before even a drop could spill. He smiled at me.

" 'Thanks, Rham Nous, that will be all for now,' he said.

"And I said, 'You're welcome, Master.' Well, my mouth said that—I didn't have a thing to do with it. Then I bolted, straight out the back door and into the jungle. It wasn't until I got out there that I realized I was wearing the wrong clothes, those awful monotone things with the jacket and—oh my. This is the strangest place I've ever seen."

We had passed around the side of a low hill and found ourselves facing an ancient oak forest with trees four and five feet across at the base. It almost looked like something out of a historical painting. I say almost, because this was Garbage Faerie and nothing was quite as you would expect. In this case, all of the tree trunks had neon graffiti on them, reaching from the roots up to about ten feet. It looked as though a veritable army of urban vandals armed with an infinite supply of spray paint had swept through the forest.

Something wasn't right about that. I walked to the nearest tree for a closer look. As I got closer, I saw that the colors were too vivid and the coverage too complete. The paint looked as it would have on a primed and perfectly flat concrete wall. There were no cracks or dim spots, no places where moss had obscured a bit of paint or the moisture in the bark had caused it to peel up.

I put my dagger into a crevice and pried a chunk of bark loose. It fell away, but made no change in the graffiti, a segment of the words "big bad wolf." The color was just as vivid beneath the bark.

"That's just bizarre," said Haemun . . . the Aloha shirt-wearing satyr.

I jabbed the dagger into the exposed wood and gouged out a big splinter. The color went at least a half inch deep and possibly all the way to the tree's heart. I really wanted to see how it looked on a sapling, but there were none around, just the ancient oaks and a litter of dead branches and leaves.

"Come on," I said. "Let's go deeper."

"You're the boss," Haemun replied, somewhat dubiously.

"So, you were back in the jungle behind the house again," I prompted.

"I was. I spent the whole day there until I fell asleep. When I next came back to myself, I was carrying a couple of dirty plates back to the kitchen. Ahi tuna—cooked very rare—asparagus, rice, and another mojito."

"Sounds familiar," I said.

"It should. His tastes were an almost perfect mirror of yours. Lots of fish and rice, fresh steamed vegetables, mojitos, daiquiris, the occasional beer. Desserts heavy on the chocolate and ice cream. In many ways it was like I was still working for you. He ate the same foods, wore the same clothes—though in different colors. He even spoke kind of like you do."

"He did?"

Haemun kicked a fallen branch aside with one cloven hoof, startling an oily-looking rainbow bunny who departed for parts less inhabited at speed. "I think so. That's how I remember it anyway, what I *can* remember."

I raised an eyebrow.

"It's strange," said Haemun. "I ran away again, and not just once. But I kept waking up in the house, and not always after going to bed. A lot of the time I was asleep on my feet—I don't have a better way to describe it than that—and things from those periods are very blurry and distant. Almost as though I were a passenger very far back in my own head and looking out through a distant windshield—a drunk passenger at that. Although, toward the end—when you found me—I felt as though I was moving back toward the front, as though soon I'd be seeing out of my own eyes again, except . . ." He shivered.

"Except?"

"Except it wasn't going to be me anymore. It was going to be Rham Nous, and Haemun—" He swallowed hard. "Haemun wasn't ever going to be coming back. Can we stop talking about it for a little while?"

"Sure." We walked on in silence for a time, and I decided that the graffitied woods had a bizarre sort of beauty all their own. Twisted and slightly off, but haunting. Like everything in Garbage Faerie, really.

"It was the differences that really got to me though," Haemun said abruptly, "more than the similarities. Somewhere in there, I came to know that it was Nemesis I was serving and that he was a she. That's kind of muddled, but so was I. There was no moment of realization, no 'aha,' just the sense that I knew what she was and always had known it. That was the biggest difference, of course, vengeance personified versus . . . well, you."

"Meaning improvisational screwup lad?"

Haemun grinned. "That, too, but that's just the way you operate, not who you are. Down underneath it all is a sort of tarnished nobility, a cynical Prometheus if you will."

"Me?" The idea made me squirm. "I'll pass. Look what it got Prometheus."

"I didn't claim you were the original," said Haemun. "More like he who would steal fire from the gods for the benefit of man . . . knowing that not only were the gods going to kick the crap out of him, but that mankind's response was going to be a mix of yawns and complaints that now they have to keep feeding the damn thing."

"That's sweet, Haemun. I'm touched you see me that way, but you've got the wrong guy."

"Maybe," said Haemun, "but it seems to me that if that were the case, you'd be quietly fixing bugs for Lachesis in a place with no free will and long, bitter winters."

I didn't have an answer to that. I wasn't a hero, not really. Just someone who kept getting stuck between a bad decision on the one hand and a worse on the other. Right? But the trees, for all that they were covered by words, held no fresh answers, and I'd already rejected Haemun's.

"Tell me about Nemesis, about the differences," I said into a silence that had grown uncomfortably long.

"As you wish. The main thing after simple identity was the emotions. Nemesis has no sense of humor. All she has is hate. Every second of every day, she radiates hate the way the sun radiates heat. It's awful. I'm a house spirit. I serve Raven House and its master. That defines both who I am and how I act. Part of that is an ability to sense the moods and anticipate the needs of my house's master."

"Like the way you always wake up in the middle of the night to get me a drink when I can't sleep," I said.

"Exactly. In order to do that, I have to be in touch with the emotions and physical needs of the master of the house. When that was Nemesis, I was constantly awash in her hate and her anger—her need for revenge. At the moment those emotions are mostly directed at you."

At the moment? Mostly? I stopped and leaned against an

oak that declared, "Eris wuz here" in a warped-text rainbow. Since there was no golden apple to go with the words, I decided the tree didn't know what it was talking about.

"I'm not sure I understand," I said.

"I . . . This is hazier." Haemun paced back and forth in front of me. "Both because of my own haziness and because of the nature of the beast. Nemesis is two creatures in one skin right now—the goddess and the body."

"Dairn."

"Yes and no. Most of Dairn is gone. I couldn't sense his thoughts or personality at all—only his hates are left, only the emotions that feed Nemesis. And more than anything else, he hates you. I don't know if Nemesis hates you because of that or if there's some deeper reason. I just know the hatred because I felt it, too." Haemun hugged himself. "I hated you so much it burned me, burned my soul. I will carry the scars as long as I live."

I reached out and touched his shoulder. "You don't have to talk about this any more if you'd rather not."

"No, I'll keep going. It's important. If anything I know could help stop her, stop that hate . . . I, well I just have to do what I can, that's all." He took several deep breaths. "Better. There is another hate underneath the hate for you, older, colder, more patient, like something waiting in the darkness. Waiting for a chance at Necessity."

"Waiting for what?" I asked. "My death? Does she have a checklist, and she needs to write me off the list before she goes after Necessity?"

"It's more complicated than that," said Haemun. "The two hates are intertwined somehow, tied together. Again, it's hard to explain. It's all emotion, all hungers and drives, no thinking. All I know for certain is that Nemesis sees you as the key to getting her revenge on Necessity."

"I suppose that could make a twisted sort of sense if she sees me as a link to Shara and the damage the Shara virus has already worked on Necessity, but I really wish the giants of the pantheon would go back to swinging at each other and leave me out of it. I'm fighting way above my weight class in these battles." I shook my head. "Let's get back to Dairn. Do you think the goddess's hate for me comes more from him or more from this perceived link to Necessity?"

"I don't know. She lives to hate and destroy. I'm not sure it matters who or what, with the possible exception of Necessity. It might be that her hate for you came from Dairn, that all she needed was the pointer, but it could just as easily be whatever link she sees between you and Necessity." He sighed. "I wish I could be more help, but that's really all I've got." He grinned morosely. "Unless you think a longer recitation of her menu would help."

"I doubt it. Thank you, Haemun. I don't know what I'll do with all that yet, but everything I can learn about Nemesis in her current incarnation helps. Why don't you head back to the hill house, and I'll follow along behind. I need to think."

"All right, but don't take too long. You're hungry, and you need a good breakfast. Here, this will take the edge off." He handed me a pear and walked away.

"Thanks," I called after him, and he waved over his shoulder.

So what did I have after all that? Not much really. Nemesis hated and mirrored me to some extent. I'd known that already, hadn't I? I took a bite of the pear. It was soft and sweet, lovely really. I started walking back toward Chez Ahllan, eating as I went.

There was just too much that I didn't know. Why had Nemesis merged with Dairn? Was it his idea? Hers? Some combination? Was that merging the way Necessity and I had gotten tied together in her mind? Did that even matter? Where had Nemesis been all this time? Not dead, obviously, at least not in the conventional sense. But how did you imprison a bodiless goddess? And how did *that* work? What was Nemesis? A goddess certainly, one with enormous power, who lived for revenge. But beyond that?

All I could say for sure was that she hated me, which emotion might or might not have come from Dairn. That and she was one hell of a coder. I stopped chewing. Nemesis had vanished over three thousand years ago, long before anyone had proposed even the idea of the computer. Where had she learned to code? That was a very interesting question, and I didn't have an answer.

"Maybe she didn't," said Tisiphone, "learn to code that is. Maybe she's just mirroring your divine spark." She looked quite bemused.

"Maybe," I said. "Certainly all I've seen her do so far are really spiffy hacks, which *is* my department, but I can't help feeling there's more to it since she's performing magic that's well beyond what I could manage even with serious goblin help."

"Do you always start conversations like this?" asked Tisiphone. "The last thing you said to me before dashing back in here and asking about Nemesis and coding was that I'd have to ask very nicely if I wanted to be forgiven."

"It's well within his normal range," said Melchior. "I occasionally suspect that Scattered ought to be his middle name." The goblin was standing on the workbench, having put aside a soldering pencil and a fragment of circuit board.

I ignored him and decided not to answer Tisiphone's question. I still wasn't happy about what she'd done to Cerice, but it was worse than what I'd done only in degree. Besides, apologies were probably not a part of Fury nature, and I didn't want to push that conflict right now.

Instead, I said, "Look at that self-harmonizing thing Nemesis does. I've only ever seen Fates and webtrolls manage that. I sure as hell couldn't do it. The way she crashed Melchior—same thing."

"That *was* nasty," said Melchior, "and there's no reason to believe she can't do it again next time we see her. She's seriously out of our league."

"Leave that to me," said Tisiphone. "She'll have a tough time whistling through a broken jaw."

"That'd be nice," I said. "It might be a good idea to have a backup plan, though. It's too bad we can't turn Mel into a webtroll."

"I don't much like the look." He mimed big shoulders and dragging knuckles. "Hulking just doesn't suit my dashing personality." Then he sighed. "Of course, I wouldn't mind a little more crash resistance."

"Maybe we can think of something," I said. "You're about due for an upgrade anyway."

Tisiphone caught hold of my shoulder, hard. "I hate to interrupt, but Shara's sending again."

"On it," said Melchior, as a slightly green Tisiphone began pointing directions. "I wonder what she wants; she isn't scheduled to check in for another hour."

"What's going on out there?" sent Shara. *"I want to talk to Cerice."*

"What do I tell her?" asked Melchior as he set up the wards.

"Oh hell." I sighed. I'd known this was coming at some point, but I'd rather hoped it would be later. "Better tell her the truth, that Cerice is with Clotho and that she and I are no longer an us."

"Will do," said Melchior. "I'll break it to her as gently as possible."

Because of the nature of the system, with Melchior flicking the wards on and off to send information to Shara, we could transmit much faster than we could receive. Now he launched into a long explanation, one that left Tisiphone looking queasier by the minute.

"I hate this," she whispered, but she didn't throw up. She *was* getting better at dealing with it, and I said so.

She nodded. "I think at this point, I could actually cope pretty well with not knowing where I was all the time. It's this flickering back and forth between the two states that makes it so hard. Wait, incoming."

"I knew it!" sent Shara. *"Stupid, both of you."* There was a brief pause. *"Nothing to be done about it while I'm locked in, and you're locked out. Have to fix that. Soon!"*

"Why soon?" sent Melchior, at my request. *"Has anything changed?"*

"Calendar, of course."

"Huh?" I said. "Ask her what she means."

"Spring," she sent.

Shit. I'd forgotten about that. While we'd been sitting

here talking at our glacial pace, the days had gone drifting by, bringing spring ever closer until . . . what? We didn't know what would happen when Persephone's annual release date arrived and with it the temporary expiration of Shara's forced tie to Necessity.

"How much time do we have left?" I asked.

Melchior shrugged. "We're off the mweb here. I haven't been able to query the Fateclock."

I turned to Tisiphone. "Does Necessity run on Olympus Standard Time? How did she decide when to release Persephone?"

"She has her own internal clock that she keeps synched with the Fateclock. Actually, it's the other way around. She dictates mweb time, and the Fateclock cues off her."

"Melchior?"

"On it."

"Five days," sent Shara.

"We've got to find some way to get in before time's up. What if Necessity spits Shara out and can't draw her back when the time comes? This could be the only shot we've got."

"But how do we find out where she is?" demanded Melchior. "We can't do thing one until we can get to Shara and Necessity, and all this *point of maximum uncertainty* jazz isn't very helpful."

"Not without some way to predict or tune in on the thing," I said. "How would we do that? Tisiphone?"

"No idea. All I can tell you is that's how the system works, all chaos flows and quantum uncertainty and the math of randomness."

Melchior got a thoughtful look. "Actually, that sounds right up your alley, Boss. Isn't being the Raven all about hacking chaos? You did a pretty good job with Clotho's quantum computer chip maze."

"That's different," I said.

But was it?

I thought about it for a minute. A while back, Clotho had locked Cerice, Shara, Melchior, and me into a magical hedge maze on the grounds of Clotho House. The maze could assume the shape of any computer chip, and to keep us trapped there, she'd had it take on the form of a quantum processor so that every gate in the maze was simultaneously open and closed. It would have taken most people, most gods even, a lifetime to find their way out. Not the Raven. My power over chaos had allowed me to shape the maze to my whim, and we had been able to escape only a few minutes later. If I could do something like that here . . . but no. What we needed now wasn't some way to make an already-existing quantum computer do what we wanted, because we didn't have the computer. Then a thought occurred to me.

"Uh, Boss," said Melchior. "I don't like the expression you've got on your face. I've seen it before, and every time it's meant trouble for me. What are you thinking?"

"I'm thinking that several problems might just solve each other."

"Like what?" He crossed his arms over his chest.

"Like we need a quantum computer that can connect to the mweb and touch chaos at the same time. Like Nemesis is an evil bastard of a hacker, and you need crash protection and an upgrade. Like I'm a chaos power, and you're fundamentally a creature of order, a conflict that's already causing problems."

"You're not suggesting . . . ?"

"That we upgrade you into a brand-new type of webgoblin, the very first quantum laptop. Oh yes, that's exactly what I'm suggesting."

Melchior sat down on the bench with a little thump. "I knew I wasn't going to like what came of that look."

"Does that mean you don't want to do it?" I asked. "You're my partner now, not my servant. If you don't want to try this, I won't force you."

"No, the reason I don't like it is that you're right. It would solve a lot of problems all in one go, and we really don't have time to look for a better answer." He sighed and closed his eyes. "I can't believe I'm saying that. Or this: we'd better start working on the plans."

That was going to be an interesting problem. I'd coded

Melchior myself years ago, crafted him by magic from blue-prints drafted by Lachesis, then modified to suit my needs. This was a bigger problem.

"We'll be able to use some of your original specs, since we won't want to make any changes in the goblin side of you," I said. "Or will we? If you've ever wanted to be a little taller or a little prettier, now's the time to speak up."

Melchior made an *eeping* noise and shook his head. "Thanks, but I'd rather not change anything we don't absolutely have to." He forced a smile and tossed his head. "Besides, I'm beautiful just the way I am."

"Done, though the head-tossing thing would work better if you had hair. We could include that in the new plans—thick, luxurious hair . . ."

"No thanks." He rubbed the top of his head. "This is much-lower maintenance."

"Uh, guys." Tisiphone put a hand on my arm.

"What is it?" I asked.

"That." She pointed toward the back wall. A ball of blue light was slowly growing there—the spinnerette. I felt a whisper on my skin as of invisible plumage ruffling.

"I wish I knew what that thing wanted," I said.

"And whose side it's on," said Melchior. "Every time it's shown up, Nemesis has been right behind it."

"Has she?" Tisiphone smiled. It wasn't the kind of smile I'd have wanted directed my way. "Good."

The spider-centaur faded into view, and Tisiphone started toward it, claws extended. I caught the tip of her wing as she went by me. It was hot, but it didn't burn me. Tisiphone had taught it not to.

"Wait a moment," I said. "Let's see what it wants." Cerice's comment about spinnerette activity had started my curiosity bump itching.

Tisiphone looked back at me. "Can't we just take it apart and figure out our answer from the pieces? It'd be simpler."

"Call that plan B," said Melchior.

"Oh, all right, but if it tries anything, I'm going to tie its legs in knots."

"Fair enough," he agreed.

I stepped around Tisiphone. This was the first chance I'd gotten to really look at the thing. Female, at least the human part of it, and about eight feet tall, though I suspected it could easily go higher if it fully extended its long spider legs. The spider body was massive, a shiny black ovoid as big as a golf cart. The woman's torso above that, likewise black, was similarly large—sized for a seven-foot female linebacker. The head was an attractive woman's with the exception of the arachnid mandibles growing out of her cheeks.

"******?" she chittered at me.

It was obviously a question, but beyond that . . . I had no idea what she'd said, though again, the voice sounded almost familiar.

"******?" Louder this time, less querulous.

"I don't understand you," I answered.

"******!"

"Nope." I shook my head. "Afraid not."

"****** . . ."

She shrugged. Then, without any warning, she was leaning down toward me. I assume she'd crossed the intervening distance, but if so, it was too fast for me to follow. Big, shiny black hands caught my shoulders, lifting me off the ground. A bubble of blue light formed around us, and the world began to fade.

CHAPTER FOURTEEN

Fire engulfed me, and I fell. When the flames subsided, I found Tisiphone standing over me, her wings spread like a shield between me and the world. The spinnerette clung to the ceiling on the far side of the room, though whether she had leaped there or been thrown I didn't know.

"*********?" she chittered—a new question.

Tisiphone growled and moved toward her.

"Wait," I said. "We still don't know what she wants."

"*I don't care* what she wants," said Tisiphone, though she checked her advance.

"*********?" The question she chittered this time sounded almost exasperated. She dropped back to the floor and reached a hand out toward Tisiphone.

"That's it," she said, and her internal fires flared higher. "You have ten seconds to get out of here. After that, I start taking you apart."

"*********!"

Tisiphone stalked forward and the spinnerette retreated.

"*********?" Then she was gone, fading away in a bubble of blue light.

"OK, that tears it," I said. "We've got to find out what those things are up to."

Melchior raised an eyebrow. "So, when exactly do you plan to slip that into our schedule?"

He had a point. We were already overbooked—what with having to design or steal a new chipset for Melchior's upgrade and only days to do it in.

"I'll look into it," said Tisiphone. "I'm not going to be much help with the upgrades, and I want to have a word with that thing or its boss anyway." She paused and sniffed the air, then smiled gleefully. "I'd better get going while the trail's fresh. Oh, this will be fun."

She sliced a hole in reality and plunged through.

"Not much for long good-byes, is she?" asked Melchior. "No smoochies or anything. You sure do have a fine eye for the romantics."

"Mel?"

"Yeah."

"Shove it."

He grinned and, somewhat ruefully, I grinned back. As usual, he had a point. Tisiphone was a challenging lover on all sorts of levels, witness her treatment of Cerice.

The next thirty-six hours were very blurry. Melchior and I madly scrambled to design and assemble Melchior 2.0. More than once, I missed the distractions Tisiphone might have provided, but it was probably better that she remained away, considering the workload. We were able to find most of the framework and peripherals among Ahllan's stores, with some notable exceptions that would require both a trip to someplace still linked to the mweb and some spell work.

If we'd had more time, we could have done the whole thing with spell work, but conjuring up things as complex as the drives and processors was a lot harder than whistling up a fresh set of clothes—the less of it we had to do, the better. Besides, it introduced another point along the way where a minor mistake could lead to a major failure.

Most of what we wanted we could get pretty easily once we had mweb access—the latest drives and such would be basically off-the-shelf parts and could go in as is. We could pick up a case the same way, though we planned on doing a custom mod once we had it.

The one really tough thing on the list was the master processor. Getting or making that promised to be a special kind of nightmare. There just weren't many possible sources for either blueprints or hardware that could do the level of quantum processing we needed—the only ones I knew of were in Athena's latest security servers and Fate's newest webtrolls.

"That does pose a bit of a problem, doesn't it?" said Melchior. "I don't much want to have a go at cracking either place, not with Cerice tuning Fate's security system for maximum Ravirn blockage and Athena's promises of death." He made an axing gesture.

"I don't know, Mel. After a day and a half bent over a workbench, the idea of taking some weight off my neck sounds almost pleasant." I was deadly tired but not the least bit sleepy, and I *ached*.

"I suppose it would solve almost all of your problems . . . with one notable exception."

"You mean Hades," I said.

"I do. Dead is just not a good option for you right now."

"OK, so I'll have to scratch dying off the list, but I'm only doing it for you. So, what else have we got? I suppose Eris probably has copies of both Athena's and Fate's blueprints."

"Veto," said Melchior. "I'm not letting the Goddess of Discord inside my head, and there's no way she'd share unless she'd had time to install back doors in the plans."

"Well, that takes us back to Fate or Olympus."

Melchior paced back and forth on the workbench. "Fate's going to be the better bet. It's the hardware we're most familiar with and much more likely to be compatible with the rest of my specs. You know Athena's stuff would require all kinds of last-minute modifications, and I'd rather not have too much untested hardware go into my head."

"How about Asalka?" I asked.

"What do you mean?" Melchior's face closed up.

"Relax. I'm not talking about breaking her up for parts or anything like that. I'm just wondering whether she might not be able to get us what we need. She seemed awfully sweet on you. What do you think?"

"I don't know," said Melchior. "I hate to put that kind of pressure on any AI. Besides, if we ask Asalka and she tells Cerice, you can bet Cerice will make getting what we need that much harder."

"Did Asalka strike you as a rat?" I asked.

"Despite everything, no. I don't think she'd have told Cerice if she'd known we wouldn't want her to. She could save us a world of trouble. . . . All right, I'm willing to ask her, but if she says no, that's it. We find another way."

I agreed, and we temporarily reactivated the beer can faerie ring, flicking from there to a very vanilla DecLocus just a few hundred dimensions away from prime. With my eyes and ears temporarily rounded to mimic the human norm and Melchior in laptop shape, we blended right in at the local-reality equivalent of Starbucks.

We had visual mail waiting, three messages. I put my back to a wall and plugged in a set of headphones so as not to share with the natives. I decided to go newest to oldest in hopes that some of my problems might be self-solving. Yes, really. It *had* happened before, just not to me. In grad school, Cerice had always had a million messages waiting, and she'd discovered that sometimes, if she just let the ones with questions or requests ripen a bit, someone else would deal with whatever needed doing.

My first v-mail was from Thalia, "Ravirn, please visit me as soon you can. Zeus contacted me looking for you, and I'm worried." Her face gave nothing away.

"That's interesting," said Melchior's voice through the headsets.

"Which?" I asked very quietly—best not to draw too much attention to the fact that I was talking to my laptop. "That Zeus is looking for me? Or that Thalia is worried about me?"

"Both, about equally, but for very different reasons. I wish we had time to follow up on that."

"Me, too," I said. "Especially since she specified a visit. I don't think that was an accident, and I really don't think we ought to just send a message. For some reason, I'd rather she didn't know where I was right at the moment. At the same time, I'm thinking any follow-up should start from a safe distance."

"Yeah," agreed Melchior. "That one's got all my paranoia alarms ringing double time. We still don't know how Nemesis got loose, where she's been, or who sent her after you."

"Though Fate's the most likely evil genius behind our current mess, this sets my teeth on edge for some reason. I guess I have a certain wariness about grandmothers."

"I wonder why." Melchior laughed. "Next message?"

"Sure."

This one was from Eris and very simple. "Trust no one." Great. That was a big help. Besides, I was already on it.

"Next," I said, and Zeus's beaming face filled my screen.

"Athena's pestering me to get you to stop in and have another chat with her. If she calls and asks you to drop by, don't answer."

"Does he think I'm an idiot?" I asked.

"Why should he be any different?" Melchior painted a grinning version of his own face on the monitor. "Most of the evidence supports that hypothesis."

"Thanks, Mel. I'm so glad you've got my back."

"Webgoblin sidekick only here to help. Do you want to do anything about any of that?"

"No, let's call Asalka."

"How about you sit here and drink coffee and play solitaire, and *I* call Asalka? It'll go smoother and faster that way."

"Fair enough."

Melchior's face went slack and the eyes of his image started to roll sarcastically—his version of a loading screen. I sipped my coffee, though I no longer felt any real need for it. Maybe I was finally getting used to this not-sleeping stuff. I didn't actually get much more than a swallow or two down before Melchior returned. AIs can speak very quickly if they don't have to slow the process down for us poor old analogue-type creatures.

"Well?" I asked.

His image grinned, and he flashed a series of schematics across his screen. They looked nothing like normal chips. Hell, they looked nothing like normal schematics. They had all sorts of what should have been irrational notations and the like. And yet . . .

"Mel, could you give me a graphic view of this? As though I were actually looking down on the real chip with the top sliced off?"

"Hang on a moment. When I look at these too closely, they start to give me a headache and I'm not sure . . . Wait. There."

The view he gave me was hideously complex, with lines that seemed to fold back in on themselves and some things represented in more than the normal three dimensions, yet it made perfect sense. I got it on some deep level, a sort of gestalt-form comprehension. Hmm.

"Melchior, Vlink; Ravirn@melchior.gob to Eris@discord.net. Please. Oh, and let's go flat panel rather than 3-D so as not to frighten the locals, OK?"

"Aren't you even going to ask me what happened with Asalka?" He sounded as though he felt a bit slighted.

"I'm sorry, I'm just a bit distracted. I promise to ask you all about it right after we get done with Eris."

He sighed. "There's not that much to tell really. She felt so bad about what happened when she told Cerice on us the last time that she said yes before I'd even finished the question. I did have to promise to have a serious live chat with her at a later date, but that was afterward. I could probably have gotten out of it, but I felt kind of guilty about it and . . ."

"And you think she's kind of cute," I said with a grin.

Melchior spluttered. "We're not even the same species."

"Uh-huh, and that's such a huge barrier in the electronic world that it would never occur to you to cross the line. That's why you always blush when Kira flirts with you, right?"

"Searching for discord.net," he said, his voice going flat and mechanical and his face taking on its loading aspect again.

"You're not fooling anyone, you know that, right?"

Seconds slipped past with his eyes rolling steadily and snarkily away. "Contact. Waiting for a response from discord.net. Lock. Vtp linking initiated."

A circle of white light appeared on his screen with Eris's face in the middle. On her end, the image would be the usual 3-D globe, but that would have caused unwanted questions here.

"Raven, how delightful to see you. How's?" Eris's hair burst into flames and her clothes vanished, exposing an absolutely perfect body that evoked but didn't mimic Tisiphone's.

Even through the screen, the impact of her sexuality took my breath away. It only lasted for an instant, then she shifted back to a more distant sort of beauty wrapped in a sharp black skirt-suit with gold pinstripes. It took me a moment to get my breath back, and my voice squeaked a little when I spoke next.

"Tisiphone's fine, thanks."

"Only fine? That's a pity. Considering how long it's been for her, I'd have hoped for mind-blowingly exhausting at the very least, to say nothing of insatiable. I suppose it's possible she's forgotten some of the basics through lack of practice." She cocked her head to one side and put on an expression of coquettish concern. "What do you think?"

"I think I'm not going to discuss my sex life with you," I replied. "Fine is how she is out of bed. In is not an acceptable subject of conversation."

"Why, Ravirn, you're a gentleman. Who could possibly have guessed?"

"Look, I don't have any time at all really, and I was wondering if you could do me a favor."

"How could I possibly resist after you ignore my questions and frame your request in such a bracingly abrupt way." She acquired a pair of stereotypical librarian glasses and frowned over the top of them at me. "What do you want?"

"The blueprints for Fate's latest run of webtrolls."

"What makes you think I've got a copy?"

I just looked at her.

"Oh, all right. But what do you want them for? I insist on knowing that at least."

"What if I told you I wanted to upgrade Melchior?" I asked.

"I'd say you were mad. The chip runs way too hot for either a laptop or a webgoblin. You'd fry his brains in no time." She paused for a moment. "I suppose you could leave the top of his head off . . ."

Shit. I hadn't thought about heat. From the look the webgoblin logo below Melchior's screen gave me, I had to assume that he hadn't either. We'd have to fix that.

"All right," I said. "You've got me. I'm just planning on making a little trouble for Fate, and I thought that knowing exactly what I was up against would make things a bit easier."

"Why didn't you say so in the first place? I'm always willing to snag the weave of Fate. The plans are on their way."

"Thanks, Eris."

She smiled. "You're welcome. Do you know that's the first time you've ever called me anything other than Discord? I wonder why that is. Maybe my being able to do this?" She flicked herself into naked Fury shape, grinned lasciviously, and vanished from the screen.

"Got them," said Melchior.

"What?" I asked.

"The plans, as you'd have realized if you put your tongue back in your mouth and used your brain."

"Sorry, Mel." I sighed. "I wish she wouldn't do that kind of thing. Could you bring her version of the schematics up for me? Graphic view, same as the others, please."

"Working on it." His eyes rolled for a few moments. "There. I couldn't detect any changes, but they feel different somehow, even more headache-inducing."

"That's because of this." I touched a spot on his screen without even really thinking about it first. "Here's where she inserted her back door. It's very subtle." I looked more closely. "Very."

In a normal computer, information was processed using binary gates that were either open or closed. In a quantum computer those gates had three states—open, closed, and simultaneously open and closed. Eris had changed the configuration of one of these quantum gates so that in addition to the three normal positions, it could also . . . There was no word for what I wanted to say. Become more *cosmically open* was the best I could do. That gate didn't just function as a processing point: it also allowed for intrusions from outside the system. It was almost diabolically elegant.

"I don't see it," said Melchior. "What did she do?"

I tried to explain it, but after a while he just shook his imaged head. "Thinking about it makes my mind want to split itself into little tiny pieces. How about I just agree to believe you, and we move on to the next question?"

"What's that?" I asked.

"How can *you* see it?"

"I don't know. I think it's part of being the Raven. I . . . Quantum effects just make sense to me in a very deep way, almost subconscious."

"You may be the only person who's ever said that," said Melchior.

"I don't think so. I bet they make sense to Eris, too, and probably a few other folks who play on the chaos team. You know, I think Fate might be making a mistake by getting into quantum computing. It may allow for much more efficient processing, but it's also at root an irrational process, something that works outside of the macroscopic rules of order that my grandmother and her sisters so love."

"I wonder if that's got anything to do with the problems in the Fate Core?" asked Melchior. "It's their biggest and most constantly updated system. Wouldn't it be funny if they introduced randomness into the system while trying to get ever-finer and more-thorough control?"

"Somehow, I don't think they'd be laughing."

"No," he agreed. "I hate to bring this up, as I'm really enjoying having a connection to the data flow of the mweb, but now that we've done the hard bit, don't you think we'd better finish our shopping and get home?"

"You're right, Mel. Let's order you up a case and some drives."

No sooner said then done, though the ordering system for the computer-parts center we went through objected rather strenuously to the fact that the address we asked it to ship to didn't actually exist in this world. It was nothing that an elegant hack couldn't fix—we just needed it to firmly identify the exact location of the parts in a way that connected them to an mweb-accessible system so that we could use a bit of transportation magic on them—but it did take a few minutes. Hopefully, no one noticed when the packing boxes simply appeared beside Melchior's laptop shape. Just in case, we went out the door and back to the coffee-grounds faerie ring in the alley as quickly after that as ever we could.

Once there, I paused because I felt bad about leaving the ring behind—it was too much like setting a pit trap for the unwary. The thing had formed when a magic-touched barista dumped a batch of Colombian ruined by a failure to insert a filter. The slurry of ground beans and water had splashed to form a near-perfect circle, and my questing mind had touched it in the minutes before the barista's quickening touch had evaporated along with the water. A ring only in potential, it had opened to the touch of the Raven.

I stepped through into Garbage Faerie, then paused again. I was feeling incredibly up and right with the world, and an idea had occurred to me.

"What are you doing?" Mel asked from the depths of my bag. He quickly shifted back to goblin form, the tension in his voice showing his alarm at lingering in the heart of the circle's chaos magic.

"I want to try something." The ring behind the coffee shop had only existed in potential—like a locked and hidden door—before I'd used my Raven magic to turn the key. "Maybe I can *close* rings from a distance, too."

"That sounds kind of dicey," said Mel. "You won't mind if I skip this bit, will you?"

He hopped from the bag to the ground beyond the circle of beer cans, but I wasn't really paying attention. Instead, I was extending my mind back through the network of rings to make contact with a magically charged circle of soggy coffee. There. I twisted with my will and . . . a perfect ring of bone-dry coffee drifted to the ground around me. The ring was shut, its magic returned to chaos, and its substance sucked through to my current here and now.

"It worked!" I whooped. Then I did a little dance.

"Ah, Boss?"

"Yes."

"I hate to bug you when you're obviously having such fun, but could you *please* step out of the ring? The sight of you wandering around in there without going away is giving me the screaming creepies. Besides, we need to take it apart and close the door to Nemesis."

"Oh." I'd actually forgotten I was still in the ring. "Sure."

I hopped over the edge—and staggered as I cut off my connection to the ring network and my sense of the universe contracted back down to the immediate. It made me feel heavy, and slow, and small, and that made me worry. Normal people could lose a part of themselves forever in the confusion of the rings. I had changed in such a way as to preclude that particular danger, but for the first time it occurred to me to wonder if maybe I hadn't acquired a whole new set of risks. The electric charge I felt as I caught hold of the first can in the ring underscored my concern.

Tisiphone still hadn't arrived back at Garbage Faerie by the time we finished disassembling the beer-can ring, so we headed downstairs to see whether we couldn't do something about the overheating issues. I was really feeling energized.

"It's a good thing you're happy with bald," I said to Mel—he was in laptop shape—after a couple of hours of working on the schematics. "Because any hair you had would start on fire."

"That's not funny," he said. "You know that, right?"

"It wasn't a joke. I'm getting nowhere with this."

"It's too bad Eris didn't solve the heat problem while she was hacking up that gate," said Melchior.

"What did you say?" I asked. There was something . . .

"I said, 'It's too bad that Eris didn't—"

"That's it!" I yelled. "You're a genius, Mel. Why didn't I think of that? It's so simple. I should have seen it before."

"You've lost me, Boss." His tone suggested that he thought he wasn't the only thing I'd lost—my marbles maybe.

"Look." I called up Discord's version of the plans and started drawing on Mel's screen. "Eris set up this gateway so that she could magically pass information into and out of the chip from a point outside the built-in channels—from the Primal Chaos really. What if I take her modification and flip it so that nothing can get in?" I did that. "Then I pop in copies at the appropriate nodes." I tapped a couple of dozen points. "And finally, what if I tweak it like so?"

Melchior's eyes popped in his screen image. "I can't get my head around the quantum stuff—it's too alien to the way I think—but did you just figure out a way to bleed all the heat out of the system and directly into the Primal Chaos?"

"Uh-huh. I think I did."

"Oh."

"Yeah," I agreed. "That pretty much sums it up."

"Sums up what?" asked Tisiphone's voice from behind me.

Even though I'd grown used to her silent comings and goings and not only familiar with, but deeply fond of, her voice, I still just about jumped out of my skin.

She laughed and wrapped her arms around me from behind. "I love it when you do that."

"I don't," I grumped, but then she started nibbling on my ear. "OK, so it's got its rewards. What did you find out?"

Tisiphone stiffened. "Nothing."

"Really?" I turned in her arms and looked into her eyes.

She closed them wearily and leaned her forehead against mine. "Really."

"Tell me about it." If someone else had joined the very small club of Fury escapees, that was big news. "What happened?"

Tisiphone let go of me and started to pace. "It's hard to explain really. It went where I couldn't follow."

"How is that possible?" I asked. "The only place that I know of that you can't get to at the moment is wherever Necessity is. Surely you're not suggesting . . ."

"No, of course not. There are all sorts of places the Furies can't go, or at least we can't go uninvited or unsent. Hades is a good example. That's why we didn't just follow you through the gates when you went there the second time. Well, that and a bit of complicity on my part and that of your doggy friend. Megaera argued for hot-pursuit rules, but I insisted otherwise, and Cerberus refused to acknowledge a warrant issued by Fate instead of Necessity. Alecto agreed with me and Cerberus for reasons of her own."

I felt something like an icy hand touch the back of my neck. That possibility had never even crossed my mind at the time.

"So, where *did* the spinnerette go?" I asked. While I might never want to return to Hades, my experiences over the last couple of years suggested that knowing someplace the Furies couldn't follow might come in handy.

"I'd rather not say."

I don't know if my face gave me away or what, but Tisiphone laughed then and bent to kiss my cheek.

"You're too transparent, my dear. We shall never again come after you without orders from Necessity herself." She looked very sad for a moment. "Were it her hand that had signed your death decree, no power of the heavens or Earth could stop us."

I decided that I didn't like the way the conversation was turning and aimed it back at the spinnerette, "So, it got away?"

"For now," growled Tisiphone, "only for now. When we have Necessity restored, things will change. In the meantime, I've been too long away and too long without satisfaction."

She scooped me into her arms as easily as I might pick up a cat and started toward the stairs. As we entered the bedroom, the cynical side of my brain wondered if she had wanted to change the subject as badly as I had or if maybe this was just her way of sublimating for a failed hunt. Then I was too busy to wonder anything at all.

Tisiphone sat on a stool in the corner of the clean room while Melchior and I put the finishing touches on his shiny new home. Once we had all the parts, most of the construction was utter simplicity. Even working out the spellcode for customizing the case and motherboard hadn't involved anything all that difficult.

The one really tricky bit of coding had been modifying the assembly spell that had come with the schematics for the quantum-processor chip so as to accommodate my new cooling scheme. But I felt pretty confident of the result. It was, after all, a hack job rather than a ground-up design task and, therefore, right up my alley.

"What do you think?" I asked Melchior after I put the last screw in place and covered it over with a rubber foot.

"Pretty spiffy," he replied, though the slight shake in his voice belied his grin.

I couldn't blame him on that front, although it really was a spiffy job. We'd ditched the rounded clamshell shape for a slightly more conventional but significantly smaller rectangle, making him more of a subnotebook than a true laptop. Made of Kevlar and carbon fiber, his computer form would weigh in at just under a pound and measure less than a half inch thick.

To make up for the lack of style in shape, we'd modded the hell out of his color scheme and added a bunch of LED telltales and translucence effect. His top surface was a very pale blue with the outline of his face etched into it. That made the area within the etching just enough thinner that the screen brightness could be stepped up to show through. For privacy reasons it wasn't on all the time, but if Mel wanted to, he could put up text you could read without actually opening the case.

Underneath, we'd gone for a much deeper blue, with loops of superbright LEDs embedded in the surface. When he activated them, they looked vaguely like glowing scales edged in whatever color struck his fancy. The extrathick rubber feet we'd put on raised him just enough so that in a dark room, an eerie glow would show from underneath.

The new case was banded in hardened anodized aluminum. Edge on, you saw two mirror-bright strips of cobalt blue metal. Likewise, his screen was surrounded with a border of brightly finished aluminum, natural silver this time except for the goblin-head logo below the screen, which matched the cobalt of his outer rim.

His keyboard was a block of white surrounded by blue, with keys that lit up from underneath and a goblin-head trackpad. The ears provided left and right mouse buttons. With the assembly finished, all that was left to do was a full test run and the transfer itself. For the former, we hooked the laptop up to a bank of Ahllan's diagnostics and controllers and set it to running. Over the next hour, it cycled all sorts of spellcode through the processor and drives and shifted the box back and forth into goblin shape a half dozen times.

That was downright creepy. Since we'd left Mel's goblin shape essentially untouched, I kept getting moments of what felt like double vision as a comatose Mel would appear on the table beside the original, upright, version.

"Oh my," said Haemun, who'd just brought a tray bearing a pitcher of lemonade and glasses for all as the next round of shape-shifting hit.

I took my glass with a stifled sigh. I just didn't have the heart to tell him he shouldn't be bringing them into the clean room.

The worst though was when the test bank ran short phrases of spoken text through the goblin form. Watching the blank-faced webgoblin's lips move seemingly without any animating will evoked a talking corpse. Finally, the bank whistled a snippet of test spell, and we all startled.

"Really," gasped Mel. "That's so cool!" The new Mel self-harmonized. Or at least, the test run did.

"Makes sense," I said, "since the processor's a webtroll model."

A moment later, the test bank beeped itself into silence, and the diagnostics screen started scrolling information. There was a lot there, and we read it all, but the key phrase came at the very end. "Unit is fully functional and ready for transfer."

I turned to Melchior. "Are you *ready*?"

"As I ever will be," he whispered.

"You don't have to do this," I said. "You know that, right?"

"I'm scared," he replied. "But I want to do it. Hook me up."

He climbed onto the table and shifted into laptop form, opening his external drive bay. I took one last look at the memory crystal we'd selected and placed it in the bay. A bright rich blue, it was the cleanest and clearest of all the crystals in Ahllan's stores, never before used and still in the original packaging until we'd plugged it in for a function check. It wasn't the biggest unit she'd had, though it *was* huge—about six terabytes capacity—because what was important was the least possible corruption and cross contamination.

The drive closed and I plugged Melchior into the controller bank, then did one last check on the transfer program. Everything looked good.

"Take care, my friend."

I hit the button that would copy Melchior into the crystal, erasing each individual bit of information from his online memory as soon as it had verified the write function in the crystal. A cumbersome and dangerous process—any information that miscopied would be lost forever—but a necessary one.

For many years, the Fates had copied files across to a new troll each time they upgraded, discarding the old hardware and personality rather than performing this sort of transfer. That hadn't always been the case, or so I'd learned from Ahllan. In the beginning, there'd been multiple attempts to copy the contents of the old drive over the new one via a networking cable. They had always failed, with resultant massive data loss in both computers. Restoring from backups could usually reproduce all the files, but it always left both systems as plain old computers rather than AIs.

The reason for that—unknown at the time—was the soulware, the actual extraphysical entity of the original AI. It couldn't exist in two places simultaneously, and when it was forced to try, the soul died. The only exception to that rule in the history of the multiverse to date was Shara, when she split herself because of the Persephone virus, and we still didn't fully understand what had happened there. Only by completely transferring the soul to an internal vessel—the memory crystal—and then moving that across to the new body could the transfer be effected safely.

The Fates had discovered the process through trial and error—though they still hadn't known about the souls—but decided it risked too much data loss and opted for the more wasteful but reliable cycle of junking the old trolls, personality and all.

"How long will it take?" Haemun asked after a while.

"About twenty minutes of write time, thirty seconds to move the crystal, another twenty minutes of read time, and at least an hour for system initialization on the new body."

"When will we know if it worked?" Haemun's voice sounded very small and worried, and I was forcefully reminded that his own personal magic gave him special insight into my emotional states and needs.

"Not until the very end," I replied. "Not until he—"

I was interrupted by a crash as Haemun dropped the drinks tray he still carried. The heavy earthenware pitcher burst apart, spraying lemonade everywhere. I had just an instant to regret not telling him to wait outside the clean room before he fell to the floor, curling into a ball in the mess and slipping quickly into unconsciousness.

"What's wrong?" I asked, kneeling and putting a hand on his shoulder.

It was Tisiphone who answered after sniffing the air for a moment. "Nemesis is here."

CHAPTER FIFTEEN

I glanced from Haemun's crumpled form to the table that held Melchior's body in mid–soul transfer. Nemesis would be knocking on the door any second, and in my whole life I'd rarely felt more helpless.

"How much longer?" Tisiphone jerked her chin at Melchior.

"I don't know." I shook my head. "Ten minutes? Maybe a bit more. It's hard to say. But that's just the write function—you heard what I told Haemun."

"Once he's written into the crystal, will he be stable?" she asked.

A boom sounded from upstairs—the front door shattering.

"For a while at least, but I don't know how long. No one's ever tested what happens if you delay the transfer. I'd rather not be the first."

Tisiphone shrugged, her face grim. "I can buy you ten minutes; that I swear. I don't know if I can do more, but I'll try. You'd better get some sort of exit strategy going in the meantime." She turned toward the door. "Good-bye."

I leaped up and caught her arm, and she let me spin her back to face me.

"Good luck," I said, and kissed her.

She leaned into the kiss for just a second, then pulled away. "Thanks, but don't worry so much. This will be the most fun I've had in years." She winked. "Present company excepted, of course. Bar the door." Then she was gone, moving with that insane speed that dazzled the eye.

I locked both the wardroom and clean-room doors, then set about crafting a faerie ring. As I worked, the sounds of violent destruction filtered down from above, along with the occasional puff of dust from the ceiling after a particularly loud and destructive impact. The horrible screams and howls sounded worse yet, something like a Hollywood director's fantasy of fifty giant alien cat creatures in the midst of a drug-fueled interstellar gang war.

Then the ring was finished, manifesting as a perfect circle of circuit-patterned mushrooms. I'd performed the task often enough now that I managed not to scorch the ceiling or knock myself over. Next, I checked the telltales on the controller to see where Melchior was in the process—perhaps three-quarters done.

I hate waiting. My eyes fell on Haemun, and I had an idea for reducing the total number of hostages. Half-lifting the satyr, I very gently slid him over the edge of the faerie ring. I could feel the magic tugging at him, ready to tumble him randomly through the infinity of the multiverse, but I didn't let him go. That would have been almost as bad as anything Nemesis could do. Instead, I sent my awareness into the network, creating a set of conditions rather than searching for a specific ring. When I thought I'd achieved them, I gave him a gentle nudge, and he was gone.

If things worked as I intended, he would in the very same instant have appeared in a temporary ring on Olympus, one tilted steeply enough to tumble him out of the ring and into the grasses beyond. It was the best I could do at the moment and a whole lot better than what he might have had to face if he stayed with us.

After that there was nothing left to do but wait. I put my

body between Melchior and the clean-room door and kept one eye on the monitor as the seconds ticked away. The transfer was almost complete when the first impact struck the door of the wardroom beyond.

"Come on, little buddy," I whispered. "Hurry." Then I drew my sword and my pistol, the latter left-handed.

I wouldn't have much time. As the door cracked under a second blow, I whistled a spell significantly shorter than its name: "Safeties? We don't need no stinking safeties."

A moment later I heard the outer door shatter. Only one thin panel now stood between me and my Nemesis. I took a firm stance and pointed my pistol at the door even as it bowed inward with Nemesis's first strike. Three more blows broke the door in two, sending the upper half tumbling into the clean room. For a second Nemesis's torso was silhouetted in the opening. I centered my sights on her chest and pulled the trigger, emptying my .45's clip at a magically enhanced full auto.

A human wouldn't have been able to hold the pistol on target. Even my wrist ached at the recoil, but it only lasted for an instant. Without waiting to see what damage I might have done, I threw the gun at her face and went for my dagger.

She caught it out of the air and snapped it back at me—so much for any hopes that the bullets would accomplish what Tisiphone had not. Reflexively, I dodged aside, then winced as I heard the pistol hit the equipment behind me. Breathing a little prayer to the goddess of fortune that it hadn't destroyed anything involved in Melchior's transfer, I took a long, lunging step forward, trying to skewer Nemesis with my rapier as she burst through what was left of the door.

There was a snap and a flash of numbing pain in my cheek as the world tumbled around me. Somewhere in there I lost my grip on my sword's hilt. It was only as I hit and shattered the legs of the table where Melchior's new body rested that I realized I was flying through the air. With a convulsive effort, I caught the falling subnotebook before it could hit the floor. Together, we slid into the corner. I ended up flat on my back, with my legs pressed against the wall amidst the wreckage of the table.

Nemesis stood just inside the doorway, a brutal smile twisting the bloodied lips she'd borrowed from Dairn. I did have the satisfaction of seeing a foot or so of my sword's blade standing out from her left side below the ribs—apparently the snap had been the sound of the blade breaking. She had other marks of having been in a fight as well. Besides the split lip, her nose was flattened, and she had a line of bullet holes running across her torso from right hip to just above the sword blade. She also had a set of deep claw marks on her left thigh—so deep, in fact, that I could see exposed bone—and I wondered sickly what had become of Tisiphone. With all of her injuries, Nemesis should have been dead. Unfortunately, it didn't look like anyone had explained that to her, not if the smile and the lack of significant bleeding were anything to go by

"Oh, look," she said, stepping deeper into the room and circling to her left—taking her farther away from me, "a faerie ring." She whistled something complex and self-harmonizing. The ring and the stone on which it stood dropped into a great pit that opened in the floor. "You should have used that before I came through the door. Now, why didn't you? I wonder."

I didn't want her thinking along those lines, not when I couldn't tell if Melchior was done with his transfer or not. Bracing my feet against the wall, I shoved, sending myself sliding across the floor toward Nemesis, dagger extended in front of me. With almost contemptuous ease, she stomped on the blade, pinning it to the floor and arresting my progress.

"Didn't like that question much, did you? Could it be because your familiar is over there on the slab, utterly helpless?" She twisted her heel, breaking my dagger, and stepped toward Melchior.

I whipped the subnotebook at the back of her head as I might have thrown a discus. I didn't want to give it up, but better that than let her put a finger on Melchior. She batted it away without even looking my way. It struck the wall with a sickening crunch. I rolled backwards onto my feet and lunged at her with the broken stub of my dagger.

With as little effort as she'd expended on the thrown computer, she caught my left wrist and twisted. My world blurred as the bones in my wrist broke, and I dropped the weapon. She twisted again, and I fell to my knees, darkness edging my vision and a rushing sound filling my ears.

"Naughty boy, mustn't get in Nemesis's way," I heard her say as if from a great distance.

Then she shoved me so hard that I almost tumbled into the pit. I lost track of things for a moment then, but came to on my feet. For reasons I could no longer understand, I had picked up the broken subnotebook and was clutching it to my chest. Across the room, Nemesis mirrored my pose with Melchior's laptop shape. Shredded cables dangled from his case, and I could only hope the copying job had finished running before she'd torn him loose. Now I just needed to figure out how to get him away from her.

"Did you want this?" she asked, holding him up in front of her. "Is it precious to you?"

"*He* is," I replied, meeting her mirrored eyes. "You know that, or you wouldn't be doing this."

"True enough," said Nemesis. "What would you give for it?"

I opened my mouth to answer, then paused for a split second as I saw movement beyond the doorway. The fight had shifted us so that I was in the farthest corner from the entrance, and Nemesis stood half-turned away from it.

"Anything," I said, forcing my eyes to move back to her face despite what I'd seen through the door. "I'd give anything to have him back."

Tisiphone stood in the room beyond. She didn't seem as bloodied as Nemesis, but the entire right side of her head looked black and blue. The wing on that side hung broken and limp, trailing behind her with its flames barely visible. Even as I registered that, she lifted her left hand to her mouth and touched her lips in a shushing gesture. Then she faded from view—the chameleon effect.

"Anything?" asked Nemesis. "Really? How about your right hand?" She pulled the hiltless blade from her side—no blood followed it.

Pinning the subnotebook to my chest with my broken left arm, I extended my right. "Melchior *is* my right hand."

"How nice," said Nemesis. "Well, that's a start then."

She raised the blade, and I braced myself for the pain. Then she lowered it again.

"No, if he really is your right hand, it seems only fair that I take that instead."

Before I could move, or even breathe, she brought Melchior's case down on the corner of the table with tremendous force. The laptop exploded into a million pieces, and I screamed. As the parts shot outward in all directions, a nearly invisible hand caught the most vital piece—the memory crystal—out of the air and flipped it in my direction. Tisiphone's toss was so accurate that I didn't even have to move my hand, just open it, and the crystal landed neatly on my palm. I gripped it convulsively as Tisiphone popped fully into view halfway through a spinning kick aimed at Nemesis's head.

"Run!" shouted Tisiphone, and I did, even as Nemesis brought up an arm and deflected most of Tisiphone's attack.

If Tisiphone hadn't dropped her camouflage, the kick might have landed true. She'd *chosen* to draw Nemesis's attention away from me. I was just ducking through the doorway when I heard a terrible screech. I looked back. Tisiphone was on her back now, with her head and shoulders hanging over the pit. Nemesis had hold of a table leg that she'd stuck deep into Tisiphone's shoulder and was using it to slide the Fury farther over the edge.

"No!" I yelled, and Tisiphone's eyes flicked toward me.

"Run, damn it!" she screamed.

Then she caught hold of Nemesis with the claws of her feet and jerked, tumbling them both into the pit. As I heard a scrabbling sound dropping away from me, I ducked back into the room. There, I saw a hand clutching the lip. It did not have claws. A half second later, another appeared beside it. Running wasn't going to be enough, but Tisiphone had bought me time to think, something I should have done from the start.

Working quickly, I opened the front of my jacket and

tucked both the crystal and what was left of the subnotebook inside. Then I pulled out my athame and slashed across the palm of my left hand. It jarred my broken wrist, and I couldn't help whimpering, but it also sprayed blood across Nemesis's groping hands. Reaching inward, I opened a channel to the interworld chaos and let it rip a hole in the walls of reality. This time, I didn't wait for the stuff to devour me as I had in Hades. Instead, I stepped through the rift into the nowhere beyond, leaving Nemesis to face the growing sphere of destruction.

Chaos whispered to me, trying to incorporate my own chaotic identity into the greater sea around me, trying to make me one with itself. I could feel the mad, pulsing vitality of it across the whole of my being just as I had when Tisiphone brought me here before. It was like being immersed in a mix of Dionysus's finest vintage and pure liquid music. All I had to do to experience it to the fullest was to let myself go and become part of the song. But I couldn't. Not if I wanted to meet Shara's deadline and not if I wanted to save Melchior.

I had to hold myself together until I could figure a way out of this, and I had to do it fast. I had no idea how much time Mel had, or even if he had any time at all. I needed to stay me.

"Me," I whispered to myself. "I. Me. Me. My."

It helped, but only a little. Asserting my me-ness wasn't going to do it for long. *Think, Ravirn! Come on, you can do this. Think!*

That was it! I had to *think*—to use the one part of me that made me who I was. My brain. I needed to think and keep thinking until I found a way out of this. Nothing was coming, though. If I were a Fury, I could have simply cut a hole in the stuff of nothingness and let myself leak into some-thingness, or something like that.

But I wasn't a Fury, and I wasn't going to be able to lay my hands on one either. The only Fury who really cared about me had fallen into a pit in my stead, and I had no way of knowing if she'd even survived the experience. Sure, she was immortal, but she'd been fighting another immortal at the time, and her own immortality was built on the power of

Necessity, who had withdrawn from the world. Maybe that made her killable. I just didn't know and . . . I was drifting away from the point again, chaos unraveling the pattern of my thinking.

It tugged at my thoughts, trying to remake them in its own image. Look at all the pretty colors and then bye-bye.

"Focus, Ravirn. How do you get out of here?"

For that matter, how had I gotten there in the first place? Not into chaos—that I knew, at least—but into the mess that led to the chaos. How had I ended up on Nemesis's hit list? Who had set her after me?

"No," I tried to force myself to focus, "that's not the right question. *Why* did they set her after me? Who has something to gain by setting Nemesis on me? Who wanted me dead?"

That wasn't it either, though. There were easier ways to kill me than resurrecting a dead goddess. There had to be. That was too much like using Zeus's lightning as a bug zapper. Well, if they didn't want me dead, what did they want? What was I good at? Hacking, which nobody hired out. Cracking, maybe. And bug fixes. Hadn't I heard that song somewhere before?

I just didn't get it, though. If someone was really trying to use Nemesis as motivation, shouldn't they have given me some idea of what they wanted by now?

"Come on, give me a sign!"

That was when Megaera arrived. At first I thought I was hallucinating, that my brain had made a pattern out of the tumbling shapes and forms of the chaos passing before my eyes—calling up Tisiphone to save me despite everything.

Then she spoke. "Looks like somebody could use a lift." She was wearing a smile, but it wasn't a very good one—she was no better at lying than her fiery sister.

"Megaera?"

"In the flesh." She nodded, and her green hair did intensely strange things in the gravityless nonspace of chaos.

"Here to rescue *me*?"

The smile slipped. "I could leave you here to die."

"Could you really? Could you just fly away and leave me to dissolve in chaos?"

"Of course. It's not as though I like you, little runaway."

"Do it," I said, because I suddenly didn't believe she would. I almost had the answer now. I could taste it, though I couldn't articulate it, like a word that was hanging just beyond the tip of my tongue.

"What!"

"Fly away. Leave me. I don't want your help."

She growled and extended her claws, but she neither left nor gutted me. I mentioned that, and she growled some more. Then she grabbed hold of my arm.

"Let go!" I demanded.

"Or what? There's nothing you can do that could possibly hurt me."

"Or I'll let go . . . of myself, and you can try holding on to chaos amidst chaos."

"You might be surprised what I can hang on to," she said. "We were built to catch even the slipperiest fish." She didn't let go of my arm, but she did stop trying to move me. "What do you want?" she sighed.

"Answers to life's persistent questions."

"Not my department," said Megaera though she still made no move to force me.

That told me a lot. I believed her when she said that she could catch even chaos hiding in chaos. That meant she had some other reason for wanting me to retain my shape and myself. The only thing I could think of was Melchior in his crystalline container, who might not take the transition so well. That's why I hadn't simply made good on my threat. I wasn't willing to risk him either, but that was because I loved him. Why should Megaera care? That had to be tied in to all the other questions.

"How much has Tisiphone been keeping you up to date on our efforts to fix Necessity?" I finally asked.

"She's told me everything."

"Everything?" I waggled my eyebrows suggestively.

"Everything." Her voice was rich with disgust.

Combine her expression with the fact that she didn't seem as worried about her sister as I might have expected, and I had to assume that she believed Tisiphone would be all right—an enormous relief. And one that left me with only one question, one that would point the way to the prime mover here.

"Who are the Furies working for now?"

"What? What do you mean? We serve Necessity."

Truth mixed with fiction: gods but she was a bad liar. I'd almost had it there, even without a real answer.

"Necessity's been off-line a long time," I said, "and I know for a fact you and your sisters don't much like autonomy. You turned away from service to the Fates because you believed they didn't have Necessity's best interests at heart, but you wouldn't have stayed free agents for long. Maybe I can figure it out without your help. You must be working for someone who you believe will help you fix her, someone with both the power and the motive. Who could that be?"

"I—I can't . . . believe you're asking that. We don't serve anyone but Necessity."

And now I thought I had it.

"Really? You're as bad a liar as your sister. I'll come with you if you'll give me a ride to the right place."

"Where?" She sounded wary.

"How about if you take me to Zeus?"

Megaera blinked, then nodded. "You are a clever one, aren't you. Maybe they were right to choose you." Then, with one great beat of her seaweed wings, she started us moving through the Primal Chaos.

So, I *had* guessed right, though I didn't feel all that clever. I should have seen it much earlier, probably would have if I were less suspicious of family—Thalia to be specific. She'd called me with a warning about Zeus, though I hadn't had the wit to recognize it as such at the time.

Zeus had set me up with the party—I was as sure of that now as if I'd seen him ordering the floral arrangements—but I still hadn't figured out why. It had to do with Necessity. He wanted her fixed, and he wanted it badly. Otherwise, he couldn't have persuaded the Furies to his side. But what was in it for him? He was perhaps the most self-interested of the gods, and he would never have put that much work into anything without a damn good reason.

I needed to know the answer to that in order to figure out
how to play this, but I hadn't come up with anything by the
time Megaera cut us a door into Olympus. She took us
straight to the top, the little round temple that sat on the roof
of the great palace of Zeus like a cupola—the thunder god's
personal office.

The big guy was in, sitting at his desk in all his
bronze-skinned, vacant-eyed glory, complete with dumb
grin. This time I wasn't buying it.

"Ravirn, my boy, how are you?" He boomed. "And Megaera, my favorite Fury. So good to see you both! If you'd
called ahead, I'd have arranged a party."

He stood up and drew us both into a huge hug. My broken
wrist screamed, but not nearly as loudly as I would have
expected, and I somehow managed not to let the sound reach
my mouth. Instead, I kept it firmly shut.

Megaera said simply, "He knows."

That was good. It saved me some time, a commodity I
was very concerned about at the moment. As soon as Zeus
let us go, I went straight to the smaller desk on the other side
of the office where his computer sat.

"Hello, Zeus, how are you?" the god said to himself in
my voice as I walked away, the tone jovially sarcastic. "Oh,
I'm fine." He turned his head back and forth as he spoke,
mimicking a conversation with himself. "And you, Ravirn?
Never better, Zeus. Good to hear that, my boy. Let me get
you a drink."

I ignored him as—one-handed—I pulled his personal
computer out from under the desk and started checking
ports and connectors. I was pleased by the results. The box
looked state of the art. I hadn't really expected anything
less, what with Zeus's fixation on power and potency, but I'd
had to make sure.

"So," said the god, after a moment, "are you going to talk
to me? Or are you just going to tear my office apart until I
smite you?" His voice remained boisterously genial, but I
detected a growing edge underneath.

I was getting to him. That was good. Dangerous, but
good. I wanted him off-balance when we started this con-

versation. It would give me an advantage, and I needed every one of those I could get. Especially since I still hadn't figured out his true agenda in all this.

"Smite him," interjected Megaera. "Please. Or if you'd rather not do it personally, I'd be happy to play your proxy."

"You want to give me a reason to hold her back?" asked Zeus, his voice cold and serious.

That was what I'd been waiting for. I turned around. Zeus had settled with one hip leaning against his desk, his position studiedly casual. All trace of vacancy had left his eyes and taken the idiot grin with it. He was still bronze, but now instead of evoking too much time spent on the beach, it reminded me of Spartan spearheads.

"We could talk," I said, "but at the moment, I'd rather do some dealing."

"What makes you think you have anything I want?" he asked, and I knew that I had him.

If he didn't need me, he would have simply refused. OK, why did he need me? And how much? I had to figure that out, or I was going to get taken to the cleaners. Somehow in my earlier encounters with him, I'd managed to let the hyper-frat-boy act blind me to the fact that Zeus had managed to retain control over a pantheon of fractious and clever gods for ten thousand years. He might play the idiot for public consumption, but he'd won every fight he'd ever gotten into all the way back to the Titanomachy. It wasn't Zeus trapped in Tartarus. It was his father. Then it hit me.

The Titanomachy and Tartarus! Cerberus had given me all the clues I needed, and I hadn't really listened. Since Persephone's virus was designed to destroy the information about who belonged where in the pantheon, Zeus was afraid that the problems with Necessity were going to free the Titans and restart the war of gods against Titans. That still didn't explain why he'd brought Nemesis into the equation, but it took me much closer.

"Well?" asked Zeus.

I scrambled to answer now that I had something to say, "The fact that you haven't already fried me with lightning is suggestive in itself, but I've got some other thoughts on the matter. I'd love to go over them in detail, but I have a problem that needs solving *right now*. If you help me with that, *right now*, then later I'll be much more open to helping you with any problems you might have with . . . oh, say, the Titans? What do you think?"

A small thundercloud formed over Zeus's head, and he frowned mightily. I didn't make the mistake of believing it was an accident or for anything other than effect. Not this time. Despite the fact that precious seconds were ticking past, I sat myself down in the chair in front of the computer desk and crossed my arms. I didn't dare blow this, so I kept my mouth firmly shut. It had a tendency to write checks the rest of me had trouble cashing. Melchior would have been proud . . . and thinking about him cut at my soul.

"All right, tell me what you need," said Zeus after a few seconds.

I half unzipped my jacket and pulled out the busted-up subnotebook, setting it on the desk. I took the opportunity to tuck my broken arm into my jacket, then opened the laptop. The screen was completely shattered, and a couple of keys were broken or dislodged. The case looked all right—no surprise with all that Kevlar and carbon fiber—but the anodized aluminum trim had some nasty scratches, and I suspected internal damage. It was all stuff I could repair given time. But I didn't have time, or at least, I didn't know how much time I had. I needed to get Melchior out of the crystal and into his new body before anything further went wrong.

I looked Zeus in the eye. "You are the embodiment of creation, the pole power of life. I figure that means you can fix this a whole lot faster and more easily than I can." I tapped the case.

"It's a computer," said Zeus. "What do I know from computers? You've debugged software problems for me before." His porn browser had broken, and he hadn't wanted to get Athena to do it. "You should know that."

"Uh-uh. This is the broken body of a living being." I pulled out the crystal. "His soul is right here in my hand. Don't tell me you can't heal him. We both know it's not true."

"When you put it that way . . ." Zeus stood up and walked over to look down at the subnotebook. "Hmm." He gazed downward for several seconds, then nodded. "You want me to do that broken wrist of yours at the same time?"

"That'd be nice," I said, "but it's not my main concern at the moment."

"Of course it's not," said Zeus. "Not after your little jaunt through chaos."

"What?" I couldn't help myself, it just burst out.

"Ah-ha," said Zeus. "Mister smarty-pants-wet-behind-the-ears-demigod doesn't actually know everything yet, does he? I take it you haven't noticed that you feel recharged and rejuvenated every time you use chaos magic? That it substitutes for the sleep you now find so hard to achieve?"

He'd hit a nerve and I wanted to know more about that; but it wouldn't fix Melchior and I really didn't know how much time he had, so I put it aside for later thought.

"My familiar?" I prompted.

He placed the palm of his right hand in the middle of the keyboard, and shouted, "Heal!" with the deep tones and Southern accent of a revival tent preacher.

The subnotebook slid halfway across the desk, making an awful crackling noise as it went. Contrary to the noise, though, all of the visible damage began reversing itself. It looked like film of an accident being run backwards. Before I could think to say anything, the god placed his hand on my forehead, and shouted "Heal!" again.

My chair went over backwards, and I landed hard, but I didn't pay nearly as much attention to that as I might have in other circumstances. I was too distracted by the sensation that someone had poured hot maple syrup into my veins—warm, wonderful, sugary goodness filling me up to the point of pain, with hot spots in my wrist, my bad knee, and my left pinky. A few seconds later, it had all faded away, and I felt as though my body had been returned to original specs. The feeling was reinforced by the totally unexpected restoration of the fingertip I'd lost more than a year ago in my fight with my cousin Moric—a small price, considering he'd died.

"Wow!" I said, though it sounded terribly uncool in my own ears. To make up for that, I quickly lifted an eyebrow at Zeus and asked in my best snide tone, "Did you have to do the 'heal' thing, or was that for my benefit?"

"Neither. I've just always kind of wanted to try it, and now seemed as good a time as any."

I laughed, and in that moment I found that despite everything, I still liked Zeus. It was an uncomfortable feeling. "Fair enough. Now, if you'll excuse me for a moment, I've got to do my part."

Opening the drive tray on the subnotebook, I set the crystal within. The shiny black plastic that lined the sides of the surprisingly deep bay flowed around the crystal, conforming to its shape. Once it was firmly seated, I closed it up and started connecting cables from Zeus's desktop to the little laptop. After that, it was all software.

Since Zeus's machine hadn't been designed for this sort of task, I had to hack some of the existing disk utilities to perform the soul-write. Then, I didn't trust them to do the job without careful monitoring, so I spent the next forty minutes ignoring Zeus and everything but getting the job done right. At the end of that time, I had a subnotebook whose hard drive held whatever was left of Melchior—*please be all there*—and only one thing left to do.

I hit the start button.

CHAPTER SIXTEEN

The small laptop chimed gently as the boot process began, and I forced myself to lean back in the chair. What I could do for Melchior, I had done. Now it was all over but the waiting. An hour at least because of the recompile made necessary by the quantum hardware. That's what I'd told Haemun, and it was likely to be more, what with all the jostling and delays. An hour or more till I found out whether I still had a best friend. I'd have screamed, but that was only going to work for a few minutes at best—the throat just isn't built for an hour of sustained ululation.

Instead, I turned back to Zeus and Megaera and tried desperately not to think about all the things that could possibly go wrong with a soul transfer onto largely untested and experimental hardware. Hardware that, by the way, had been shattered by Nemesis, then repaired by the king of the gods through pure wild magic, and using a soul that might or might not have finished its transfer protocol.

"Are we ready to talk now?" asked Megaera, her voice dripping poison. "Have we finished playing with our silly toys and having a temper tantrum?"

I didn't remember crossing the distance between us or grabbing her throat in my hands. Everything between her comment and Zeus shouting, "Don't kill him!" was a blank. Almost simultaneous with the words came a gentle impact on my chest and a circle of searing pain. That brought me fully back into my right mind. I looked down to find the fingertips of Megaera's right hand pressed into the flesh above my heart.

"Please," said Megaera. "I just want to tear his heart out a little bit."

"No," replied Zeus, and she pulled her hand away, leaving five bleeding punctures where her claws had bitten into my flesh.

"I suppose you want that healed as well?" Zeus didn't sound amused.

"No. I think I'll keep it for now. It'll help remind me to think before I act."

Zeus sighed. "It's a good idea, but somehow after reading Athena's reports on you, I doubt it'll be enough. Megaera, why don't you find someplace else to be for a while. The two of you don't play together well, and I'd rather not have to keep pulling you apart. It's extra effort, and I'm not a big fan of extra effort."

Without so much as a good-bye, Megaera stepped between two pillars and leaped into the sky.

"Good riddance," I whispered under my breath.

"Could we just skip all that?" asked Zeus.

"All right." I returned to the chair beside Melchior's new case—close enough to touch but facing away so as not to allow myself to get too distracted. "Where shall we start?"

"I don't think that's how it goes," said Zeus. "We've already started. I did something for you, now it's your turn to do something for me."

"Fix Necessity, you mean? So that the Titans don't break themselves free of Tartarus?"

"In a nutshell," Zeus said, nodding, "yes."

"I'm already on the case, but you knew that. As soon as I leave here, I'll get back on it, assuming Melchior survives his upgrade, that is." I swallowed hard.

I would not break down in front of Zeus. I would not break down in front of Zeus. Not now, not knowing he was my . . . well, not enemy exactly. Adversary sounded about right. Especially considering the fact that he'd set Nemesis on me.

"Why did you do that?" I asked.

"Do what?" He assumed a puzzled expression. "It may surprise you to know this, but I'm not omniscient. Cronus's teeth, I don't even do divination. That whole Delphic oracle shtick is Apollo's thing, not mine. It's always sounded like far too much work for my tastes."

"Why did you set Nemesis on me?"

"I wasn't sure Tisiphone would be able to convince you to the cause. Especially not as you were still attached to that girl of Clotho's when I set the plan in motion."

"Cerice?" I tried to keep my voice polite, though I felt more than a little sick at his mention of Tisiphone.

"*That's* her name, yes." He theatrically slapped his forehead.

"Could you please stop doing that?" I asked.

"What?"

"Playing stupid. Neither one of us believes it. Not anymore. Doesn't that make it count as wasted effort? That's your idea of a cardinal sin, right?"

The god became perfectly still, and his face lost the vague look it had assumed. "Point to the Raven. You're right; it's wasted effort now. I won't even pretend to have forgotten where we were. You were about to ask whether Tisiphone knew about Nemesis and why on Earth I'd thought setting Nemesis on you would motivate you to repair Necessity."

"Exactly," I said.

"Of course she didn't, and it's because I thought you were smarter than perhaps you are."

"Pardon?" I asked.

"I didn't tell Tisiphone about Nemesis, nor Megaera or Alecto. To do so would have set them to wondering about my motives, and that has everything to do with the reason I arranged for Dairn to make a visit to Tartarus and, with it, Nemesis's acquaintance."

"I still don't . . . Oh." I almost had it all. "Nemesis was trapped with the Titans in Tartarus. When Necessity was damaged, that loosened the chains of all who are bound there." Zeus smiled at me like a teacher whose student has just grasped the lesson. "Nemesis will kill me if I keep going head-to-head with her, and she'll keep coming after me as long as she's free. The only way to stop her is to reimprison her in Tartarus, which means fixing Necessity."

"Precisely. The biggest problem with the plan is that you didn't figure it out anywhere near as quickly as I'd expected."

"Is that why you went to plan B and set Tisiphone to wooing me to the cause?" I made the question as light as I could, but I didn't fool Zeus.

"No, Tisiphone's wooing was all on her own behalf. Convenient for me, but not my fault. The only thing I did on that front was suggest to Alecto that you'd make a good choice for fixing Necessity. I figured that if she agreed, that would make a two-to-one vote in your favor and give Tisiphone the freedom to pursue you without the worry that Megaera would kill you for spite."

Another piece fell into place. "That, and you arranged for Nemesis to attack me while I was in Tisiphone's presence. You knew that the return of Nemesis would force her and the other Furies to work faster on getting Necessity repaired. That's what the spinnerettes have been about, lighting me up so that Nemesis could find me. Right?"

"Not quite," said Zeus. "I did arrange for that encounter, but I don't control the spinnerettes. They're working for the Fate Core."

"I notice you didn't say for Fate," I said, thinking back to Cerice's suggestion that the Fate Core was becoming sentient.

Zeus shook his head. "Not as far as I can tell."

"Huh." That could get very ugly. "Well, what are they doing for it, and why?"

"I don't know." The statement was flat and unaccompanied by one of his patented dumb looks, and I found that I believed him.

"But didn't you make Tisiphone stop chasing the one that visited Garbage Faerie?" I asked.

"Yes, but not because I was protecting the spinnerette. I just wanted her back with you, solving the Necessity problem and guarding you in case Nemesis showed up. Vengeance is a very hard goddess to control. I didn't want you dying without solving my problem."

"You know," I said, putting the issues of the spinnerettes aside for the moment, "for someone who claims to be lazy, that all sounds like a *lot* of work."

Zeus chuckled. "You'd be surprised. All I had to do to make Nemesis work for me was give the faerie-ring network a tiny nudge so that it spat what was left of your cousin Dairn out at the right place for him to meet and offer himself to Nemesis—less work than you expended sending your Haemun here to protect him. I didn't have to do much more with the Furies. They want the same thing I do, and they're willing to do all the sweaty running-around parts."

I opened my mouth to ask another question, then closed it with a snap when I felt a tap on my shoulder.

"Boss?"

I spun in my chair and found Melchior—in goblin shape—staring at me from a distance of inches. I snatched him into a hug.

"What did I miss?" he asked, when I loosened up enough to let him breathe.

"Everything," I said, suppressing tears once again. "How are you? All the right parts in all the right places?" I set him down and tapped his shoulders and hips.

"Sort of," he said, "but I feel really, really strange."

"Could you be any vaguer?" I asked.

"I don't know, I could try if you really want me to . . ." He winked. "It is actually hard to explain. Maybe it'd be better if I showed you."

With that, he changed back into laptop shape. Only he didn't. Unlike the old change, this was instantaneous, complete, and—strangest by far—no change at all. On the desk in front of me stood something that was Melchior, the open laptop, and both simultaneously. At least that was how I saw it. I imagine someone who wasn't a chaos power would have been getting a really nasty flickering effect as their eyes tried to process the three overlapping entities as distinct images. Even for me, it was a little rough on the digestion.

"I don't suppose you want to stop that," I said. "It's kind of hard to look at."

"You think you've got problems," he said as he suddenly became only the webgoblin. "Imagine how it feels from the inside."

"I'd rather not, if that's all right with you. How are you doing it?"

"I'm not sure. I was all set to transform the old way when . . ." He frowned. "It's strange really. I just got this wild impulse to try something different and, presto!" He snapped his fingers and shifted back and forth again. "Is that what it's like to be the Raven? All weird intuitions and sudden impulses?" He shuddered.

"It does have moments like that, yes. While we're on the subject of weirdness, that was no hour. How can you be back with me so soon?"

"Blame me," said Zeus. "I maybe should have mentioned it before, but creative processes, like births—even electronic births—tend to go more quickly and easily in my presence. It can be a bother really. Take a nap in a just-planted field, wake up to find very confused farmers harvesting all around you. Oh well, at least it doesn't involve any work. Now, where were we?"

"Arranging for me to get from here to Necessity, if that's possible. It looks like it's my turn to pay up." If he'd saved that one to increase my gratitude, it had worked.

"So quick to agree to my terms?" mused Zeus. "And that despite all the trouble I've caused you. It almost makes me want to ask for more."

I growled. "Don't push your luck. At the moment, our needs and wants on the subjects of Necessity and Nemesis are in concert. That doesn't mean I'm going to forget or forgive the fact that you've endangered my life and the lives of my friends. I'm putting it aside, not dropping it."

"Uh, Boss?"

"Yes, Melchior?"

"Please tell me that you're not threatening Zeus."

"All right. Melchior, I'm not threatening Zeus."

"You're lying," he said with a sigh.

"I'm lying, but not much. It's not like I'm planning genuine retaliation or anything. I'm just making vague, menacing sounds in the hopes that it'll make him think twice about pulling this kind of crap on me again later. It not like I have any real power to harm him."

"You are aware that I'm still in the room, right?" asked Zeus.

"Of course I am. This is as close as I can get to admitting Mel's right that threats were a bad idea and maybe I should retract them. It saves face, you see?"

"Even when you explain it like that?" Zeus sounded bemused.

"Oh, especially when I explain it," I answered. "That makes it all a joke between friends. Speaking of which, now that we're past the parts you didn't want her to hear, maybe we should call Megaera back. Unless, that is, you've done more double-crossing of the Furies that you don't want them to know about." I cocked my head to one side and took my chin between finger and thumb. "You know, I hadn't thought about that."

"What?" asked Zeus, suddenly sounding more than a little wary.

"Assuming I get Necessity fully repaired, neither she nor the Furies are going to be particularly pleased about the way you've brought Nemesis into all this. They're bad enemies. I know *I* wouldn't want my girlfriend, Tisiphone, really mad at me."

"That's a much better threat," said Zeus with a tight smile. "I especially like the subtlety of mentioning, as if in passing, that you're romantically linked to one of the Furies. For such a young godling, you're learning how to play the game quite quickly. I will have to watch you more closely in the future."

"I'm a fast learner, and I keep ending up across the table from the best—you for example. Now, where were we?"

Melchior put his face in his hands.

"I was calling Megaera back so that we could see about getting you on your way," said Zeus. "At least, I presume that's why you wanted her back. You think you'll need her to get to Necessity."

I nodded. That, and I was worried about Tisiphone. I hoped Megaera would be able to tell me whether she was all right or not.

A few minutes later, Megaera nodded cautiously to the latter question, though she looked worried. "I think so. Tisiphone's angry, and she's in some pain, but not a lot." My expression must have shown my shock, because she laughed and directed her gaze my way. "We heal very quickly. Even with the injuries you described, I would expect her to bounce back fully within a matter of hours at most. No, it's not her physical condition that concerns me. It's the weakness of the link between us. I can't tell where she is, and that's never happened before."

"Do you suppose she's with Necessity?" asked Melchior.

Megaera turned to him so quickly that she blurred. "What makes you ask that?"

"The impression I got from Tisiphone was that right at the moment you can find anything in the multiverse but Necessity. Since you can't find Tisiphone now . . ."

"How would she get there?" asked Zeus. "That's a problem no one's been able to solve for some time."

"Which is why you brought Ravirn into the equation," said Melchior, "for his skills—skills currently mirrored by Nemesis as part of her quarrel with him. If Tisiphone is with Nemesis—"

"She'd never betray Necessity that way!" snarled Megaera.

"Who says she's anything but a key?" I said very quietly. "Tisiphone told me that I'd have to bring a Fury along when I went to fix Necessity, that without her, I wouldn't be able to get past the physical security, or even get in for that matter. What did she mean?"

"She shouldn't have told you that," said Megaera.

"It was when she was trying to convince me to take the job, and you didn't answer the question."

Megaera closed her mouth and crossed her arms.

"If I'm going to crack my way into Necessity for you, I need to know," I said.

"Tell him," said Zeus.

"All right, but under protest. Necessity's physical form is a computer. You know that. Tisiphone told you that she exists at the point of maximum improbability? The place where DecLoci are formed, where new Earths split away from the old?"

"She did."

"Did you ever wonder about what physical shape such a place might take?" asked Megaera.

"Not really. I was mostly focused on finding a way to get there. I figured that sort of thing could take care of itself. Are you going to get to the point anytime soon, or should I get myself a drink?"

"What was the first DecLocus to split off from the world of Olympus?" asked Megaera as though she hadn't heard me.

"I don't know." I shrugged. "Prime +1, I guess, the place where humanity first came into existence."

"No," said Megaera. "It was Prime/?, the decision point, where Necessity made her home. The alternate Olympus."

"Wait a second," interjected Melchior. "Are you suggesting that Necessity has an entire copy of the planet Earth to herself?"

"Close," said Megaera. "Though I don't see why that should surprise you given the empty world where Raven House sits. No, Necessity has an entire universe to herself. The Earth is merely the vessel that houses her spirit."

"A planetwide computer?" I gasped.

Megaera nodded. "One that is within its own closed universe with no faerie rings and no physical entry other than this." She extended one claw and cut a tiny slice in the stuff of reality. "With the mweb portals shut, you would need a living Fury to open the way if you wanted to enter the House of Necessity."

"Nemesis has a living Fury," I said, though my stomach dropped at the thought, "for now. We've got to find out where they are and get moving."

"You'll be taking me with you," said Megaera, "of course. How soon can we leave?"

"That depends on whether Melchior's upgrade actually bought us anything." I looked at him.

He shrugged. "I don't know. What are we hoping for?"

"Deep insights into multidimensional quantum uncertainty," I replied.

"Oh, good," said Melchior. "Then we're screwed. Unless feeling really strange counts as a deep insight."

"Probably not, but maybe it'll be a place to start. In the meantime, why don't we check in with Shara and find out whether Nemesis and Tisiphone are really there. Megaera?"

"You want me to play signal fire like Tisiphone did, don't you?"

"Unless you've got a better suggestion."

She sighed. "Better get me a barf bag then. I was only getting it secondhand when you ran Tisiphone through the ringer, but that was bad enough to send me running for the porcelain more than once."

"Wait," I said. "You were feeling what Tisiphone felt?" I didn't like that idea at all.

"Echoes of it. We are all part of the same being."

"Even when we . . ." I couldn't help it; I blushed.

"Only a little, by accident. I mostly tried to block it out. Believe me, I like the idea even less than you do. Your hands on my—ugh!" She shivered. "Look, I don't want to talk about it, and you can't make me. Not if you want to keep all of your bits where they currently reside. Let's just make the damn call, OK?"

A few minutes later we had Megaera positioned in a small pentagram drawn on Zeus's pristine white marble floor with permanent ink. He'd winced at that, but hadn't suggested we stop.

"Here goes," said Mel. Then he began sending, *"Shara, are Tisiphone and Nemesis with you?"*

Several long seconds ticked past before Megaera—looking even greener than her normal seaweed-and-saltwater self—jerked and pointed to her left.

I barely noticed, because at the very same moment Melchior jumped a good foot into the air.

"What's wrong?" I caught him by the shoulder.

He held up a hand. "Hang on a second!" Then he started pointing in synch with Megaera. "I can hear her! I can hear Shara! It's like she's right"—he turned slowly in place—"over . . . there."

He pointed—sort of. His finger was doing something quantum, simultaneously aimed at something that was both of this dimension and outside it.

"Megaera, can you follow his bearing?" I asked.

"I don't know." She looked even greener than usual. "Not from here, but maybe within chaos."

"Hang on a second," said Melchior. "I'll tell her we're on the way and to keep sending." His expression went thoughtful and abstracted. "There."

"Then let's go." I scooped him up and stepped in close to the Fury.

With a distinct look of distaste, she put her left hand on my right hip and tore a hole in the universe with her right one. Then, pulling me tight against her, she leaped into nowhere.

It wasn't until the hole closed behind us that I realized we'd forgotten to say good-bye to Zeus. Somehow, I figured he'd get over it.

Once again, the creation-in-destruction that was chaos tugged at my sense of self. The sheer power of it felt seductive and intoxicating—pure raw magic, forever and always only a hairbreadth away from the real world. All that separated the two was the swipe of a Fury's claws. I tore my attention free of the dance and forced myself to think of other things as a queasy Megaera began to follow Melchior's guidance through the joyous madness.

Still, I couldn't stop feeling the chaos thrumming across my skin like a song in the back of my head, a chorus in some alien tongue I could almost make out. I found it very hard to keep from humming along, and so I didn't pay much attention to the trip. Not until Melchior jerked in my arms, though he didn't stop pointing.

"What's wrong?" I asked.

"The signal's getting kind of ragged, like something's interfering with it or with . . . Shara!"

"Can you tell which it is?"

"Is something wrong with Necessity?" demanded Megaera, her face sheened with sweat.

"I don't know," said Melchior. "I can't signal her back without a set of wards to modulate, and that's impossible here."

"Fly faster!" I said.

Megaera shook her head and spoke through clenched teeth, "I wish I could."

A few more minutes passed, moments in which I found it easier to stay tuned in to the here and now instead of the chaos chorus. The tension and worry seemed to help.

"I'm losing her," Melchior said abruptly. "The signal cut out completely for a moment there."

Megaera nodded. "I can barely keep track of where I am."

"How far do we have left to go?" I asked.

He shushed me and looked thoughtful, and I found myself wishing I could hear her with his ears, because the chaos chorus had picked up a bit of volume again. Finally, he shrugged. I swore. Megaera hissed. Time passed.

Then, "Gone," said Melchior.

Megaera shrieked something inarticulate, thwarted rage plain in her face, then turned away and vomited into the void. I wanted to shriek, too. Chaos whispered to me through every pore, and this time I listened. It wasn't like I had anything better to do.

"Now what?" asked Melchior.

"I . . . Hang on." I had just had one of those belated realizations, where something has happened that you register but don't notice. "The chaos chorus has changed."

"The what?" Melchior looked bewildered.

"Don't worry about it. Just ask me another question."

"Are you out of your mind?"

That was it. "No." Yes! The chaos song changed, I could feel it echoing through me. "Megaera, go that way." I pointed along a bearing slightly to the left of the one Melchior had been holding us to.

"Why?" She sounded positively defeated.

There, stronger. "Because I can feel the flow of chaos, and it's telling me to go that way."

"All right," she said, though she looked worn and doubtful.

I might not be able to hear what Melchior had, but I could listen to chaos, and it had been talking to me all along, telling me things about probability and uncertainty and potential. When an uncertainty was introduced into the matrix of the universe—would we or wouldn't we make it to Necessity, was I insane—it rippled through chaos. I could feel my way into the uncertain, and if Necessity really was the point of maximum uncertainty . . .

"Keep asking questions." They both looked at me as though I'd answered the madness question the other way, but I ignored that and made them keep asking questions until . . . "Here. Cut us a hole right here. This is Necessity." I was sure of it.

"You're a funny one," said Megaera, her voice weak and thready, "but what the hell."

Before I could respond, she'd sliced a hole into the universe and pulled us through.

We emerged in a room that was large and white and utterly wrecked. It had been a computational center once, the kind you might find in any large institution, with dozens of server racks arranged in neat rows beneath an acoustical-tile ceiling, though it appeared to be older equipment. Now it looked as though a minotaur with anger-management issues had decided it looked like a great place for experimenting with vandalism therapy. The racks had literally been pulled apart. The computers lay shattered and scattered about the room, and a huge hole gaped in the near wall. Parts of the dropped ceiling had collapsed, and a thick layer of fresh dust covered everything. I suspected that we had arrived at the ELF control center.

Megaera made the sort of noise you might get if you doused a lion's tail with gasoline and lit it on fire. It was somewhere between a snarl and a yowl, and I felt it in my spine. I'd have pulled away from her then, but the hand curled around my hip had grown six-inch razors at the tips of its fingers and I didn't want to self-amputate any of the things those points were resting near.

"I hate to be a bother, but could you maybe move your . . ." I raised my eyebrows and pointed downward.

Megaera didn't answer, and she didn't move, just stood there and sniffed the air. I was trying to decide what to do next when she let out another yowling snarl, and I found myself spinning half-around and sitting down. On the floor. Hard. But not bleeding, which was a fair trade in my book. I landed facing the hole in the wall and Megaera's rapidly receding back.

"Was it something I said?" I asked aloud.

"Maybe it was your breath," said Melchior. "I've been meaning to talk to you about it."

I laughed, though I didn't find the situation the least bit funny. If you'd asked me the week before what view I would most like to see of an angry Megaera, I'd have described the scene as it stood, with her heading away at speed and me not bleeding to death behind her. Now, with Nemesis running around somewhere in the vicinity, I found that I really wanted Megaera back.

I said as much to Melchior as I climbed to my feet, and he nodded. "Me, too. Unfortunately, it looks like we're on our own. So, now what? Do we follow Megaera?"

"I don't know, Mel. On the one hand, that's probably the path Nemesis took, and if we follow it, we might catch up with her."

"And on the other?"

"That's probably the path Nemesis took, and if we follow it, we might catch up with her."

"There is that," he said. "What about Tisiphone?"

"She's a big girl. She can take care of herself."

"So why are we walking that way?" he asked.

"Because I'm a freak of nature," I answered.

"I can't argue with that, but did you want to be more specific?"

I peered through the hole. A dark hallway lay beyond, its floor marred by deep gouges as though someone had dragged a clawed and unhappy something away down its length.

I sighed. "It's a horrible birth defect, actually; I was born with no sense of self-preservation."

"So we're going after them?" he asked.

"Yep." I stepped through into the hall.

"I was afraid of that."

"Me, too, Mel. Me, too."

About a hundred yards farther along, we came to a series of doors and another nexus of destruction. It was hard to tell with only wreckage to read, but it looked as though Tisiphone had decided to fight back again, and the battle had crashed through into several of the rooms off the hallway, destroying their contents, including a small router closet, a bank of uninterruptible power supplies, and another server array. Again, it looked like older units.

A freshly torn-off door opening onto a utility-type stairwell suggested that the trail led up from there. Broken-off bits of railing and chunks of concrete cluttering the steps seemed to confirm that as we followed the damage upward. After a dozen or so flights, I noticed a change in the air.

"Mel, does it seem to you as though there's a bit of a draft? And not the sort that comes from an out-of-control air-conditioning system?"

He nodded. "Not unless Necessity has a sea-scents attachment built into her climate-control system."

Another couple of turns confirmed it. There was a cool breeze blowing down from somewhere above, a distinctly temperate and ocean-smelling breeze. That was wrong. Salt air and computers of the sort we'd been passing did not mix well. I reached for my sword, and only when I found the sheath empty did I remember I'd lost it to Nemesis. Along with my pistol and dagger. I was unarmed.

I looked at the empty sheath. "That's not good. Mel, do you think you could do something about it?"

"Sure. Let me just try a spell." He let out a burst of whistled code that switched from his normal style to self-harmonizing halfway through.

Sudden cold weight dragged my empty hand down. A sword . . . fish? I let go with a startled yelp and leaped up several stairs as the rather large and angry fish started flopping wildly on the landing.

"Oops!" said Melchior. "Sorry. I guess I'm not used to this quantum stuff yet. Let me fix that."

He whistled again, this time with harmony right from the start. The fish vanished, hopefully back to wherever it had come from.

"Now, a sword." He pursed his lips for a third whistle, one that again sounded slightly off.

"Not in my"—something filled my hand—"hand."

It was a slender black cane with a glittering grip like a diamond grown into the shape of an angel with wings of fire. Tisiphone.

"That's not right," said Melchior. "It's like I'm getting some sort of interference. Hang on, and I'll try again."

"Wait a moment," I said. "The weight on this feels a little off. Let me just check . . . Ahh, nice." With a push and a twist the grip slid away from the wood, revealing a gem-bright blade. "A sword cane, and a very nice one, too." The blade was four-edged. Bad for slicing, but a thrust would leave a wicked wound with a cross section shaped like a plus symbol.

"But it's not a rapier," said Melchior. "Let me give it another shot."

I shook my head, then tried a few experimental thrusts before taking the point between two fingers and trying to flex the blade. It didn't move, so I jabbed the tip into a gap in the wall for added leverage. The concrete cracked instead.

"It's OK, Mel. The balance is good and the—it's sure not steel . . . the whatever it is of the blade is better." I slid the sword back into the cane and locked it in place, giving the figure of Tisiphone an extra squeeze. "Why not quit while we're ahead?"

He looked disgruntled but finally sighed his agreement. "You're probably right. I can see this is going to take practice. Do you want I should try for a pistol?"

"Maybe we'd better leave things that go bang for a later

date and a less-enclosed space." I pointed upward with my new sword. "I'd rather not experiment with explosives until you're very confident about the results."

"Fair enough."

A few moments later, we turned the corner on the last landing before the top. Before what was left of it, really. The stair had clearly once ended in a rooftop enclosure of some sort. Now it ended in empty air. Climbing over the broken remnants of a concrete wall, we stepped out onto a large meadow of dune grass. Bits of the stairhead littered the field around us, but they were the only evidence of artificial construction. Beyond the edges of the meadow, there was nothing but sky and sea. If I hadn't just climbed out of it, I wouldn't have believed I was atop a building. Nor was there any evidence beyond the broken concrete that either the Furies or Nemesis had passed this way before me.

I walked to the nearest edge and looked out and down. It was a hundred-foot straight drop to the gently rolling surface of the surprisingly weedy water, and nothing more than a few grassy islands were visible between me and the horizon. I made a quick circuit of the island and found the view similar in every direction—no way to tell where we were, beyond someplace mild on an ocean. The illusion of a purely natural setting was reinforced by the irregular shape of the tall island and the lack of windows in the stone of its sides.

As for Megaera, Tisiphone, and Nemesis—there was no sign of any of them or any way of guessing in which direction they might have gone.

"So now what?" asked Melchior after we'd circled the island a few more times.

"I don't know, Mel. I really don't."

CHAPTER SEVENTEEN

"Maybe Shara can help," said Melchior.

"Huh?" I'd been watching the thick weeds drifting back and forth in the surf—there was something familiar there, though I couldn't quite decide what.

"Shara? Webgoblin. Curvy, purple, about so tall." Melchior held a hand up to his own height. "The one who's currently running the show here. You remember her, right?"

"Yes, Mel. Sorry. I guess I'm just tired. That's a great idea, but how do we reach her? We don't have a Fury to play walkie-talkie with anymore."

"No, but we do have a huge building filled with computers that are hooked up to the giant, networked entity that is Necessity. At least we do if Nemesis didn't destroy them all."

"Why didn't I think of that?"

"Because you're an idiot?" he said with a smile.

"Oh, that's right." I grinned back, but I wasn't happy about missing something that obvious.

Melchior started down the stairs, and I followed after. Why was I so distracted? I felt almost as scattered as I had in the Primal Chaos.

"How about this one?" said Melchior, as we came to the first door on the stairs, three landings down from the roof.

I shook my head. "It doesn't feel right."

"Are *you* feeling right, Boss?"

"I'm fine."

He gave me a worried look, and it wasn't until we'd gotten several floors farther down that I realized it was because he'd called me Boss again and was waiting for my response. What was up with me?

When I finally figured it out, I wasn't sure I wanted to tell Melchior. It was my nonexistent feathers acting up again. The reason it had taken me so long to recognize the feeling was that it was somehow related to the song of chaos. It wasn't Ravirn's skin the stuff had spoken to, it was the invisible feathers of the Raven—all fluffed up and acting like thousands of tuning forks, vibrating at the same frequency as the stuff of chaos. I'd brought the feeling through into this world without really noticing it till now.

So what were they trying to tell me? I closed my eyes and focused on the sensations flowing across my skin. There was a slight increase in the fluffiness factor down and to my left, as though chaos, or whatever else they were sensitized to, was stronger in that direction. I thought back over the other times I'd felt this way and realized that many of them had come in concert with the arrival of a spinnerette.

"Come on, Melchior." I scooped him up. "I think we're about to have company."

"Oh goody," he said. "Who, and how do you know?"

"Our friend the spinnerette." I took a deep breath. "I can . . . feel it in my feathers."

"If you hadn't gotten us here after Shara's signal zorched out, I'd figure you've finally lost it. As it is, I'm going to give you a chance to explain that."

As we retraced our steps back to our point of entry, I told him everything I'd figured out to date about the feathers and their relationship to chaos and the spinnerette.

"Huh," he said, as we reached the threshold of the trashed server room, "that's truly bizarre." We entered, and he glanced around. "One problem."

"What's that?"

He twirled a finger in the air, encompassing the room with a gesture. "No spinnerette."

The room was empty of anything living, but I wasn't so sure I agreed with him just yet. My ruffled plumage was telling me something very different from what I could see with my eyes. Following its pull, I crossed to the point where our own footprints appeared in the dust. The feeling grew stronger and lost its directionalism.

"It's here, but it's not." I set Melchior and my new sword cane down and pawed the air with my hands, feeling the outline of the spinnerette through the feathers on my palms.

"That's an interesting statement. Care to elaborate?"

"I can feel a presence with my feathers. It's just a hair-breadth away." Like the distance between reality and chaos! "That's it! Except we don't have a Fury, and that means no way to make a safe breach in the wall. Damn it."

As I looked around for something to throw in my frustration, my eyes fell on my cane. My *new* cane. The one produced by chaos magic gone awry. The one with the grip in the shape of Tisiphone.

"Not really." I bent and picked it up, noting anew the diamondlike sheen and organic lines of the figure of the Fury.

Carefully, almost reverently, I drew the shimmering blade. Then, before I could change my mind, I thrust it straight into the concrete of the floor. I felt the impact all the way up my arm and shoulder into my skull, but the blade didn't break. In fact, it sank a good inch into the floor. I jerked it free and examined it closely. Not a scratch. No maker's mark either, no hint that it had ever been shaped by hand. No, it looked grown. Diamond-bright and at least diamond-hard, yet organic, it very much resembled the claws of a Fury.

"Here goes nothing." I raised the blade and drew a vertical line through the air, picturing the kind of rip the Furies made in space-time.

Nothing happened. I glared down at the sword. I was sure I'd gotten that bit right. I even had a pretty good idea of why

I'd been given the sword and by whom—Necessity, or what was left of her, interfering with Melchior's whistling. So what was I doing wrong? The claws of a Fury were a part of her, and the sword was definitely not a part of me. If I was right about this, the sword was an artifact of chaos—the stuff of creation pretending to be normal matter . . . just like I was. At least according to Eris. Maybe . . .

I switched the hilt to my left hand and very carefully drew the tip across the palm of my right as I might with an athame. Instead of blood, a thin line of chaos appeared behind the cutting edge.

"You didn't happen to install Windows when you upgraded me, did you?" whispered Melchior when nothing more happened. "This isn't just some kind of really spectacular crash?"

"Nope."

I switched the hilt back to my right hand. When it touched the chaos there, I felt a shock of connection, as though I were momentarily one with the blade. Darkness edged my vision—the Raven's shadow. I could feel that the sword and its grip were a single continuous piece of organic crystal in that brief moment while both were a part of me.

Quickly, before that connection could fade, I made a vertical slice in the air. Shocking heat traced the slice in my hand, like a hot iron cauterizing a wound. I dropped the sword in surprise, looking at my palm. The line of chaos was gone, replaced by a much bigger one hanging in the air beyond. The shadow faded.

A pair of hands reached out of chaos and pulled the rip wider, allowing the spinnerette's broad spider-centaur body to pass through.

"*******!" it said. "**'* ***** **** ****."

"Hello to you, too." I bent and retrieved the sword, slipping it back into its cane-sheath. "You realize I can't understand a word you're saying, right?"

"***!" It nodded vigorously.

"You've been trying to communicate with me all this time, and I've just been too stupid to figure it out."

Again the nod, though less emphatic.

"Uh, Boss, would you care to let me in on this?"

"Certainly. Melchior, this is . . . call it The Left Hand of Necessity. Necessity's hand, Melchior."

"What!" squawked Mel, as the spinnerette bowed a greeting at him. "Wait, I thought this thing came from the Fate Core."

The spinnerette nodded, though it looked impatient.

"I'm confused," said Melchior. "How can it be both from Fate and Necessity? And if it really is an agent of Necessity, how come Shara didn't warn us?"

"I only just figured it out myself. You remember Cerice saying that the Fate Core was doing things on its own, possibly even becoming self-aware?"

"Yes, and . . . ?" asked Melchior.

I continued despite the spinnerette's increasing fidgets. "Shara said she had trouble communicating with Necessity proper, that it seemed almost like Necessity'd had a stroke? Well, depending on which parts of the brain are hit by a stroke, things can get very strange. There's something called . . ." I snapped my fingers a couple of times trying to jar the memory loose. "Damn, Alien Hand or something like that? You've got an encyclopedia in there somewhere, don't you?"

"Hang on." Melchior's expression went slack, and his eyes flicked back and forth as though he were reading from an invisible page. "Strokes . . . Alien . . . Got it. Apraxia and Alien Hand Syndrome. Let's see. The phenomenon is usually brought on by damage to the corpus callosum . . . disconnecting the two hemispheres of the brain . . . so that one hand literally doesn't know what the other is doing."

"That's the one," I said. "I think Necessity's been trying to work around the damage done by the Persephone virus by annexing space in the Fate Core, but the disconnect has kept Shara from finding out."

"That, or Necessity just didn't want to tell her," said Melchior.

Just as I opened my mouth to respond, the spinnerette reached out and picked up both Melchior and me. It was gentle but firm as it tucked us under its arms and started running. It ducked through the hole in the wall, turning away from the path followed by Nemesis.

"Do you think we should argue with it?" asked Melchior.

"No. We don't know where Nemesis went. There's a good chance the spinnerette does, and that's where it's taking us."

At the end of the hall, we passed through a door into a smallish room with a big hexagram built right into its concrete floor. As soon as we hit the center of the diagram, the spinnerette whistled a spell for activating permanent, hardwired gates, and we went zipping along a communications cable to somewhere else.

We emerged through another spellgate into a nearly identical room, but the spinnerette didn't even slow down there, nor for several minutes and many twists after. Only when we passed through a pressure hatch to arrive in a stadium-size space filled with what looked like a complete replica of a living coral reef did it come to a halt. There, in front of a yellow trunk of pseudocoral with a big glass cat's eye protruding from it at about chest height, it set us down.

"Now what?" I asked the spinnerette.

"********* ** * ******," it said.

"Thanks."

It ignored me and turned to the eye. "**** **, **** ** **** ****." That was the last thing it said that even resembled language before speeding its syntax up into a range where it sounded like gigabyte data bursts sent over a voice line.

The eye lit up, looked at the spinnerette, turned to me, rolled down to stare at Melchior, blinked once, then shot an intense beam of white light into the air in front of us. The beam stopped about three feet from the source and formed a glowing globe with an image of Shara in the center.

"It's about damned time," she said.

"Good to see you, too," replied Melchior.

"Sorry, lover, but Nemesis is on her way, and you need to do a bunch of work before she arrives. Besides, I've got no body to give you a proper greeting, and that makes me snippy."

"This is all some kind of computer?" I swung my arm to take in the coral.

"Quantum organics and specially grown," said Shara. "It's supposed to be the successor system for the pantheo-management system—Necessity's been moving all of her systems over from the more traditional legacy hardware. This block was going to be replacing the machines Persephone gorked. It's got a whole new type of architecture, and if Necessity'd had it in place at that time, the virus probably would have failed. Unfortunately, it hadn't finished growing. Your job is to set up a software port from there to here once I've got this place flooded again and the weednet in place."

"Weednet?" asked Melchior.

"Seaweed as multipath network cable," said Shara. "I'll tell you more later if we all survive the experience. For now, memorize this."

A series of computer and network schematics flashed in the air too fast for me to do more than get a rough gestalt of a really complex intranet work-around at the hardware level combined with some sort of insanely hacked software bug fix.

"Got it?" She looked at Melchior.

"Uh-huh."

"Then good-bye for now."

"Wait a second, why good-bye?" I asked.

"Because I can't go where you need to be. If the pantheo-management servers weren't cut off from the main system, you wouldn't need to go to them. The Persephone virus destroyed the weednet interface, and the old-style copper connections had been long since disconnected."

"What about Tisiphone . . . and Megaera?" I asked.

"They can take care of themselves. Now that they're here, Necessity is communicating with them directly. I can hear echoes of it, though it's not in a form I can understand."

"I thought Nemesis trashed the ELF system?" I'd assumed that was why the signal went dead.

"She did, but there are in-DecLocus work-arounds."

"******* ****."

Shara's projection nodded. "The spinnerette tells me Necessity's got the Furies playing a distraction game, sort of like human targets and . . ." Her expression went abstract for a moment, indicating an inflow of data. "Sorry, but that's all the time we have, kids." Her eyes flicked to the spinnerette. "You, ***!"

It picked us up and bolted for the door as a gurgling noise started. By the time we reached the exit, the floor was already ankle deep in water. The spinnerette splashed as it ran. It paused only long enough to close the hatch and dog it shut. Since it had eight limbs in addition to the human ones, it didn't even have to put us down to do it. Then, back to the gate, and poof.

This time we appeared in an area heavy with dust and lit only by dim emergency lights. The spinnerette carried us through perhaps a mile of steadily rising corridors and stairs, passing numerous closed pressure doors, eventually emerging onto the top of another island, this one dotted with olive trees. The weather was wild, with huge storm clouds chasing a gale-force wind in from our left. The spinnerette set us down and began drawing silk out and making big balls that it attached to its feet.

"Why do I think I'm going to hate the reason for that?" asked Melchior.

I looked out over the mad chop and sighed. "Because we're going over there." I pointed toward an island halfway to the horizon.

"Why do you . . . Oh."

He'd seen the island and the thick mat of dead weeds surrounding it. It was a perfect black hexagon as shiny and slick as tile, a lovely terrazzo actually. I'd visited the virtual version of that island twice before while dealing with the Persephone virus. Underneath its surface lay the computing center devoted to the fates of the gods.

He nodded. "You're right, I'm going to hate this." He paused for a moment and scratched his cheek. "Somehow it looks wrong without the Shara-gorgon."

I thought so, too, despite the fact that the hundred-foot-tall, mirror-shade-wearing, animate statue had only existed in the virtual world. It was hard to forget.

Moments later, the spinnerette had once again picked us up. "*****?"

"Sure, whatever you say."

It nodded and leaped over the edge. We dropped fifty feet in a few seconds, stopping only inches above the water. Reaching back with one foot, the creature snipped off the dragline and dropped us onto the waves. The water bowed under each of the eight web-wrapped feet, and the spinnerette started to sink. But before the surface tension could break, the thing started running again, this time skipping along the wave tops.

Between the storm and the lack of anything remotely resembling traction, we spent a lot of time moving in directions other than forward—most notably up and down, with seriously ugly consequences for the contents of my stomach—but somehow we got steadily closer to our goal. That might have been the strangest thing of all. Despite the fact that the island stood barely a yard above the surrounding water, no waves broke over its surface, leaving it bone-dry. Eventually, we arrived.

"**** ******!" Nothing happened. It started dancing in place to keep from sinking. "******* ********* ******** *******."

"I'm not sure what it just said, but if that wasn't swearing, I'll eat my slipcover," said Melchior.

"*****?"

With a creak, the top of the island opened, exposing a flight of stairs. Down we went. At the bottom, we had to pass through another watertight pressure door. I couldn't help but notice an increase in the ruffled-plumage factor as we did so.

Beyond lay a big tomblike room filled with racks and racks of slick-looking black multiprocessor servers, each with its own bank of blinking red LEDs. Imagine Giorgio Armani designing the interior of the great pyramid of Cheops as data center—sober and clean-lined, and this was the *old* hardware. It read as professional but also shockingly cool right up to the point where I realized that all that red was alert lights. The whole damn server farm needed a reboot.

I walked to the nearest box and held down the power button. For several seconds nothing happened. Then, with a swooshing-boooong sort of noise, the computer reset itself. The red light went out, replaced by a lambent purple one.

"I love that," said Mel. "Very power geek."

I imagined all the red replaced by that deep vivid purple. OK, it was still a pretty cool design statement. Much more so than the coral-reef thing that was replacing it, but hey, in the IT biz, if you don't move with the times, they bury you.

"So now what?" I asked.

"You look for any live machines while the Left Hand of Necessity here puts all those limbs to use doing manual reboots."

"*** **, **** ********?"

Either the spinnerette was getting better at tone, or I was starting to get used to its subtleties, because that almost made sense.

"Because somebody's got to do it, and Ravirn and I both have other jobs," said Melchior. Apparently it was starting to make sense to him, too.

The spinnerette sighed but walked to the nearest server bank and started pushing buttons. By balancing on four legs and stretching, it was able to hold down six at once. As the boooong noise sounded in chorus, Melchior turned back to me.

"The live boxes are running all that's left of the master control program. Shara didn't know much about it, so you get to try to parse it on the fly, then package it for porting."

"Doesn't that just sound like fun?" I suppressed an urge to make raspberry noises. "From the way you say that, I have to assume you won't be looking over my shoulder and helping me make sense of the thing."

"No, because someone also has to reconnect the old copper trunk lines so that once you've figured out the ways, there's also a means. According to the schematics Shara showed me, I go this way." He pointed along the wall to left.

"Write if you find work," I called after him, "especially if it's got happy little purple running lights." Then I turned the other way.

"Mail's dead," replied Melchior, his voice receding, "but I'll keep an eye out."

"So e-mail me," I tossed over my shoulder.

"Will do."

The first couple of dozen rows of racks were a solid mass of winking red eyes. I finally saw my very first spot of purple way down at the end of row thirty or thereabouts. I made a mental note of it and moved on. I'd work off a single box if I had to, but a cluster would be much better. I passed a couple more singletons and one triplet before I hit the jackpot, a row where about half the computers looked to be in working order. Now I just needed an interface device. Unfortunately, there was a distinct lack of keyboards and monitors, though there was an abundance of networking cable.

I checked the far end of the row but didn't find anything there either. That didn't leave me a lot of options—one really, and I didn't like it at all. Jacking my one and only soul into a badly virus-thrashed multibox supercomputer system designed to control the destiny of the gods seemed like the worst idea I'd had in years. Not that that kind of thing had ever stopped me in the past.

I pulled out my athame and collected a length of cable. I plugged one end into the closest active machine and the other into the athame. Then I sat down on the floor, my back braced against the nearest rack, my new sword cane lying across my knees. As I set the narrow blade of the athame against my palm, my stomach replayed a sort of highlights reel of the way it had felt during our recent spider-dance across the waves.

"I don't like it either," I said to my stomach. Melchior wasn't there; who else was I going to talk to?"

I pressed the blade into my skin. Blood welled . . . and I screamed, yanking the athame free and throwing it away. Tethered to the cable as it was, it didn't go far.

"What the hell was that?" I whispered.

As the point entered my flesh, I'd felt as though the universe had split in two, with me straddling the divide. In one version, I'd sunk the athame in quickly, catapulting myself into . . . madness! There was nothing sane in the virtual environment I'd entered, no hint of normal structure, and I'd felt it pulling me under, devouring me. At the very same time, looking out through my other eye, I saw myself doing what I had just done, pulling the blade free before the irretrievably cracked system could swallow me.

Sweat covered me like a second—liquid—skin, and I could feel all of the Raven's feathers, as though they'd gone beyond standing on end and actually tried to flee my body in search of a safer location. It seemed like a fabulous idea. I wanted to do a little fleeing myself. Dead was one thing. Trapped forever in a program gone insane, entirely another. I couldn't even bring myself to pick up the athame as I got shakily to my feet. I was not going to try that again, not for love or money or threat of death. I would turn up a keyboard and monitor or get Melchior to whistle me up a set if that didn't work.

I passed the spinnerette on my way back to let Melchior know what happened. It had continued methodically down the rows, leaving a trail of purple lights behind it. It took me a little longer to find Melchior because he'd crawled several yards down a huge conduit that came in through the far wall. I'd have missed him completely if I hadn't noticed the ragged end of a huge tangle of cables twitching occasionally.

"Hey, Mel, we've got a problem. I need to talk to you."

"Just a second. See that pile of cable?"

"Yeah."

"Pull on it."

I grabbed and yanked. Slowly, a couple hundred pounds of bundled cable slid out into the open, with Melchior riding it. I got about ten feet free before it jerked to a stop.

"That's all there is this side of the firestop," said Melchior. "I just hope it's enough. Help me get it over to the router cabinet."

As we wrestled the mass into place behind an old-fashioned patch panel, I quickly and briefly told Melchior about my run-in with the system.

He grimaced before wedging himself into the narrow gap at the back of the panel. "Nasty. Try the next cabinet over. There's a bunch of odds and ends in there, and I thought I saw a monitor."

We didn't have much time, so I left him to his task and went to check out the cabinet. As I hurried away, I heard him whistle the opening code of Snake Charmer. The cable ends rose up around him like so many dancing cobras, suggesting that this spell was going to work a whole lot better than his attempt to conjure me a rapier.

Two minutes later, I was plugging a badly scratched monitor and a keyboard missing its caps lock key into a machine a couple over from the one I'd tried earlier. I left it and my athame right where they were. Unfortunately, the alternate interface couldn't help much with the content. The image on the monitor was just as crazy as the one that had almost consumed my soul. On-screen it read as a sort Brownian sea of alphanumeric characters in every ethnic flavor from Roman and Arabic through Korean and Chinese to Greek and Russian. All in shades of pink for some reason.

It wasn't chaos—that I could have dealt with. It was order gone horribly wrong. Looking at it made my brain hurt. I tried hitting escape, and command-escape, and control-alt-delete and every other override I could think of for a dozen operating systems, all to no avail. Then I tried simply staring in the direction of the screen, trying to see without looking so that my subconscious could search for hidden patterns. All I got out of that was a strong urge to return my last meal to the wild and an ever-increasing paranoia about the approach of Nemesis.

I wasn't going to get anywhere from the inside. That was as certain as Dionysus's morning hangover. I hurried to the nearest of the machines the spinnerette had reset to see what the reboot looked like. Same thing, only considerably less so. Still pink, still running the Brownian-motion screensaver, but this time with fewer characters and all of them native to a Greek keyboard, though as I watched, the whole thing seemed to shift steadily toward the wilder scene of the original.

All right, so whatever it was, it infected or reinfected new machines added to the system. In that it acted like a virus. I knew beyond any shadow of a doubt that Persephone's effort was long since departed, but maybe it had left something behind that acted like an after-infection. I picked up monitor and keyboard and moved again, this time choosing a rack of crashed machines in the line opposite from where Melchior was working. After I'd held down the power button long enough to generate a boooong, I checked in with him.

"I've got all the connections to the patch panel reattached. I'm working on a kludge to get from there to the computer side while bypassing the weednet interface. Then I have to reset the switching computer for the old network, and we'll see what happens. Hopefully, that'll give Shara access. You?"

"I'll tell you in a minute."

As the server finished its boot cycle, rational text started scrolling by on my salvaged monitor, black letters on a blue background reading off system resources and . . . as it hit the network queries, the text blinked once, turned pink, and started to slither away from the rational. With a sigh, I physically removed the next box over from the network and hit reboot.

While I waited, I stuck the end of the sword cane through two of my belt loops and loosened the grip so it would draw easily. A few minutes later and closer to the inevitable arrival of Nemesis, I had a working machine. That lasted from the time I turned on every security measure I could think of until I reconnected it to the network. At that point: happy, dancing pink letters.

I had just gotten up a really good head of profanity when a hollow boom sounded from somewhere above.

Into the silence that followed, Melchior—still working madly away—said, "Don't stop. If ever there was a reason to swear, it's the one knocking on the front door right now."

Another boom, this one followed by a sharp crack like shattering tile. A third, and sea air suddenly stirred the room. I drew my sword and moved to a point where I could see the base of the stairs. I was wishing we'd redogged the hatch, though that probably wouldn't have held for long.

"What's the word on the connection work-around?" I called over my shoulder, all the while keeping my eyes fixed on the entrance.

Boom.

"Hope," replied Melchior.

"Care to elaborate?"

"Everything's done except flipping the switch and hoping for a miracle."

Smash. Thud. Howl. Something above had changed.

"Maybe that's the cavalry arriving," said Melchior. "Have you got a plan for the port?"

"Yep," I said.

More crashes and howls sounded above, followed by the roar of the storm. Water started to dribble down the stairs. Apparently, whatever protected the island from waves had just broken.

"What's the plan?" asked Melchior.

"You flip the switch, and we hope for a miracle."

"I was afraid that was what you were going to say. Here's hoping."

I heard a click from behind me. It was followed by a tremendous crack from the top of the stairs. The flow of water increased, forming a large puddle. A limp bundle of green and beige tumbled down the steps to land with a splash. Megaera. Unconscious. Or dead.

Another bundle followed a moment later, this one snarling as it fell. At the last minute, it turned the tumble into something more like a roll, landing on its feet next to the fallen Fury. Nemesis.

Orange light flared in the stairwell, and a seething mass of flame dropped into view, completely enveloping Nemesis. Tisiphone, I assumed, though I couldn't make out anything resembling human shape in that great, writhing ball of fire. As it hit the puddle, water hissed into steam, briefly obscuring my view and no doubt wrecking the closest racks of servers. I winced then and again as the two combatants slammed into a row of computers. A horrible clanging started up then.

"Oh shit," snapped Melchior from behind me.

"What?" I risked a glance over my shoulder.

He was standing on the console of the switching computer. Behind him, lights danced across its face. Whether those meant that the computers in this room were once more connected to the main network of Necessity or just that the system was slowly shorting out was an open question. And the alarm?

"Halon system," said Melchior. "Fire suppression."

That was bad. "Can you find the override or whistle one up?" A halon system would flood the room with an inert nonflammable gas, one that would starve any fire of the air it needed to burn, suffocating it . . . and us.

"Working on it." Melchior scrambled toward the back corner of the room, where a flashing light accompanied the alarm.

If we were lucky, there would be a switch there, one that would delay the halon release for as long as it was held down plus some very short number of minutes afterward to allow the button pusher a chance to escape. If we were unlucky—

"Got it!" yelled Melchior. Then he let out a quick burst of codespell. "Damn."

"What?" I yelled.

"Magic doesn't seem to work on the system. I'm going to have to stay here and hold the button if you don't want to give up on breathing."

That made us safe, for the moment, from the halon, at the cost of immobilizing Melchior. I was still trying to figure out what to do next when I realized the light had changed. The fires had gone out.

I turned back toward the door. Nemesis stood alone at the base of the stairs. I couldn't see Tisiphone. Nemesis smiled and stepped over Megaera's crumpled form, sauntering in my direction.

As she got closer, I couldn't help but blanch at the ravaged condition of the body she animated. It had once been my cousin Dairn. No more. Half of his face was gone, exposing raw bone, though both mirrored eyes remained. His hair and clothes had burned away completely, and the flesh underneath was charred black where it wasn't torn. I could still see the holes made by my gun in our last encounter and the deep gouge Tisiphone had torn in his side.

"Why aren't you dead?" I whispered.

"Hate." The voice was female but not feminine, and it didn't come from the body's closed mouth but, rather, from somewhere in the chest.

"For me? You shouldn't have. I mean, I'm flattered and all, but—"

"For you?" growled Nemesis, still advancing. "No. For Necessity. For this." She threw an arm out to take in the racks and racks of servers. "For three thousand years bound and bodiless in the pits of Tartarus." She was only a few yards away by now.

"You're barely an afterthought, the last petty wishes of this"—she pinched the flesh of a cheek that had once belonged to my cousin, tearing a piece free—"sad thing." She opened her fingers and let it fall wetly to the ground at my feet. "Its wants and needs are no longer important. As soon as I've finished my business here, I'll be moving to a new, far more appropriate, home. Do you prefer water?" Her eyes flicked back toward Megaera. "Or fire?"

I whipped my sword across her abdomen in a drawing cut. Designed for thrusting, the blade should have done little more than leave a bloody slice. Instead—maybe because of the abuse she'd already taken—it opened her up so that . . . things fell out. I tried not to look at them as I hopped backwards to give myself room.

As I began a lunge, I heard a self-harmonizing whistle start up behind me—Melchior—just barely audible over the continuing alarm bells. Nemesis whistled back, though otherwise she didn't move, seeming to ignore me. I drove my blade straight at her left eye. Almost casually, she brought her open palm up between us so that my point slid between the bones of her hand and out the other side. Perhaps a foot of it had gone through when she twisted her wrist, yanking the hilt free of my grasp. She looked speculatively at it.

"You're hardly worth the effort." The words continued to echo out of her chest and didn't even slow the speed of the whistled code coming from her lips as she dueled magically with Melchior. "But you are between me and my rightful prey." She caught the hilt in her own right hand and yanked it free.

With a move as fast as any Fury's, she thrust the point through my right biceps and deep into the stone wall of the room. Then, leaving me pinned like a butterfly, she passed me by. Whistle and counterwhistle continued as she headed for the connection Melchior had put together.

The pain from my arm was nauseating. I had to keep swallowing to hang on to the bile that threatened to rise up from my much-abused stomach. I turned as far as I could without twisting the blade in my wound. She had reached the switching computer and seemed to be examining the pattern of the lights. Why? It couldn't actually be working could it? Making the port I had failed to set up?

"Hello, my old enemy," said Nemesis, her voice too loud, "my old master—my thousand-times-damned mother. How does it feel? Alone and defenseless? Voiceless even? Knowing that I am wholly without mercy? It hurts you, doesn't it? It certainly hurt me when you threw me in the pit."

I was still trying to make sense of that, of the idea that the Furies were not just the successors to Nemesis but her sisters as well, when the spinnerette arrived, leaping at her over the top of the row of servers. Nemesis spun on her left heel, whipping her right foot around in a kick that connected brutally with the side of its head. There was a horrible crack, and it dropped and went forever still, its neck bent at an impossible angle.

"Pathetic," said Nemesis as she turned back to the console. "Is that really the best you can do, Mother? Throw a toy at me? And one stolen from Fate, no less? How far you have fallen. It will be almost a mercy to put you out of my misery."

I looked away, trying to find Tisiphone with my eyes. Nothing. The only Fury I could see was Megaera, and she had not moved. I had to do something. Had to stop Nemesis from destroying Necessity and possibly the universe with her. I had no idea how I was going to do it, but I knew where I had to start. Moving as gingerly as possible, I lifted my right leg and braced my boot against the wall. Then, catching the grip of the sword in my left hand, I yanked with my whole body.

Black lightning and agony. The blood-slippery sword came free of my hand and slid through my arm until the hilt struck my flesh and brought it to a sudden, breathtaking stop. I convulsed with pain but somehow managed to get my other foot up on the wall, putting the whole of my strength into straining against the trap that held me. The sword grated free of the wall, and I fell.

I lost a couple of seconds when the end of the blade dragged along the floor, though I didn't quite pass out. I spent a few more seconds on throwing up, then forced myself back to my feet. Ten staggering steps brought me up behind Nemesis. She was still talking to the computer, though I couldn't seem to make sense of the words, and still whistling away. As was Melchior in a sort of magical stalemate.

Whether she hadn't heard my approach over the alarm and her own gloating, or whether she just didn't consider me enough of a threat to bother with, I don't know. For whatever reason, she didn't so much as turn an eye in my direction.

I paused for a moment, looking for some weapon to use on her. There was nothing. Nothing except the blade still sticking through my arm. I wanted to cry then, or simply walk away. I couldn't. I had a job to do.

I braced the sword's grip with my left hand and sort of lurched into her point first, aiming for the heart. The blade slid home well enough, but I didn't have sufficient control to stop there. Together we toppled into the computer, driving the sword into the front panel.

As its point punched through the plastic casing and grated across the electrical connections beyond, I felt a touch of that same giddy sense of dislocation that came when I drove the athame home in my palm. The sword, lodged deep in my flesh, acted as a magical conduit, connecting me to the computer that was Necessity. Information flooded into my brain so fast that I felt as if it might burst. Images, thoughts, emotions. It was far too much for me to process or even hold on to, save only one thing. One thing that lay at the heart of the current conflict.

Pain.

The pain of a mother driven to the ultimate conflict with her firstborn daughter by the necessity of being Necessity. A pain that had prevented her from striking the killing blow she knew she should have. Pain at knowing that she had earned the hatred of a daughter who, driven by her own nature and role, must forever after become her mother's ultimate Nemesis.

I was still trying to cope with that idea when the universe seemed to split in two, just as it had when I'd tried to jack in earlier. Again I found myself straddling the divide. In response, my nonexistent feathers decided to stand on tippy-toe and do their impression of the Bolshoi Ballet performing *Swan Lake*. In one universe, I fell through the connection into the heart of Necessity and was lost forever in that wild flood of information. In the other, I grabbed hold of the naked blade where it stood out from Nemesis's back, intentionally slicing my hand open to expose . . . chaos?

In that instant, I understood the mystery of the two universes. It was the point of maximum uncertainty, and I had only one hope. I caught the blade, squeezed, and slid my hand along the edge. The blade, made of Fury-stuff and activated by my willing connection, exposed the chaos within me. The Raven's shadow seemed to fill the room, bigger and darker than it had ever been before, as though the night sky had taken bird shape.

I was the Raven, a power of chaos, and what was chaos but the stuff of uncertainty itself? The blade Necessity had sent me was a key of sorts, a codespell in physical shape that allowed me to touch the power of Necessity, to play system administrator with the universe. For that brief moment *I* became the point of maximum uncertainty, the place where DecLoci were split one from the other, the bridge between order and chaos.

Reaching through the sword, I took control of the system and started making decisions. In one universe, Nemesis moved quickly enough to pull us free of the computer, and I died. In the next, I acted more quickly, twisting the point deeper into the system and creating a massive magical short, a surge of chaos so great that it fried the heart of Nemesis, bursting her body asunder and leaving her soul naked and unhoused. With no host prepared, she was powerless to prevent me sending her back to Tartarus and bondage.

I used my brief stint as administrator to choose the latter universe, and Dairn's body came apart in an explosion of silvery lightning that banished its occupant. Instantly, a second split appeared in my mind. In one fork, the surge that destroyed Nemesis took me as well. In the other, Tisiphone, who had been sneaking up from behind, caught the blade between Nemesis and me, grounding the magical charge and frying the entire row of servers touched by her trailing wings. Again, I took the second path. Tisiphone screamed.

Even as the shorting switch console died, and the power faded away, I had a final choice. Allow the surge to stop her heart or take the last of the feedback into my own body and me into a long darkness, walking just this side of the border between life and death.

Lights out.

EPILOGUE

The lanai of Raven House is a beautiful place to eat and watch the sun go down, especially in company.

"Lovely," said the redhead sitting across the table from me.

I nodded, but didn't respond aloud. I was having a bad week. For starters, I was having dinner with the wrong redhead. Don't mistake me, the more I see of Thalia, the more I like her, but I'd really been hoping for a very different evening with a very different titian-haired goddess.

"Such a frown," said Thalia. "Someone might think the world had ended rather than that you had saved it."

"Sorry," I said, "I guess I'm just not in a smiling mood."

"And why, pray tell, is that?"

She knew very well what was bothering me. I raised an eyebrow at her, but she just smiled.

"You can be a silly boy sometimes."

"What's that supposed to mean?"

"You're all bent out of shape because your new lover is angry and not talking to you, right?"

"Why is that silly?" I asked.

This time she laughed out loud. "She's a Fury, oh, Raven."

"And?"

"Furious? Being angry with a goddess of anger because she's angry with you doesn't strike you as the least bit silly?"

"Well, when you put it *that* way . . ."

"What other way is there to put it?" she asked. "Tisiphone is angry. It is her job to be angry. If you're going to have any kind of relationship, you're going to have to learn to live with the occasional round of the grouchies."

"But I didn't deserve this one."

"That's my cue," said Thalia.

"For what?"

"Either my exit or extreme measures." She snapped her fingers, and a heavy chocolate silk pie appeared in her open hand. "Which would you prefer? Whine again, and I'll make the choice for you."

I grinned at the absurdity of it. How many people have been threatened by a goddess wielding a pie? "You're right, I sounded all of eleven years old there, and it's not the first time this week. I guess I've earned the pie." I braced myself for impact.

"Better," she said, setting the pie on the table instead of hitting me with it, much to my surprise. "Your sense of humor is restored, and that means it's time for me to go." She stood and turned toward the faerie ring.

"What about the pie?" I asked, as she started walking away.

"You could always hit yourself with it, but I'd recommend you eat it." She stepped into the ring and winked. "Humbly." And she was gone.

The pie was delicious.

The sun set but I didn't move. Haemun brought me a mojito, and I sipped it in the dark. Thalia was right, but that didn't change the fact that I missed Tisiphone.

"I'm sure she'll get over it," said Melchior from the depths of the porch. "She did let you stay long enough to put together a kludge for the subroutines for Tartarus and its inhabitants and to fix the ELF."

"Only because Alecto and Megaera insisted," I replied. "Doesn't it bother you that she's the one who actually threw us out at the end, Melchior? Not Alecto. Not even Megaera. Tisiphone."

"Not really, but then, I'm not dating her, so I've got a bit more perspective. She feels guilty." He emerged onto the lanai with Shara trailing behind him—they'd made themselves scarce during Thalia's visit, though from the mussed look about them, they'd probably been looking for some private time, anyway. I raised an eyebrow, and Melchior flushed indigo, but continued, "The battle did an awful lot of damage to Necessity, and Tisiphone is the one who brought you in, and in her eyes, the one responsible for all the harm done to her mother."

"And the one who loves you," interjected Shara, "at least a little, and that makes her doubt her judgment where you're concerned."

With the official end of winter, Necessity had spat Shara back out into the real world. That was two weeks ago now, and she'd been visiting with Cerice's grudging approval. A thought that made me feel doubly girlfriendless. I looked at the pie and grinned. Still enough to hit myself with if I got too far down pity-party lane.

Maybe my current time alone was for the better. I still had a lot to learn about all this Raven stuff. Witness how I had been able to wield the power of Necessity, if only for an instant and with her consent. What that meant I hadn't begun to understand.

"Tisiphone will come back," said Melchior, his voice laced with both sympathy and sarcasm. "You're irresistible."

"I don't think Cerice would agree with that," said Shara. Then she winked at me. "But he might be right."

Haemun arrived with more drinks then: another mojito, Drambuie for Melchior, and something with rum and a little umbrella for Shara.

Melchior raised his glass. "Absent friends."

Shara nodded. "Ahllan."

"Ahllan," I said, and drank. She had been the subject of

much conversation over the time Shara had been visiting. "Speaking of which, tell me again what you found out about her disappearance while you were running the show for Necessity. It didn't make much sense the first time through."

"All right, but it'll take a while."

Much, much later, I crawled off to bed. When winter came again and Shara returned to Necessity, we would have to see what we could do about Ahllan. The troll vanishes and is never seen again was not a satisfactory result. I glanced over at the rack where my new sword cane, Occam, rested beneath the nameplate Melchior had insisted on. I had a feeling it might come in handy on that trip.

Finally, I shut off the lamp and settled back into bed, only then noticing that Haemun had been through and tidied the room. On my bedside table lay the slightly creased card that had started it all. By the light of my eyes, I reread it for the umpteenth time.

Zeus wants you!

KELLY McCULLOUGH has sold short fiction to publications including *Weird Tales*, *Absolute Magnitude*, and *Cosmic SF*. An illustrated collection of Kelly's short science fiction, called *Chronicles of the Wandering Star*, is part of InterActions in Physical Science, an NSF-funded middle school science curriculum. He lives in western Wisconsin. Visit his website at www.kellymccullough.com.

**Explore the outer reaches
of imagination—don't miss these authors
of dark fantasy and urban noir that take you
to the edge and beyond.**

Patricia Briggs	Karen Chance	Anne Bishop
Simon R. Green	Caitlin R. Kiernan	Janine Cross
Jim Butcher	Rachel Caine	Sarah Monette
Kat Richardson	Glen Cook	Douglas Clegg